Notorious Eliza

A NOVEL ABOUT THE WOMAN WHO MARRIED AARON BURR

BY

BASIL BEYEA

SIMON AND SCHUSTER · NEW YORK

PUBLISHED BY SIMON AND SCHUSTER

A DIVISION OF GULF & WESTERN CORPORATION

SIMON & SCHUSTER BUILDING

ROCKEFELLER CENTER

1230 AVENUE OF THE AMERICAS

NEW YORK, NEW YORK 10020

DESIGNED BY EVE METZ

MANUFACTURED IN THE UNITED STATES OF AMERICA

1 2 3 4 5 6 7 8 9 10

LIBRARY OF CONGRESS CATALOGING IN PUBLICATION DATA

BEYEA, BASIL.

NOTORIOUS ELIZA.

SEQUEL TO THE GOLDEN MISTRESS.

I. JUMEL, ELIZA BOWEN, 1775?–1865—FICTION.

I. TITLE.

PZ4.B5733NO [PS2552.E87]   813'.5'4   78–2629

ISBN 0–671–22470–0

To Thomas A. Flanagan, M.D.
in appreciation of his understanding and patience
and
Affectionately to Geneviève Claussen
for her encouragement and editorial advice

FOREWORD

THERE HAVE BEEN many books written about Aaron Burr and at least two novels about Madame Eliza Jumel, the notorious and beautiful woman he married in his later years. The facts about Burr's life have been well established; however, most of Eliza's real story came out only after her death, and there are some gaps and much speculation about her.

In my earlier novel, *The Golden Mistress*, Eliza's life until the age of nineteen was covered in detail. The daughter of a prostitute, she was born as Betsy Bowen in 1775 in Providence, Rhode Island. She was separated from her mother and adopted by Samuel Allen and his wife, Lydia. Sam taught her to read and write, but he also developed a passion for the child and after his wife's death made her his mistress. She ran away from him at the age of fifteen and was supported by Jacques de la Croix, a French sea captain, who furthered her sexual education.

When Betsy was eighteen, she fell in love with Matt Wyatt, son of a socially prominent family. Although she became pregnant by him, Matt's father forbade a marriage. Still, she bore the child, named George Washington Bowen, and left him in the care of Freelove Ballou, a midwife, after making financial arrangements for his future care by the Wyatt family.

Eliza (or Betsy) was as ambitious as she was strikingly beautiful. In the fall of 1794 she left Providence to better herself in New York City.

This novel begins shortly after her arrival there under the name of Eliza Capet: a name that was later to become Madame Stephen Jumel, and finally Mrs. Aaron Burr.

PART I

Eliza

CHAPTER 1

BETSY BOWEN SAT in the parlor of Mrs. Cuyler's boardinghouse on Wall Street and asked herself how she was going to survive in New York City. Two days earlier, Captain Curry had brought her here, and from the fare that he had returned to her in exchange for her favors in his bunk aboard the *Roger Williams*, she had paid her rent of four dollars a week plus another four dollars for firewood. It was only later that she had learned that Mrs. Cuyler kept what she referred to as "a respectable abode for ladies and gentlemen" and that no man could visit a lady in her room.

Back in Providence, Rhode Island, where she had come from, there would have been no problem. She would have walked the streets at night until she found a man who would pay for the use of her body. But now, here in the bright sunlight of the parlor, she recalled with horror her experience on the street the night before. She had accosted a young man and had promptly been taken in tow by a constable.

She could still hear his voice as he said, "Solicitin' on the street, eh?"

"Oh, no, sir. I was on my way home and that man accosted *me*!"

He had looked at her cynically. "And where is home?"

When she told him that her name was Eliza Capet and that she lived at Mrs. Cuyler's on Wall Street, the constable had held his lantern up to her face and looked at her curiously.

11

"You talk with a funny accent. Where do you come from?"

"Providence, Rhode Island. I just got here yesterday."

"Well, young woman, I'm a-goin' to let you off this time on account you're a stranger here. But I warn you—we don't allow whores on the streets of New York. If that's your business, then go to a whorehouse to work, but stay off the streets at night."

The constable had escorted her home, not so much out of politeness as to make sure that she really lived at Mrs. Cuyler's.

But Eliza did not want to go into a whorehouse. She had done that out of necessity in Providence, and she had no intention of repeating the experience here in New York. After all, she had come here in quest of fame and fortune, and a brothel did not offer a chance for either.

She remembered how Captain Curry had taken her on a tour of the city on the day they had arrived. What had impressed her most was Battery Park, where, in the late-afternoon sunlight of a sparkling fall day, the young ladies and gentlemen of the town were strolling in all their colorful dress. The ladies wore hoopskirts of satin, silk or brocade, drawn in tightly at the waist. They glided along so smoothly that it seemed to Eliza that they moved on wheels. Even though she was dressed in her very best gown, she felt like a wren set down in an assembly of peacocks. She had no hoopskirt.

Her only chance of survival was to join the daily parade at Battery Park in the hope of finding a gentleman who had a room. But she could not go to Battery Park dressed as she was. It seemed silly to her, but everything depended on the acquisition of a hoopskirt. The alternative was to seek out a madam and enter a whorehouse.

Her thoughts were interrupted by the opening of the parlor door. A fellow lodger who had been introduced to her as William Dunlap stood in the doorway.

"I hope I am not intruding," he said politely.

Eliza gave him a warm and welcoming smile. "Oh, no, do come in. I was feeling a bit lonely."

He sat down in a chair opposite her. He wore a black patch over his right eye, which he had evidently lost, and although he was not handsome, he had a genial, friendly face. In introducing him to Eliza, Mrs. Cuyler had said that he was the stage manager at the John Street Theatre.

And so, Eliza said, "Tell me, Mr. Dunlap, do you often play *Hamlet* at your theatre?"

He looked at her with quickening interest. "Ah, you like *Hamlet*, Miss Capet?"

"I like all of Shakespeare's plays," she said. "But I have never seen them performed on a stage. We have no theatre in Providence. The stage is considered immoral there."

William Dunlap laughed, and his single brown eye twinkled in amusement. "It was considered immoral here until President Washington came to New York to live. He loved the theatre and attended regularly with 'Lady Washington.' Even after he left to go to Philadelphia, the theatre continued, except for the summers, when the yellow fever regularly plagues us, and people move to the north, as far as Greenwich Village or farther. Even I go to my house in Perth Amboy."

Eliza resolved that next summer she would somehow leave the city to escape the plague. She had no intention of dying of yellow fever. "It is horrible," she said. She paused and then changed the subject. "What is playing at your theatre now, Mr. Dunlap?"

"*Much Ado About Nothing.*"

"And are you playing Benedick?"

He laughed. "Oh, no. I'm not an actor. I'm only the stage manager."

"Oh, how I should like to see it! But I cannot afford it, and I would need a hoopskirt and a new dress. Where would I find a shop that sells women's clothing?"

"On Pearl Street, I would think."

"Your city is so confusing for a country girl like me." She sighed. "I wouldn't know how to get there."

"If you would permit me, I would be happy to escort you."

"You are very kind, but in this clothing—"

He rose and, bowing, he said, "You would be beautiful in any kind of dress, my dear Miss Capet."

She gave him a fetching smile. "Oh, thank you, Mr. Dunlap."

"I would be more comfortable if you called me William."

"Only if you will call me Eliza," she said.

As they turned right onto Broad Street, the full din of the city struck them. Men and boys carrying huge pails of milk suspended from poles slung across their shoulders shouted, "Milk, ho! Milk, ho!" There were knife grinders wheeling their machines, ragmen carrying large bags, wood vendors pushing carts of firewood in front of them, girls selling oranges from trays suspended by a rope around their necks, and men with brooms and brushes crying, "Sweep, ho! Sweep, ho!"

Everybody seemed to be selling something and making a lot of noise about it. And through it all the ever-present pigs, eating, squealing, fighting for the garbage, and even copulating.

"Is it always so noisy?" shouted Eliza in order to be heard above the clamor.

"It will get worse the closer we get to the Merchants' Exchange," he shouted back. "They had to put chains all around the front of it so that the people inside could hear one another. And they had to ban the tolling of church bells for funerals."

As they reached Pearl Street, William pointed out Fraunces Tavern and explained that this was the terminal for coaches leaving for Boston, Albany, and Philadelphia, where the President and Congress were.

After they had walked a short distance, William said, "Well, here's a dress shop for you."

"Oh, those are dresses made to measure. I just want to get some material. I sew very well, but first I'd have to buy the hoop."

The shops on Pearl Street fascinated Eliza. There was almost nothing that one could not buy here, but the prices were much higher than in Providence. Her remaining four dollars would not go very far here, and she dared not even ask the price of a hoop for a skirt.

William pointed with pride to the newly finished Tontine Coffee House, which had replaced the old City Hotel torn down two years before. It was a large and handsome brick building.

Eliza looked at it in admiration. "Does it cost much to live there?" she asked.

14

"Oh, yes," said William, "about twice what you're paying at Mrs. Cuyler's. The place is frequented mostly by businessmen. The food and drink are most elegant—and most expensive."

Shortly after they had passed the Tontine, Eliza paused. "I am tired, William. Could we go back to Mrs. Cuyler's?"

"But you didn't get a dress."

She looked at him in embarrassment. "To be honest, William, I haven't the money. I have just enough for another week at Mrs. Cuyler's."

"But how do you expect to live?" When she did not answer him, he said, "Well, there should be no difficulty for a pretty lass like you in finding a—a benefactor.'"

She nodded, and her eyes filled with tears. The tears distressed him, and he felt that he had said a clumsy thing.

"I'm sorry if I have offended you, Eliza."

"You haven't offended me. What you said is only the truth. I shall have to find what you call a benefactor."

"He would be a lucky fellow. If I weren't married—"

She looked up in surprise. "You're married?"

"Unfortunately, yes. I have three children."

"But I don't understand. If you are married, why do you live in a boardinghouse?"

"I don't really. I sleep there and take my breakfast there. I am a writer of plays, you see, and I must have my mornings free of squalling children. At noon, I go home for lunch."

"And then do you come back to Mrs. Cuyler's to write some more?"

"No. My earnings as a stage manager during the theatre season are not enough to support my family, and so I work with my father-in-law, who imports fine china and sells it."

Eliza was disappointed not only to learn that William was married but also, more important, that he was poor. After a pause, she said, "But you should be doing your writing now, shouldn't you?"

"Yes, but even writers must take a holiday, particularly when a beautiful young lady needs an escort."

They were near the John Street Theatre now, and on impulse, William said, "Would you like to see the theatre? I have a key."

15

"Oh, I would love that. I have never seen the inside of a theatre."

Eliza stood in an aisle of the pit of the theatre and looked in awe at the stage. In the dim light she could see a backdrop of a street. It was crudely painted but for Eliza the effect was breathtaking.

"Oh, it's beautiful!"

"Let me show you the stage," he said as he led her up the steps at the side. "Now be careful, Eliza. It's very dark here, and the stage is already set for Scenes Two and Three of the rooms in Leonato's house in Messina." He reached down to the footlights and picked up a candle, which he lighted. "There, now you can see better."

"Oh," she breathed ecstatically as she looked at the furnishings on the set. She seated herself on a sofa, which was hardly Italian in style, since it had been designed by George Hepplewhite before his death some ten years earlier.

Eliza looked at William in delight. "I feel as though I were Beatrice herself."

William raised his voice theatrically. " 'I will hold friends with you, lady.' "

Eliza thought for a moment and replied, " 'Do, good friend.' "

William's eyes lighted in astonished pleasure as he continued, " 'You will never run mad, niece.' "

" 'No,' " she said, " 'not till a hot January.' "

They both laughed, and then William looked at her intently. "Now, how did you remember those lines?"

Eliza shrugged. "It is one of my favorite comedies. I remember little bits of the dialogue very easily. I love plays, even if I've never seen one."

He stared ahead thoughtfully as he seated himself beside her. "You remind me of myself when I was very young. I went to the theatre as often as I could scrape together three or four shillings for a seat in the gallery. I decided to write a play myself. I called it *The Father; or, American Shandyism*, and they played it right here on this stage in 1789 to great acclaim."

"Did it make you very rich?" asked Eliza.

16

"Hardly. Very few writers become rich. Right now I'm working on a tragedy called *Fontainville Abbey*. But that's enough about me. Tell me about yourself." He moved a little closer to her on the sofa and took her hand in his.

"There isn't much to tell," she said. "My father was a French sea captain, and my mother was English. I was born at sea on a French ship that was carrying troops to the West Indies. My mother died not long after I was born, and my father put me to stay with a family in Providence. He died in a sea battle when his ship was captured by pirates. I was only twelve then, and since there was no one to pay for my lodging, I went to work as a maid. I didn't like that kind of work, and so I decided to come to New York to better myself."

"But where did you learn to read and write—and read Shakespeare?" asked William.

"I was tutored by Captain Jonathan Clarke, who had been a friend of my father's. He was a shoe cobbler and had little money, because he was drunk most of the time." Her eyes took on a gentle expression. "He gave me something more important than money. He taught me to read books and gave them all to me when he left Providence to go to Massachusetts. I still have them."

There was a puzzled look on William's face. "But how did you get enough money to come here?"

Eliza lowered her head and did her best to look ashamed. "I—it is hard for me to say this, William, but—well, I am not a virgin, and I had a gentleman friend who helped me."

This remark had its calculated effect on William, and he moved closer still to her and ventured to put his arm about her waist.

"You poor child," he said gently. "Fate has not been kind to you."

He lifted her face toward his and kissed her gently at first and then with growing passion. It was not difficult for her to respond, for she found this young man attractive. When one of his hands slid down her bodice and began caressing a breast, she did not push him away.

The candle, which had been placed on the floor, began to

17

flicker as it reached the end of its wick. William leaned over and with a wet finger and thumb extinguished it.

"I don't think we need any light, do we?" he asked. The sofa was rather short, and he pulled her to the floor. "The floor is well swept. You don't mind?"

As he lifted her skirt and began to caress her between the thighs, she sighed.

He was a gentle but passionate lover, and she responded to him readily but with the reserve that she considered appropriate to a girl who was not overly experienced.

He reached his climax too soon for her, but she pretended that she was in ecstasy in order to please him. Her interest was not in making love. She wanted a hoopskirt. While he lay beside her, still kissing her and murmuring grateful endearments in her ear, she was trying to figure out how to broach the subject.

Smiling, she said, "I never did this on a stage before."

He laughed. "I daresay it's been done here. No doubt, it's been done everywhere."

He lighted another candle, and they got dressed.

Eliza looked wistfully out toward the auditorium, her eyes moving from the pit up to the gallery. "Oh, how I wish I could attend a performance and see Benedick and Beatrice. But without a hoopskirt—"

"I think we can remedy that situation," he said, looking at her with admiring eyes. "God, you are beautiful! With eyes like yours, you need no hoopskirt, but we'll get you one anyway, so that you can attend the theatre."

"But William, you are not rich—"

"But I'm not so poor that I cannot buy you a hoopskirt!"

It was reassuring for her to know that the rules of the game were the same in New York as they were in Providence.

The dress was of light-green silk decorated with bows of dark green, and the bodice, of bright golden velvet, fitted snugly, so that her breasts were outlined seductively. The silver necklace that Jacques had given her on the day they parted in the Bulldog Tavern was around her neck, its pendant of cut green jade glowing against the bodice of gold velvet.

It had taken Eliza almost a week of steady sewing to finish the dress, and her last four dollars had gone to Mrs. Cuyler in payment of a second week's rent.

And so, without a penny to her name, she went to the John Street Theatre to see *Much Ado About Nothing*. William had given her a ticket in the gallery and arranged to meet her when his duties backstage were over. She was enthralled by the performance and laughed merrily at the swordplay in words between Benedick and Beatrice. But she was even more enthralled by the audience.

During the entr'acte, while three musicians in the pit played romantic music, the audience strolled in the area at the back of the theatre. Gentlemen and ladies gathered in small groups and talked about the play and the players. They were all brilliantly dressed, the men in waistcoats of brocade with silk shirts ruffled with lace. Highly ornamented silver buckles were pinned to the knees of their bright-colored breeches and were sewed to their shoes. Most wore their hair powdered or wore white wigs.

But it was the women's clothing that held Eliza's eyes. Their hoopskirts seemed to her to be masterpieces of dressmaking. They wore their hair, curled and arranged by professional hairdressers, in high masses on the top of their heads, all surmounted by lace caps pinned with jeweled clips or by small fanciful hats.

Her own comparatively simple gown struck her as almost drab by comparison, but at least she had a hoopskirt and did not feel conspicuous, and she had learned how to walk with tiny steps so that she seemed to glide over the floor.

When the orchestra stopped playing and three loud thumps from the area of the stage signaled that the play would soon begin again, the strollers moved in an unhurried fashion to return to their seats.

Eliza's companions in the gallery were not the fine ladies and gentlemen she had seen in the lobby. They were noisy and unrestrained in their approval or disapproval of what took place on the stage. And Eliza, caught up in the plot of the play, found herself responding verbally along with them.

At the conclusion of the performance, after the actors had taken bows in acknowledgment of the applause that filled the theatre, the musicians played "Hail, Columbia," and the audience rose to its feet.

Eliza left the gallery before the presentation of the "afterpiece," since William's duties as stage manager would then be concluded, and he had arranged to meet her in the theatre lobby.

He was there, waiting for her, and she ran to him, throwing her arms around him.

"Oh, William, you have given me the most enjoyable night of my life! To see those characters come to life and hear them speak—it was like a miracle!"

William smiled with pleasure. "I am so glad that you enjoyed it, my dear. And now, I think we should crown the evening by going to Ranelagh's Gardens for refreshments."

"But I have no money, William."

"I have. You must remember that during the theatre season I receive money from two jobs."

The air was chill, and so he called a hackney. But even inside, Eliza shivered and had difficulty in keeping her teeth from chattering.

William looked at her in concern. "I see that we must buy you a wool shawl or perhaps even a winter coat."

"Oh, no, William. You have already been kind enough to me."

"Tush. We must not let our Eliza take cold."

When they arrived at the Gardens, Eliza looked about her in wonder. The place was not large, but it resembled a garden with its large boxes of evergreens set between the many small tables. Light was provided by scores of Japanese lanterns with candles inside them. There was a light breeze coming from the bay, and the lanterns danced on the wires from which they were suspended.

A waiter in a red waistcoat approached their table, which was decorated by a vase of dried flowers and a candle for light.

William ordered. "A negus for the lady—very hot, if you please. And I'd like a flip."

"What is a negus?" asked Eliza.

20

"It is made of hot wine, hot water and sugar, with nutmeg and lemon for flavoring. I think it will warm you."

Conversation lagged while they waited for the drinks, and Eliza looked studiously at the face opposite her. It could not be called handsome, as she had noted before, narrow and with a long, thin nose, but the left eye was expressive and alive, whether pensive as it was now or twinkling as it did when he laughed. She judged him to be in his mid-thirties, but his manner was so boyish that he could have been thought younger. She found him, in an odd way, physically appealing, but it was his mind and his humorous outlook on life that attracted her.

Jonathan Clarke had introduced her to reading what he called "lit-er-a-toor" and had a limited fund of knowledge, but William was the first man of education and culture that she had ever met, and he had both magnetism and charm.

When the waiter returned with the drinks, he brought with him a quart-size pewter mug half full of beer laced generously with rum and sugar. He then plunged a red-hot poker, popularly called a "loggerhead," into the mug. The mixture foamed and swirled as it was set before William, who picked it up and toasted Eliza.

"Do you like the negus?" asked William as he set down his mug of flip.

"Oh, 'tis delicious," she said, "and the warmth will take care of my chill, I'm sure."

The concoction did indeed warm her, and she gulped it down eagerly. William beckoned to the waiter and ordered a second round of drinks.

When it was time to leave, Eliza felt a bit tipsy, and William steadied her as she rose to her feet.

While they waited for a hackney to appear, Eliza turned to him. "This has been a most enjoyable evening, William. I don't know how to repay you."

He looked down at her and smiled. "I think you do, my dear."

She was not displeased by his directness. "I know," she said and paused. "But where?"

"I see no reason why our own little play should not have a

21

second performance, since the first one was so well received."

She laughed. "But, William, the actors and actresses are at the theatre—"

"Not now," he said. "I have learned that at the conclusion of a performance, actors and actresses flee the theatre as though it were contaminated by yellow fever."

And so once more Eliza found herself on the stage of the John Street Theatre giving a second performance in the setting for the room at Leonato's house. She carefully stepped out of her prized hoopskirt, and William helped her unlace her bodice. Without ceremony she lay down on the floor and waited for him.

Leaning above her with his breeches undone, he paused and said, "Did you pleasure yourself fully last time?"

"Well—almost. If you could take a little longer, perhaps. I am very slow—in—arriving."

And so, by using his hand to prepare her more fully, he waited before entering her.

Their second performance was a great success. As William lay above her, panting and exhausted, he whispered, "All the play needed was a dress rehearsal."

"An undressed rehearsal," said Eliza.

CHAPTER 2

FOR THE NEXT THREE DAYS Eliza did not have a chance to be alone with William. He left immediately after breakfast to go upstairs to work on his new play and then went to his father-in-law's china business. On the afternoon of the fourth day he returned to the boardinghouse at four o'clock and asked Eliza whether she would like to go for a stroll with him.

She had dressed in her hoopskirt, and since the day was cool and overcast, she found herself shivering.

William was not long in noticing this. "We must buy you a shawl, Eliza. You are cold."

"But you're not a rich man, William. You have a wife and children to support and must needs work with your father-in-law as well as stage manager at the theatre."

"That is true, but just the same—"

He took her by the arm and led her into a shop that sold woolens. She chose a not-too-expensive scarf of bright-green wool, voluminous and warm. William put it over her shoulders, and she snugged it around her eagerly.

When they reached the street, she looked at him gratefully and said, "I don't know how to thank you, William. For keeping me warm, I could almost fall in love with you."

"But you mustn't," he said seriously, "because then I might fall in love with you, and that would be a great mistake, if only because I cannot afford to keep you." He paused and smiled at her. "But I cannot help falling a *little* in love with you, not just because you are so beautiful, but because of your charm and intelligence."

Nobody had ever called Eliza intelligent before, and she was pleased. "Why, thank you, William. You could not have said anything that would make me happier—that I am intelligent, I mean."

"But you are, and it would be an insensitive man who did not appreciate it." His face became suddenly sad. "I suppose, then, that our 'play' has closed after only two performances."

"Oh, no," said Eliza. "I enjoyed performing on stage with you, and I hope we'll have many repeat matinees."

"Now?" asked William. "The actors' rehearsal for the new play should be over by this time."

"What's the new play?"

"*As You Like It*," he said.

Eliza laughed. "I do like it," she said as they turned their steps toward the theatre. She was pleased to know that the rules of the game would be observed and that the new green scarf would be honestly earned.

But Eliza was not really happy with her lover. He was not rich, and she was looking for someone who could keep her. She wanted more clothes: gloves, another dress, and especially a hat to top her lustrous red-gold hair.

The next afternoon, when the weather was fine, she wandered into the Merchant's Coffee House at the corner of Wall and Water Streets. There were few women there, and the possibility of finding a gentleman friend there was unlikely. The men were too busy with their transactions in real estate, insurance ventures, Western land grants and the cargoes on incoming ships.

And yet they could not help staring at this lovely intruder on their affairs and wondering what she might be doing in their almost exclusively male precincts. Eliza was not ill-at-ease and walked about slowly with complete unconcern.

She stopped before a large easel that bore a poster on which had been written under the heading "Marine Register" the names of ships soon due in port. She feigned interest in reading the names, when her attention was fixed by the words "*L'Étoile de Marseilles*," beneath which was printed "Capt. Dellycraw." Her heart beat quickly as she noted the probable time of arrival as ten the next morning at Peck's Slip.

As soon as Eliza had finished breakfast the next day she went to her room to prepare herself for a reunion with Jacques. She curled her hair with her tongs which she had heated in the fireplace. She washed herself with the water from the pitcher and then squirmed into her hoopskirt and golden velvet bodice. She made up her face in a modest fashion, using very little rouge. With the green shawl over her shoulders, she descended the staircase and left the house hurriedly.

She inquired from a passer-by the way to Peck's Slip and learned that it was on Water Street near the Walton Home. At last she saw the familiar outlines of *L'Étoile de Marseilles*, but she looked in vain for Jacques. The cargo was already being unloaded, and she approached one of the sailors.

He recognized her and said, *"Je vous connais. Vous êtes Mademoiselle Bowen. Comme vous êtes belle! Plus belle qu'autrefois, je crois!"*

She curtsied in acknowledgment of his compliment and then asked, *"Mais où est le capitaine—dans sa cabine?"*

"Mais non, mademoiselle. Il va déjà à la taverne Tontine pour faire des affaires."

"Merci, monsieur."

She retraced her steps westward on Water Street until she reached the Tontine Coffee House, which housed the Stock Exchange. As she entered, she hesitated, because the room was large and full of men, all of whom seemed to be shouting numbers at one another. Her presence was not even noticed. She despaired of finding Jacques in this boisterous crowd. There was a doorway at the side that seemed to lead to a room where refreshments were served.

The dining room was crowded, too, with many tables at which businessmen sat and had liquid refreshments. She finally sighted Jacques, who was sitting alone at a table, busily writing with a quill pen. As she approached his table, he looked up and regarded her curiously, wondering what a woman would be doing in this place. Then his eyes widened in recognition. He got up from the table and came over to her.

"Betsy!" he said, and both surprise and delight were in his voice. "What do you do—here in New York?"

"I left Providence two weeks ago. I came to live here."

Jacques was so overjoyed that he could not restrain himself from embracing her. He kissed her full on the lips, and she did not resist him.

Then he held her off at arm's length and studied her. "What a fine lady you are now—a woman, not a girl anymore. And in a hoopskirt! You are very *à la mode, ma chère*."

Eliza twirled around in front of him. She enjoyed showing off, and his response was immediate.

"*Tu es ravissante!*" he said. "And your husband, this Matt that you love so much, he is here with you?"

"He didn't marry me. His family objected. I bore his child—a *bâtard*. The child is in Providence, being taken care of by Free-love Ballou."

"You have left your *bébé*?"

"*Oui.* I wished to have a new life. I am not Betsy Bowen anymore, Jacques."

"Not Besty Bowen? Then who are you?"

"Eliza Capet."

Jacques smiled. "Capet—the royal family! That is not a very popular name in France now."

Eliza nodded and then turned, preparing to leave.

Jacques thrust out his hand to hers and pulled her toward him. "But you cannot go now, just when I have found you."

"But you are busy with *tes affaires, mon capitaine*. I live in a boardinghouse—Mrs. Cuyler's at 49 Wall Street. You may come to visit me this afternoon, perhaps, and we can talk."

Jacques looked at her playfully. "Only talk?" he asked.

" 'Tis a most respectable boardinghouse, Jacques. I am a lady, *tu vois*."

Jacques looked at her skeptically. "Then where did you get such fine clothes, *ma fille*?"

Eliza, to her surprise, found herself blushing. "I have—a friend,

26

Jacques. Or perhaps you thought I worked as a chambermaid?"

Jacques' laughter exploded from him in the way that she remembered. "You—a chambermaid? Never—at least until you have fifty years, *peut-être!*"

Eliza tilted her head and said, "When I am fifty years old, Jacques, I shall be very rich."

Late that afternoon the maid knocked on Eliza's door and said, "There's a Frenchie sea captain downstairs. He's asking to see you, mum."

"Tell him I'll be right down, Lottie."

Jacques rose to his feet as Eliza appeared in the doorway of the front parlor. He rushed forward and kissed the hand that she extended toward him. She had noted that this was the way a lady greeted a gentleman in New York.

Then he took her in his arms and kissed her with passion. "We can perhaps go to your *chambre?*"

She did not need to ask why. Gently pushing him away, Eliza said, "But it is not allowed here for a lady to entertain a gentleman in her room. Mrs. Cuyler's boardinghouse is most respectable."

"Then we must find other lodgings for you, *ma chère* Betsy."

"Lodgings and board are very expensive in New York. This costs me four dollars a week plus the cost of wood for the fireplace."

Jacques scratched his head thoughtfully. "*Oui, c'est cher.* In Providence you had lodgings with your mother." He shrugged. "Well, *en ce cas*, I must entertain you on my ship, *comme autrefois.*"

Eliza nodded and they moved to the door.

As they walked toward Peck's Slip, Eliza told him what had happened since she last saw him in Providence: about the baby and the murder of Michel, and of her final decision to provide for the child and leave Providence forever. She told him of Captain Curry and his generosity. Last of all, she mentioned William Dunlap.

27

Jacques looked at her acutely. "This Monsieur Dunlap—I think you like him very much."

"Yes. It is not that he is such a good lover, but he has a fine mind and he is educated."

"Ah, *je vois*. Your old Jacques—he is not a man of books. I cannot make competition with him there."

Eliza felt that she had unwittingly criticized him and said hastily, "Perhaps not. But he is not a man like you in the bed."

Jacques beamed. "I am glad to know that. But this Monsieur Dunlap—he reads books to make money?"

Eliza laughed. "Oh, no, Jacques. He writes plays for the theatre."

"An *écrivain de pièces*? And he has much money?"

"No, he is poor. He must help his father-in-law in the china business to support his wife and children."

Jacques shook his head disconsolately. "He is not a man for you, Betsy. You must find a man of some money to make you his mistress."

She nodded and said, "I know. But meanwhile, perhaps I shall find myself a 'madame' who will take me into her whorehouse the way Sally Marshall did."

Jacques snorted his contempt. "A beautiful woman like you must be a whore? No, you must do better than that, Betsy. *Bien entendu*, when I am in port, you will dine well and I will give you lodging on my ship. But what will you do when I am not in port?"

"I told you," she said sadly.

They had reached Peck's Slip, and Eliza followed Jacques up the gangplank and into his cabin. She looked around her at the familiar furnishings: the bunk bed and its red quilt, the mahogany desk with its brass knobs, the corner cupboard where Jacques kept his wine, and the porthole on the other side of the room. For a moment she was transported backward in time to the night when, as a girl of fifteen, she had first seen this room. It was incredible to her that four years had passed since then.

She turned to Jacques. "Your cabin is exactly the same, and I still love it." She paused and then turned her eyes to the wine cupboard. "Do you still keep Madeira in there?"

"*Mais bien entendu.* Would you like some?"

She nodded, and he fetched two glasses and poured the wine. He raised his glass in a toast to her. "To *ma bien-aimée* Betsy."

"Not Betsy, Jacques. You must remember that I am now Eliza Capet."

He laughed gently. "By any name, to me you are the most beautiful woman in the world, *ma chère* Eliza."

They drank, and the wine was no sooner finished than he went over to her, drawing her toward the bunk.

"We can make love now?" he asked and kissed her ardently.

Her answer was to open her bodice quickly so that her breasts protruded voluptuously. He began kissing them, and soon he had undressed her, hoopskirt and all, so that she lay naked on the red quilt of his bunk. Then he tore off his clothing until he stood nude before her. He had put on a bit of weight, she noticed, as she surveyed his hairy, stocky figure, and his manhood was as large and hard as she remembered it. She reached out her hand and grasped it, pulling him toward her.

Jacques was immediately astride her, pressing himself slowly but gently into her. She sighed with pleasure and was surprised that for the first time she was actually enjoying contact with him. In the past, in the days before Matt had awakened her, love-making with Jacques had been not unpleasant but neither had it been really enjoyable. All that had changed now, and she gave herself up to him ardently.

Jacques was aware that her response was different from before, and the thought that she was enjoying herself renewed his desire and made him all the more anxious to please her. He kissed her tenderly on the mouth, on her nipples, and in that sensitive spot between her neck and shoulders. She responded ecstatically, lazily sure that with Jacques her pleasure would be prolonged. Unlike William and Captain Curry, Jacques could control himself indefinitely, and when at last she did reach her climax, she arched herself up to meet him, moaning and sobbing with passion. Jacques let forth the bull-like roar that always accompanied the consummation of his lust, and he lay limply on top of her while he regained his breath.

When he had rolled himself away and lay quietly at her side, he turned his face toward hers. "You have become much more wise in the making of love, Betsy—I mean, Eliza. In Providence you were like a wax doll in the bed. Now, you are alive—like a woman. Who has learned you this?"

She did not want to mention Matt or even to think of him. She said, "It is the years going by, Jacques. I have grown up. I am nineteen now."

He surveyed her nude figure on the bed with a contemplative and admiring look. "*Oui*, you are a woman now, more beautiful than you were before, and I think I love you even more."

She acknowledged his compliment with a smile that was almost smug, pleased by the knowledge of her power over him. It was a power that she intended to use.

That night Jacques took her to dinner at the Tontine City Hotel. In the parlor reserved for gentlemen dining with ladies, she had her first full dinner in New York. It began with a punch made with rum and "sourings": lemon, orange and lime juice which had been imported in casks. This was followed by lobster and terrapin served in a delicious cream sauce. The meat course was venison and bear steak, which Eliza had never tasted before. For dessert there was a syllabub, its creamy curds flavored with sherry, and a plate of sweet cakes iced with rich chocolate.

During dinner Jacques again brought up the subject of William Dunlap. "This man of the theatre—this Dunlap—you will still make love with him on the stage of the theatre?"

Eliza laughed. "Oh, no. Now that you are here, I will not need him, will I?"

Jacques became uncharacteristically firm, striking the edge of the table so forcefully with his hand that the glasses shook. "I will not share you, Betsy!"

Eliza's response was cool. "My name is not Betsy, Jacques. You must learn to call me Eliza. Betsy Bowen is as good as dead."

"Very well, Eliza. But you have not answered my question."

"No," said Eliza. "I will not make love with him. But I will still see him. He is a friend, and there is much that I can learn from him."

"You have already learned the most important thing for a woman to know—how to pleasure a man in bed."

"There are other things. A woman is not only for making love. She must know about books—the things that Jonathan Clarke taught me."

Jacques shook his head in a puzzled way. "But you already know enough of those things. Why do you need to know more?"

Eliza spoke slowly and seriously. "Because I intend to become a lady."

"And when you become a lady, then you will say goodbye to Jacques."

"Perhaps," she said quietly.

Jacques became angry and pounded the table again. "I see that I cannot trust you. You think only of yourself—not of me."

Eliza reached out and covered his hand with her own. "But I do think of you, Jacques. You know that I have always been fond of you. I still have gratitude for your taking care of me in Providence, and as a lover, you are—well, *parfait*."

His anger vanished, and he smiled at her. "I am *cochon* to be jealous of this Dunlap. I will pay your board."

"It is very expensive, Jacques."

"Yes," he admitted. "But tomorrow I will find a place not so expensive, and not so respectable that a man is not allowed to visit a lady in her *chambre*."

Eliza's new quarters were in a boardinghouse at 32 Beekman Street, which ran between Nassau and Pearl Streets and was far to the east of Mrs. Cuyler's house. Nearby was the district known as Beekman's Swamp, close to the ill-smelling tanning vats owned by Jacobus Roosevelt. The Almshouse, Bridewell and the jail, which faced Chatham Street and the park, were near enough to make Eliza uncomfortable.

She was the only woman among the six boarders, who were dealers in cattle, leather, glue, tallow and wool. They were rough, good-natured men who were so absorbed in business affairs carried out in the Bull's Head Tavern that they seemed scarcely to notice her presence.

She had two rooms on the second floor: a large bedroom and a small sitting room. The food was plentiful, though plainly prepared. But she felt a freedom and lack of constraint here that was more to her liking than the strait-laced atmosphere at Mrs. Cuyler's. The board was only two dollars a week, an amount that Jacques could well afford.

Daniel MacAllister, the proprietor of the house, was a corpulent, dour-faced Scotsman who was never without the smell of rum on his breath. Every Sunday he attended services at the Presbyterian church near St. Paul's, but his religious convictions did not extend to a concern for the morality of others. He was perfectly aware that Eliza was the mistress of a French sea captain who paid for her board and room, but as long as the payments were made regularly he shrugged his shoulders at the arrangement and made no comment.

Sometimes Jacques would take Eliza for an elaborate dinner at the Tontine, and on some nights Édouard, the ship's cook, prepared a repast of simple elegance aboard ship.

With the move to Beekman Street, Eliza had no occasion to see William Dunlap. She had no need for him now, although she did miss the hours she had spent talking with him about Shakespeare. She had settled into a domestic routine with Jacques, usually seeing him only at the end of the day.

Meanwhile, she had persuaded him to buy more material for dresses, and she busied herself with needlework. As the days moved deeper into winter, she was in need of winter clothing and gloves, and these items were generously supplied by Jacques during trips to Pearl Street. And at long last, Eliza had acquired a hat, an elaborate concoction of bows and ribbons and Belgian lace. It sat rakishly on top of her curls and was fastened down with pins of ornamented silver, so that it would stay fast on her head against the stiffest breeze that blew in from the bay.

Within two weeks *L'Étoile de Marseilles* was loaded with a new cargo, and it was time for Jacques to leave for the West Indies.

The night before he left, they dined royally at the Tontine, and later, in Jacques' cabin aboard the ship, they talked about her future during his absence.

After they had made love, Jacques looked at her seriously. "I will leave twenty dollars with you, Eliza. That will be more than enough for you while I am away."

She did not feel especially grateful for his generosity. It was, for her, only a fair trade for her favors. But she threw her arms about him and said, "Oh, Jacques, you are so good to me—and so generous!"

A note of sternness crept into his voice as he said, "But I trust you not to go to the bed with other men while I am gone, especially with your friend who makes *pièces de théâtre. Compris?*"

"Oh, yes, Jacques, it is *compris*, just as before, when we were in Providence. I will not even look at another man."

"*Bien*," said Jacques, and took her once again to his bunk for a final bout of love-making.

But Eliza had no intention of keeping her promise. She saw no reason why she should belong exclusively to Jacques as she had in Providence. If William should want to take her to the theatre, she would certainly accept his invitation. And she would reward him in the usual way.

She did not think it would be prudent for her to receive a man in her room at the new boardinghouse, for fear Mr. MacAllister would report it to Jacques on his return. It occurred to her that Mr. MacAllister, in an alcoholic mood of lust, might blackmail her into going to bed with him in return for silence.

And so, Eliza continued to see William. He had a way of rewarding her for playing the game with him, and that was what counted most.

William's new play, *Fontainville Abbey*, was produced, and it was a great success. Eliza was there at its début and was very proud when the audience brought William before the curtain many times.

She had an occasional pang of conscience for her infidelity to Jacques, especially when she remembered how in Providence she had saved herself only for him. But during the last year her views had changed. She would give nothing to any man without a suitable and immediate reward. Her only regret was that she could not accept gifts, articles of clothing or trinkets that Jacques might question her about when he returned.

She was also sure that William would not infect her with disease, because he did not consort with whores. It was possible, of course, that she might become pregnant, but she would deal with that situation if it arose. Of one thing she was certain: she would never go through another childbirth, and abortion would be the only way out. But she did not become pregnant, and soon she no longer worried about it.

CHAPTER 3

WITH THE COMING OF JUNE and the first outbreak of yellow fever in the city, Eliza became panicky and told Jacques that they would have to move north, where people seemed to be safe from the plague that swept the city so regularly during the summer months.

"But my dear Eliza," said Jacques, "I cannot afford the high rents up near Greenwich Village. I am not a man *très riche, comme tu sais.*"

"But I cannot stay here," said Eliza. "It's dangerous, and I don't want to get the sickness and die. If you cannot afford accommodations in the north, then I must find a benefactor who can!"

Jacques was surprised and even shocked. "You are now become *une femme dure, ma chère,* not like the little girl I knew in Providence."

"I have learned since then that I must take care of myself in my own way. I cannot trust any man again—not after Matt."

Jacques shook his head sadly. "You make me *triste,* Eliza. What am I to do? I do not want to lose you to another man."

She faced him. "But you would not mind losing me to the yellow-fever plague, *n'est-ce pas?*"

Jacques was troubled, and he sat down in the chair at his desk in the cabin. His brow was furrowed, and he rubbed the back of his head thoughtfully.

"*Très bien,* Eliza. What you say is the truth. I would not like losing you to another man. But to lose you by death—that would be even worse. Tomorrow we look for a room north of the city."

35

Eliza, as though on impulse, but quite calculatedly, threw her arms about him. This display of affection aroused Jacques, as she had known it would. It meant that she had to go to bed with him again. The prospect was far from exciting at the moment, but she had had her way over him once again, and that made her happy. At least she would not die of yellow fever.

The house at 14 Moore Street was small and dilapidated. It was of Dutch design, and even the present owner, an elderly widower named Hans Van Zandt, was of Dutch ancestry. He agreed after much haggling to rent the two rooms on the second floor for fifteen dollars a month.

There was a fireplace to provide heat on chilly days, and cooking could be done on the large hearth on the ground floor. Mr. Van Zandt was delighted to learn that Eliza could cook and would provide his meals if he covered the cost of wood and food. His grandson, Pieter, a strapping boy of sixteen, would do the shopping and bring the necessities of life from town.

Eliza was delighted with the situation of the house, which was not far from the Hudson River. Nearby, there was Hudson Square, an overgrown and ill-kept open area where there were some trees and a few crudely made wooden benches. During the hot months of the summer, Eliza often sat there to enjoy the cool breeze from the river.

It was pleasant enough for Eliza, but for Jacques the new location had disadvantages. To get to the southern tip of the island, where *L'Étoile de Marseilles* was docked, he had to walk through Hudson Square to Leonard Street and thence more than a mile along Broadway. When the weather was fine, he enjoyed the walk and the exercise it provided. But the heat of summer sometimes made it necessary for him to get a hackney to complete the journey, and this meant an additional outlay of money.

Eliza did not dare go south to the city, and indeed there seemed little point in making the trip. Half of the inhabitants had fled in their fear of yellow fever. Occasionally, when Jacques returned from the port, he brought Eliza a copy of *The New York Advertiser* with its news of the many deaths. Most of the dead were poor Irish immigrants who were buried in the potter's field east of Bowery Road. Those who gave signs of recovery from the illness were isolated on Nutten Island in New York Bay. Toward the end of the summer, a hospital was opened on the Bellevue estate northeast of the city. Here the victims were cared for and given the usual remedies of garlic, vinegar and gunpowder. It was popularly believed that the smoking of tobacco and the burning of tar would prevent infection, and small fires were kept burning in the area of Bellevue to protect the lives of the doctors and nurses who cared for the afflicted.

Eliza was bored, especially during those times when Jacques was away at sea, and was grateful for the company of Hans Van Zandt and young Pieter. Hans was about seventy. He had been born in Manhattan of Dutch parents and was in his early fifties at the start of the Revolution. He believed that the city rightly belonged to the original Dutch inhabitants. It did not matter to him whether the English or the Americans won the war. He lived contentedly in his parents' house on Moore Street.

On some days, when Eliza had finished the household chores, she listened to the old man reminisce about the days of his youth. He had once been married, but his wife had died in childbirth with their second child, Willem, and he had not married again. Just before the Revolution Willem had married and moved out of the house to live in the city and had continued to live there during the British occupation. His wife had left with a British officer at the end of the Revolution, leaving Willem to bring up his only son, Pieter. She was never heard from again. Then, four years ago, when Pieter's father died of yellow fever, the boy had come to live with his grandfather and had stayed with him ever since.

Pieter adored Eliza from the moment of her arrival. He had never seen such a beautiful woman before, and he regarded her as an unearthly creature who had been magically set down in his grandfather's house. He watched her every movement, and when her eyes met his, he blushed to the roots of his hair. Often, he helped her with some of the heavier household chores, and she rewarded him with a smile that set his heart pounding.

37

Eliza was, of course, well aware of her effect on him. He was a bright boy and would one day become a handsome man, if he did not become fat the way so many Dutchmen seemed to do. She curbed his appetite by not refilling his plate at mealtime. When she learned that the boy could neither read nor write, she decided to teach him, and he readily agreed, if only to be close to her.

And so on warm summer days they sat in the tall grass near the river and pored over her books. He was as eager a student as she herself had been when she lived with the Allens, and within a few weeks, Pieter had mastered the alphabet and could add by counting on his fingers.

But on some afternoons, he was so overwhelmed by Eliza's closeness that he could hardly concentrate. He tried to conceal the shameful bulging in his pants, but Eliza saw it and made a decision. In the interests of Pieter's education she would seduce him.

So one day, when the boy was especially aroused, she casually reached over and unbuttoned his pants. He was amazed and frightened, but did nothing to dissuade her. When she touched him, he immediately had a spontaneous climax and pulled away from her in shame, covering himself with his kerchief.

Eliza waited a few moments and then touched his shoulder. He turned and looked at her intently.

"Why did you do that?" he demanded. " 'Tis sinful to touch that thing. My father told me so."

Eliza smiled gently and took his hand in hers. "I knew what was bothering you, so that you could not keep your mind on your book."

Pieter looked puzzled and embarrassed, and to distract himself, he buttoned up his pants. At last he said bluntly, "Why did you say it was not sinful, when my father said it was?"

"Many people believe what your father said, but I do not. That's all. People say it is wicked, but they do it just the same. They are hypocrites."

"What's hypocrites?"

"A hypocrite is somebody who says something is bad, but does it anyway, and makes believe he don't."

"Some of the boys I know in the city do it with girls, but I never dared to."

"Why not?"

"Because my father told me that they would make me sick down there. Is that true?"

"Yes. You must be careful, Piet."

He frowned in thought. "But it *do* feel good. I would like to do it again sometime." He blushed at his boldness.

"We can," said Eliza. "But you must remember this, Pieter. When the Captain is here, we cannot do these things. If he found out, he would horsewhip you."

"Why?"

"Because he is my husband, and he would be jealous. A husband don't want his wife doing things with other men. He looks at his wife as his property."

"Are you his property, madame?"

"I am no man's property," said Eliza slowly. Then, with a smile, she added, "But he thinks I am."

"I don't understand it, and that's the truth."

She kissed him lightly on the cheek. "You will understand someday."

He was thoughtful for a moment, and when he spoke, his eyes had a faraway look that was also sad. "My mother ran away with a British officer and never came back. Why did she do that?"

"Maybe she loved the British officer and had stopped loving your father."

Pieter looked at her straight in the eyes. "What is love, madame?"

The question took her by surprise, and she did not know how to answer him.

At last she said, "I don't know, Pieter."

CHAPTER 4

ELIZA HAD PLANNED to move back into the city when autumn came, but the long Indian summer and its warm days brought a renewal of the yellow-fever outbreak.

Eliza was bored. She longed for the life of the town, the opportunity to buy new clothes, and to resume her friendship with William Dunlap, who during the summer had taken his family to the house in Perth Amboy where he was born.

Meanwhile, there were old Hans and Pieter for company during the times when Jacques was away. Pieter by this time had become Eliza's devoted servant. Three times a week he ventured into town to bring back food, ice, and wood for the hearth, where Eliza did all the cooking. He looked forward to the times when Eliza tutored him in reading and writing, as they lay in the long grass near the river. As a reward for being a good student he was given a full initiation into the art of making love, also under Eliza's instructions.

When Jacques returned from a voyage and lived at the house, the boy never indicated that there was anything in his relationship with Eliza that went beyond that of a servant.

But Jacques was aware of the boy's devotion and questioned Eliza about it.

"This *garçon* Pieter is in love with you, did you know it?"

"I know that he is fond of me," said Eliza casually.

"*Ah, non, chère Eliza*. It is more than that."

Eliza looked at Jacques impatiently. "Now what would give you an idea like that?"

"It is the way he looks at you."

"No doubt he is very grateful to me, Jacques. During the summer days when I was bored, I have been teaching him to read and write. He has never been to a school, *tu sais*."

Jacques smiled. "It is good of you, *ma chère*. But *prends garde* that the reading and writing are the only things you teach him. He is a grown boy, almost a man."

Eliza turned on him angrily. "*Vraiment*, Jacques, you have a *mentalité vicieuse*! If I were to take a new lover while you are away, it would not be a boy with no money! So get these foolish ideas out of your head!"

"I make apologies, Eliza. I have forgotten that for you love is a game—with a reward afterward. You make explanation to me a long time ago in Providence." He could not help smiling at the memory.

"Well, it's still true, *mon brave capitaine*. It will always be true!"

Although Jacques had believed her, Eliza took no chances. When she was able to have a few moments of privacy with Pieter while they swept up the ashes from the hearth, she cautioned him about the Captain's suspicions.

Pieter was alarmed. He remembered that Eliza had told him that Jacques would horsewhip him if he found out what was going on.

"But, madame, why should he think such things? I do not touch you or come near you."

"It's not that, Piet. It's the way you look at me."

"I can't help the way I look at you."

"Then keep your eyes on what you are doing."

"Then I mustn't look at you at all?"

Eliza smiled. "No, that would be worse. Then the Captain would be sure that I had spoken to you and would become more suspicious than ever."

His eyes filled with tears, which threatened to spill over.

Eliza's voice became suddenly sharp. "Now, none of that, young man!"

"But—but I love you, madame."

"Then if you love me, you will do as I say! You must learn to hide your feelings. Make your face like a dumb boy's." She illustrated this by making her face into a mask.

Pieter laughed and then imitated her. "Is that it?"

"Very good!" said Eliza. "Maybe someday you will be an actor on the stage."

With the coming of a heavy frost in November, miraculously yellow fever left New York. Eliza decided to return to the city, and Jacques arranged for them to have their old rooms at Daniel MacAllister's boardinghouse on Beekman Street.

Pieter was heartbroken, and old Hans desolate, for he was losing his housekeeper and cook. But Eliza assured both that she would visit them and gave them the address on Beekman Street. Privately, she assured Pieter that once a week he could continue his lessons in reading and writing on afternoons when *L'Étoile de Marseilles* was not in port. The boy nodded gratefully and was able to hold back his tears when the day of her departure arrived.

Back in her old quarters on Beekman Street, Eliza began acquiring new clothing for the winter season: two new gowns, a warmer winter coat, new shoes with silver buckles, and even two pairs of woolen gloves. Jacques reproved her for her extravagance but smiled indulgently when he saw her in her new clothes. He was proud to take her to dinner at the Tontine and was flattered by the jealous glances of the men at other tables.

When *L'Étoile de Marseilles* left for the West Indies early in December, Jacques paid their board for six weeks in advance and left twenty-five dollars for Eliza's personal use. This was kept in a locked tin box to which Eliza carried the key.

Jacques had a lavish farewell dinner prepared by Édouard aboard ship on the night before he sailed. As usual, on the eve of his departure, Jacques was insatiable in his love-making, and Eliza endured it without pleasure. She had learned by this time to feign an ecstasy that she did not feel.

At last, she said, "Jacques, you must not do it again. I am tired, and you must think of your health. You are getting older and should not strain yourself so. Your health—"

Jacques roared with laughter. "*Ma santé?* It is better than ever.

I will never lose health when you are near."

The situation resolved itself when Jacques tried to make love again, and both of them fell asleep before he reached his climax.

The days of December grew colder, and on the day after New Year's, 1796, there was a heavy snowfall, which marooned Eliza in her room on Beekman Street for almost a week. She was bored, and her only diversions were reading and those times when Pieter came to visit. He did errands for her, slogging through the slush-filled streets, where traffic almost came to a standstill. Horses fell, carriages were overturned, and walking became almost impossible. But Pieter always returned, eager for his lessons in reading and writing—and for the reward that awaited him.

In the middle of January there was a sudden thaw, and Eliza's spirits rose at the thought that very soon the John Street Theatre would begin its deferred season. She dispatched Pieter with a note to William Dunlap, in the hope that he still spent his mornings at Mrs. Cuyler's boardinghouse. The response was immediate. Pieter returned with a note from Dunlap, asking whether he might call on her, and her answer was, of course, yes.

When he came to visit the next afternoon, she was wearing one of her new gowns and looking lovelier than ever. He was overjoyed to see her and talked enthusiastically about the new plays he was working on: *The Mysterious Monk*, based on a novel by Mrs. Radcliffe, and some adaptations of Kotzebue's German plays.

Eliza listened attentively, but while he talked, she was studying his face. It was pale and tired-looking, and the circles under his eyes told her that he was not sleeping well.

At last, during a pause in the conversation, she said, "William, you don't look at all well. I think you are working too hard."

"It is true, but I must work, Eliza, not only for my future income, but it is all that really interests me." He paused. "Except you, my darling."

He moved from his chair over to the bed, where she lay back against the pillows. His kiss was passionate, and she responded to him eagerly.

"Where can we go, Eliza, for a bit of love? The theatre is too

43

cold, and anyway it is locked, because the season has not begun."

"We could stay here," said Eliza.

"But your sea captain might find out—"

"I don't care if he does. I told him that I will continue to see you, because you are a good friend."

"Am I? I cannot even bring you a gift, I am so poor."

Eliza looked at him affectionately. "The gift you bring me is yourself, and the chance to talk to you about the theatre and things that are more important to me than love-making."

He looked at her with a rueful smile. "But I am not a good lover, I fear."

"You will do very well," she said.

She stepped out of her hoopskirt with a flourish and at last stood before him, naked and inviting. Gently, he pushed her back upon the bed and unbuttoned his trousers. As he placed his hand caressingly between her legs, she lay back with a sigh. His gentleness as a lover stirred her, and when at last he had thrust himself into her, she responded almost with ecstasy.

Later, Eliza prepared tea from the kettle that she kept on a trivet over the fire in the hearth, and they talked.

"But how do you manage here alone?" William asked. "When the Captain is away, you must be very lonely."

Eliza pointed to the row of books on a table. "I don't get lonely when Shakespeare is with me, and then there is Pieter Van Zandt who lives in the place on Moore Street. He comes once a week, sometimes oftener, and I teach him how to read and write."

"How old is he?"

"Seventeen. He's a fine boy. He adores me and does errands when the weather is bad."

William looked thoughtful. "Seventeen. I suppose your course of instruction has not limited itself to reading and writing. Do you sleep with him, Eliza, or is that an impertinent question?"

"Of course I sleep with him," she said with a laugh. "I had to. When he was with me, his trousers bulged so bad that he could not concentrate on his lessons."

William threw back his head and laughed. "Eliza, you are incorrigible! You sleep with this dolt of a boy so that he can learn to read and write!"

44

Eliza did not join in his laughter. "It is not funny, William. Don't you think it's important for a boy to be able to read and write?" She paused, then added, "And he is not a dolt!"

"But he is a good lover, I gather."

"Not yet," said Eliza with quiet seriousness. "But one day I think he will be."

"With you as his teacher, how could he help it?"

Eliza shrugged. "But enough about Pieter. I want you to tell me about the new theatre season. What plays will you be performing?"

"Well, we are opening on February tenth with *The Provoked Husband*. It's not a very good play but it's popular, and the afterpiece will be *The Spoiled Child*, which always amuses the audience."

"Will there be any Shakespeare this season?"

"Very little. I think Hodgkinson will do *Macbeth* in the spring and also *Much Ado About Nothing*."

Eliza clapped her hands in delight. "*That* performance will be one that I'll certainly not miss, even if Jacques doesn't want to go. He doesn't like Shakespeare, poor man. The language is too fancy for him to understand."

"It's hard enough for some of our Americans to understand."

"But won't they be doing any of your plays, William?"

"Only one that I know of—*The Archers, or The Mountaineers*, Benjamin Carr's opera with my book. But it promises to be a good season."

"Oh, how I do wish I could go to that opening on February tenth, whether or not Jacques is here."

"I will get you tickets for that, come what may!" He extended his hand to hers and clasped it firmly in his own. "Here's my oath on it!"

"Oh, thank you, dear William!"

Eliza's smile was not only one of gratitude. It was a smile that was also triumphant. She would receive her reward for playing the game, after all.

CHAPTER 5

On the night of February 10, 1796, Eliza attended the opening performance of the John Street Theatre's new season. True to his promise, William gave her a ticket for a box seat to see *The Provoked Husband*. Jacques was at sea, and so Eliza went to the theatre alone.

She spent the whole day preparing herself for the occasion. First, she washed and curled her hair and took a bath from the large bowl in her room. Then she carefully pressed all the clothing she would wear: her underthings, her lace cap, and last of all a new gown that she would wear for the first time, a dress with a bodice of brilliant green velvet and a hoopskirt of expensive yellow brocade. For jewelry she would wear a new necklace of glowing red coral with silver pendant earrings to match, each studded with a small brilliant diamond.

She was so excited that she had no appetite for dinner and ate lightly of cheese, bread and an apple. When Pieter appeared at a quarter before seven, bearing her ticket, he was overcome by her appearance. He had never seen her in full regalia before, and the sight left him momentarily speechless.

Finally, he was able to say, "A hackney is waiting at the door, madame. You look to be a true queen. You look—"

As words failed him, she gave him a ravishing smile and patted him on the shoulder. "Thank you, dear Pieter. It is late. We must leave now."

She descended the narrow staircase slowly, lifting her hoopskirt so that it would not be soiled. Pieter followed her, still wide-eyed with wonder. He opened the door of the hackney, and she entered. He turned as though to leave, when she stopped him.

"Surely, Pieter, you will come along as far as the theatre?"

He jumped into the cab eagerly, but settled himself far to one side so that he would not touch her lovely clothing. He looked at her carefully coiffed red-gold hair, which was topped by an elaborate lace cap ornamented with a small cluster of bright-green feathers pinned to her hair with a gold clasp.

"What kind of bird has feathers like that, madame?"

Eliza laughed. "Maybe they came from the tail of somebody's parrot."

This idea threw him into a fit of giggles that lasted almost until they reached Ann Street and the theatre. He sprang from his seat in the cab so that he could open the door for her.

Before she went up the stairs that led to the theatre entrance, she turned to him with a gracious smile and said, "Some day, Pieter, you will be my footman and wear a beautiful uniform with many buckles." This remark made him straighten up as though standing at attention, and he gave a vigorous nod of his head.

Eliza pressed through the crowd of people waiting in the lobby. For the first time she felt herself to be the equal of ladies of fashion and society—at least in appearance. The appreciative stares of the men and the envious looks of the women told her that her gown was stunning. She was aware that ladies did not usually attend the theatre without an escort, and this only added to the attention that her arrival created.

When she was ushered to the box to which her ticket entitled her, she noted with disappointment that its four chairs were not occupied. Soon a handsomely outfitted young dandy arrived and took the chair on her left, but the two chairs on her right remained empty.

The orchestra began to play a sprightly overture, and the candles that lighted the auditorium were extinguished one by one. Suddenly, a man of imposing appearance and bearing entered the box and took the seat on her right. Before sitting down, he gave her a slow, appraising look, and his eyes, which were large and gray in color, told her that he liked what he saw.

He nodded to her in a dignified but friendly fashion, and she nodded back. He was dressed formally in an expensive waistcoat of black brocade, and he wore a powdered white wig. His face was an extraordinary one, with a massive leonine head and a full brow. The features had a chiseled quality, from the full curving lips to a nose that was long and sharply cut. But it was his lustrous eyes that were most striking.

As the curtain rose on the first act of *The Provoked Husband*, the audience burst into applause, with those in the gallery exceptionally boisterous and approving. The play was amusing and obviously one that was highly popular. Laughter and loud clapping greeted the funny lines, and it was clear that the opening of the season, after its long postponement, was ecstatically welcomed by a city that had always loved theatregoing. Almost any play would have received a rousing welcome.

During the intermission after the first act, the gentleman to Eliza's right turned to her and said, "Very amusing, is it not?"

"Yes, I am enjoying it, but truth to tell, I am happier with the comedies of Shakespeare."

The man took out a snuffbox of filigreed silver, opened it and extended it toward her.

"No, thank you," said Eliza primly.

He took a pinch of snuff between his thumb and forefinger, sniffed and inhaled deeply. He took a lace-embroidered kerchief from his pocket, sneezed in a genteel manner and delicately dabbed at his nose.

"I beg your pardon," he said. "Does snuff offend you?"

"Not at all, sir."

He moved a little closer to her chair and sat sideways so that he could look at her. "I have not seen you at the theatre before. Are you lately come to New York?"

"Yes. I am from Providence, Rhode Island."

"A most delightful and beautiful city. I have many friends there."

Eliza favored him with a polite smile. She had decided not to be overly friendly with this distinguished gentleman and did her best to be reticent and ladylike.

48

"And do you like New York?"

"Oh, indeed I do. It makes Providence seem rather backward. There is no theatre permitted there, you know."

"Not? The Puritan heritage is still strong there, I would imagine—a quality that extends itself, no doubt, to its inhabitants?" He accompanied the question with a raised eyebrow and a look that was faintly suggestive.

She returned the look in an open, matter-of-fact way. "Yes, I suppose that we are all rather puritanical in our ways and shall never outgrow it. They are snuffing out the lights. The second act will soon begin."

The gentleman leaned back in his chair with a sigh. He felt that this beautiful young woman was keeping him at her distance, and his spirits were dampened. Impatiently, he waited for the next intermission and looked at the play with boredom. He squirmed in his chair, but made sure that in doing so, the chair moved always slightly closer to Eliza. Her response to this maneuver was to move her own chair slightly away and closer to the young gentleman on her left.

When the intermission came, Eliza was ready for the byplay that she knew would be renewed.

"I find the second act rather tedious," said the gentleman, "but I have seen the play before." He smiled at her archly. "But then, I suppose the play would be more interesting to one who has not endured in reality the trials of married life."

"Oh, I am married, sir. I am Madame de la Croix."

He nodded his head in acknowledgment of her introduction and said, "I am Alexander Hamilton. You have heard the name?"

She managed to control her surprise and the quickened beating of her heart and was able to say, "Indeed, who has not heard the name?"

He paused and then said casually, "But your husband, he is not with you tonight?"

"No. He is a French ship's captain, presently at sea."

He sighed. "Alas, I, too, am alone." He pointed to the empty chair on his right. "My wife is ill with a severe cold and could not attend."

49

She foresaw his next remark, and it was not different from what she expected.

"After the theatre, perhaps we could have some refreshments together, since we are both so very much alone."

She was ready with her reply. "That is very kind of you, Mr. Hamilton, but I am going to dine with a friend, Mr. Dunlap."

His disappointment was evident, but politely he said, "Mr. William Dunlap, the playwright?"

"Yes. He is stage manager for the performance, and I shall meet him outside when the afterpiece is concluded."

Mr. Hamilton was silent for a moment, during which he gazed into her eyes with unconcealed ardor. At last he said, "Mr. Dunlap is a most fortunate fellow to be escorting a lady as lovely as you."

She lowered her eyes. "Thank you, Mr. Hamilton," she said demurely. "I am most flattered by your generous compliment."

"I assure you, madame, that it was not generosity that prompted it."

He became silent as the candles were snuffed out for the beginning of the third act. Eliza stared at the curtain, but her interest in the play, slight as it had been, had now disappeared entirely.

The fact that she was sitting next to the great Alexander Hamilton set her thoughts whirling. She knew that she had only to accept his invitation and she would very quickly find herself in bed with him. She had heard of his reputation as a lecher and rakehell, but she had no intention of becoming just another lady of the evening in the long list of his conquests. She found him attractive but certainly not irresistible. She could conceive of herself as this man's mistress, but she would not settle for less.

At the conclusion of the afterpiece, the trifle called *The Spoiled Child*, Mr. Hamilton repeated his invitation to have refreshments with him, and she again politely declined. He accompanied her to the lobby, hoping that William Dunlap would not put in an appearance.

When they reached the entrance to the theatre, Eliza was dismayed to find that William was not there. Mr. Hamilton waited with her as the long line of coaches drew up on the street to pick up ladies and gentlemen of the audience and take them home.

Suddenly, William was at her side, and she greeted him with a sigh of relief.

"William," she said, "I would like you to meet a gentleman who has kindly escorted me this evening. This is Mr. Alexander Hamilton. Mr. Hamilton, I believe you know Mr. Dunlap?"

Mr. Hamilton's smile of greeting was only polite, and William was so surprised that he could hardly stammer out words of greeting.

Mr. Hamilton made his *adieux* to Eliza in formal manner, doffing his hat and bowing from the waist. Eliza curtsied.

"Meeting you, Madame de la Croix," said Hamilton softly, "has greatly enlivened an otherwise dull evening. Perhaps one day you may stand in need of legal advice. My office is at 58 Wall Street."

"Thank you," said Eliza. "I will remember that."

Then Hamilton nodded farewell to William and went in search of a hackney. He had not come in his own coach, because his destination, since no other diversion presented itself, was the brothel kept by Mrs. Elizabeth Carr on Vesey Street.

William turned to Eliza and said, "And how, pray tell, did you manage to meet Alexander Hamilton?"

Eliza laughed. "But you yourself arranged it, William. He was sitting next to me in the box you provided."

"Not knowingly, my dear Eliza, I assure you! To introduce you to a gentleman so noted for his conquests of women—well, how long do you suppose it will be before you become his mistress?"

"I am quite well provided for," said Eliza, and then added, "at least for the present."

While William went in search of a hackney, she waited on the steps of the theatre. She was thoughtful. To be the mistress of Alexander Hamilton—well, it would be a step up the ladder from being mistress to a French sea captain.

CHAPTER 6

THE SPRING THEATRICAL SEASON at the John Street Theatre was a varied and successful one, and Eliza attended many of its performances. When Jacques was in the city, he paid for the tickets himself, although his unfamiliarity with the language made it necessary for Eliza to whisper occasional interpretations of the action on stage.

In April William Dunlap's *The Archers, or The Mountaineers* was performed and proved to be an overwhelming success, much to Eliza's delight.

But it was Mr. Hodgkinson in *Macbeth* that was most moving to her. Macbeth's overweening ambition struck a responsive chord in her, and Mrs. Melmoth as Lady Macbeth filled her with horror in the sleepwalking scene.

In the latter part of May, when *L'Étoile de Marseilles* was in port, Eliza insisted that Jacques accompany her to a performance of *Much Ado About Nothing*. Even though she had carefully outlined the plot to him in advance, he found the archaic language too hard to understand, and during the third act he fell sound asleep. Fortunately, he did not snore, and Eliza did not awaken him until the play had reached its happy conclusion with the reluctant declaration of love by Beatrice and Benedick. When she roused him, Jacques apologized profusely.

That was the last performance until the reopening of the season in the fall, because summer as usual would bring with it not only warm weather but yellow fever.

Eliza urged Jacques to move back to Moore Street to avoid the plague, but Jacques refused.

"I am well and in good health," he said. "And the walk from Moore Street to the port is long and tiring, especially in hot weather."

Eliza herself was not anxious to move. A return to Moore Street would bring with it all the duties of housekeeping, which she detested. Somehow, her early fear of contracting the disease had lessened, especially when Pieter taught her how to smoke the cigars that were said to prevent it. She did not enjoy smoking tobacco and felt that it was distinctly unladylike, but she did it anyway.

When Jacques' ship returned in July, the outbreak of the plague was at its height, but Jacques still refused to move north to the safety of Moore Street.

One day not long after his return, he complained of having chills and fever and did not go to the port.

In response to Eliza's concern, he said, "It is nothing, *ma chère*, just a cold. *Il va disparaître tout de suite.*"

But the chills and fever did not disappear; they became worse. And soon he began having pains in his muscles, and his skin turned yellow. When congestion developed in his throat, Eliza was sure that Jacques had yellow fever, and she went to the Columbia College medical school in search of a doctor.

By the time Dr. Romayne arrived, Jacques had begun having "the black vomit," popularly believed to be a definite symptom of yellow fever.

Dr. Romayne cupped Jacques and bled him and gave Eliza some laudanum to ease the stomach cramps that racked his feverish body.

After they left the bedroom, Eliza confronted the young doctor. "Is it yellow fever, Doctor?"

Dr. Romayne nodded his head.

"Is he going to die?"

"I fear that he will, Madame de la Croix. Though he is evidently a man of robust health, he is not a young man, you know."

"But there must be something we can do!"

"If we knew how to cure yellow fever, madame, there would

not be the terrible toll of death every summer. I have done what I could. Are you willing to nurse him at the risk of your life, or shall I have him removed to the Bellevue estate? I would advise the latter course for your own safety."

"He will stay here. I will nurse him, if there is any chance that he will live."

"The chance is but a very slim one. I must tell you the truth."

Eliza clenched her teeth in determination. "I will take that chance, Doctor."

"You are a brave woman, madame, and I wish you great luck. But I must warn you—death by yellow fever is not a pretty sight." He paused. "I was forgetting. My fee for the visit, plus the cupping and medicine, is five dollars."

Eliza opened the tin box where Jacques kept his money and paid the doctor.

"When will you visit him again?" she asked.

"Regretfully, I do not think that will be necessary. But if he should still be alive tomorrow, let me know."

She watched the doctor as he walked down the stairs. Then she lighted one of the cigars that Pieter had brought her and puffed on it vigorously, although the smoke choked her and made her feel nauseated. Alone with Jacques, she was frightened, but she did not dare call Mr. MacAllister for fear that the presence of yellow fever in his boardinghouse would alarm him and cause him to evict her. She thought of going to Moore Street and getting Pieter, but she feared that exposure to the illness might cause him to become infected too.

There was nothing to do except stay where she was and do what she could to save Jacques. But she did not know what to do. He had already vomited up the laudanum that the doctor had given him, and there seemed little point in giving him more of it. He was for the most part unconscious and delirious from the fever. Occasionally, he would attempt to rouse himself and talk incoherently in French, calling out the name of his wife, Hélène. But the only other words that she could distinguish were "*Aide-moi! Aide-moi!*" Then, exhausted, he would fall back on the pillows, his breath coming jerkily through the clots of phlegm in his lungs and throat.

54

The day was hot and fair, but the breeze that floated in through the windows could not dissipate the foul stench that rose from the dying man's bed. He had developed a bloodstained diarrhea and had lost all control of his bowels and bladder.

He lay on his back, and Eliza had tried in vain to move him, to roll him over so that she could place clean towels beneath him. But his body was too heavy for her, and she could not budge him from his position. Her efforts to urge him to move met with no response.

Nightfall renewed her terror, and the light cast by the flickering candles made grotesque shadows on the wall. Although she had no appetite for food, she went downstairs to the dining room, if only to escape the horror she felt in the confines of the bedroom.

When Mr. MacAllister inquired about the Captain's absence, Eliza said casually that he had a cold and was in bed. She ate silently, toying with her food. At last, after a second cup of tea, she returned to the bedroom. From the bed came the continued sound of stertorous breathing, and Jacques was still unconscious.

Into his ear she whispered and then shouted his name. *"Jacques! Jacques! C'est Eliza qui parle. Dites, dites quelque chose, pour l'amour de Dieu!"*

Her words echoed in the room, and then there was silence again, except for the terrible rhythm of the labored breathing.

The fetid reek from the bed had become so overpowering that Eliza could no longer stand it. She went into their small sitting room and closed the door. A wave of guilt passed through her, because she felt that she was deserting him. But the knowledge that there was little that she could do by way of nursing him was somehow comforting. She knew now for a certainty that Jacques was dying, and she hoped only that his suffering would be brief.

She curled herself up on the small sofa and tried to read. But the words, even from her beloved Shakespeare, were meaningless, and she gave up at last. For the first time, she began thinking of herself. What would happen to her when Jacques was gone? Life without him seemed an impossibility. But somehow, some way, she would manage. She always had.

She tried to sleep but could not. She kept thinking of the past:

her first meeting with Jacques, when he had rescued her from rape by Bobby Brown, the town sergeant. She remembered that first night with him, his lust and his tenderness. Especially his tenderness. It had always astonished her that a man so rough and uncouth in his ways could at the same time be so gentle. And when she had said goodbye to him in Providence because she had fallen in love with Matt, he had not caused a scene or reproved her. Instead, he had given her the jade necklace that he had brought as a gift, with his best wishes for happiness.

But the real proof of his love for her came when she learned from Nate Mason that the Captain's ship would no longer be coming to Providence and would dock instead in New York. Nate's comment came back to her as clearly as though he were there in the room. "A man sometimes steers his ship to another port to forget a face," he had said.

A feeling of shame swept through her as she thought of how little she had given Jacques in return for his love and generosity. And yet she knew that she had not merely used him. In a curious way, she had loved Jacques, if only because he was the only kind and benevolent father she had ever known. Her body had attracted him, but there had been more than that in his devotion to her.

Now, she could not believe that he was dying. She got up hastily and went into the bedroom. One look told her that Jacques' condition had worsened. Unconscious though he might be, he was now fighting for life, desperately trying to get air into his congested lungs. His arms flailed frantically, almost angrily, about him, as though he had been attacked by some savage beast intent on devouring him.

Eliza watched in fascinated awe at first, and then she was filled with a rising pity for the dying man who wanted so much to live. She turned away and began to cry bitterly for the first time. She did not know whether she believed in God, certainly not in the God that Sam Allen had told her about. But there might be a God who was merciful and compassionate.

"Dear God, if you are there, please let Jacques live!" she whispered hoarsely. "They say you perform miracles. Please, God, perform one now." She paused and then added, "But if it is your will that he die, let it be soon, so his suffering will stop."

She looked back toward the bed, half hoping that her prayer would have an immediate answer. But Jacques still fought for life, and there was no sign that he was winning the struggle.

She went back to the sitting room and closed the door. She sat down on the couch and cried until she had no more tears. As she stared unseeingly at the window, the words of Hamlet unexpectedly came to her. Jacques was going to "the undiscover'd country from whose bourn no traveler returns."

The phrase echoed and re-echoed in her mind like some monotonous litany, and she thought now of all those she had known who had gone to that undiscovered country: her little drowned kitten, Blackie; Lydia, her bruised and broken body lying at the foot of the stairs; and most painfully, her poor dear Michel, so still there on the street with that stain of blood across his beautiful face; last of all, she remembered her beloved monkey, Danton, limp and lifeless on the hearth of the Ballou house.

Yes, she had seen death many times and feared it. But never before had she watched the struggle of someone who was dying slowly, fighting an unseen adversary in primitive combat.

The undiscover'd country from whose bourn no traveler returns . . . the words kept reverberating in her mind. Soon their very monotony soothed her to the point where she nodded in exhaustion and finally slept.

She was awakened by the light of the new day that was dawning. She stirred herself sleepily, for the moment forgetful of Jacques in the next room. But there was a feeling of oppression in her, a vague dread of something fearful that had happened. And then the memory of Jacques flooded through her, and she arose hastily and went into the bedroom.

Jacques was dead. She did not need to listen to his heart to tell her. The figure on the bed was quiet and did not breathe. She moved slowly toward him and took his limp hand in hers. It was still slightly warm but unresponsive and lifeless.

She turned away and hurriedly went back to the sitting room. She did not cry now. Jacques had gone, and there were things that must be done, and no one to do them except her. Soon the yellow-fever wagon would be coming past the house, and in her imagination she could already hear the hoarse, loud cries of the men, "Bring out your dead! Bring out your dead!"

The thought of Jacques being carried from the bedroom to be hurled into the wagon with all the stinking corpses filled her with loathing. Jacques was a man of the sea, and he should be buried at sea, as all sailors were. She went to the washbowl and washed her hands and face in the cool water. Then at the mirror she combed her tangled hair into some semblance of neatness. She left the house and almost ran down Beekman Street on her way to Peck's Slip, where *L'Étoile de Marseilles* was docked.

The men of Jacques' crew arrived at the house within the hour. With reddened eyes and tear-stained faces they wrapped his body in burlap and carried it down to the street. They put him gently in a wheelbarrow and stuffed the soiled linen under him as a cushion.

She turned to the first mate and talked hurriedly in French. They would bury the *capitaine* at sea? The safe in the cabin—did he know how to open it? Did he know the address of Mme. de la Croix in Marseilles? Was there a will? She promised to come to the ship before it sailed to arrange whatever legal matters might be necessary.

As the men lifted the wheelbarrow and prepared to move, one of Jacques' arms broke loose from the burlap and fell to the side, dangling limply.

Impulsively, Eliza ran to the wheelbarrow and seized the arm, as though to prevent their taking Jacques away. She took his bloodstained hand between her own and planted a kiss on the palm.

"*Au 'voir, mon cher Jacques,*" she mumbled, her voice stifled by sobs. The men paused, turning their heads away. Finally the first mate placed his hand on Eliza's and brought her to her feet.

"*Ma chère, ma chère. Il faut accepter la volonté de Dieu. Notre capitaine est en ciel.*"

He embraced her, placing his arms around her with a great gentleness. At last she stood away from him, her head still bowed in grief.

58

"Au 'voir, mes braves garçons . . ."

She turned quickly and fled into the house.

In a daze she looked at the empty, silent rooms. She had never felt more alone. She told herself that she should have insisted on moving back to Moore Street. Jacques had not wanted to go, but if only she had been firmer in her demands, if only— She stopped suddenly, as she heard Freelove's voice after Michel's murder . . . *"There ain't no sense saying 'if only' every time life kicks you in the arse, blaming yourself instead of the Almighty. . . . He ain't even got the common decency to warn you so you can watch out."* And when she had asked Freelove if she believed there was a God, she remembered with a smile Freelove's answer. *"Yep. But He's a bastid."*

Out on the street she heard the groaning wheels of the yellow-fever wagon, and the cry of "Bring out your dead! Bring out your dead!"

She ran to the window and looked out. The wagon, half full of corpses in grotesque positions, was almost opposite the house.

She stuck her head out of the window and screamed, "You won't get him, you sons of bitches! He's gone to the sea he loved, not to your stinking potter's field! So the hell with you!"

The driver of the wagon looked up at her and then grinned. "The hell with you too, ma'am."

The wagon rolled on, and Eliza turned back to the room. "I must think, I must think," she told herself. She knew that she could not stay on in these quarters, not only because of the memory of Jacques, but because of the danger of becoming infected with yellow fever herself.

She lighted one of the cigars she hated and puffed on it furiously, expelling the clouds of smoke into the still air of the room. A mosquito hummed about her head and finally lighted on one of her forearms. She slapped at it in fury and killed it. The sight of the blood from its body filled her with grim satisfaction.

That afternoon Eliza went to the house on Moore Street in search of Pieter. When she told him what had happened, his eyes grew big and serious.

"But why didn't you tell me, madame? Maybe I could have helped some way."

"There was nothing to be done except for me to sit there and watch him die. He was past all nursing."

Pieter's eyes filled with tears. "But you were there all alone. I could have stayed with you."

"Thank you, Pieter. But it's all done now, and I'll be moving back here to stay with you and your grandfather."

His tears stopped immediately, and his mouth broadened into a grin of pure joy. "Oh, it will be good to have you here again! Oh, madame—"

She smiled, but it was a smile tinged with irony. "I suppose you will be glad to go on with your lessons."

"Oh, yes, madame!" He impulsively flung his arms about her and hugged her. Then he stepped back and said, "We won't lose any time. I'll go get my wheelbarrow and tell Grandfather."

Looking at the boy's departing figure, Eliza thought to herself how odd it was that out of one person's grief happiness for someone else could blossom.

When Eliza arrived at Beekman Street with Pieter, she went to see Mr. MacAllister. He was furious with her for not having told him that Jacques had died of yellow fever and had thus endangered all their lives.

He had been drinking heavily, since some people believed that this was not only an effective but pleasant way of avoiding infection.

"Get your things out as quick as can be, especially the Captain's clothes, which should be burned right away!" he bellowed.

"The rooms will be cleared as quickly as possible, Mr. MacAllister, and I shall pay you for an extra week's board."

At the mention of money, Daniel MacAllister's eyes lighted. "Good! I must get up there with garlic and vinegar and burn some tar. The rooms will not be fit to live in for another week."

Eliza went upstairs and looked disconsolately at the empty rooms. Her first thought was of Jacques' money box. She opened it hastily with her key and found that it contained forty-one dollars in silver. There would be more in the safe in the cabin aboard ship, and she intended to get it. But the lock might have to be forced, and she did not know how this could be done legally. There was also, she supposed, the question of a death certificate, and a will, if there was one. She needed a lawyer. Suddenly, Alexander Hamilton's words came back to her: *"Perhaps one day you may stand in need of legal advice. My office is at 58 Wall Street."*

Late that afternoon Eliza knocked on the door at 58 Wall Street. It was opened by a neatly dressed young man.

"Yes?"

"I wish to see Mr. Alexander Hamilton, if you please."

The young man surveyed her, obviously impressed by her fashionably clothed figure and her beauty. He smiled, revealing tobacco-stained teeth that somehow gave his mouth a vulpine look. He arched an eyebrow and said, "And whom shall I say it is that wishes to see Mr. Hamilton? He is very busy today."

"It is a matter of great urgency. I am Madame de la Croix," said Eliza majestically.

The man ushered her into a small sitting room and then departed in the direction of what she judged must be Mr. Hamilton's office. He returned in a few moments.

"Mr. Hamilton will be delighted to see you, madame."

She got up and followed him.

Alexander Hamilton was sitting behind an enormous desk littered with papers, letters and legal briefs. He rose when Eliza entered. In spite of his small stature, he exuded an air of superiority and an oddly gracious manner.

"Madame de la Croix! I dared not hope to see you again so soon."

Eliza was so awed by the man's presence that she found it difficult to speak. At last she stammered, "I am—I am in a state of great confusion, Mr. Hamilton. You must forgive me. Captain de la Croix is dead of yellow fever." Tears trickled down her face, and she dabbed at her eyes with a lace handkerchief.

"Ah, madame, I am sorry. You must be desolate with grief. Come, sit in the chair over here, where we can talk more easily."

Eliza sat in the chair next to his desk. Hamilton's luminous eyes stared into hers in a sympathetic way, but still she found herself unable to speak easily.

Hamilton cleared his throat in a businesslike manner. "You have come to see me, madame, in regard to his will, no doubt."

"Yes. You see, I am not sure if he left a will. Perhaps it is aboard his ship—I don't know." She swallowed hard and decided to tell him the truth. "You see, Mr. Hamilton, I am not his—his wife."

Hamilton's eyes flickered with interest, but he said nothing, waiting for her to continue.

"I am—or was—his mistress for many years. My name is not Madame de la Croix; it is Eliza Capet."

"French?" he asked.

"My parents were French. I was born in Providence, and so I am an American. My mother died in giving birth to me, and my father died not long after. I was adopted by a kind family, and then, when I was seventeen, I met Captain de la Croix. His ship docked in Providence harbor."

Hamilton looked at her in a puzzled way. "But I cannot understand why he did not marry you. You must know that you are a woman of great beauty with both charm and intelligence."

She ignored the compliment and said, "But he was already married. His wife lives in Marseilles. There are—there are children."

Hamilton was silent and thoughtful for a moment. At last he said, "A wife—yes, that does complicate matters unless he left you something in his will."

"Mr. Hamilton, I am not a greedy woman. It is not my wish to deprive his family of its due. I have some money that the Captain had on hand when he—when he—"

"How much do you have?" The voice was curtly matter-of-fact.

"Thirty-six dollars."

Hamilton leaned toward her, his eyes warm and sympathetic. "But that will not last you very long. What will you do?"

"I don't know, sir. I don't know," she said sadly.

62

"Well, madame—or should I call you Mademoiselle Capet?—first we must find out if there is a will. I shall take the necessary measures and inform you. Where do you live?"

"To the north—at 14 Moore Street. It is a house owned by an elderly gentleman named Van Zandt. We stayed there last summer to avoid the yellow fever, but this year Jacques insisted on our staying in town on Beekman Street. If only he had listened to me—"

Eliza began to cry again, and Hamilton got up and patted her on the shoulder.

"There, there. You have been through an ordeal, but you must be brave now and think of your future. The Captain is dead, but you must go on living."

He helped her to her feet and gently steered her to the door. As she prepared to leave, he said, "I will take care of things, my dear, and you will hear from me soon."

He bowed to kiss her hand, and as he did so, she was aware that his eyes lingered for a moment on her bodice. That made her feel more cheerful.

Eliza did not know how soon she could expect a visit from Hamilton, but each day she carefully groomed herself, dressing as she thought a newly bereaved widow should: a plain gray hoop-skirt, a bodice of black velvet, and a lavender kerchief tied loosely about her neck. The dark clothing only served to accentuate her red-gold hair and draw attention to her face, which was pale and without rouge.

Two days after her office visit, Hamilton arrived at dusk in his coach, drawn by a pair of matched bays. Eliza opened the door when he knocked. She curtsied, and he bowed in a formal manner.

"Good afternoon, Mademoiselle Capet," he said.

She acknowledged his greeting, noting that he did not call her Madame de la Croix. She ushered him into the downstairs sitting room and asked Pieter to bring tea.

"Well," said Hamilton, "I fear I am the bearer of ill tidings. The Captain did indeed leave a will, which we found in his safe.

63

He left all his possessions, including the ship, to his wife in France."

"I am not surprised," said Eliza. It was odd, she thought, how her name never appeared in the wills of her lovers. Sam Allen, she remembered, had left her nothing.

"But there was about two hundred dollars in silver, and when the crewmen had left the cabin, I pocketed half of it, a hundred dollars, for you. Here, please, take it."

From a pocket he took out a chamois sack that contained a hundred dollars in silver.

"But, Mr. Hamilton, is that legal? Don't it belong to his wife along with everything else?"

"Perhaps," he said, "but I believe that you are entitled to it. I suppose one might say that I had stolen it for you, but there is no one to know. Don't worry about it."

Eliza opened the sack and emptied the coins onto the table. She tried to hide the glint of pleasure in her eyes. After waiting a moment she slowly placed the coins back in the sack.

Shyly, she said, "You are very good to me, sir. I wish to thank you. There is enough here to see me through the summer."

Hamilton looked at her in a speculative way. "And what will you do when summer is over, mademoiselle?"

"Go back to town, I think. Life is very boring out here, alone with the old man and the boy."

Pieter arrived with the tea things on a tray, which he set down on a table near Eliza. Then he made a hasty departure. He knew who Alexander Hamilton was, and the presence of the man awed him. He could hardly believe that so renowned a person should be sitting in the Van Zandt living room.

Eliza poured tea and offered Hamilton some little cakes that she herself had baked in preparation for the occasion.

"These cakes are delicious, mademoiselle."

"I made them myself," she said, and added after a pause, "just for you."

"I am flattered." His gray eyes looked into hers with an intensity that told her plainly what was in his mind.

He finished his cup of tea and then leaned back in his chair.

64

Now, his eyes did not stop at her face but moved downward slowly so that they took in her whole figure. Eliza felt that his gaze had undressed her and that she now sat before him in total nudity.

"Mademoiselle Capet—may I call you Eliza?"

"Most certainly," she said. "And what shall I call you, Mr. Hamilton?"

He smiled. "Alexander, or Alex. Some of my closer friends call me Sandy."

"I'll call you Sandy, then."

"That pleases me," he said. "It is so formal sitting here at tea like this. Could we move to the sofa?"

She rose slowly and led him to the small sofa on the other side of the room, near the windows that faced west. The last rays of the setting sun rested momentarily on her hair, so that it flamed in beauty.

Hamilton, taking his place beside her, took her hand in his. "Do you know, my dear, that since that night I met you at the theatre, I have never been able to forget you?"

She turned innocent eyes toward him. "But why?" she asked. "I have a pretty face, but there are many pretty faces in your world."

"Your face is not pretty, my dear. It is beautiful, and it radiates an indefinable charm. That little upturned nose of yours—" He reached out his hand and gently touched the end of her nose.

Eliza drew away slightly and laughed. " 'Tis nothing but an ordinary Irish pug nose that I got from my Irish mother."

"But I thought your parents were both French."

"Yes," she said quickly, "but my mother was partly Irish."

"No matter where it came from, I find it—delicious."

Again, he leaned toward her and brushed the tip of her nose lightly with his full, sensuous lips.

Eliza turned her face away and was silent for a moment. At last she gazed at him directly. "Alexander," she said, "I must be frank with you. I know that you are intending to seduce me, and I find you attractive and charming, but the memory of my Jacques is still very much in my mind—and I cannot—cannot—"

65

She forced tears into her eyes and, as convincingly as she could, wept into her handkerchief. The effect on Hamilton was immediate, and he stood up.

"Forgive me, my dear mademoiselle. I am a clumsy dolt to have so little regard for the feelings of one so recently bereaved. Say that you forgive me."

She turned her tear-streaked face toward him. "But of course, you are forgiven. It is good of you to understand how I feel."

Hamilton turned abruptly. "Well, my dear, I must leave now."

Eliza said, "But your lawyer's fee. Surely, there must be expenses in procuring a death certificate and for all the time you spent on the ship—"

"Mademoiselle, if I were to charge a fee, it would be far more than a woman in your circumstances could afford. There is no fee, Eliza."

As he went toward the door, she followed him and grasped him by the arm. "But you are too kind. Surely, I could give you something to repay you for your trouble—"

He smiled, looked into her eyes and kissed her gently on the forehead. "There," he said, "the debt is paid!"

"Oh, 'tis but small payment."

As she opened the door for him, he said, "Just grant me the pleasure of seeing you some time soon, before the summer is over. May I call on you again?"

She nodded her head vigorously. He said goodbye then, got into his coach and was gone.

Eliza was thoughtful as she went back into the sitting room. She did not know how soon she would see him again, and it would be six weeks before summer would be over, but she had no intention of being an easy conquest. She could wait. She picked up the sack of silver coins, opened it and counted out the one hundred dollars. She smiled to herself, at the thought that she could afford to wait quite a while.

CHAPTER 7

THE DAYS OF EARLY AUGUST passed quickly. Eliza busied herself with the household chores and in the afternoons she went with Pieter to the tall grasses near the Hudson and gave him lessons in reading and writing.

Pieter had proved to be as apt a student at grammar as he already was in the art of making love. He could read fairly well now, but writing was difficult for him. He wrote in large, poorly formed capital letters, but he had learned to make numerals that were small and neat. He no longer counted on his fingers when doing arithmetic and could add, subtract, multiply and divide with ease.

But his favorite subject was love-making, and in this he had made considerable progress. One afternoon, as he stood naked before Eliza and had begun to put on his clothes, Eliza surveyed his lithe, boyish figure in admiration.

"Piet," she said, "you are fast becoming a man."

He grinned at her and said, "That I am, thanks to you, madame. I'll be eighteen in October, you know."

Eliza felt unaccountably sad. Why should the sight of this young man as he stood before her, so radiant with health and good looks, fill her with an inexplicable heartache? And then, quite suddenly, she knew. He reminded her of Michel. The memory of his slain body as it lay there that night on the street in Providence made her shiver with a horror that had still not been forgotten. She told herself that all that was in the past, that this was Pieter, not Michel. Actually, there was little resemblance between them: Pieter, blond and fair-skinned with his typically

67

square Dutch face, and Michel, who had had dark curly hair and a more muscular figure. She found herself smiling wistfully as she remembered Michel's concern about his "smallness." At least Pieter did not need to worry about that.

Pieter, fully dressed now, kneeled down before her. "What's the matter, madame? You look very sad."

Eliza smiled up at him. " 'Tis nothing. I was thinking of someone I loved—who is now dead."

"Oh, you mustn't do that. When I think of a sad thing, like how my mother ran away and deserted me, I just make myself think of something else, something good that is happening to me *now*."

"You are wiser than most people, Piet," said Eliza.

As he helped her to her feet, he looked at her in quick concern. "Madame, it's not that I didn't pleasure you, is it?"

Eliza laughed, her mood of sadness utterly dissipated by the boy's anxious question. "Oh, no, dear Piet. I would only wish that your handwriting was as good as your love-making."

Pieter smiled in relief. "Oh, it *will* be, madame! I promise you that one day soon I'll be writing as well as—as the town clerk!"

Eliza patted him affectionately on the cheek, and then together they walked back, hand in hand, toward the house.

In mid-August Alexander Hamilton decided that Eliza's period of mourning for the Captain might well be over, and so late one afternoon he made an unannounced appearance at the Van Zandt house. Eliza was not prepared for his visit. She had spent most of the day cleaning the house, and she was far from ready to receive her caller.

After apologizing for her appearance, she settled Hamilton in the sitting room and went upstairs to her bedroom. When she reappeared twenty minutes later, she had bathed and changed into one of her more fetching gowns.

Hamilton stood up as she entered the room. "You are like Cinderella," he said. "I arrive to greet a scullery maid, and within moments you are transformed into a princess ready to go to the ball."

68

"And do you have a glass slipper ready, Alexander?"

He laughed and went over to her, taking her by the hands and drawing her toward him. She broke away and moved to the door.

"I'll get Pieter to prepare us some tea," she said.

"I really do not stand in need of tea—unless, of course, you would like some."

"No. The day is really too warm for tea. Let's sit down and talk."

"Only providing that you will sit next to me on the sofa so that I may look into those lovely violet eyes at close range."

She smiled and sat down next to him.

"How beautiful you are, Eliza! You seem to have recovered from your time of sorrow."

"Yes. I have come to accept the fact that my dear Jacques is gone, and all my tears will not bring him back."

He leaned toward her and whispered, "You are wise. You have many years of life ahead of you, many hours of happiness— which I would like to share."

His arm went around her waist and he pulled her toward him. She did not resist. Encouraged, he moved his face close to hers and kissed her, gently and then with passion. With a forced patience she waited for the usual male routine in love-making: the hand on her bodice, which was quickly unlaced; then the lips kissing the nipples of her exposed breasts; and finally, the slow exploration of her under the skirt and between her legs.

Almost against her will, she found herself responding to him. At least, he did not hurry, and his hands and his lips performed with a practiced finesse that she could not help admiring.

His mouth, wet and caressing against her ear, whispered, "Your bedroom—it is upstairs?"

She nodded and then, breaking away from him, led the way upstairs. She lay back on the bed, and slowly and with trembling hands, he undressed her. His trousers were quickly taken off, and he stood expectantly before her.

"Sandy," she said, "are you going to make love with your waistcoat on?"

69

His waistcoat and shirt came off almost as quickly as his trousers, and he stood before her nude for a moment before he joined her on the bed. Then he renewed his caresses, more passionately now, and again she found herself responding to him without really wanting to.

Physically, he was most attractive to her. His skin was as fair and smooth as a woman's. Indeed, there was something almost voluptuously feminine in the way he made love. Gentle and unhurried, he continued to fondle her body. He ran his tongue over her breasts, then down her belly until he reached the sensitive spot between her legs. When at last he entered her, she was ready to receive him. Once he was astride her, his lust seemed to madden him. Gone was the gentleness and the leisurely caress. As though she were a horse that he was mounted on in a mad race, he rode her hell-for-leather in quick jabs. And then, suddenly, he gave a quick groan of pleasure and fell away from her, gasping for breath.

Eliza lay quietly on her back. She had been greatly stimulated but had not reached a climax. Frustration touched with anger filled her, and she looked at him coldly. But Hamilton had already risen from the bed and stood before the mirror above the washstand. He was arranging his mussed hair, patting the strands into place and then tying them neatly at the back with a firmer knot of the small black bow.

Finally, she said, "Alex, I have not been fully pleasured."

He looked toward her casually. "I am sorry, my dear. I was too much hurried. I have an engagement to take my wife to dinner at the Livingstons, and I am already late."

"How unfortunate," she said. The irony in her voice was lost on him, because he was now busily putting on his clothes.

She got up and began to dress, calmly and deliberately, but inwardly she was seething with anger. Fully dressed now, he moved toward her to give her a goodbye kiss.

She moved away from him, and in a cold voice, she said, "You might at least have the grace to wait until I am dressed."

"Oh, I am sorry, my dear. I trust I have not offended you." He waited impatiently for her to finish dressing, but she said nothing.

At last she stood before him, fully clothed. "No, my dear Alex, you have not offended me."

He came over to her and took her hands in his. "Oh, thank God for that!"

He moved to kiss her now, but she turned her face away so that his kiss brushed her cheek and did not reach her mouth.

"That will be three dollars, if you please," she said in measured tones.

He looked at her in bewilderment. "Three dollars? What are you talking about?"

"I am talking about the cost of pleasuring yourself on my body."

"But my dear Eliza, you cannot be serious. You speak as though you were a—a whore."

"Yes. I have been treated like a whore, and so I will behave like one. Three dollars, please."

He was annoyed. "But I gave you a hundred dollars only six weeks ago—"

"I have what is left of the hundred dollars, Alex. It is almost time for me to return to my rooms in town and to buy clothes for the fall season, and I stand in need of cash."

He shook his head back and forth in disbelief. Then he fumbled in his purse and produced three dollars, which he placed in her outstretched hand.

"I hope," he said, "that this does not mark the end of our—our friendship."

Eliza gave him a warm, ingratiating smile. "Oh, no. I would enjoy seeing you again, now that you know the terms of that friendship."

Hamilton put his arms around her and attempted to kiss her again. She did not turn her head aside and kissed him full on the lips. When he turned toward the door, she followed him downstairs. Then she watched him get into his coach, and as it drove away, she waved to him cordially.

Hamilton was thoughtful in the coach that was carrying him back to town. "Damn the woman!" he said to himself. "Behaving like a whore, when she is most certainly not one. Damn her eyes!" And yet, he found himself admiring her for the way she had so openly defied him. He was not used to having women who showed such spirit. He had grown weary of ladies, including his wife, Elizabeth, who behaved with humility and subservience, as though grateful that the great Alexander Hamilton had deigned to bed with them.

He knew that he would arrange to see her again—and soon. She was a challenge, and in love-making as in politics, he relished challenges.

After Eliza had closed the door on her visitor, she went to the kitchen, where Pieter was rekindling the fire for dinner. Old Hans sat in his chair near the hearth. He dozed, snoring lightly.

"Pieter," said Eliza, "I am feeling faint. Would you bring a cup of hot tea to my bedroom?"

He looked up in surprise. "Tea? Yes, of course, madame."

In her bedroom, Eliza sank wearily to the bed. "Well," she thought to herself, "I have been to bed with the great Alexander Hamilton. So much for that. It is an honor that I could well have done without." As she remembered him primping before the mirror, she laughed at the vanity of the man. And in his haste to be off and return to his wife and dinner, he reminded her of those men of position on the hill in Providence: the men who, once their lust was sated with a whore in Sally Marshall's brothel, were in a great hurry to return to a respectable life with their wives and children.

When Pieter brought her the cup of tea, he lingered, obviously full of curiosity about the recent visitor to the house.

Eliza sipped her tea and looked at Pieter with an amused smile. "What's on your mind, Pieter?"

Pieter looked away in embarrassment. "I just was wondering if—if—" he stammered.

"If I had gone to bed with Hamilton?"

"Well, yes. Truth to tell, madame, I felt—well, a little jealous."

"Well, you have no need to. I bedded with him, and a very poor lover he is!"

Pieter grinned. "You mean he is—is not as good a lover as me?"

"Not by half. He did not pleasure me at all. In fact, dear Piet, you might like to finish what he only started."

Pieter's mouth dropped open in surprise. "You mean—you want—"

Eliza pulled the boy toward her and unbuttoned his trousers.

"But, madame, your tea. It will get cold—"

"Dear Piet, I don't need tea right now as much as I need you."

She rose and stepped out of her hoopskirt. Pieter rushed to her, flinging his arms around her.

Eliza responded to his passion with more than usual abandon. Part of her pleasure, she knew, was the feeling that she was taking further vengeance on Hamilton's treatment of her. She was replacing him with an uneducated and unsophisticated boy of seventeen, and very satisfactorily too. But after all, he had had an excellent tutor.

A week passed before Alexander Hamilton paid another visit to the house on Moore Street. He could not have come at a more inopportune time, because Eliza was busy packing her belongings in preparation for a move back to the rooms on Beekman Street.

Eliza's greeting was casual, and Alexander appeared nervous and ill at ease.

"I see that my visit has been ill timed," he said.

"Well, frankly, Alex, it is. As you can see, I am in the midst of getting my things together to move back to my rooms on Beekman Street, where I stay during the winter."

"My, what a great lady you are—rooms in the country for the summer, and another place in town for the season."

She laughed. "Great lady I may be, Sandy, but it is still necessary for me to pay lodging and board. Since the death of dear Jacques I am without a provider."

She looked at him pointedly, and he turned his eyes away. "I would like to keep you, my dear Eliza, but it would be difficult for me financially."

"That is an odd statement," she said, "coming from a former Secretary of the United States Treasury. My Jacques was only a French sea captain, but he managed very well."

"I'm sure he did." He went over to where she sat on the floor before an open suitcase. Pulling her to her feet, he put his arms around her. "Eliza, my dear Eliza," he murmured into her ear. "I have been in torment since I last saw you."

"Torment?" she asked incredulously.

"Yes. I have been haunted by you. You are like a powerful drug that runs in my veins. I find it hard to get to sleep nights. I am tortured by the memory of you—" He broke off, his voice choking with emotion.

She looked at him curiously. Was he telling her the truth, or was this an elaborate bit of playacting, part of a plan to get her into bed again?

He continued to hold her in his arms, whispering endearments into her ear and moving his hands toward her breasts. Abruptly, she broke away and looked at him levelly.

"Alex," she said. "I am forced to be blunt with you. I like you; you are attractive to me, but—"

"Oh, I know. I proved to be a very poor lover the last time we were together. In the future—"

Eliza's voice was not cold, merely matter-of-fact. "That is of little importance, Sandy. I am sure that with more time with me, you would have proved to be a very good lover. I am not concerned about that."

"But what is bothering you, then?"

She looked at him with directness. "Do you want me to be your mistress, Sandy? My needs are few, but I must have a man who can at least assure me of board and lodgings." She paused, and then, with a note of pride in her voice, she added, "I have no intention of taking to the street like a common whore or entering a brothel in order to survive."

He looked shocked. "Oh, my dear, that must not happen. Yes, yes. Be my mistress. I shall take good care of you, be sure of it. But I must have you! I need you. There is no woman in my life so important to me as you. You must believe me!"

She gave him a smile of gratitude. "Oh, thank you, dear Sandy. It will be an honor to be the mistress of so notable a man—and a man so full of warmth and affection."

They kissed now, and she surrendered herself completely to his growing passion. He held her close to him, and then he whispered, "Shall we go upstairs now?"

"Why not?" she said.

"Why not, indeed?" she thought to herself. She had won, at least for the time being. She knew that she would be cared for, and this gave her a sense of great well-being, even happiness. But she dared not ask herself how long she could depend on this strange man of mercurial passions, a man who kept as tight a rein on his own money as he had done on the silver in the United States Treasury.

CHAPTER 8

ELIZA'S OLD ROOMS at Mr. MacAllister's on Beekman Street were occupied, but there was a single room on the floor above that was vacant, and Eliza took it. In fact, she preferred it, because it was cheaper.

When Hamilton paid his first visit to her new quarters, she told him that the rent was three dollars. This meant that she would have an extra dollar a week to spend on clothes. She foresaw, quite correctly, that Hamilton would be stingy about buying her presents in exchange for her favors.

Once, after a session of love-making, she had plaintively mentioned that she needed a new dress for the fall, and Hamilton had immediately changed the subject. Curiously, his ardor seemed to grow each time he saw her, and he was stopping by, usually late in the afternoon, three times a week.

Eliza felt this arrangement was unfair. For a mere three dollars a week he was bedding her three times, which brought her remuneration to a dollar each time, a sum much lower than a common prostitute would receive.

One afternoon, before they had made love and when he was at his most amorous, she suddenly turned away from him.

"Wait, Sandy. Before we go on with this, I think we should have a business discussion."

"Business discussion?" he asked with feigned bewilderment.

"Yes. I am your mistress. I see no other men who might help me with my expenses. You are here at least three times a week, and all I receive is three dollars. That amounts to one dollar per night."

"Oh, please, Eliza, don't use such offensive words. It is not becoming in a young lady of your—your—"

"Of my what?" she asked. "Of my accomplishments? They consist, so far as you are concerned, of my lying on my back on this bed while you satisfy yourself!"

He was silent, his ardor dampened by all this talk of money. Finally, he said, "But, Eliza, what do you want me to do?"

"I want you to do what any man does for his mistress—give me presents of clothing and jewelry, tokens of your affection and of your desire to see that I am attractive, a woman you can be proud of."

"But I *am* proud of you, my dear. And you are already the most attractive woman in New York. Were it possible for me to be seen with you in public, take you to dinner or the theatre, I would do so, but—"

"But you fear gossip. You are afraid that your dear wife, Elizabeth, one of the aristocratic Schuylers, might hear that you were keeping a woman on Beekman Street."

He nodded, his head bowed. He hated to admit it, but she had challenged him again, and she had won.

"Very well, dear Eliza. You shall have a new gown. How much will it cost?"

"Five dollars would be enough, I would think."

He smiled. "And now, my dear, may we continue with what we had so enjoyably started?"

Eliza lay back on the bed and opened her arms to him. Words seemed scarcely necessary. In her mind, she was already deciding on what color dress she would buy and what kind of headdress would match it.

A few days later, while Eliza was shopping on Pearl Street, she paused before a clothing shop. Displayed in the window was a pair of shoes so beautiful that the very sight of them made her catch her breath. They were of a dazzling scarlet satin, dotted with gleaming rosettes of knotted gold thread. They cost more than she could possibly afford.

Suddenly, there was a light tap on her shoulder, and she turned around. William Dunlap stood before her.

"Shopping again, I see," he said. "And pray tell, what is there in that window that has hypnotized you so?"

"Those little red shoes. Aren't they beautiful? I especially like red shoes, because I can walk faster in them."

William laughed. "Well, my dear, I would like nothing better than to buy them for you, but I am penniless."

"Oh, drat the shoes. I'll find another way of getting them."

"I heard that Jacques had died of yellow fever this summer. It must be a new gentleman friend, then."

"Yes, dear William. I am Alexander Hamilton's mistress," she said, trying to sound casual.

"Well," said William, "you certainly believe in starting at the top of the ladder!"

"It's just as easy as beginning at the bottom, but it's not as exciting as it sounds."

"Not?"

"Alexander Hamilton is a skinflint. He pays my board and feels that is enough to keep me happy. I must beg for everything else. He makes me feel like a whore."

"But he is, I expect, a good lover. At least that is his reputation."

Eliza snorted her contempt. "Reputation! As a lover, he is like a puppy dog—jab, jab, jab, and goodbye. But tell me about yourself. It has been a long time since I've seen you."

"Things go well for me. My play *The Mysterious Monk* will open the season on September twenty-sixth, and, Eliza, I am now a partner with Hodgkinson and Hallam in the management of the John Street Theatre!" As her face showed her pleasure, William added, "And I am still almost penniless."

"But why?" Eliza asked. "If you are a partner—"

"I had to borrow the investment money, and I am a partner with two men who are always at loggerheads. Mrs. Hodgkinson and Mrs. Hallam are as jealous as cats, with Mrs. Hodgkinson overbearing and Mrs. Hallam drunk. I sometimes think I was taken on as a peacemaker rather than a partner."

"That is a role," said Eliza, "that I am sure you play well. You are a most congenial man, you know. At least I have always found you to be."

William looked at her silently for a moment and then said, "Congenial enough so that you would invite me to tea?"

Eliza laughed. "You are becoming very bold, William. How could I refuse to have tea with the new partner of the John Street Theatre?"

"The penniless partner, remember."

"You won't stay penniless very long, I'll be bound. It's after two o'clock. We could have an early tea right now."

"Now?" he asked in surprise.

"Perhaps you have another engagement."

His eyes regarded her affectionately. "For you, Eliza, I shall never have another engagement."

They walked along Pearl Street and then turned right on Beekman Street. They talked about the coming theatre season, and Eliza was delighted to learn that both *Much Ado About Nothing* and *As You Like It* would probably be performed before Christmas.

While they talked, Eliza asked herself why she should be going to bed with William Dunlap without any thought of reward, except possibly a few theatre tickets. He had little or no money, and as a lover—well, even Pieter was better at love-making. She decided that she had only two reasons: she liked William, and she had great respect for his talent as a writer. It was as simple as that.

Eliza had begun to dread the days when Hamilton visited her. She hated the humiliating position she found herself in financially. It was not only necessary for her to ask him directly for money for a new article of clothing; she even had to remind him when the weekly amount for her board and lodgings was due. Then, begrudgingly, he would fumble in his purse for the requested amount, his fingers parting with the coins or bills with a lingering hesitancy. His miserliness provoked a fury in her that she controlled with difficulty. And one day in mid-September, she did not control it.

As he placed the money in her hand, counting out the coins and bills carefully, she said acidly, "Watch out, Alexander—you might give me too much."

"Eliza, what do you mean?"

"I mean that your tight-fisted ways give me a pain in the arse!"

He drew himself up proudly and looked at her in disdain. "I am not tight-fisted. I am merely prudent, as every man should be. How do you think I was able to set up our country financially and get us out of the red and into the black?"

"I am a woman—not the United States of America's bank."

"My wife, Elizabeth, has never felt I was ungenerous."

"No doubt. She stands in such awe of you that she would be grateful for whatever pennies you might dole out to her."

"Elizabeth, unlike you, loves me, my dear."

"Then she must be a harebrained bitch of a woman!"

Hamilton became suddenly furious, his face suffused with blood. "I forbid you to speak of my wife in such terms!"

Eliza was becoming more angry herself now. "Nobody forbids *me* to do anything, you niggardly penny pincher! Who do you think you're talking to?"

Hamilton's voice was icy. "I thought I was talking to my mistress, but I see that I am attempting civilized conversation with a common whore!"

"You make me feel like a common whore, and I've had enough of it! Get out of here and don't come back!"

He patted his hair into place and said, "My hat, if you please."

"It's over there where you put it on the table. I'll not get it for you!"

Hamilton walked with slow, mincing steps to the table and put the hat carefully on his head. Then he turned to her, his voice conciliatory now. "I am sorry it has come to this, Eliza. I loved you—"

Eliza laughed derisively. "Loved me! You have never, my dear Mr. Hamilton, loved anyone but yourself!"

He moved toward her and extended his hand in a friendly way. Her response was cynical. "I won't shake hands with you. The only reason you're trying to be sociable is that you've paid my lodging for a week, and you'd like one more bedding to get your money's worth! You've got your hat on, so just leave!"

Her words nettled him, because they happened to be true. He

walked sedately to the door, opened it and banged it shut after him.

Eliza sat down on the bed. "Well," she thought, "now you've done it—lost your only means of income all because of your blasted pride."

But she soon became cheerful. It was a relief to her to be rid of the man and to feel free again. She was not, after all, entirely destitute. She still had fifty-two dollars left from the hundred that she had received from Jacques' safe.

There was merely the question of finding another lover, a rich and generous one. She did not know how she would find him or where, but it never entered her mind that she wouldn't. New York was a big town.

William Dunlap saw to it that a ticket for the performance of *The Mysterious Monk* was delivered to Eliza, and on September twenty-sixth she spent the better part of the day in preparation for the occasion. William had told her that he would not be able to take her to Ranelagh's Gardens for refreshments after the play because he was low in funds. Eliza had laughed and, snapping her fingers in a reckless way, had said that his escort was all she wanted and that she herself would pay for the refreshments and the cost of a hackney.

Eliza's newest gown was her most expensive one, all in black velvet, with a brilliant red rose in the lace cap on her head. A large piece of cut red glass that resembled a glowing ruby was suspended around her neck on a gold chain, and her shoes were the scarlet ones that she had looked at so enviously in the shop window on Pearl Street. It was the first time that she had worn a black gown, and it had the effect of drawing attention to her face, which achieved a cameolike clarity.

Pieter was overwhelmed by her appearance when he arrived in a hackney to take her to the theatre. He found it hard to believe that this wondrous creature had taken him as a lover, that he had seen her stark naked on a bed with arms stretched out toward him in a gesture of welcome. It was as though she were a stranger, and he did not know how to talk to her.

81

In the cab, Eliza turned to him. "Pieter, why don't you say something?"

"I—I don't know how to, madame. You are so beautiful tonight that it's like I never saw you before, like I don't even know you."

Eliza laughed. "Oh, you know me right enough, my lad." She seized his hand and thrust it into her bodice so that it touched a breast. "Maybe that will refresh your memory!"

With that Pieter burst into an unrestrained fit of laughter that was both joyous and full of wonder. He withdrew his hand quickly and said, "Oh, madame, you must not do things like that! Supposing the driver should look back and see—"

"Oh, to hell with the driver. He's being paid, and I daresay that worse things have happened in this cab!"

When Eliza arrived at the theatre, she paid the driver, tipping him handsomely. She left Pieter at the curb gazing at her fixedly, as though in a trance. His eyes followed her as she moved to the entrance of the theatre and up the steps toward the lobby.

Eliza walked regally, more sure of herself and her beauty than she had ever been. She was aware that her entrance created something of a sensation, for the eyes of the theatregoers turned toward her and their conversation ceased abruptly.

Eliza was ushered to a box in the center of the theatre. It was a box for two, and the seat beside her was empty and remained so for the entire performance. She smiled to herself as she recognized that this time William was taking no chances of having her meet some eligible gentleman. It was curious that he was jealous of her interest in other men and was, in his quiet way, possessive of her.

Eliza liked *The Mysterious Monk* and responded to its eerie mood and its melodramatic twists of plot. She gasped when she was supposed to gasp and shivered in apprehension along with the audience in the moments of suspense.

The reception of the play was rapturous. The audience applauded long and loudly. They stamped their feet with pleasure, and also to keep them warm. There were fourteen curtain calls, and finally, when William Dunlap was dragged before the curtain, the applause became deafening. William bowed gracefully. He was astounded at the play's reception, since it had been performed several times before, but never to this applause.

Eliza was delighted with the play's success, and when William appeared outside at the conclusion of the performance, she threw herself into his arms and hugged him close to her.

Later, as they sat at a table in Ranelagh's Gardens, she was still full of praise for the play, and he acknowledged her compliments in a rather bored way.

"But, Eliza, it is not really a good play, you know."

"Well, it's not Shakespeare, William, but it's very entertaining."

"I know," he said despondently. Then brightening, he added, "But its success will bring the money that I need so badly that I cannot even afford to take my dear Eliza to Ranelagh's Gardens, and particularly on a night when she looks so ravishing!"

"We will not talk of money, William."

He looked around the room, aware of the admiring stares of the gentlemen at other tables. "Do you realize, my dear, that I am the envy of every man in this room?" He paused, and then, with a smile, he added, "I see that you got the scarlet shoes that make you walk faster. Now, how did you manage that?"

"Well, I have a little money saved, but I'll have to walk very fast to find a new gentleman provider."

A waiter approached their table and took their order: a negus for Eliza and a flip for William.

Eliza leaned forward earnestly. "Is there no way for me to earn money, William—just enough to survive? I could do housekeeping for someone perhaps or—"

William's laughter interrupted her. "Somehow, Eliza, I cannot see you as a charwoman. It would have to be something where your beauty would be recognized—" He stopped, as a sudden thought occurred to him. He looked at her studiously, even critically. "Eliza, had you ever thought of going on the stage?"

She looked at him in astonishment. "But I have never acted. Being on a stage before a lot of strangers would frighten the wits out of me."

"Can you sing?"

"Oh, I can carry a tune, but I would never call myself a singer. My voice is low and not very loud."

"All actors are frightened when they first come on stage, but they get over it. As for your voice, I will be your coach."

When Eliza saw that he was serious, she became alarmed. "But, William, I could never—"

"We shall see about that. Come to the John Street Theatre tomorrow afternoon at two, and we'll see if you can sing. Later, I can arrange for you to meet my partners, Mr. Hodgkinson and Mr. Hallam."

"Oh, no! I just couldn't. Please, William—"

William nodded his head decisively. "No more excuses. I'll see you at two."

The waiter arrived with their drinks, and Eliza drank her negus, hot though it was, in almost one nervous gulp. William raised his mug of flip in a toast. "To Madame Eliza de la Croix, the new theatrical sensation of New York!"

Eliza was still protesting. "But, William, I cannot be an actress, I truly cannot!"

William set down his mug and with a smile said, "No, not as Madame de la Croix—as Mademoiselle Élise Capet, newly arrived from France, yes!"

He raised his mug again and, smiling joyously now, he said, "Ladies and gentlemen, may I present Mademoiselle Élise Capet, who has come all the way from France to entertain us!"

"But what shall I wear, William?"

"Exactly what you are wearing now. You are irresistible in that black velvet gown!"

"Oh, my God," Eliza murmured to herself. "I shall not sleep a wink tonight!"

It was true. Long after William had left her room on Beekman Street, she sat in a chair by the open window. Her worry was not so much that she doubted her ability to sing as it was the prospect of doing it before an audience.

But at two the next afternoon she kept her appointment with William at the theatre. He greeted her warmly and introduced her to Joe Malloy, who played the pianoforte that had recently been bought from Thomas Dodd.

William was more enthusiastic than she had ever seen him, and his one eye gleamed with excitement. After introducing Eliza to Joe Malloy, who would accompany her, he said, "Now, sit down, Eliza. I want to tell you about the songs you're going to sing. I found two that ought to do very well. The first is a Portuguese song called 'The False-hearted Lover.' "

"But I can't sing in Portuguese," said Eliza.

"It's translated into English, and it goes like this." In a thin tenor William sang:

> " 'I don't weep because you leave me,
> I don't weep because you leave me,
> Nor for all the lies you tell;
> Other men would not deceive me,
> Other men would not deceive me,
> But who would love you half so well?
>
> Oh, false heart, false heart,
> You light-hearted lover,
> Who loves girls and leaves girls,
> You gay deceiver rover!' "

William paused and looked toward Eliza, who had been listening intently. "Do you like it?"

"Not much. I haven't much use for girls who wail and moan when their lover betrays them. Why don't she find another one?"

William was disappointed. "Well, I have another one here. It's Irish, called 'Shule Agra.' Maybe you'll like it better. Listen."

William sang again.

> " 'His hair was black, his eye was blue;
> His arm was stout, his word was true.
> I wish in my heart I was with you.' "

85

William stopped singing and looked at Eliza questioningly.

"Well," said Eliza reluctantly, "I like it better, but I'll never be able to sing it."

"Yes, you will. Stand up now. Sing a scale so that Joe can place your voice."

"I don't know how to sing a scale."

Patiently, William taught her to sing do-re-mi-fa-sol-la-ti-do. Joe decided that she was a contralto, and at last, with William accompanying her, she got through the song. Her voice was not strong, but it was clear and sweet, and William was pleased.

When she sat down in discouragement, William said, "Your voice is fine, Eliza. Not a great voice, mind you, but very sweet and charming. Now, get up and stop complaining."

For the next two hours Eliza sang the song again and again, until she had memorized the words and the tune. She did, in fact, improve greatly, and William was encouraged.

When she protested that she was tired and could sing no more, William sat down next to her. "We are not through rehearsing yet, my dear. Just once more, and I want you to sing the song with a French accent. After all, you are supposed to be Mademoiselle Capet, just off the boat from France."

The accent was not difficult for her. Two of her lovers had been French, and she found that she could mimic them very well.

William went into gales of laughter. "You will be a sensation, Eliza! They will love you!" He turned to Joe. "Thank you, Joe. Can you be here again tomorrow at the same time?" As Joe nodded, William said, "They've decided to do a repeat of *The Mysterious Monk* next Friday night, because it was so well received. Do you think our mademoiselle will be ready by then?"

"Why, she's almost ready now," said Joe. "Sure an' she's a charmin' colleen." A broad grin spread over his good-natured Irish face as he got up to leave.

Alone with William now, Eliza rose to her feet, moving toward the door.

"Come now, you haven't even got a kiss for your voice coach?" asked William.

She went over to him and embraced him. It was a long kiss, and she felt his tongue pressing against her teeth insistently. Then he drew her to him.

"You didn't think, did you, that I would not ask for a reward for my work?" he asked.

She smiled, then stepped back from him and began to undo her bodice. She sighed. "Oh," she said quite seriously, "if only I could sing as well as I can pleasure men."

On Friday night Eliza saw *The Mysterious Monk* from backstage. William had provided her with a chair in the wings, because he felt that watching the play would divert her from the sense of gloom and fear that pervaded her at the thought of going before an audience.

But when the play was over, and the time approached for her own performance, her nervousness had become sheer terror. She had an almost irresistible desire to run from the theatre, go home and pull the bedclothes over her head.

But William had already stepped before the curtain to introduce her. "Ladies and gentlemen," he was saying, "we have a great treat in store for you. Tonight we shall introduce a great French *artiste* who will sing for you!"

Eliza stood stock-still in the wings, incapable of moving. It was Mr. Hodgkinson who got behind her and literally shoved her onto the stage.

She looked out at the audience. It seemed to her to be a great black monster ready to devour her. But people were applauding her entrance, and that calmed her somewhat. At least they liked the way she looked.

She began singing in a faltering voice, which trembled uncontrollably whenever she had to sustain a note.

> " '*I don't weep because you leave me,*
> *I don't weep because you leave me,*
> *Nor for all the lies you tell . . .*' "

The audience was restless; people shuffled their feet and coughed. Toward the end of the first verse, there were some faint boos from the back of the pit. She decided not to go into

87

the second verse. She didn't like the song much anyway, and neither, obviously, did the audience. She nodded to Joe Malloy and then announced, "I will sing you another song."

Somebody in the pit yelled "Why?" and the audience laughed. When quiet was restored, she announced, "I will now sing you an Irish song."

Again there was the voice from the pit. "I thought you was supposed to be French." Again the audience guffawed, more unruly than before. To silence them, Joe began the introduction, and then Eliza started to sing in a small and frightened voice. The audience was still noisy and unsettled, and suddenly Eliza's fear gave way to rising anger. Her voice became louder, almost belligerent.

> " *'His hair was black, his eye was blue;*
> *His arm was stout . . .'* "

Another voice from the pit bellowed, "How big was his cock?"

At this, the audience broke up completely and laughed long and loudly. Even the ladies in the boxes giggled softly behind their fluttering fans.

Eliza was furious now, and rage brought the blood to her cheeks. Her face was damp with sweat. Suddenly, on impulse, she jerked at her bodice and then stepped angrily out of her hoopskirt. She stood before them clad only in her shift.

"All right, you bastids!" she screamed, and without a French accent she said, "I'll sing you a sea chantey that my mother taught me!"

A shocked hush had fallen over the audience. It was not usual for a performer to divest herself of clothing, and even the vulgar-tongued men were struck dumb. Eliza glowered at them challengingly, and without Joe's accompaniment, she sang:

> " *'Oh, Lily was a sailor's lass,*
> *She liked the boys to pat her arse.*
> *She allus took 'em to her bed,*
> *And when they got undressed, she said,*

"Ho, sailor boy! Heave it to!
Your mainmast's swingin' in the breeze—
So reef your sail and bring it down—
Down right into me!"' "

Midway through the song, the audience's shock gave way to raucous laughter. People clapped their hands wildly and stomped their feet. As she started to leave the stage, they screamed for her to come back and cries of "Encore! Encore!" reverberated through the theatre.

When Eliza reappeared, the reception was deafening. She did not know a second verse for the song, and so she repeated the only one she knew. This time Joe, who had picked up the melody, accompanied her.

Eliza was supremely confident now and was actually enjoying herself. She embellished the song with improvised movements. When she said "arse" she gave herself a loud whack on her thigh. When she reached the words " 'Ho, sailor boy! Heave it to! Your mainmast's swingin' in the breeze—' " she thrust out her right arm straight in front of her and raised it rigidly until it was over her head. And at the song's conclusion—" 'So reef your sail and bring it down—Down right into me!' "—she made vague circles with her hands in front of her, moving them as though to go downward, but then, instead of lowering them, she flung them into the air straight above her head and stuck out her tongue impudently at the audience.

The theatergoers went wild. They demanded three encores and would not let her off the stage until she had given them a fourth.

It was a dazed William who at last came before the curtain to quiet them. "I am glad that you liked Mademoiselle Capet, but we must go on with the performance. There is still the afterpiece to come—that delightful musical play by Benjamin Carr, *The Lyar*."

It was only the raising of the curtain on *The Lyar* that finally brought the audience to silence.

William was waiting for Eliza offstage. He said, "Where in God's name did you get that bawdy song?"

"From my mother, like I said."

"Your mother?"

"Yes, she was a whore in Providence, and I learned it from one of her sailor friends who used to sing sea chanteys."

"Well," said William, "I don't think you'll need to worry about money for a while, my girl."

"How much will I get, do you think?"

"I'm going to arrange with them to put you on a regular salary, not only for singing your sea chantey but as a supernumerary in other productions."

"What's a supernumerary?"

"One of those actors or actresses who are in a scene just to be there, like one of a crowd. Usually, they don't have any lines to say."

Eliza lifted her head in a new and proud way. "But I think I would *like* some lines to say. I like acting now."

William was thoughtful. "In our next production, which will be *As You Like It*, there are a couple of small speaking parts: Phebe, a shepherdess, and Audrey, a country wench, who has a scene with Touchstone."

"I shall play Audrey," said Eliza confidently.

When Eliza and William were ready to leave the theatre, a man and a young girl were waiting at the stage door.

The man stepped forward and bowed to Eliza. "You must forgive me, mademoiselle, but I so much enjoyed your performance that I wanted to tell you in person."

Eliza curtsied and said, "Thank you, sir." She looked at him and smiled, but somehow she could not turn her eyes away from him. He was a man in his early forties, handsome and attractive. But it was his eyes that held her. They were as nearly black in color as a human eye could be, and they fastened themselves upon her face with such fixity that she stood there a moment, hypnotized by their unwavering, intense gaze. Finally, she turned away in distraction and made a move to join William, who stood waiting nearby.

But the man stood in her path and was obviously not going to let her get away so easily.

"I am Aaron Burr," he said casually. Nodding to the young girl at his side, he added, "And this is my daughter, Miss Theodosia Burr."

After they had exchanged greetings, Burr said, "We would be honored if we could take you to Ranelagh's for refreshments."

Eliza, as though waking from a dream, said, "I am sorry, Mr. Burr, but I am going to Ranelagh's with my friend, Mr. William Dunlap."

"What a shame!" said Aaron Burr. "But, mademoiselle, let me assure you that you have not seen the last of me." The statement was made casually, as though it were an already established fact.

"Perhaps not," said Eliza abruptly and added, "Good evening to you, sir, and to you, Miss Burr."

She moved decisively away from him. William had found a hackney, and she got into it with him. As they drove off, Eliza said, "William, that was Aaron Burr."

"I know," said William.

"Aaron Burr! And he wants to see me again!"

"I'm sure that he does, and no doubt you will."

"Yes. What a very attractive and charming man he seems to be."

"He is both—and a devil with the ladies to boot. God help you, Eliza!"

"Why do you say that?"

"Because you will need His help." He paused and then added, "Eliza, I think you have met your match in the game of love."

"Nonsense!" said Eliza. But she was not so sure that William's prophecy was nonsense at all.

CHAPTER 9

ON THE ADVICE OF William Dunlap, Eliza's singing act was thereafter repeated just as it had occurred at its début, and Eliza was aware that at every one of her performances Aaron Burr sat alone in a center box, his gaze fixed on her every movement. This pleased her, and she came to look for him. And he was always waiting for her at the stage door. She would greet him and then leave with William.

On December fourteenth the season's début of *As You Like It* took place, and Eliza played Audrey, as she had intended to. Under William's careful coaching, she learned the lines in her scene with Touchstone and Jaques in Act III, and in her shorter appearances in Act V.

But on the night of the performance, William was taken ill with a cold and could not be at the theatre. His absence made Eliza nervous, but she need not have worried.

As she sang her sea chantey, she looked toward the box where Aaron Burr always sat. He was there, and she put more than usual ebullience into her singing. There were five encores, more than she had ever received.

After the performance, Burr was waiting to greet her at the stage door. When he saw that William was not present, he boldly stepped forward.

He bowed and kissed her extended hand. Then, looking at her

with his piercing black eyes, he said, "You were especially magnificent tonight, Mademoiselle Capet. I laughed until there were tears in my eyes."

Eliza acknowledged his compliment, still unable to move her eyes away from him. She shivered, because she felt that his gaze had stripped her naked there on the freezing street.

"I see that your customary escort is not with you tonight," said Burr casually.

"No. Mr. Dunlap is in bed with a cold."

"Then perhaps you will allow me to accompany you to Ranelagh's for refreshments?"

She started to shake her head negatively but found that she could not. "Why, thank you, Mr. Burr. That would be very kind of you."

When Eliza and Aaron Burr entered Ranelagh's and took a table for two, everyone's eyes turned toward them and the place became suddenly silent. Burr drew a chair for Eliza, and she sat down. Now the people in Ranelagh's whispered excitedly to one another.

They were used to seeing her with William Dunlap, but now she was with Aaron Burr, well known as the most relentless woman-chaser in town.

Eliza, dressed in the black velvet gown that she always wore when she sang, had never looked more beautiful. Her face was slightly flushed from the excitement of her début as an actress in *As You Like It*. But the high color in her cheeks was due not only to her success, it was also induced by the exciting presence of the man who sat opposite her. Her feelings about him were confused: she was nervous and excited, but at the same time she had an unaccountable sense of being at ease with him, as though he were someone whom she had known a long time.

After they had ordered drinks, Burr leaned toward her and said with an ironic smile, "Now, tell me, *ma chère* Mademoiselle Capet, are you really French with that royal last name?"

Eliza decided to tell her usual lie about her background. "No, I am an American. I was born in Providence. My mother died giving birth to me, and I lost my father not long after. I was adopted by a kind family, and then, when I was seventeen, I met Captain de la Croix. His ship docked in Providence harbor, and I—and I—became his mistress."

"But you still have not answered my question. Are you French?"

She met his persistent gaze without flinching. "Yes, my mother and father were both French, and so pure French blood runs in my veins."

"Your French accent sounded very genuine when you sang your songs. Do you speak French?"

"*Un peu*—what I learned from Captain de la Croix. I continued to be his mistress after we came to New York in November of 1794." She paused dramatically. "He died of yellow fever last summer."

"And how did you manage then? Mr. Dunlap?"

"Oh, no. He is merely a very good friend. The Captain had left me some money, you see. And now, Mr. Burr, don't you think you have asked enough questions? You make me feel as though I were in a courtroom."

He smiled his apologies. "I am sorry. I am, after all, a lawyer, and a good one. But your story fascinates me, just as you fascinate me. Furthermore, there is little point in my questioning you, since you lie so very easily."

"Sir!" said Eliza indignantly.

He smiled again, this time in a kindly way. There was silence between them, until the waiter arrived and set their drinks before them.

After Burr had raised his glass in a toast to her, Eliza broke the silence by saying, "You have questioned me quite thoroughly, Mr. Burr. I think I will now question you."

"Please do. And I promise not to lie."

"First," said Eliza, "where do you and your daughter live?"

"I live in a small house on Partition Street, but my real home is on a large estate called Richmond Hill, north of here. I live mostly on Partition Street, while my daughter, Theodosia, manages Richmond Hill."

"But your daughter looks to be no more than a young girl."

"She was thirteen on June twenty-first of this year, but she is a most extraordinary child. In addition to being my beloved daughter, she is probably the best-educated female in this country—the result of my own experiment."

"Experiment?" asked Eliza, not understanding the word.

"Yes. There is a brilliant English writer by the name of Mary Wollstonecraft who wrote an essay called *Vindication of the Rights of Women*. It made a great impression on me, and I decided to bring up my daughter by its precepts, as an experiment."

"I still don't understand," said Eliza.

"Well, from the age of nine, Theodosia has been treated as though she had a boy's mind. I hoped to convince people of something that neither sex wishes to believe: that women have souls. I hired a host of tutors to teach her languages, such as Greek, Latin, German, and French, as well as philosophy, and to say nothing of riding horseback, dancing, and playing the harpsichord and pianoforte. I can say now, only four years later, that the experiment has been completely successful!"

"But how could she learn all that in only four years?" said Eliza incredulously.

Burr took a deep breath, and when he spoke, the tone of his voice had altered. It was stern, unyielding. "She arose at dawn, and every minute of her day was laid out in a rigorous program from which she was not allowed to vary without my permission."

"Oh, the poor girl!" said Eliza. "Why, it's not right for a child to have no time for fun!"

"Fun was part of the program, too."

Eliza was silent again, looking at Burr's determined face in awe. At last, she said, "The child must hate you, Mr. Burr."

"On the contrary," said Burr proudly, "she adores me. No two human beings could possibly have a closer relationship. And so, my dear, you can see that Theodosia is quite capable of managing Richmond Hill, the servants and all the details of maintenance. She even presides, and most graciously, at the head of my table when I have dinner parties."

"I would not know how to talk to this strange child," said Eliza.

"That would be no problem, for she is most kind to people who do not have her learning. There has been only one difficulty. Theodosia's education has made me a pauper. I am constantly overwhelmed with debt, as I am now."

"Then how can you afford to go to the theatre and take me here as your guest?"

Burr laughed. "I borrow. I will not forgo the pleasures of this world for lack of money. Money can always be had."

"But if you borrow, you must pay the money back."

"Unfortunately, that is true. But enough of this talk of money. It is time for us to leave and be alone together."

Burr beckoned to the waiter and paid the bill. Eliza pondered how she would respond to the invitation that she knew was coming. She wanted him as a lover, but she did not want to be just another conquest for him.

When they reached the street, Burr hailed a hackney. As they got settled in the cab, Burr said to the driver, "Number 30 Partition Street!"

"But I live on Beekman Street," Eliza protested.

"Perhaps so," said Burr. He turned and drew her to him. He kissed her passionately, and her lips were unable to resist his.

Then she felt his mouth against her ear as he whispered, "Tonight, my dear, you are spending with me."

She bowed her head in happy assent.

PART II

Aaron Burr

CHAPTER 10

BURR'S HOUSE at 30 Partition Street was comfortable, but not large. The lower floor consisted of a small drawing room, off which there was a little room that served as a study. As Burr busied himself lighting candles, Eliza looked about her at the charmingly furnished room. She was in a daze at the quickness with which the man had made her decision for her. She half resented his assumption that she would come here with him, but the masterful way in which he had acted inspired her admiration. He was like her: he knew what he wanted and he acted decisively to get it.

He stood before her now, smiling down at her. His face showed no pride in his conquest as he gazed steadily at her upturned face. She felt again the curious magnetism of his dark eyes.

"Would you like some wine or spirits?" he asked softly.

"Some Madeira, please."

He went to a cabinet and took out two bottles and two glasses that sparkled in the candlelight. "My favorite wine comes from Spain," he said. "It is a claret called *tent*."

"Let me taste it," she said.

He offered his glass, and she sipped the wine.

"It is a bit too sour for me."

"All claret is sour, my dear, but there are degrees of sourness, and every good wine has its own special bouquet."

A silence fell, as they drank. She could feel his eyes studying her. She was uncomfortable and wished he would say something, anything to break the tension between them. At last, he drained his glass at a gulp and stood up.

"The bedchamber is upstairs. Shall we go now?" he asked.

She finished the madeira. He took her hand and she rose, following him like an obedient spaniel and hating herself for it.

Aaron's bedroom was larger than the other bedroom on the second floor. In the center of the room, there was an enormous bed, with four posts and a red velvet canopy. Curtains of heavy Belgian lace were at the sides and could be drawn to shut out the light.

She stood hesitantly in front of him, unsure what to say, what to do. Burr set down the candle and went over to her swiftly, taking her in his arms. Again she felt his lips pressing against hers, and again she found herself responding without quite knowing why. It was as though her mind had stopped working, and she reacted only with her body, spontaneously and automatically.

He drew her to the bed and began to undress her. In an unhurried fashion, he opened her bodice and covered her breasts with kisses that lingeringly caressed her skin. All the men she had known had done this as a preamble to making love, but they had done it voraciously, as though seized with an insatiable hunger.

When she was at last completely nude, she drew back the bedclothes and got beneath them. She shivered, not merely because the room was cold but in anticipation of making love with this strangely alluring man who seemed to have a power over her that she could not explain.

She watched him as he took off his clothes, swiftly but methodically, meticulously laying the garments on a chair next to the bed. Last of all, he took off his powdered wig and placed it carefully on the bedside table. She saw now that he was partially bald in front, with a forehead that extended backward some three inches, almost to the middle of his head. But the hair at the sides and back was full, black and wavy. Oddly, the bald forehead did not detract from his handsomeness. Instead, it gave him the look of a scholar. His figure was lithe and trim, and he was rather short in stature, only a few inches taller than she, and this had the effect of making his head seem too large for his body. His geni-

100

tals, too, seemed too large for the smallness of his body, and she was disappointed to note that he did not have an erection.

But this situation rapidly corrected itself when he slid down beneath the bedclothes next to her and took her in his unexpectedly strong arms. Again she was surprised at the leisurely way in which he made love. There was no part of her body that he did not caress with his hands, and often with his tongue. Passion had stirred in her as soon as she felt his body pressing against hers, but now it began slowly to increase to a pitch that became a fever.

Finally, in a voice choked and thick with desire, she moaned, "Oh, Aaron, Aaron! Take me, take me!"

He responded by thrusting himself into her, slowly because he knew that he was large and that women sometimes had difficulty in accommodating themselves to him. When at last she held him completely, she threw her hips up to meet him and curved her legs over his hard buttocks, which now were moving rhythmically over her. She sighed with a pleasure that she had not known since her affair with Matt so long ago. As he continued to ride upon her, she began to moan softly.

His mouth was on hers, his tongue moving insistently past her teeth until it almost reached her throat. She could feel him reaching farther into her, until her rapture became almost too great to bear, a kind of joyous pain. His movements were still deliberate and languorous, as though there were all the time in the world. She found herself reaching a wild and sobbing climax before he had shown any signs of reaching his own. Breathless and sweating now, she still responded to his movements. Astonished, she felt a new passion rising in her. She tossed and turned under him, but he held her firmly and relentlessly, like a rider who was breaking in a wild horse, a rider who had no intention of letting his steed escape him. Merciless, he persisted in postponing his own consummation, although his movements now had slightly accelerated, as though he were gathering force for the inevitable conclusion.

She was in an endless, delirious state of joy that took over her body, from her breasts down her arms to her fingertips, and to her belly and legs and even her toes, but it was a joy that was

101

becoming intolerable. She wanted to cry out for mercy, and she screamed, "Finish it, finish it, let me go!"

Without warning, he slapped her on the cheek and increased the speed of his movements. Then he seized her roughly by the shoulders and pulled her so close to him that she could hardly breathe.

"Take me, you bitch, take me!" he shouted. As he reached the pinnacle of his lust, he gave a final violent thrust that went deep into her, and she could feel the rhythmical throbbing of him inside her as he roared, "Take me! Take all of me!" Suddenly he released her from his viselike grip, and his head fell against her breasts, but she could still feel the throbbing inside her, as though he had not yet spent himself.

Their bodies were slippery with sweat, glued together, so that when they moved apart, there was an explosive sound as air rushed in. He threw back his head and roared with laughter.

The laughter broke her own tension, and she lay back in happy relaxation. As he withdrew himself from her slowly, she wanted to cry out, "Don't take it away from me!" But she did not, because she was already exhausted, and the prospect of more love-making was unthinkable. At least for now.

He stayed close, showing no inclination to leave her. Tenderly, he kissed and caressed her, nibbling gently at her ear as he whispered endearments. She had the strange feeling that he was grateful to her, that he was somehow asking forgiveness for his roughness during passion.

Before they slept, Eliza could not resist asking a question purely out of curiosity. "Tell me, my dear Aaron," she said, "how can you last so long before you—you—"

"Before I come, do you mean? It is no trick, if that's your thought. It is just a matter of will power."

"Will power? But in making love, the will power disappears."

"For most men—and women, too—that is true. But will power, dear Eliza, is like a muscle. It develops only by the exercise of it. At the height of passion, when I am momentarily quite mad, my will power is still in command. Without will power, little of moment is possible. With it, all things are possible."

He turned away from her then, after a good-night kiss, and was soon asleep, snoring softly. But Eliza, exhausted though she was, could not sleep. She lay awake, pondering Aaron's statement about will power. It was a new idea for her. She knew that she had a will, to the point where Sam had often called her willful. But she also knew that she had never been able to command her will to do something against her immediate wishes.

She resolved to cultivate her will power, so that she could use it—perhaps even as a weapon against this man beside her, so peaceful in his sleep.

He was her lover, the most exciting lover she had ever had. But instinctively, she knew that he was also her enemy.

When Eliza awoke the next morning, the place beside her in bed was empty. Aaron was already up and half dressed. As she watched him, she felt a new desire to have him make love to her again.

"Aaron!" she called softly.

He was knotting his cravat and turned toward her. "Ah, so you are awake. I tried to be quiet so as not to disturb you." He came over to her and took her in his arms. He kissed her gently, and she moved her body toward him voluptuously. He patted her playfully on her buttocks.

"Not now, my dear. I must be off to my work, so that I can pay some of my debts." He moved away from her and back to the mirror, where he finished tying his cravat.

She concealed her disappointment. "But when shall I see you again—and where?"

He looked at her in surprise. "Why, right here, of course. If you are going to be my mistress, and I trust you will be, you will live here with me. I shall send one of my men to help you move your belongings. Meanwhile, I suggest that you have breakfast in bed. What would you like?"

She was annoyed by his brisk tone of voice and was silent.

"Well, what shall it be? Coffee? A corn muffin, perhaps, or a bun? Eggs?"

He sounded as impersonal as a waiter in a restaurant, and she said, with an attempt at irony, "What do you recommend, *garçon?*"

"Everything that my maid Molly prepares in the kitchen is excellent," he said, ignoring her sarcasm.

"Well, I prefer *chocolat* to coffee—and perhaps a sweet bun with icing, and some bacon. I love bacon."

He smiled at her warmly. "Your every wish shall be granted, mademoiselle. *Ce que tu desire est un ordre!*"

He bowed elegantly from the waist, fixed her for a moment with his compelling gaze, and then added, "Goodbye, my best love." He left quickly.

She dozed, and it seemed that only a few moments had passed when Molly, a broad-beamed Irishwoman of middle age, appeared at her bedside with a breakfast tray.

"Good mornin' to you, madame. Here's your breakfast. Would you like me to open the draperies to let the sunshine in?"

Eliza roused herself and sat up. "Please do," she said.

The room was filled with morning sunshine, and Molly turned to leave. "If there's anything else you'll be needin', there's a bell on the tray."

"Thank you. What's your name?"

"It be Molly O'Hara, madame. What's yours, if I may be so bold as to ask?"

"I'm Madame de la Croix."

"Hm. French. Mr. Burr likes the Frenchies."

After Molly had left, Eliza began eating her breakfast. Her appetite was good, and the luxury of breakfast in bed made her feel like royalty.

While she ate, her mind raced, skipping from one thought to another, sometimes nonsensically. Her night of love with Aaron seemed an incredible dream now in the sunshine-filled, elegantly furnished bedroom. She found herself wondering if she were pregnant. Certainly, if any man could get her with child, Aaron Burr was that man. But she dismissed the thought, because it had long since become for her an accepted fact that she would never become pregnant again. Freelove Ballou had told her that it was unlikely that she would ever conceive again, because her difficult labor in bearing George had tipped her womb. At the time, Eliza had paid little attention, but now she was ready to believe it. She had made love with William Dunlap, Alexander Hamilton, Jacques, and Pieter. Surely, if she were going to conceive, there had been plenty of opportunity for her to find herself "in a condition."

Her thoughts turned again to Aaron. She had not imagined that she could respond to any man the way she had with him. It seemed impossible that she could experience such ecstasy in love-making, and the thought filled her with joy, but also with a curious fear—the fear of becoming in bondage to him. The memory of Matt and the eventual heartbreaking end of that affair was still as alive as though it had happened only yesterday.

But her feelings for Aaron were deeper than those she had had for Matt, who, by comparison, seemed only a cardboard figure, in two dimensions instead of three. Aaron Burr was a man whose attraction was not merely physical. He had a mind that was like a fine instrument, tuned exquisitely by education and sensitivity, and it gave forth a music that was overpowering in its brilliance and virtuosity.

She knew instinctively that she would have to meet him on his own ground, openly and honestly, for he would see through her lies and her wiles with complete clarity. This thought, too, frightened her. With all the other men she had known, she had always felt herself in complete control, confident of getting what she wanted, of making them do whatever she pleased, even though they might be unaware of it. For the first time now, she felt utterly helpless and without weapons.

She tried to dismiss this uneasy foreboding and almost succeeded in assuring herself that Betsy Bowen still rode her horse proudly, even royally.

But this horse, named Aaron Burr, was high-spirited and untamed and might easily break loose, race away violently—and throw her ignominiously to the ground.

CHAPTER 11

THAT AFTERNOON ELIZA WENT to Moore Street and got Pieter to help Aaron's manservant move her possessions from Beekman Street to Burr's house on Partition Street. Pieter was astonished at the news that Eliza had become Aaron Burr's mistress.

"You mean you're going to live with him just like you was his wife?" he asked.

"Yes, Pieter. I don't know whether you can understand this, but I—I am in love with Mr. Burr."

"In love? I thought you never fell in love with men. Just went to bed with them to pleasure yourself, or to get presents from them, like new clothes."

Eliza smiled. "That's true enough. But with Mr. Burr it's different. I wouldn't care if he never gave me presents. I love him."

Pieter pondered this. At last he looked up at her with questioning eyes. "Does that mean that you will not make love with me? Or give me lessons?"

"No. The lessons will go on, if you wish." She paused and then added gently, "But not the love-making."

The boy looked at the ground. She knew that he was hurt and disappointed, and she wanted to say something to console him.

At last, with a cheeriness that she did not feel, she said, "I will be giving up my work as an actress too. Why, Pieter, you have never seen me on the stage, have you?"

"No, ma'am," he said glumly.

"Would you like to?"

"Yes, ma'am, but I ain't got the money for a ticket."

"Well, that's no matter. You will have a box seat tonight for my farewell performance. I'll have a ticket reserved for you."

"Not in a box seat, madame. I don't own any fancy clothes for sittin' in a box with ladies and gentlemen in all their finery. A seat in the pit would be good enough."

Eliza decided not to give him money for new clothes, because she knew that he would still feel uncomfortable in the company of what he called "ladies and gentlemen in all their finery."

"Thank you, madame. I will like seeing you on the stage." He paused and then impulsively, with a note of jealousy in his voice, he said, "This Aaron Burr—does he love you like you love him?"

"I—I think so," said Eliza.

"Because if he don't and if he treats you bad, I will kill him with my jackknife!"

"You mustn't say things like that, Pieter."

"Why not? In case you didn't know, madame, I love you even more than he does! I will love you all my life. I will never stop loving you!"

Eliza leaned toward him and kissed him tenderly on the forehead. "I know you do, Pieter, and I am—I am very grateful for your love."

Her kiss had the effect of moving him to tears, and he fled from her in embarrassment.

By six o'clock Eliza had hung up her clothing in an empty closet in Aaron's bedroom and had stored her other belongings in the bottom drawer of a large chest. Aaron had still not returned, and so she went downstairs to ask Molly when he might be expected.

Molly was noncommittal. "The time when the master returns is something that only God knows. It's easier when he's in Philadelphia and I know he won't be comin' home."

"But I must leave to go to the John Street Theatre. I'm an actress there."

Molly surveyed her with a new interest. "An actress, hey?

107

Well, he never brought home an actress before. Well, if I was you, I wouldn't wait for him. He's in politics, you know, and when them politicians get to schemin' and plottin' over their drinks, time just don't exist no more. Would you like some supper before you go?"

"Yes. Something light, just enough to carry me through till after the performance, when I can have dinner."

"How's about some cold sliced roast beef, with some corn muffins, and an apple for dessert?"

"That would be fine, Molly. And some hot tea."

As Eliza ate the supper that Molly spread out for her on the kitchen table, she was nervous. Would Aaron be annoyed to return and find her gone? She had forgotten to tell him that she would have to be at the theatre, because *As You Like It* was being given a second performance, and she would have to be on hand to play Audrey. She decided to write a note asking him to meet her after the performance.

Molly provided her with a sheet of paper, a quill pen and ink. "Dearest Aaron," she wrote, "I must go to the theatre to play the roll of Audrey and could not wait for you. Please to meet me when the performance is over outside the theatre. Love from your Eliza."

She folded the note and put it in an envelope, on the outside of which she wrote "Kernel Aaron Burr." She gave the letter to Molly and then left to search for a hackney to take her to the theatre.

She was pleased to find that William Dunlap was waiting for her backstage. He looked pale and had obviously not recovered entirely from his cold.

"Oh, William," said Eliza, "you should not have come out on this cold night. You are still sick."

"Not so sick that I could not stay away from the theatre. It is only a cold." His voice was hoarse, and he coughed repeatedly. "How did it go last night with you as Audrey?"

"Oh, very well. Why, they even applauded me when I made my first entrance!"

"Good!" said William. "I think you may yet have a career as

108

an actress. You have good looks and that inborn talent for engaging an audience."

Eliza was silent for a moment. "William, I have something that I must tell you. I don't think I will continue on the stage. Last night I went home with Aaron Burr."

William shrugged. "Well, that hardly astonishes me."

"But it was not just an affair of the night, William. I love him. I have become his mistress. Today I moved all my things from Beekman Street into his house on Partition Street. I will live there with him."

"But I fail to see how this will affect your career as an actress. Surely Mr. Burr would not object to your continuing here."

"Perhaps not. But I wish to devote all my time to him, even help him, if that should be possible."

William shook his head sadly. "Eliza, you are a fool. How long do you think he will keep you as his mistress? Only until he meets another pretty face and makes a new conquest."

"That's not true!" protested Eliza. "I know that he loves me, and that's all that matters!"

"Is it? Even supposing that you stay with him for six months, even a year, what do you think will happen when he decides to run for President of these United States—and I am sure that is his aspiration."

Eliza paused, because she had no answer. At last she said rather lamely, "Well, I will stay with him, that's all. He is already a senator, and a mistress in his house does not disturb him."

"There is a great deal of difference, my dear Eliza, between being a senator and the President of these United States."

"He could marry me, you know."

"He could, but he won't." William paused and then continued in a gentle voice, "In the eyes of society, you are a tainted woman, and no President can marry a tainted woman."

"Tainted woman be damned! Then I shall live with him as a tainted woman. I don't care what society thinks, and neither will he!"

William sighed and shrugged his shoulders again. "Well, there is small point in my arguing with a woman in love, and I can only say 'Gather ye rosebuds while ye may, Old Time is still a-flying, And this same flower that smiles today Tomorrow will be dying.' "

"Is that Shakespeare?" asked Eliza.

"No. Those lines were written by Robert Herrick, a seventeenth-century poet. And they are as true today as when they were written."

"Then I guess I'll just gather the rosebuds, and when the flower dies, it will die, and I'll have to make the best of it."

William smiled. "That may mean that you will have to come back to the stage, just to support yourself. I will be waiting." On ·impulse, he put his arms around her and kissed her chastely on the cheek. "I will miss you, and I think the audience will, too."

Tears came to Eliza's eyes. "It is good to have a friend like you," she said.

After the performance, Eliza hurried out of the theatre. Aaron was there, pacing up and down with a measured step, his hands clasped behind him, and as soon as he saw her, he rushed to her. His eyes smiled into hers, and he took her into his arms and kissed her.

They had dinner at the Tontine, because both of them had eaten a light supper. Aaron ordered a lavish dinner, beginning with turtle soup, then oysters and roast pheasant, and ending with a creamy dessert made with preserved black cherries.

Their conversation was light and bantering as Eliza told him that she had made her farewell appearance at the theatre and had been greeted with an extraordinary demonstration by the audience, who demanded encore after encore.

"But why are you deserting the stage?" asked Aaron.

"So that I may devote myself to you," said Eliza.

"I am flattered, but in truth, you know, I don't require that much devotion." He paused reflectively. "On the other hand, there is one very good reason for you to give up your theatrical career. I refer to your education."

"My education? But I don't need any more education. I can read, and I can write—"

110

"Yes, but can you spell?" He reached into a pocket and brought forth the note she had written him. "Now, let us begin with the envelope. It is nice of you to refer to me as Colonel, but I was not at all pleased by your quaint spelling of the word."

After he had given her the correct spelling, she looked at him in annoyance. "It is a silly way to spell the word."

"Nevertheless, it is the correct way."

"It isn't even sensible," Eliza said.

"The English language, my lovely Eliza, is probably the least sensible language in the world."

While they ate the roast pheasant, Aaron continued with his spelling lesson, pointing out her misspelling of the word "role."

Eliza listened attentively, but she was growing more and more annoyed. Finally, she said angrily, "I thought I had come to have dinner with you, sir, not for a lesson in English!"

"I apologize. It was rude of me to interfere with your enjoyment of this delicious pheasant."

He spoke in a soft voice and with sincerity, and Eliza quickly responded, " 'Tis no matter, Aaron. I must improve myself."

He looked at her thoughtfully. "You have a lively intelligence, Eliza, and it should be cultivated. There is no reason why the accident of being a woman should mean that your only purpose on earth should be the bearing and rearing of children. I foresee the day when there will be women lawyers, women doctors, even women senators."

Eliza laughed. "A woman lawyer! You are daft, Aaron."

"Portia in *The Merchant of Venice* made a good lawyer."

"Yes, but she was dressed as a man."

"But that is not the point, my dear. She had the natural wit and intelligence to win her case, so that Shylock could not take his pound of flesh."

Eliza was thoughtful. After a few sips of wine, she looked at Aaron quizzically. "Then it is your plan to have me become a lawyer?"

Aaron laughed. "Hardly. I fear it will be many years before women will be accepted in the professions. And yet, we could as easily be governed by Abigail Adams as by her illustrious husband, our President-elect. Indeed, she is a woman of such excellent intellectual powers that she might be a better President."

"You don't like John Adams, do you?"

Aaron looked thoughtful. "I don't dislike him, although he is too much a Federalist for my taste and leans rather heavily toward consultation with Alexander Hamilton. But to give the man his due, he will have a difficult task steering a middle ground between France and England, when we cannot wage war with either."

"I do not like Mr. Hamilton," said Eliza firmly.

"Because he is a Federalist?"

"No. Because he is a very poor lover who thinks only of himself and never of his partner."

Aaron's heavy eyebrows were raised in genuine surprise. "You went to bed with him?"

"Yes. Only a few times. Aside from his love-making, the man is a pinchpenny. I sent him packing finally."

Aaron roared in delighted laughter. "What I like most about you, Eliza, is your blunt honesty, even though you have not yet told me the truth about yourself. But I trust that will come later."

"I will tell you the story of my life tonight, if you wish, but not until after we have made love."

And Eliza kept her promise. That night, after a bout of making love that was even more unrestrained than it had been the night before, Eliza propped herself up on pillows in the large four-poster bed and told him the truth about herself.

"To begin with, my name is not Capet, and neither of my parents was French. My mother was a whore in Providence, and her name was Phebe Kelly, although she adopted the name of Bowen, a sailor she said she was married to. He died before I was born. She told me that my real father was George Washington, and I believe it is true."

Aaron sat up in bed and looked at her in astonishment. "You mean I am sleeping with the bastard daughter of the father of our country?"

"Yes," she said with calm assurance. "It's too bad that there's no way of proving it."

"When were you born?"

"Sometime in August 1775. My mother was not sure of the date, and so I have no birthday."

Aaron thought a moment. "It's true that Washington was in that area in the latter part of 1774. He might have met your mother. Of course, he did not bed women to any great extent, but when he was away from Martha, he might have had the amorous needs that all men have. Let me look at you."

He took her face in his hands and stared at it intently, first in full face and then in profile.

"Egad, there is some resemblance in the cut of your jaw, but that nose, that pretty little uptilted nose—that has to be Irish, a Kelly nose for sure."

Eliza smiled at him, pleased that he had taken her seriously and had not dismissed a relationship to George Washington as absurd, the way most people did.

"I am honored to be your bed partner, Miss Washington. But pray, continue with your story."

And so Eliza told him about her early life in Providence: the burning of the brothel at the old gaol and her adoption by Sam and Lydia Allen; how she became the mistress of Jacques de la Croix; her love affair with Matt and its unhappy ending.

Until now, her voice had been matter-of-fact, as though she were telling the story of someone else. But as she recounted her brief affair with Michel and its tragic outcome, followed by the birth of her son, she became emotional and sometimes wept. She ended her story by describing her struggle to survive during her two years in New York.

When she finished, Aaron was silent. She was fearful that she had bored him, or worse, that he was shocked and would end their relationship.

At last, unable to bear the silence any longer, she whispered, "Aaron, are you asleep?"

"No," he said. "How could I sleep listening to the sad tale of your life in Providence? You have much courage, Eliza—as well

113

as ambition. Your foster father taught you to read and write, to say nothing of taking your maidenhead. And Jonathan Clarke introduced you to Shakespeare and to read for pleasure. But your education has only just begun."

"I think I am enough educated," she said defensively.

"Nonsense! Next week you will begin work with an English tutor who will teach you something about grammar and spelling. And I shall hire another tutor to teach you French."

"But I already know how to speak French!"

"Yes, a little bit, and your accent is extremely good. But there is much, much more for you to learn."

"But I don't want to study, Aaron."

"Perhaps not. But you will. The matter is settled. And now, let us get some sleep. I must go to Philadelphia tomorrow, because Congress is in session. Meanwhile, you will stay here. I will leave twenty dollars with Molly for spending money—a new gown, perhaps, or whatever else you may need."

"But when will you be back?"

"In two or three weeks, and then I will take you to Richmond Hill so that you can meet Theodosia."

He kissed her tenderly, said good night and almost immediately fell asleep.

Eliza could not sleep. She was disturbed by the way that Aaron had taken command of her life, but she was more disturbed by the fact that she was letting him do it. With other men she had always been in control. It had been she who called the tune that they danced to.

But it was not the nature of the new relationship alone that made her wakeful. The prospect of meeting Theodosia at Richmond Hill filled her with uneasiness and dread. Although she had been introduced to Aaron's daughter that night at the theatre, it had not occurred to her that she would ever see the child again.

Now, she saw Theodosia as an adversary. Eliza was not only envious of this precocious child and her many accomplishments, she was also jealous because she knew that for Aaron his daughter was an idol, a model of feminine perfection that he himself had created and therefore worshipped.

Eliza knew that competition was out of the question, and that however much Aaron might desire her and love her, she would always be second in his heart.

This role was not to her liking, and the knowledge that she would have to make a friend of Theodosia was even less to her liking.

Already, she found herself hating the child and all that she stood for.

CHAPTER 12

Two DAYS AFTER AARON LEFT for Philadelphia, Eliza's education began. At ten o'clock in the morning Molly announced that there was a Mr. Courtenay asking to see her. She went downstairs and was greeted by a plump bald man of middle age. He wore spectacles and looked over the top of them at her in a studious way.

"I am Mr. Thomas Courtenay, madame. Mr. Burr has engaged me to tutor you in French and English."

"I am happy to make your acquaintance," said Eliza, although she was not at all happy to meet him. She had enjoyed Jonathan Clarke as a teacher because of his informality and his often drunken declamations of Shakespeare. But this man was a scholar, a professional teacher, and his serious air made her uncomfortable.

"Where shall we transact our lessons?" he asked.

Eliza looked about her distractedly and finally said, "Why, in Mr. Burr's study over there, I suppose. There are many books on the shelves."

Mr. Courtenay rubbed his hands together gleefully. "Ah, books! Yes, we shall need books, many of them. I have brought with me an English grammar and a French grammar for us to start with."

They seated themselves in the study, and without further preamble Mr. Courtenay began his course of instruction.

"We shall undertake a review of English and French grammar, but first I must tell you that the most important thing is for you to read aloud to me in both languages. Later, we shall begin writing little compositions in English and in French."

116

"I can read quite well in English," said Eliza, "but Mr. Burr says that my spelling is bad when I write it. As for French, I can speak it a little, but I wouldn't know how to write it at all, let alone spell words in it."

"All in good time, my dear, all in good time. It will not be easy; you will have to work very hard."

He tested her on reading from the Bible, and she did reasonably well. Then he tried speaking to her in French, and she responded haltingly to him in her limited vocabulary.

Eliza had had no idea that there was such a thing as an English grammar, let alone a French one, and conjugations puzzled and dismayed her, especially if they were of irregular verbs. She was bewildered but Mr. Courtenay was patient and encouraging.

She was glad when it was twelve o'clock and time for luncheon. To her dismay, she learned that Mr. Courtenay would dine with her, holding conversation only in French. She was even more dismayed to learn that lessons would continue for another two hours after lunch.

Before Mr. Courtenay left, he gave her written assignments in both English and French, to be completed in two days, when he would return. On the point of leaving, he turned to the bookshelves in search of a book that she might read. He had correctly assumed that she was Burr's mistress, and so he pulled down a copy of Defoe's *Moll Flanders*. Mr. Courtenay believed that his students should read books that might interest rather than elevate them, and the first-person memoirs of a London prostitute seemed altogether fitting for his new pupil.

After Mr. Courtenay had left, Eliza developed a headache and retired to the bedroom for a nap. Her head was so full of words that she wanted to escape from them, and so she slept.

After supper she sat down with the grammar books and made an attempt to memorize conjugations and grammatical rules. She was determined to get the education that Aaron was offering her, not merely to please him, but because she knew that if she was going to become a lady, she would need to talk like one, whether in French or in English.

Before going to bed, she opened *Moll Flanders* and started to

117

read. She was astonished to find that Moll's adventures fascinated her and she continued to read until it was bedtime. She had finished perhaps a third of the novel with enjoyment.

At the end of two weeks Mr. Courtnay was delighted with Eliza's progress, and he told her so. He was particularly pleased with her interest in reading for entertainment. She had read Defoe's *Robinson Crusoe* and *Roxana*, but his *Journal of the Plague Year* depressed her, because it reminded her of the death of Jacques. He then tried her on Samuel Richardson's *Pamela*, but she did not even finish the first of the four volumes.

"But why did you not like Pamela?" asked Mr. Courtenay.

"Because she is a silly woman," said Eliza. "Always having the vapors and fainting for no good reason. Women like that are nothing but playacting fools, and they bore me."

Mr. Courtenay nodded his head sympathetically. "I must say that I half agree with you. But Mr. Richardson's novels have been very popular both in England and here, and whatever else they may be, they are well written."

He got up and went over to the bookshelves in search of a book that might please her. He saw an almost-new copy of Mrs. Radcliffe's *The Mysteries of Udolpho* and took it from the shelf.

He presented it to Eliza with a flourish. "Here is a Gothic novel that is full of action and mystery. Perhaps you may like it. When its ladies faint, it is for a good reason—they are constantly confronted with horrors."

Mr. Courtenay's choice had been astute. Eliza loved the novels of Mrs. Radcliffe, and she read all the popular Gothic novels that were being imported from England as fast as they could be printed.

When Aaron returned from Philadelphia, he received Mr. Courtenay's favorable report and was pleased.

"I am very proud of you, Eliza. You are indeed applying yourself assiduously to your studies, but I could wish that you would choose to read books that are not merely entertaining."

"It is good of you to educate me, Aaron, but can you really afford to pay this tutor?"

"No, of course not."

"Then you must dismiss him. I can study by myself now that I have gotten started."

"No. Without a tutor, you would become lazy, I fear. It is true that I am heavily in debt. But recently, I have had a friend of mine, Colonel Lamb, consolidate all my debts and provide me with an advance."

"And how much do you owe this Colonel Lamb?" asked Eliza.

Aaron waved his hand in a airy gesture of dismissal. "Only twenty-two thousand dollars."

Eliza gasped. She had never known anyone who even possessed that much money, much less owed it.

"Oh, my dear Aaron, we must cut expenses. I can go back to the stage and—"

His fist came down hard on the table. "You will do no such thing! You will continue to study, and your only role will be to play Galatea to my Pygmalion."

She had not the vaguest idea who Pygmalion and Galatea were, but she did not have time to ask, because Aaron had seized her in his arms and was carrying her to the bed. He had been home only two hours, and Eliza had imagined that he would be too tired from his journey for love-making.

She had not yet learned that Aaron Burr was never too tired to make love. That afternoon he proved it. His time away from her had made him insatiable, and when it was time for dinner, she wondered if she herself was not too exhausted to rise from the tumbled bed.

That night they dined at the Belvedere and consumed a lavish dinner that began with a clear soup and went on to a fish course of broiled bass, roast beef, and for dessert a floating island flavored with Jamaica rum.

Eliza was beautiful in a new gown that she had made during Aaron's absence. It was of shining red satin with a ruffled white bodice, and her hat was a dazzling *pouf* of French blue gauze, pinned to her hair with tiny red, white and blue cockades.

"You have a new dress," said Aaron. "You look ravishing in it."

"I made it myself," she said demurely.

He smiled. "Well, at least we shall not have to give you lessons in sewing. The color scheme is no doubt in tribute to France."

"Yes. I like the French," she said.

"I am a Republican myself. But France is not behaving as a friend to us now. The Federalists would like us to make war with France, you know, and it might come to that."

"I don't understand why."

"When the French Revolution began in 1789, Americans were very sympathetic. We had just recovered from a revolution of our own, and we remembered that the French had helped us. But the French Revolution became a reign of terror and blood. Many people were beheaded, and the government was unstable. People here, especially the Federalists, lost their sympathy. But the real trouble began when France went to war with England and began to raid our ships, especially those carrying cargoes to England. And so," he concluded, "we are arming ourselves for war with the French, and the English, too, since John Jay's treaty with them has not prevented their acts of piracy and the impressment of our sailors."

"Oh, dear," said Eliza, "now I'll have to change the colors of my new dress."

He patted her hand. "No need for that, my dear. Red, white and blue are *our* colors too."

The waiter brought the bill for their dinner, and Aaron passed it over to her with a roguish smile. "Pray, tell me, Madame de la Croix, is the addition correct?"

She looked at the bill in bewilderment and blushed. "I don't know, Aaron. I cannot add or do other arithmetic."

As they rose to leave, Aaron said, "That situation will be remedied immediately. I shall speak to Mr. Courtenay in the morning."

Eliza sighed at the prospect of even more studies. She suddenly understood how Pieter must have felt when he did his lessons in anticipation of making love with her. And she wondered how long Aaron would love her if she stopped her education.

As they settled into the carriage for the ride to Partition Street,

Aaron kissed her. And then he drew away, as though a thought had occurred to him.

"By the way, Eliza, you must start reading the newspaper every day, and not just the latest fashions. History is not only something that happened yesterday. It is happening right now."

She nodded, bowing her head in assent. She longed for the moment they would be in bed together later. Then, at least, her education would stop. She needed no lessons in love-making.

The next day Aaron announced that they would be driving out to his country estate, Richmond Hill, and would have dinner with Theodosia. Eliza dreaded the meeting with Theodosia, but she dressed for the occasion in her new gown.

It was a drive of almost two miles, but Aaron's shining black coach trimmed with gold and drawn by two handsome black Arabian horses got them over the icy roads in half an hour.

The sight of the house and its spacious grounds made Eliza cry out in surprise. The house, large and with a portico at the entrance, stood on a hill near the Hudson River. To the right of it there were pastures where cattle grazed; and to the left, a grove of pine and oak trees. The Minetta Brook had been dammed to form a small pond on which ducks, geese and two swans glided on the icy waters.

Eliza clasped Aaron's hand in excitement. "Oh, Aaron, it is beautiful! I had no idea that Richmond Hill was a real mansion."

"It is not so beautiful now as it is during the spring and summer, when everything is in bloom. Then it is as much of paradise as I ever expect to see."

When they alighted from the coach and went up the steps to the entrance, Eliza became apprehensive. As Aaron pounded the ornate brass door knocker, she whispered, "Oh, Aaron, do you think Theodosia will like me?"

"How could she help liking you?"

"But does she know that I—I am your mistress?"

"Of course. I wrote her all about you. I have seen to it that she has received instructions on the relations between men and women. She has met other lady friends of mine and was most gracious to them. You see, we have no secrets from each other."

The door was opened by a footman who ushered them into an opulently furnished hallway from which a handsome mahogany stairway rose to the second floor.

Theodosia came running into the hallway from the drawing room on the left. She threw herself into her father's arms and they embraced warmly.

"Oh, Father, it is so good to see you. It has been so long. It seems years since I last saw you."

Eliza watched them as they exchanged greetings and endearments. Aaron's eyes, she noticed, glowed with love.

At last he turned toward Eliza. "Theodosia, I would like you to meet my dear friend Madame de la Croix."

Theodosia curtsied, as did Eliza, and they clasped hands.

"Oh, Papa has told me so much about you, how beautiful and charming you are. And I loved your performance at the theatre!'"

Eliza smiled at Theodosia and said, "Why, thank you, Miss Burr. I have heard most complimentary reports about you, too, especially your accomplishments in learning."

They moved into the drawing room, which was the most exquisitely furnished of any Eliza had ever seen. The drawing room at Matt Wyatt's house in Providence seemed dreary and cold in comparison. The highly waxed pine boards of the floor were covered by a thick Turkey carpet of brilliant colorings. There were oil paintings on the walls, mostly portraits, one of them of Theodosia herself. The fireplace, in which a log fire was burning briskly, boasted of gleaming brass andirons ornamented at the top by hand-wrought eagles.

But it was the window at the end of the room that caught Eliza's eye and held it. It was large and was trimmed with sumptuous red velvet draperies, and through it there was a breathtaking view of the Hudson River. The sun was setting in the west over the majestic Palisades of New Jersey, and the golden light settled in gleaming puddles on the room's elegant furnishings.

Quietly, Eliza watched Aaron and Theodosia while they chatted about her studies. He cross-questioned her about what she was reading, from the philosophical writings of Jeremy Bentham to Gibbon's *Decline and Fall of the Roman Empire.* Theodosia answered his questions with vivaciousness and pride.

Aaron was like a stern schoolmaster, but he was obviously delighted by the girl's display of knowledge. And always, there was that look of unwavering love in his dark eyes.

That same love showed in Theodosia's eyes, and it was evident that the bond between the two was deep and abiding. Eliza knew that no matter how hard she might try, she could never be first in Aaron's heart.

She recognized her jealousy and reconciled herself to the fact that it would always be there. Meanwhile, she concentrated her attention on this remarkable thirteen-year-old and marveled at her display of knowledge and her eloquent vocabulary. In appearance, Theodosia was not quite pretty, but her finely chiseled features and her clear ivory complexion indicated that within a very few years she would be beautiful. Her most striking feature was her flashing black eyes, very like Aaron's own. Her curly hair was like his, too, but not quite so dark, and she wore it long, over her shoulders, and tied at the back by a small scarlet bow. In front, she had bangs, cut squarely over her forehead.

Suddenly, Theodosia addressed Aaron in an almost scolding voice. "Papa, we are being very rude. We have been so busy talking about my studies that we have quite left Madame de la Croix out of our conversation."

Eliza protested that she did not mind, but Aaron turned to her. "Theo is quite right, Eliza. Her manners, you see, are better than mine."

And so Eliza was drawn into the conversation, and Aaron encouraged her to talk about *Moll Flanders* and the Gothic novels of Mrs. Radcliffe. Soon she and Theo were deep in conversation, while Aaron remained silent, looking at both of them proudly and smiling to himself.

At teatime they were joined by Natalie de Delage, a girl of Theo's age. Her parents were French refugees, and Aaron had adopted her as a companion for his daughter. Unlike Theo, she was blonde and blue-eyed and shy in manner, and it was clear that she was pleasantly dominated by Theo, who treated her in an indulgently maternal fashion.

Tea was served by Peggy, an ancient and faithful servant who had attended Mrs. Burr during her long and painful last illness.

The tea was sumptuous, with muffins and jam and small iced cakes. Eliza ate ravenously, and the food tasted especially good because it was served on hand-painted plates imported from China, and the tea service itself was of sterling silver.

Eliza remarked on the beauty of Theodosia's oil portrait, which hung over the fireplace.

"Oh," said Theo, "our dear John Vanderlyn painted it last summer. He is one of Papa's many protégés. Last September he arranged for John to go to France to study, and is paying all his expenses. He did a portrait of Papa, too."

Eliza was beginning to understand now why Aaron was so greatly in debt, especially when Theo described the excellent care that was given their horses. Ten dollars a month was paid just to have their teeth scrubbed and their hoofs polished.

After a magnificent dinner, which had been meticulously prepared by Aaron's chef, Alexis, they relaxed once again in the drawing room, where brandy and cordials were served. Even Theo and Natalie were given small portions of crème de menthe in tiny crystal cordial glasses. Eliza was persuaded to sample crème de cacao, which she had never before tasted.

Bedtime came soon for the girls, both of whom would rise at dawn to begin their round of studies and the supervision of household duties.

When at last Eliza and Aaron were alone, he said, "Well, Eliza, what do you think of my Theo?"

"I have never seen the like of her. It is hard to believe that she is only thirteen. Her manners and speech are those of a young lady. She is altogether charming, and I can see now why you take such pride in her."

Eliza was speaking the truth. To her surprise, she had found Theo very likable, even delightful. It was impossible for her to hate the child, as she had anticipated, but she did envy her, not only because of her education but because of Aaron's adoration of her. She was thankful that there was at least one part of Aaron's life where Theo could not be a rival.

And that night, in the large double bed in Aaron's bedroom, she was more than usually responsive to the ardor of his love-making.

CHAPTER 13

THE DAYS OF WINTER dragged on, and the weather was so bad that Eliza did not often leave the house on Partition Street. In her studies with Mr. Courtenay she continued to make progress in French and English grammar. Her new subject of arithmetic became easy for her when Mr. Courtenay slyly converted the figures into dollars. This had a practical effect, and she quickly learned the multiplication tables, and how to add, subtract and divide. She was pleased when Mr. Courtenay one day declared that her ciphering, as he called it, was superlative.

She still read books, for pleasure and to pass the hours when she grew weary of studying. She sampled Gibbon's *Decline and Fall of the Roman Empire*, but it bored her almost as much as works of philosophy. Otherwise, most of her reading consisted of the popular fiction of the day. Aaron often brought her a book as a gift, and so she added several volumes to her own small library.

Aaron took her to task again for reading mostly fiction. "But, Eliza," he said, "there are many things you should know about, not only history, but philosophy and science. Try Mr. Gibbon again."

"No, Aaron," Eliza said. "He bores me. I get all the emperors mixed up, and I hate reading about wars and people dying and famines and sad things."

Aaron relented. He was pleased at least that she continued to read and especially that she had taken an interest in the daily newspaper and was becoming aware of politics and America's relations with France and England. News of the doings of Alexander Hamilton renewed her dislike of the man, and she found herself greatly in sympathy with the political philosophy of Thomas Jefferson.

But she lived for those times when Aaron was not in Philadelphia and she could have evenings with him, dining out or going to the theatre.

On an unseasonably warm and clear day in March, she decided to drive out to Moore Street and visit Pieter. She had not seen him since the night when she had given him a ticket for her performance at the John Street Theatre.

She arrived in midafternoon, but Pieter was not there. Old Hans Van Zandt was ill and in bed. He was overjoyed to see her.

"Oh, Madame de la Croix, how good it is for you to visit me! It has been so long a time, and things have not gone good for us here." He began coughing, and it was several moments before he caught his breath.

"How long have you been sick like this, Mr. Van Zandt?"

"All winter long. I have had this inflammation of my lungs, and it does not go away. I don't know how I would ha' managed without my Pieter."

"Where is he?"

"He's working now, helping a carpenter and learning to be one. My savings are almost gone, and Pieter had to earn some money so that we could eat. He'll be home soon."

"I'll wait," said Eliza. "But meanwhile, let's have some tea, shall we?"

"Oh, that would be so good. There is some coffee on the stove that you can heat up." He paused and smiled. "We Dutch do not care much for English tea."

As Eliza got up to go to the kitchen, the old man looked at her gratefully. "You are so beautiful, madame, and I saw that you came in a coach with a pair of black horses. You are married?"

"No. Not exactly. But I am betrothed, and my—my fiancé lent me his coach for the afternoon."

When Eliza returned from the kitchen with cups of hot coffee and some corn muffins, Hans got out of bed and put on a faded dressing gown so that he could sit at the table with her. Again he went into coughing spasms and brought up phlegm, which he spat into a large handkerchief. There was blood in the sputum.

Eliza was concerned. "Have you seen a doctor, Mr. Van Zandt?"

"Oh, yes. He bled me and cupped me and gave me medicine, but nothing helps." He paused and then added, "It is my age, madame. I am seventy-four, and I don't think I will live much longer. I thank God that I own this house and that it will be Pieter's when I am gone."

"Oh, you mustn't say such things. Now that spring is coming, you will get well and soon be fit again."

The old man shook his head sadly. "I do not think so, madame."

The door opened and Pieter strode into the room. He went over to her quickly and, bowing and blushing with pleasure, he kissed her hand.

"I saw the coach outside," he said, "and I wondered who was visiting us. I did not think it would be you, madame."

"And why shouldn't it be?" asked Eliza. "We are old friends, and I have not seen you all winter long. You did not come to me for your lessons."

Pieter hung his head. "No. I was too ashamed to come visit you in your new house. And I did not have the time. I had to find work so that we could eat."

"But why didn't you tell me, Pieter? Perhaps I could have helped."

"You mean you could have gotten some money from your Mr. Burr? I would not accept it. I am too proud, madame."

Mr. Van Zandt had fallen asleep at the table, and so Pieter carried him to bed and tucked him in.

He turned to Eliza. "I would like to talk to you, madame. Let's go into the kitchen."

They sat at the kitchen table, and Pieter looked at Eliza with sad eyes. "I must tell you, madame, that my grandfather is close to death. I got a doctor from over at the New York hospital to come see him. He says that Grandpa had a bad consumption in his chest, and there is nothing to be done for it. All he could do was to give him opium to ease the pain and the coughing."

"But what will you do when he dies?"

"Well, I'll just keep working so that I have enough to eat—and live here alone." He paused and then said, with an effort to be cheerful, "I saw you on the stage, madame. You were so funny. When you sang the song about Lily, I just laughed and laughed. And you looked so beautiful. Not a man jack in the place but what fell in love with you."

"I'm glad you enjoyed it, Pieter. I am not on the stage anymore. Mr. Burr has engaged a tutor for me to learn better English and to study French and arithmetic."

"You mean *you* are taking lessons, just the way I did?"

"Yes. There is much that I do not know, and Mr. Burr has taken on the task of educating me." She paused a moment in reflection. "Mr. Burr owns a beautiful estate north of here and employs many servants. Perhaps he would give you a job caring for his horses or his gardens."

Pieter pressed his lips together in determination. "I want no favors from your Mr. Burr. I have seen his mansion at Richmond Hill." He paused. "Madame, do you still love him very much?"

"Yes, Pieter, more than any man I have ever known. He has a fine mind and is truly a great man. It would not surprise me if he one day became President of the United States."

"And how is he when he gets into bed with you?"

Eliza did not answer immediately. She did not want the boy to be more jealous than he already was, so she said, "He is a very good lover, Pieter."

"As good as me?" he asked. There was a touch of pride in his voice.

"I must be truthful, Pieter, and say yes." She rose and prepared to leave.

"Must you go so soon, madame?"

She patted him affectionately on the cheek. "Yes, it is growing late, and I must get home for dinner."

He saw her to the coach and was full of admiration for the black horses. He looked at her sadly. "I guess you have now become a great lady, madame."

"Yes, maybe. But I am still your very good friend, Pieter. If

129

you should ever need me for anything, the house is at 30 Partition Street. Mr. Burr is gone during the day, and often he is in Philadelphia, so you would not meet him."

"Why does he go to Philadelphia?"

"He is our senator from New York State, you know, and he must be in Philadelphia when Congress is in session."

Pieter helped her into the coach and closed the door. "I didn't know he was a senator, madame," he said wistfully.

Eliza leaned her head out of the coach window. "We live in a democracy, Pieter, and you are just as good a man as he is. Never forget that."

He considered her words seriously and then smiled. "Thank you, madame."

As the coach drove away, she looked back at Pieter, who stood in the road waving goodbye. He seemed to Eliza a pathetic and yet gallant figure, and she realized suddenly that she felt that he had been not only her lover, but, in some strange way, her son.

She thought of her own son, George Washington Bowen, whom she had deserted some two years ago, leaving him in the care of Freelove Ballou. She did not often think about him because the memory brought with it a feeling of sadness. Although she had never loved the child, the thought that she had deserted him nevertheless made her feel guilty. But she always reassured herself with the knowledge that at least the boy was being given good care by Freelove, who had loved him from the moment he was born.

When she arrived at the house on Partition Street, she was greeted by Aaron. She was overjoyed to learn that Congress had taken a short spring recess and that he would be with her for a few days.

He had bought tickets for the theatre, where *As You Like It* was to be performed again, and so Eliza hurriedly donned the new gown that she had bought while Aaron was away. It was more subdued in coloring than her most recent costume had been. It was in pastel shades of green and yellow, and her headdress was an elaborate affair of forest-green velvet, crowning her red-gold locks, which had been massed high on her head.

Aaron looked at her, appreciation glowing in his dark eyes. "*Madame, tu es tout à fait ravissante!*" he exclaimed.

"*Merci, monsieur, mais c'est toi qui as acheté ce beauté.*"

"Your French is improving, my dear, but it should be *cette beauté*, not *ce beauté*. *Beauté* is a feminine noun, you know."

Eliza pouted. "Even when you praise my dress, you must correct my grammar. That takes away all the pleasure of being called *ravissante*."

"But you *are* ravishing, my dear!" He strode toward her and seized her in his arms. "Take off the dress," he commanded.

"But why? You said you liked it."

"Certainly I like it, but I like the body beneath it even more, and I aim to have it."

"But not now, Aaron. Please. We have had no supper, and the theatre—"

"Damn the supper. One can eat at any time. And sometimes, the occasion for love-making is impromptu. Please to remove the dress. I would not like to muss it."

Eliza hated herself for her easy compliance as she began taking off the dress. She had not even removed her petticoat when he seized her and forced her to the floor.

"But, Aaron, we might at least go to bed," she pleaded.

As he lifted her petticoat and got astride her, he said, "Love is as good on the floor as anywhere."

His mouth on hers silenced her protestations, and almost immediately, he had unbuttoned his trousers and was beginning to enter her. She could not keep herself from giving in to him completely, and his old magic began to work in her again and she cried with pleasure.

They went without supper and were even late for the theatre. Much as Eliza enjoyed *As You Like It*, her pleasure in the performance was marred by the memory of what Aaron had called "impromptu" love-making on the floor of the bedroom. She resented his assumption that she would so easily acquiesce to him. She felt as though she had been raped, and she did not like the feeling.

After the performance, they went to the Tontine Coffee

House for a late dinner. She ate without much appetite and was unusually silent.

Aaron looked at her in concern. "Don't you feel well, *ma chère madame?*"

"I feel well enough," she said.

"What is the trouble, then? You are not your usual vivacious self. Did the play bore you?"

"No. I thought the performance was excellent."

"Then what is the matter? There is something wrong, I can see."

She did not reply right away and took a gulp of Madeira, draining the glass. She looked him in the eyes as she said, "It is you, Aaron."

"Ah, you are annoyed with me because my love-making made us late."

"I did not mind being late."

"Well, what is it then, for God's sake? It is not good for you to be nursing grievances against me."

An unexpected anger sprang up in her. "You are a hypocrite!" she said. "You talk always of how women should be the equals of men, but you don't behave that way with me. You are always superior, and especially when we make love. Tonight you did not give any thought to my feelings. You—you just grabbed me and forced me." Her voice rose in fury. "You raped me!"

Aaron remained calm and did not respond with an anger of his own. "I have been a long time in Philadelphia without the consolation of female company, Eliza. You looked so beautiful that my feelings overcame my judgment."

"And where is the will power that you have talked about so much? It is not just tonight, Aaron. You always treat me as though you were—were a conqueror."

"But I am, after all, a man, my dear," he said with a trace of annoyance in his voice.

"And must a man always be a conqueror, then?"

He smiled. "Yes. At least, when he is in bed with a woman. It is true of the whole animal kingdom. It is the bull that mounts the cow and forces her to his will, you know."

132

"But I am not a cow. I am a woman, and I do not enjoy being treated like an animal."

Aaron smiled and reached across the table to grasp her hand. "I am sorry to have offended you, dear Eliza." His voice became soft and placating. "I shall try not to be a bull in the future."

She could not resist the warmth in his smile and the mocking humor in his voice as he referred to himself as a bull.

She said, "*J'accepte ta apologie, Monsieur Burr.*"

"*Ton apologie,*" he corrected her. "*Apologie* begins with a vowel, remember."

"Oh, really, Aaron," she said in exasperation, "must you always be the schoolmaster?"

"Yes," he said seriously. "In bed I will try not to be a bull, but when it comes to your education, I shall be a schoolmaster, not because I want to be superior to you, but because I wish you to learn. Why, I even correct Theo's letters to me for errors in spelling and grammar, and she does not mind."

"Well, I am not Theo!"

"No, you are not," he said quietly, and she thought that the tone in his voice implied criticism.

"I thank God that I am not Theo!" she said.

That night, after they had returned home and were in bed together, Aaron's advances did indeed seem to be more gentle and considerate than usual. But Eliza, still nettled by their conversation, did not respond to him as easily as usual.

But she did respond eventually. She could not repel him for long, and finally she gave in to him completely. She was well aware that she loved him more than any man she had ever known.

And yet, she found herself increasingly unable to tolerate his dominance of her. She retaliated in small ways, being critical of him whenever an occasion presented itself. Usually, he took her gibes good-naturedly, and she was denied the pleasure of hurting him.

There was the night when they were getting ready to attend an assembly ball. He had finished dressing long before she had put on her gown for the evening. He appeared before her in a resplendent new costume he had just bought: bottle-green trousers and an expensive brocade waistcoat of yellow and brown.

He stood there waiting for her approval. "How do you like it?" he asked.

She surveyed his figure critically. "It is very becoming to you," she said, and then added, "But, Aaron, must you wear your trousers so tight at the—at the—"

"At the crotch? But certainly. I had the tailor make them that way."

"It is indecent, and hardly becoming in a gentleman," she said. "People cannot help noticing that—that large bulge."

"But I *want* people to notice! Surely a man must apprise the ladies of the presence of his jewels—their size and beauty. A sale is not made without a display of the merchandise."

"But such display is hardly proper!"

"Well, Miss Priss," he said, "the fault lies not with me but with the generosity of my Creator."

She turned from her dressing table and faced him. There was jealousy in her voice as she said, "And why should you care so much about making what you call 'a display of the merchandise' to the ladies?" She paused. "Are you tired of me then, and looking for someone else?"

He went over to her and put his arms around her. "Dear Eliza, I was joking. I am not looking for another woman. Why should I, when you are here?"

"Then why do you care about making such a display of yourself?"

"Vanity, Eliza, pure vanity and nothing more. Every man sets great store by his organs of virility, and if they happen to be large, he is proud of them, that's all."

"But size makes no difference to a woman's pleasure."

"You are right, and yet women often have a feeling that largeness will make love-making more enjoyable. Logic has nothing to do with it. It's merely the idea, you see."

"Well," said Eliza, "it's an idea that I have never had."

"But you are an extremely logical woman."

The compliment pleased her, and she smiled. But she was annoyed that her criticism had been turned aside so lightly, and that, as usual, Aaron had won the argument.

It was not until the end of April, when Congress adjourned for the summer and Aaron returned, that Eliza resolved to assert herself in the traditional feminine way. She would deny him her body and refuse to engage in love-making.

And so, one night she turned him away, saying, "I'm sorry, Aaron. I just don't feel like it."

He drew away from her in astonishment. "What do you mean by that? In all the time I have known you, you have never denied me."

"Well, I'm denying you now. I am just not in the mood for making love."

He renewed his advances. "I'll put you in the mood, then." He began caressing her, and she knew that if she let him continue, he would break down her defenses. She grabbed his hand and thrust it away from her roughly.

"I said no, and I meant no!"

Aaron was not easily dissuaded. He seized her by the shoulders. "You cannot behave like this with me! There are women who enjoy teasing men, but you have never been one of them, and I do not intend that you should be!"

"Damn your intentions!" she said angrily.

She got herself out from under him and ran from the bed to the sofa at the other side of the room.

He went over to her, and fury was mounting in him. "Are you my mistress or aren't you?"

"Being your mistress doesn't mean that you can have your will of me whenever it pleases you!"

He drew her from the sofa until she was on her feet and faced him. As he made another attempt to force her to come to him, she slapped him on the cheek. Stunned, he looked at her, and then automatically he smote her on the jaw so hard that she fell at his feet.

The blow had been a painful one, and she lay there whimpering. Her tears had no effect on him. If anything, they intensified his rage.

135

"You goddamned slut, you! If you don't want to sleep with me, then don't! Don't come back to bed. No woman slaps Aaron Burr, and no man either! Since you have chosen to sleep on the sofa, then sleep there!"

He strode back to the bed and poured himself a generous jolt of brandy from the decanter on the night table. He drank it in one gulp and then poured himself another. Before getting back into bed, he ripped a blanket from the bedclothes and hurled it across the room to her.

When Eliza was sure that he was asleep and snoring lightly, she picked herself up from the floor and stretched out on the sofa with the blanket over her.

She could not sleep. The quarrel had upset her. She had not anticipated that Aaron would react so violently to her rejection of him, and she realized now that this way of trying to assert herself would not be successful. It was not his vanity that had been hurt, but he was a man who was used to having his own way, not only in bed with a woman, but in his political ambitions and in his career itself.

It occurred to her that he might well ask her to leave his house the next morning, and this thought worried her most of all. She wanted to stay with him, and even at the moment when she was denying him, she was aware that, in fact, she wanted him desperately. She loved him, and that was that. Now, she had no idea of how she would cope with her feelings of resentment at his domination. And she knew that they would remain.

At last she became weary of thinking and fell into a light sleep. She was awakened by the morning light slanting through the blinds. She was cold, and she felt alone and deserted lying there on the sofa. She wanted desperately to be back next to Aaron in bed.

Finally, she got up from the sofa and quietly crept into the bed beside him. He stirred in his sleep, and it was not until she put her arms around him and kissed him that he awoke. He stared at her a moment, and then, as the memory of their quarrel returned to him, he tentatively reached out a hand in her direction. She did not push him away now and responded to his gestures of affection with warmth. He became aroused and moved closer to her.

"Eliza, my darling naughty Eliza," he murmured. "I am sorry I struck you. I had not the right to do that."

"It's nothing," she whispered. "I was asking for it."

His voice serious, he said, "Do you still love me?"

Her answer was not in words. She pressed her thighs against him and guided his member toward her until he had entered her. The bout of love-making that followed was more prolonged and more intense than it had ever been before. The reunion had been made more exciting than usual, she knew, because of their quarrel.

The next day was bright and fair, one of those rare April days when spring announces itself. Aaron had risen early, and when Eliza came downstairs for breakfast, he greeted her with gaiety and courtly manners.

"Madame de la Croix, I have decided that in view of the balmy weather we shall take a vacation. I shall not go to my office, and you will have no studies. Mr. Courtenay will be shown the door upon his arrival."

Eliza was delighted, not only because she would not be tutored, but because she would be able to spend a day with Aaron.

And so they set out in his carriage.

"Are we going to Richmond Hill?" Eliza asked.

"No, my dear. I have a little surprise for you. We are going to the studio of Charles Fevret de Saint-Mémin."

"Who is he?"

"He is a young Frenchman who has achieved great popularity during the last two years in the making of miniatures."

"Miniatures? But I don't understand, Aaron."

"It is my wish that you sit for him, so that your inimitable profile will achieve immortality. He has already made one of me, and two of Theodosia. I think it is only right that your portrait should join ours."

When Aaron ushered Eliza into the artist's small studio, she was nervous, especially since she did not feel that she had dressed for the occasion.

But M. de Saint-Mémin's gracious reception quieted her fears. He was a good-looking young man, dark in complexion and with alert brown eyes that fastened on her face.

"Monsieur de Saint-Mémin," said Aaron, "this is the young lady of whom I spoke to you, Madame de la Croix."

"*Enchanté*," said Saint-Mémin, and the admiration in his eyes left no doubt that he meant the word literally.

"*Et moi aussi*," said Eliza, curtsying in acknowledgment of the introduction.

Eliza then found herself being led by the hand to a chair that faced a large easel on which there was a tinted paper. While the young man posed her in a position that pleased him, he began describing his craft in a manner that was not so much informative as boastful.

"You see, Madame de la Croix," he said, "I must first make an *image* of you in black crayon on this paper." He pointed to the easel. "It will be the size of life. And then, *plus tard*, after *votre départ*, I will engrave it on this little copper plate, very small— *une vraie miniature*. Now, *s'il vous plaît*, madame, sit very still while I work."

Saint-Mémin's black crayon moved swiftly over the paper. He looked intently at Eliza's profile until he had completed its outline to his satisfaction. Next, he worked on her hair, which lay in curls over her forehead and then swirled in a sleek coil to her shoulders from which it was lifted by a chignon pinned at the back of her head. Last of all, he sketched in the silk neckerchief that was knotted under her chin and the plain green wool coat that she was wearing.

Eliza sat very still for the first ten minutes or so, but then she began to squirm. Sensing her restlessness, Saint-Mémin suggested an intermission before they continued. Since Eliza was turned away from the picture in profile, she had not been able to look at it until now.

"But it is beautiful, monsieur. You have paid me a compliment."

"I do not think so, madame. It is easy to make a beautiful profile when one has you to pose. Your profile is *très intéressant*, not just for its beauty, but for its *caractère—ce petit nez, par exemple*."

Aaron had come forward to look at the picture and complimented Saint-Mémin. "It is indeed a good likeness," he said, "and the nose, that is Irish. Madame's mother was from Ireland."

"*Ah, ca s'explique!*" said Saint-Mémin. "*Irlandaise*, but of course."

When Saint-Mémin was satisfied with the finished portrait, Aaron paid him thirty-three dollars.

"But thirty-three dollars, Aaron! That is very expensive."

Saint-Mémin said, "It is my usual fee, madame. But for this you will receive the paper drawing and a dozen prints from the copper plate."

"And do we get the copper plate?" asked Eliza.

"Ah, no, madame. I keep the plate—to give to history."

Eliza was pleased to know that her picture would be on record as part of New York's history.

As they were taking their leave, Saint-Mémin became extremely gallant and courtly. "I am pleased to have met you, madame," he said. "My only regret is that you already have a gentleman friend. Otherwise, I would ask you to dine with me."

Aaron smiled. "I am sure that madame is complimented, monsieur, but I am her *only* gentleman friend."

Saint-Mémin nodded his head, but he could not resist still another admiring glance at Eliza before they left.

In the carriage once again, Aaron said, "Well, you have made still another conquest, madame."

"It seems so. He is an attractive young man, and I love to feel that I am admired. And now, pray tell, where are we going?"

"We are going to a lovely little woodland glade near Minetta Brook, about half a mile to the east of Richmond Hill. There, we shall have a picnic. The coachman carries a hamper of food by his side."

Aaron's woodland glade was indeed a secluded and charming spot. It was a five-minute walk from the road where the coach waited for them, and so they were alone. The sun was still shining brightly and fell in golden patches on the rippling brook. Trailing arbutus bloomed profusely in the moist earth at the edge of the water, and its fragrance filled the air.

After they had eaten, gorging themselves on sliced roast beef and buttered slices of Molly's bread, they were sleepy and took a nap. Aaron was still sleeping when Eliza awoke. The perfume of the arbutus filled the air, and she gathered long strands of it, which she wove into a garland.

She sat down near Aaron and shook him gently by the shoulder. When he opened his eyes, she dangled the wreath before him.

"Wake up, Aaron! I am going to crown you."

He smiled and raised himself to a sitting position, while she placed the wreath on his head.

"So now I am crowned," he said. "But as what? A king? An emperor? Or perhaps a fool?"

"Whatever you would like to be!"

"I think an emperor would be enough to satisfy my excessive ambition," he said.

He pulled her toward him, so that she was lying on top of him. Then he kissed her, at first lightly and then with passion.

"I feel very lustful, Eliza. It always happens to men when they awake from a nap, you know."

"And it is only that which makes you passionate?" she asked playfully.

By way of answer, he took her shoulders and rolled her over so that she was beneath him. Within moments, they were making love with such abandon that it might have been years instead of hours since they had been together.

Afterward, they lay together and talked. At one point, Aaron took her face in his hands and looked deeply into her eyes.

As his fingers lightly stroked the black-and-blue mark on her jaw, he said, "I don't know how I could have done such a thing to you. It has not been my habit to strike women, not ever. Say that you forgive me."

"I have already forgiven you, dear Aaron. I provoked you, and you lost your temper. I tried to cover the spot with powder, so that we could both forget it."

"Don't cover it. Leave it there to remind me. That will be my penance, my love."

The rays of the sun were casting long shadows in the woodland when they rose and repacked the hamper.

"Oh, Aaron, the coachman!" said Eliza. "Did he eat?"

"But of course, my dear, I have never been one to forget that my servants are also human beings with the same needs as myself."

On the way home in the carriage Aaron was strangely silent, and Eliza became uncomfortable. At last she said, "Aaron, you are so quiet. Have I done something to displease you?"

He patted her hand reassuringly. "Certainly not, my dear. I was merely being thoughtful."

"And what were you thinking about?"

"My debts, darling. They are mounting ever higher, and there is nobody to whom I can turn for a loan."

"What will you do?"

He looked at her sadly. "It may become necessary for me to give up Richmond Hill, if only to sell its furnishings."

"Oh, but you can't do that! All those beautiful things, the Turkey carpets, the mahogany furniture, and the lovely paintings—"

"Vanderlyn's paintings of Theodosia and me I shall keep, no matter what. The rest—all of it—will have to go." He paused and smiled. "Unless the good Lord in His infinite wisdom should pass a miracle."

"We can't count on that. Meanwhile, we will have to cut expenses. I will help. No more gowns, no more eating meals at the Tontine."

"And no theatre?" he said teasingly.

"Only Shakespeare," she said.

CHAPTER 14

ELIZA AND AARON ATTENDED the performance of Mrs. Hallam in
Cymbeline, but it was a melancholy occasion for both of them.
The furnishings of Richmond Hill were to be sold the next day
to Sir John Temple for a mere thirty-five hundred dollars in
order to pay a single debt, and the house would, of course, have
to be closed.

At the conclusion of the performance Eliza and Aaron had
refreshments at Ranelagh's Gardens. They ordered drinks, but
neither of them was in a mood for conversation. It was only after
a second drink that Aaron took Eliza's hand in his and said, "I
wish you would reconsider your decision about leaving me, my
dear."

"No, Aaron. My mind is made up. The three of us living in the
house on Partition Street would not be practical."

"But, Eliza, you and I shall continue to share the large bedroom, and Theo will be quite comfortable in the small bedroom
across the hall."

"Perhaps. But it wouldn't work out. Theo and I like each other
well enough, but you must remember that we are rivals for your
love, and like it or not, we would become enemies."

"But where will you live, Eliza?"

"At the Van Zandt house on Moore Street. I have already
talked with Pieter, and there would be plenty of room there. He
called at Partition Street last month and told me that his grandfather had died, so the house is now his."

"But what will you do for food?"

"Pieter works as a carpenter, and the money will be enough for us to eat on."

Aaron was silent and stared at his glass of brandy sadly. At last, he lifted his eyes to hers and said, "This is a sad thing for me, Eliza. You know that I still love you."

"You will be able to come visit me on Moore Street."

"Yes, I know, but I want to be with you, my dear. And your education—"

"Don't worry about that," she said, trying to make her voice cheerful. "I read very easily now, and Mr. Courtenay says that my spelling has improved greatly. My arithmetic is excellent; I not only add and subtract, but I can multiply and divide. And as for French, I am not only speaking it more fluently, but I can even read it a little. We finished Voltaire's *Candide* and are half-way through Molière's *School for Husbands!*"

"*École des Maris*, you mean." He corrected her with a smile and then added, "You have proved to be an excellent student, Eliza, and I am proud of you, very proud."

They left earlier than usual and went home to Partition Street. The knowledge that this would be Eliza's last night in Aaron's bedroom made both of them linger over their love-making until dawn, when they fell into an exhausted but troubled sleep.

Pieter was, of course, delighted to have Eliza with him again in the house on Moore Street. His earnings were small and barely enough to provide for the two of them, but they managed. Eliza had hoped that she could return to the theatre in the fall, but the John Street Theatre was due to be torn down to make way for the new Park Theatre, on which construction had already started.

Eliza had begun to look upon her affair with Aaron as finished, although he sometimes arrived, unannounced, for a visit with her. She had decided to resume love-making with Pieter, because there seemed no good reason why she should not. But if Aaron visited while Pieter was at home, Pieter became so fiercely jealous that he could scarcely bring himself to be polite, let alone cordial. He would sometimes leave the house and go on long walks on the banks of the Hudson River, returning only when he saw that Aaron's coach had disappeared.

When autumn came, with its prospect of a winter during which Pieter's earnings would fall to nothing, Eliza decided that she would once again have to find lovers who would pay for her favors.

She told Pieter about this late one afternoon in September while they were having tea.

"I wish to have a serious talk with you, Pieter. I have always been honest with you, and I will be now."

"What is it, madame?" asked Pieter anxiously.

"It is simply that if we are going to have enough to eat this winter, I will have to entertain gentlemen in order to earn money."

"But you could go back on the stage, madame."

"I could, if there were a stage. But they are tearing down the John Street Theatre, and the Park Theatre will not open until January next year."

"But I'll get some work. I'll make some money. I don't want you to become a—a—"

"A whore?" she asked gently. "There is no other way, Pieter, and it is so easy. I made money that way long before I met you, you know."

Pieter was silent, scowling into his teacup. "But Mr. Burr—he don't give you money?"

"He has none to give, Pieter. He is overwhelmed with debts. I go to bed with him, because—because I still love him."

"And you don't love me. I understand."

The bleak hopelessness in his voice touched her, and she reached her hand out to his. "But I do love you, Pieter—just not in the same way."

"Well, what way then? Answer me."

She was thoughtful for a moment. "The only way I can explain

144

it, Pieter, is that you are—well, like a son to me."

He was silent for a moment and then got up from the table. He did it quickly so that she would not see the tears that were beginning to come to his eyes.

She felt sorry for him, but his feelings did not deter her from making plans to find lovers who would make it possible for her to survive. She thought of Captain Curry, whom she had not seen since she arrived in New York, and then there was Charles Fevret de Saint-Mémin, who had been so obviously charmed by her when he had drawn her crayon portrait for the miniature. While the weather remained clear, she might be able to stroll on the Battery and make new gentlemen friends.

Eliza started her campaign by finding out when Captain Curry's packet would next be in port from Providence, and she was there to greet him when he disembarked.

He was delighted to see her, and that afternoon he came out to the house on Moore Street. When he left, Eliza was five dollars richer.

A meeting with Saint-Mémin was easily arranged. She merely called at his studio on the pretext of ordering another copy of the miniature. She waited in the small reception room while he finished the portrait that he was working on. When his client had left, he greeted Eliza with enthusiasm, coming forward and kissing her hand.

"Ah, Madame de la Croix! *Je suis très content* to see you again."

"I wish to have another copy of the miniature," she said.

"For you, madame, a copy will cost nothing. I know that Mr. Burr is *bouleversé* by his debts."

"I do not stay with Mr. Burr any longer, monsieur."

Saint-Mémin raised his eyebrows in surprise. "Ah, that is too bad for you." He paused, looking at her face and then at her bosom. "Bad for you, but good for me. Now, *peut-être* you may dine with me?"

She smiled at him. "You do not lose any time, monsieur, do you?" She paused. "Yes, I would be *enchantée* to dine with you."

And so, that evening they dined together at the Bull's Head

145

Tavern on Bowery Lane. She had chosen this out-of-the-way place because there was little likelihood of Aaron's being there.

Saint-Mémin was surprised by her choice. "But, madame, this is not a *taverne à la mode* for a lady like you. The *clientèle* is very rough, men who sell cows and bulls. There is not one other *dame* in the room."

"I know," she said, and then added with a coquettish look, "but it is very near to where I live on Moore Street."

His eyes lighted up. "It is *très difficile* for me to wait until we are *fini* with dinner and I take you to your house, madame."

"But food—it is a *nécessité pour l'amour, n'est-ce pas*? And I think you must call me Eliza and not madame."

He nodded his head so enthusiastically that he choked on his wine.

"Fevret, please don't use *vous* when you address me in French. *Tutoyez-moi, s'il te plaît.* We are friends now."

Again he nodded his head vigorously, and again he choked on his wine.

Charles Fevret de Saint-Mémin proved to be as adept at love-making as he was at drawing portraits. With his lean young body and his boyish face, he was attractive to Eliza, and she responded to him with unfeigned warmth.

While he was dressing and getting ready to leave, Eliza was wondering how she should broach the subject of money.

"Did you enjoy yourself, Fevret?" she asked casually.

He came quickly over to where she lay on the bed. "Madame, you know there is no *nécessité* to ask that question. In bed you are *merveilleuse! Superbe!*" He kissed her tenderly on the mouth and then on the nipples of her breasts before he continued dressing.

"*Mon cher Fevret,*" she said softly, "I must ask of you a favor."

"And what is that?"

She forced tears to come to her eyes and began to cry softly. Wiping her eyes with a lace handkerchief, she said, "Since leaving Mr. Burr I have had no way of supporting myself. The theatre is closed, and there is no work for me unless I become a *prostituée. Après tout,* I must have food."

146

He had finished dressing now and went over to her again. He put his arms around her consolingly. *"Toi, une prostituée?* That must not happen—*jamais!"*

He reached into his pocket and brought forth five dollars, which he placed in her hand. *"Voilà,"* he said. "Now you can eat. But your rent?"

"That is taken care of. The young man who owns this house does not charge me."

"Je vois," said Fevret. "But he does not work?"

"Yes. He is very young and gets work helping a carpenter, but during the winter—" Her voice trailed off, and there were more tears.

"Do not cry, Eliza. Is it *permis* that I make you a *visite* one time every week?"

She rose from the bed, still nude, and threw her arms about him. *"Mais bien entendu, mon cher,"* she murmured.

He kissed her and then bowed before he said goodbye.

"Au 'voir," he said. "And I will see you on the Thursday that is coming next week?" She bowed her head and smiled.

After he had left, Eliza sat on the bed. She counted the five dollars he had given her. She congratulated herself on having made a conquest that assured her a regular income.

She heard Pieter's footsteps on the stairs, and he came into the room without knocking. He stared at her, his disapproval obvious in the coldness of his eyes.

"Well, madame," he said, "I see that you have had a gentleman friend to call."

She nodded and then handed him the five dollars.

"He was very generous, Pieter. He is a good young man, an artist. He made a miniature of me."

She picked up the miniature that Saint-Mémin had left and handed it to Pieter.

Pieter stared at it in silence for a moment. Then he looked up at her with a half smile. "It looks like you. He is a man of talent, not like me—a nobody, good for nothing, with no brains."

Eliza knew that there was only one way in which she could reassure him. She pulled him into the bed beside her. While he

147

allowed her to unbutton his trousers, he murmured, "Well, at least, he is not that goddamned Aaron Burr."

Eliza saw less and less of Aaron during the autumn. Every so often he would arrive unannounced, sometimes in the afternoon, sometimes late at night. She did not expect him to give her money because his debts now were greater than ever. His term as senator had expired, and he now contemplated running once again for the Assembly. Meanwhile, he was activating the Tammany Society as a political instrument, because it contained many of his devoted followers. These activities took up most of his time, as well as whatever cash he could manage to raise by his law practice. But he still, to Pieter's dismay, came to see Eliza, and she always welcomed him.

But there was one night in late November when he was not welcome. He arrived just as Saint-Mémin was preparing to leave. She heard the coach drive up, and she knew who it was.

Hastily pulling on a dressing gown, she stood up. "Fevret, you must hurry. It is Mr. Burr who is arriving!"

Saint-Mémin's face went white. "*Ah, mon Dieu*, he will kill me! I must hide."

"That would do no good. He has already seen your coach outside. I do not think he will kill you. Just leave quickly by the back door."

Saint-Mémin fled from the room, and Eliza sat down on the bed and waited.

At last she heard Aaron's step on the stairs, and then he burst stormily into the room. He stared at her in anger.

"I see that you have had a gentleman caller," he said.

"Yes."

"Then I am no longer satisfactory as a lover?"

"You have always been more than satisfactory, and as you know, I love only you."

"Only me, indeed! But this does not prevent you from going to bed with other men!"

She stood up and faced him. "I go to bed with other men so that I may get enough money to survive without taking to the

148

streets as a whore. I do not expect money from you, because you have none. The John Street Theatre is closed, so I cannot get work on the stage. What would you suggest that I do in order to eat?"

He could not meet her gaze, and he hung his head guiltily. When he spoke, his voice was hoarse with jealousy.

"Who was it?" he demanded.

"I shall not tell you, Aaron."

"That means that it is someone I know. Was it Alexander Hamilton?"

"I told you that I would not tell you, and I meant it."

He moved to her quickly and seized her by the shoulders. "By God, you *will* tell me, or—"

"Or what? You will beat me? Go ahead. You have struck me before, and I survived!"

He hit her on the jaw, and the blow made her stagger back.

With rising anger, she said, "You may leave now, Aaron. Our affair is at an end."

He slumped into a chair and rested his forehead on his hand. He was silent for a moment. When he looked up, he said, "Forgive me, Eliza. I should not have struck you—I—" Overcome by a rush of feelings, he could not finish what he wanted to say.

She went over to him and stroked him on the head. "I was speaking the truth, Aaron, and you know it. There is no future for us unless—" She paused.

"Unless what?"

"Unless you marry me."

"But, Eliza, I cannot do that. You must know that is impossible."

"Why?"

He looked at her directly, his dark eyes fixed on hers. "I have always been honest with you. I shall be so now. I do not say this as an accusation, but you must know that your reputation in New York is not—not good!"

"My reputation did not interfere with your career while you were a senator."

"No. But you were not my wife. You were my mistress." He

149

paused. "I am an ambitious man, Eliza. I would like to be President of these United States."

"And the President could not marry a woman of bad reputation. I would interfere with your career."

"Yes. It is unfortunately true."

"Society would not accept me. Is that what you mean?"

"Eliza, my dear, if you break the rules of society, you can't very well expect society to accept you."

Eliza's resentment was growing in intensity. "But society refused to accept me long before I broke any rules! I was born the daughter of a whore!"

He smiled ironically. "But that's one of the rules—one must choose one's parents more wisely."

She could not help laughing. "Oh, Aaron, you are altogether impossible!"

He became serious. "But, Eliza, what will become of you? You cannot just go along giving yourself to men for money. The day will come when you will no longer be so beautiful, and you will need someone—"

"Perhaps. But long before that has happened, I will find a man who will marry me, and he will be a very rich man."

Aaron looked thoughtful. "It is a lovely dream, Eliza, but it is only a dream."

"But you dream of becoming President, is it not *le vérité*?"

He smiled as he corrected her. "It is *la vérité*. The noun is feminine, remember."

"I shall miss not having you near to correct me, Aaron. My education is still important to me. Aside from our love, it is a debt that I shall never be able to repay."

"Next to Theodosia, you are the student I take most pride in." He broke off suddenly and went over to her, taking her in his arms. "Eliza, dear Eliza, I shall always love you best."

"Next to Theodosia," she said, gently pushing him away from her.

But he took her in his arms again, and in growing passion, he said, "Just once more—can we not make love?"

She stepped away from him. "No. It would be only a sad love-making. I could not bear it. Please go now, Aaron."

The tone of her voice told him that she meant what she said, and he recognized with sadness that she was right. He turned to leave.

"Then we shall never see each other again," he said at the door.

"Never is a long time, dear Aaron. Perhaps some day when I am very rich—"

He looked at her in admiration. "You know, it is just possible that you will be as much of a success as I myself plan to be. Remember that I shall always love you."

At the door, just before he turned to go downstairs, he said, "Good luck to you, my dear Eliza."

She could not answer, because her voice strangled on her tears. She lay down on the bed and cried. This time the tears were real.

She remembered her violent parting with Matt Wyatt. The end of this affair was different. She was not angry. She could not find it in her heart to hate Aaron, and she knew that she would in some inexplicable way always love him. She had foreseen the inevitable end of their affair on that day when he had taken her to Richmond Hill to meet Theodosia. She knew now that she would occupy only third place in his heart, after Theodosia and his career.

She washed the tears from her face and combed the tangles from her hair. She forced herself to smile at herself in the mirror. But there was no humor in the smile. It was set in hard lines, her lips drawn back in determination, so that the tips of her upper teeth showed, as though she might be a dog growling at an enemy.

And there was an enemy—all those fine gentlemen of New York and their proper, smug wives. The only way to conquer them was to become rich, with the power that riches bring.

For her, there would be no more affairs in which her heart would be vulnerable. She would settle for nothing less than a rich man, a man for whom she would always come first, not third. Her heart no longer mattered.

It was not until the spring of 1800, more than two years later, that she met the man she wanted. His name was Stephen Jumel.

PART III

Stephen Jumel

CHAPTER 15

STEPHEN JUMEL HAD ARRIVED in New York City in 1795, not by choice but by chance, and, like so many men before him, as a refugee. He came from the island of Santo Domingo in the West Indies.

The island had been prosperous with its trade in coffee, sugar and indigo, and its population had been relatively large: 600,000 people, of whom 500,000 were Congo slaves, 60,000 free mulattoes and the rest French Creoles. There were only a few hundred white Frenchmen, and they owned the plantations that dotted the island. The rest of the island was jungle.

Although Stephen had been born and educated in France, he went to Santo Domingo to rejoin his family when he was twenty years old—a tall, well-muscled young man, handsome and olive complexioned.

When his mother and father died of yellow fever in 1786, Stephen took charge of the plantation and ran it successfully with his older brother, Pierre.

And then, in 1790, came the news of the French Revolution, with its message of *Liberté*, *Égalité* and *Fraternité*. It was a message that ran like wildfire fron one end of the island to the other. The unrest caused burnings of buildings and the murder of some of the white Frenchmen who owned the plantations.

In August 1791 the half million slaves began a full-scale revolt under the leadership of Toussaint L'Ouverture. The previously peaceful island became a seething cauldron of murder and torture, a blood orgy that surpassed in violence the Reign of Terror itself.

Every building on the island was put to the torch. By the time the chanting, crazed mobs reached the Jumel plantation house, the family had already fled into the jungle in the hope of escaping to the coast. Stephen and his brother, with the latter's wife and children, moved slowly through the tangle of jungle. Their machetes cleared a path for them, and their only food was bananas and other edible tropical fruits.

Roving bands of black revolutionaries roamed through the jungle, killing anyone who was even part white, and so it was necessary for the Jumels to travel surreptitiously by night. Stephen's compass was their only guide in reaching the sea.

One morning Stephen left the group to forage for food. When he had gone perhaps half a mile, he heard screams and shouts behind him. He stopped in fear, but he did not dare return to his family until nightfall. He found all of them, even the children, mercilessly and viciously slaughtered. His brother had been tortured with fire and stabbed to death. His severed genitals, all bloody, had been stuffed into his mouth. His sister-in-law had been killed by a knife plunged into her heart and entrails. A deep cut ran the length of her body. Two of the children had been beheaded, and the baby, scarcely a year old, had been skewered on a bayonet and burned alive over a fire that still smoldered.

Stephen looked at this scene with a revulsion that made him vomit, but he forced himself to quiet his retching for fear the sound might make his own whereabouts known to whatever slaves might still be hiding nearby. He had no time for tears. They would come later, but now, like a hunted animal, his only concern was his own survival.

Later, he often wondered how he had managed to stay alive at all. Parts of his journey he did not remember, because there were times when he had been delirious with fever. By the time he saw the sea shimmering in the distance, he had lost a third of his body weight and was clothed only in a tattered pair of breeches and a threadbare shirt that had once been white.

He waited for days in the jungle near the shore. He tied the

156

remains of his white shirt to a long, sturdy pole that he had cut with his knife. He killed a snake that he found sleeping in a patch of sunlight and ate its flesh raw from trembling hands.

One morning he saw the sails of a ship on the horizon and fled to the beach, where he waved his shirt frantically. The ship did not see him, but another, several days later, did. A boat rowed to shore to pick him up.

The ship was British, bound for the island of St. Helena. By the time it reached its port, Stephen had recovered. But he did not want to go to England. He wanted to return to France, but the next ship that sailed was bound for the port of New York.

When Stephen arrived in the strange American city, he was dressed in sailor's rough garb, and he was penniless. He thanked God now for the lessons in English he had received in school in France. Eventually, he found his way to the Tontine Coffee House, and there he met some of the American customers to whom he had once shipped sugar cane and cotton from his plantation.

From that point on, his rise in the world of merchants was meteoric. He went to work in the wine shop of John Juhel, an importer of wines, brandies, cordials and gins. With his genial personality and his expert knowledge of wines and spirits, he made many friends among the customers, one of whom was President Washington himself. Within a year he had opened his own shop on Stone Street, and as his business prospered he moved to a larger shop on Liberty Street. His merchandise was shipped from abroad not only in bottles but in kegs, puncheons and pipes.

The city's foremost families flocked to him for their alcoholic supplies, and among his customers were the Livingstons, the Clintons, the Schuylers and the Jays. And he made friends with those connoisseurs of wines and spirits, people like General Alexander Hamilton of The Grange, Colonel Aaron Burr, and John Jacob Ashdor, a fur merchant who later spelled his name Astor.

As Stephen's fortunes prospered, he bought a brig of his own, named the *Stephen*, and became the owner of a two-story house on the corner of Whitehall and Pearl Streets, in the most fashionable residential district in the city.

He gave lavish dinner parties to which the city's best families came. They were charmed by this educated and well-mannered Frenchman, and the Federalists were pleased by his political leanings. French though he might be, he had little sympathy with the French Revolution. He had suffered too much because of it. But in those days of strife between the Federalists and the Republicans he tried to remain neutral.

Stephen Jumel in 1800, when he became forty years old, was undoubtedly the most eligible bachelor in the city of New York. In appearance, he was highly attractive to the ladies. He was tall and broad-chested, and was called by someone "a graceful giant." In spite of his size, he danced very well. His sympathies were as broad as his chest, and he was called "Uncle" by neighborhood children.

A trifle boisterous by nature, he was a clever practical joker in his elephantine way, and his laughter boomed out loudly from somewhere in the depths of him. And he often laughed.

And yet, there was a serious side of him, sensitive and proud. He was as popular with the ladies as he was with the men who dealt with him in business. A man of quick passion and lust, he made many conquests, but although many young ladies set their caps for him in hopes of marriage, he remained a carefree bachelor, living alone in simple elegance. When he set out to win a woman who attracted him, he was usually successful. He was used to getting what he wanted.

And then, in the spring of 1800, he met Madame de la Croix. He had first seen her at the theatre in the company of William Dunlap, and then on the stage, when she sang her bawdy sea chantey. He was aware, too, that she had become the mistress of Aaron Burr, and during that time he had not seen her.

On a day in April 1800, Stephen decided to take the day off and go to the horse races that were held when the weather was fine on the Old Bowery Road. Wagers were made at the west end of the road, and the prize for the winning horse was one-tenth of the total receipts. People stood in line for their tickets, on which were written the amount of their wager and the number of the horse on which their bet was made.

There were only four horses in the race, because even the widened Bowery Road could not accommodate more. Stephen, along with the other bettors, examined the horses. There were a handsome black Arabian gelding, a dappled gray stallion of probable English breed, a sleek brown Percheron gelding, and a black stallion, obviously of American origin.

Stephen placed ten dollars on the brown Percheron. As he turned to walk toward the finish line a mile to the east, he saw Eliza waiting in the line of bettors.

She wore a dazzling white silk dress with a red velvet bodice. Her shining crown of red-gold hair needed no ornamentation.

Looking at her, so radiant there in the spring sunlight, Stephen drew in his breath sharply. No woman had ever seemed lovelier to him, and as he moved toward the crowd of people walking to the finish line, he moved slowly, to give her time to catch up with him.

Stephen himself was handsomely garbed in a plum-colored costume that fit his huge frame snugly. He wore a green cocked hat trimmed with silver buttons, and as Eliza drew near, he doffed his hat and bowed.

Eliza stepped back and stared at him in surprise.

"Sir?" she said in a questioning tone.

Stephen's voice was as soft as a cat's purr. "You are Madame de la Croix, are you not?"

"Yes, but—who are you?"

"I am Stephen Jumel. I am a Frenchman by birth. I have wanted to meet you for a very long time. Please forgive me for being so forward."

"*Vous êtes français, vraiment?*"

"Ah, madame speaks French—and with such a pretty accent."

"I would hope that it was a good accent, not a pretty one."

He smiled a wide, genial smile. "It is that I was perhaps thinking of your face, madame."

She was walking by his side now, taking her smallest and most ladylike steps, and he slowed his pace accordingly.

"On what horse did you bet, madame?"

"On the black Arabian gelding. I know that he is fast."

"And how do you know that?"

Eliza paused. "He once belonged to a friend of mine."

"Would that be Colonel Aaron Burr?"

"Yes." Her eyes narrowed in suspicion. "How do you know that, monsieur?"

"I often saw you in his company at the theatre."

They had reached a very large puddle, left by yesterday's heavy April rain, and she had stopped, not wanting to get her new calamanco shoes wet. Suddenly, she felt Jumel's strong arms picking her up, and he carried her across.

She gave him a fetching smile. "*Merci bien, monsieur.*"

"It is said that the Englishman Sir Walter Raleigh threw his cloak into a puddle so that Queen Elizabeth could pass." He shrugged his shoulders. "But I had no cloak."

"And I am no queen."

He looked at her with warmth and admiration in his eyes. "If there were queens in America, you would be one."

"You are a man who makes many compliments, Monsieur Jumel."

"I do not make them often," he said. His eyes sought hers, but she was looking straight ahead at the end of the race course.

They reached the finish line just in time to hear the pistol shot that signaled the start of the race. Everyone's eyes were now turned to the track—everyone's eyes except those of Stephen Jumel. He was watching Eliza's face, noting the delicate color that had mounted in excitement to her soft cheeks.

Eliza's black gelding was the winner, and she jumped up and down with joy.

"Oh, I have won, I have won!"

"You have won more than the horse race, madame," said Stephen.

She looked at him in puzzlement. "I don't understand."

He bowed and kissed her hand. "You have won my heart," he said simply and with absolute sincerity.

That afternoon Eliza took special care in preparing herself to go to dinner with Stephen Jumel at the Belvedere Club. She washed and curled her hair with tongs. She dressed herself in her latest and most fashionable gown: a skirt of patterned green-and-white brocade with a bright golden bodice that laced tightly over her firm, prominent breasts. Her headdress was an elaborate affair of imported Belgian lace, pinned to her hair with shining stars of sterling silver. Around her neck she suspended the pendant of cut jade that Jacques had given her so many years ago. It was still her favorite bit of jewelry.

When she had finished dressing, she went downstairs for Pieter's inspection. As she twirled before him, his mouth dropped open in admiration.

"Madame, you have never been more beautiful!"

"Good! I am dining with a very rich wine merchant named Stephen Jumel, and I aim to hook him."

"You'll do that for sure, madame. No man could resist you."

She placed some money in Pieter's hand. "I won at the races today. Go find me a hackney, Pieter. I will arrive in high style, like a fine lady."

When Eliza reached the Belvedere Club, she found that Stephen Jumel was waiting for her at the entrance. He moved toward her quickly, and in spite of his large bulk, he bent gracefully to kiss her hand, and she curtsied.

Stephen had reserved a table for two near the large window that looked out from Cherry Street onto the East River. After they had seated themselves, Stephen gazed at her with such rapture that he was unaware of the waiter at his side, waiting for him to order.

Eliza nodded her head in the waiter's direction. "*Monsieur, le garçon vous attend.*"

Stephen gave a start. "Ah, yes," he murmured. "*Après tout*, we have come here to dine."

He ordered an elaborate dinner, careful to include only imported wines of the best vintages. The food was delicious, and Eliza ate as ravenously as good manners would allow.

In the lull between the fish course and the roast beef, he looked at her musingly. "But tell me, my dear Madame de la Croix, how did you happen to come to New York?"

161

She told him the well-rehearsed and fictitious story of her early life in Providence, her equally fictitious marriage to Jacques de la Croix, and his death from yellow fever. She said that Jacques had left her a small fortune, and on this she had managed to live.

"And Aaron Burr?"

"He is a very dear friend."

Stephen cocked an inquisitive eye toward her. "He was only a friend?"

She stared at her roast beef for a moment, and then lifting her eyes to meet his, she said, "I was in love with Colonel Burr. I was his mistress."

Stephen could not keep jealousy from his voice as he said, "And now?"

"I do not see him. It is over between us. When I realized that I could never have first place in his heart, I broke off with him."

"And who holds first place in his heart?"

"His daughter, Theodosia—and next to her, his political career."

"I have met Theodosia Burr," said Stephen. "I went one night out to Richmond Hill for dinner, and she played hostess. She is a most brilliant young girl."

"Yes," said Eliza. "She is indeed, as you say, brilliant, and adored by her father. No woman could compete with her in Colonel Burr's affections."

"And you—you do not wish to be second in a man's heart?"

"I shall be first or nothing. I shall always admire Mr. Burr, and I sympathize with his political beliefs. But as for love, it is out of the question."

Stephen leaned across the table toward her. "You would always be first in *my* heart, dear madame." He spoke in a low and intense tone, and there could be no doubt of his sincerity.

Eliza said nothing. She was outwardly calm, but inside, her thoughts raced. She knew that the man sitting opposite her was the man for whom she had searched. He was handsome and attractive; he was educated and genteel in manner. But above all, he was rich. She planned to become not only his mistress but his wife. Calculatedly, like an army general devising his attack before a battle, she would embark on her own strategy. She would make use of every weapon in her arsenal, and she would win. The thought of failure did not even occur to her. She would play the "love game" that she had used with Sam Allen. It had been successful then, and it would be successful now.

She resolved not to be an easy conquest for this man who was used to winning the favors of women with ease. She would keep him dangling. She would promise much but give little.

When they had finished dinner and were preparing to leave, Stephen suggested that she come to his house on Whitehall Street for brandy, or perhaps a cordial.

"I am sorry, Stephen. I am a bit *fatiguée* and would like to go home. Could you call me a hackney?"

He got into the cab with her, and gave the coachman her address on Moore Street. He attempted to kiss her, but she politely repulsed him.

"I cannot kiss you, Monsieur Jumel. I hardly know you. I cannot kiss a man unless I love him."

"And you do not love me, *n'est-ce pas?*"

She looked at him in feigned astonishment. "But I have only just met you, monsieur."

There was a pleading look in his eyes as he said, "But tell me that you do not find me repulsive."

She smiled at him warmly and patted his hand. "Oh, most certainly not. You are a very attractive gentleman, *très charmant.*"

She moved to get out of the cab, and he hastily went around to the other side to help her alight. She extended her hand to him, and he kissed it.

"And you will have dinner with me again tomorrow night?"

She looked thoughtful for a moment and then said, "No, but perhaps the night after that."

He smiled. "*Bien!* Then on Thursday night I will come and call for you."

He escorted her to the door of the house, but before she left him, he bowed once again and kissed her hand. "It will be *difficile* for me to wait until Thursday, but I will do it, *ma bien-aimée.*"

"*Merci, monsieur,*" she murmured and then turned quickly and entered the house. From behind the curtain of the front window, she watched him as he returned to the coach. He walked with a jaunty step, and he was whistling happily.

After Jumel had left, Pieter came into the room. He had been anxiously awaiting her return.

"Ah, madame," he said. "Did you have a good time with your new gentleman friend?"

"Oh, yes indeed, Pieter. He is a wonderful man."

"But—but you did not go to bed with him?"

"No, and I do not plan to, at least not for a good while. I shall wait and keep him on the end of the hook."

Pieter looked at her musingly. "Forgive me, madame, but you are what the boys in town call a cock-chafer."

Eliza laughed and said, "You mean a cock-teaser? Yes, that is what I'll be—but not with you, dear Pieter. Come to bed."

Overjoyed at the prospect of a night with her, he hastened up the stairs in her wake. He was undressed and standing nude in front of her before she had hardly had time to take off her hoopskirt.

Eliza played her game of love carefully and deliberately. Although Stephen would have liked to take her out to dinner every night in the week, she limited their dining together to Tuesdays, Thursdays and Saturdays. At the end of the second week, she permitted him to call her Eliza instead of Madame de la Croix, and he was delighted when she agreed to call him Stephen. He offered to take her on a shopping tour of Pearl Street, but she declined with thanks. They usually went to the theatre once a week, especially if a play by Shakespeare was to be produced. Stephen did not enjoy Shakespeare much because the archaic Elizabethan language made the plays difficult for him to understand, and he sometimes found it hard to stay awake during the performance.

At the end of an evening together, Stephen never failed to invite her to his home on Whitehall Street, but she always politely refused. She continued to make every effort to captivate him, to be as alluring as possible, both physically and mentally. She laughed at his little jokes, even though they sometimes did not amuse her. She flattered him in small ways, but never so that he would suspect it. She knew that he had a keen mind, sensitively aware of what people said, and, more important, of what they did.

Eliza was quite pleased with the success of her campaign to ensnare him. Men had loved her before, but none had adored her, and Stephen plainly adored her. She had calculated that she would make him love her, but she had not expected pure worship, and she did not entirely understand it. But she had decided long ago that love itself was a mystery. One could devise reasons for why one loved, but love itself remained inexplicable. Lust and the passion of the moment were not difficult to understand, but the feeling that persisted after lust had been sated—that was the heart of the matter. She knew that she did not love Stephen Jumel and perhaps never would, not in the same way she had loved Matt and then Aaron. It was enough for her that she found his company pleasant and that he was attractive to her physically. Mostly, it was enough for her that he was rich.

As the weeks went by, Stephen seemed uneasy and troubled when he was with her. It did not please her to know that he was suffering, but she did not swerve from her plan to ensnare him.

There was one subject that always troubled him: the specter of Aaron Burr seemed to inhabit all his jealous fantasies. And yet it was difficult to leave Burr and his doings out of their conversation. In the balloting in May, the Republicans under Burr's leadership had scored an overwhelming victory in the state of New York, and this made him a probable candidate for President.

One night Stephen said, "I think, dear Eliza, that you still love this man."

"Nonsense!" she replied sharply. "I admire Colonel Burr politically, and I like Mr. Jefferson's Republican party and what it stands for. That has nothing to do with the love I once had for Burr."

"But why do you admire him so?"

"Because he has worked so hard to achieve his ambition. Do you know that he organized the Tammany Society and visited every ward in this city to gain support for himself and his party?

165

And he succeeded, in spite of all the lies that Hamilton and the Federalists told about him!"

"And is success your only god, Eliza?"

"In politics, yes."

"And what about the principles of democracy in these United States?"

"Burr is more true to them than Alexander Hamilton, who is such a royalist that even President Adams finally broke with him. Mr. Jefferson is the champion of the common man."

"I know. Liberty, equality and fraternity." He smiled a bitter smile. "I have seen what they accomplished for my beloved France." His voice rose in anger. "In their name I have seen my whole family tortured and murdered, our home and land taken away from us—" His voice broke, and tears came to his eyes and trickled down his cheeks. He took out his kerchief, blew his nose and wiped his eyes.

Eliza was touched. To see this strong, proud man in tears was more than she could watch in silence. She reached her hand across the table and grasped his. "Stephen, I am sorry. I did not realize—"

He regained control of his feelings and said, "Of course, you didn't. I have never told you the horrible story of my escape from Santo Domingo, and I do not intend to. It is best forgotten, like all sad things. It is enough to say that I escaped to New York with only the clothing on my back."

For the first time Eliza felt admiration for him. "You had great courage, Stephen. It is a quality I admire in men, and in women, too." She was thinking of herself, of course. She, too, had faced adversity and overcome it. "It is in Hamlet's soliloquy, Stephen, that he asks himself 'whether 'tis nobler in the mind to suffer the slings and arrows of outrageous fortune, or to take arms against a sea of troubles, and by opposing end them.' " She paused. "I do not believe that suffering is ever noble."

Stephen looked at her in astonishment as she quoted Hamlet. "You amaze me, dear Eliza, with your learning and your quick mind. I have never understood those words of Hamlet until now." He smiled. "You will end by making me a lover of Shakespeare too."

166

"I plan to," she said.

"I think you have many plans for me, but none of them seem to include making me your lover. *C'est dommage, ça.*"

"But I think I am beginning to love you a little, Stephen."

He sighed. "But not enough to come and live with me in my house on Whitehall Street?"

These were the words that she had been waiting to hear—not an invitation to go home with him for the evening, but a proposal to live with him as his mistress. Even so, she demurred, holding her impatience in check.

"Sometime soon, Stephen. But I must think about it."

She didn't need to think about it, of course, and she kept him at bay for another two weeks. It was not until the latter part of May that she finally agreed to live with him, but only on a trial basis.

When she told Pieter of her decision, he was desolate at the thought of her leaving.

"Don't feel bad, Pieter, because I am taking you with me as my private footman. That will be one of the conditions of my going to Whitehall Street."

Pieter grinned in delight. "A footman! Does that mean that I will have a uniform?"

"The most beautiful that money can buy—gold braid and gold buttons!"

Pieter frowned. "But what of *this* house? Who will take care of it?"

"You can rent it, and then you will have a small income all your own, in addition to the wages that Monsieur Jumel will pay you."

"You think of everything, madame." He paused suddenly. "But you and me—I guess we'll not be going to bed together anymore."

She gave him a mischievous smile. "Monsieur Jumel often goes out of town and sometimes even to France on business. But we shall have to be very careful. He has other servants, you know."

There were three other servants, and Eliza met them as soon as she moved in. There was Henri Nodine, the butler, and his wife, Marie, the parlormaid. And then there was François, the fat and

167

accomplished chef whom Stephen had brought to America from France.

Eliza made an effort to be friendly with all of them, even though she took a dislike to Nodine on sight. She distrusted his steel-blue eyes, which looked out at the world critically and coldly. But with all of them she played the role of mistress of the house, friendly and yet formal. She supervised the ordering of food and the planning of menus. She expected and received an itemized accounting of all money that was spent.

The large kitchen occupied most of the ground floor, except for two rooms at the rear and one at the side, where the servants slept. One of these was given to Pieter, who was pleased to have a room all his own.

Although Pieter was to be a footman, his duties in full regalia were limited to those occasions when Stephen entertained at dinner. The rest of his time was spent in assisting Nodine and François with household chores, or in shopping. The only time he was permitted above stairs was to serve tea every afternoon in the drawing room. Nodine was annoyed to find that he would no longer serve tea and complained to Stephen, who promised to speak to Eliza about it.

And so one afternoon Stephen brought up the matter with Eliza. "But, Eliza, Nodine has always served tea, and I see no reason why he should not continue to do so. Besides, Pieter is awkward in his manners and does not know how to pour tea gracefully."

"Then Nodine can teach him," said Eliza decisively.

"But, Eliza, why do you insist on this?"

"First, because I do not much like your Nodine, and second, because Pieter is my good friend."

Stephen looked at her intently. "How is he a good friend? Perhaps he is *too* good a friend."

Eliza rose angrily. "I will not listen to your vile insinuations, Stephen! He provided me with shelter in his grandfather's house when I had no other place to go. I feel a debt to him for standing by me when I had no one after the death of my husband." She paused and then added in a gentler tone, "I have come to look upon him as—well, as almost my son." Tears came obligingly to her eyes.

Stephen took her hand. "I am sorry, *ma chère*. I understand. It will be as you say, but do not favor him too much. The other servants will become *jaloux*, and we must keep *harmonie* among them. As for Pieter, he is a true addition to the *ménage*. He works hard, helping both Nodine and François with their tasks. I have remarked upon this. Nodine will instruct him in genteel behavior in the drawing room."

Eliza, having won her point, gave Stephen an endearing smile and kissed him on the cheek. He responded by taking her in his arms. She knew that he wanted to take her upstairs and make love, but she gently pushed him away.

"Tonight," she whispered.

She had continued to use procrastination in her love-making with Stephen, even after that first night when she had finally gone to bed with him. It had been a memorable night for Stephen when he had at last held her naked body against his. As a lover, he had been extremely gentle. Perhaps because his large stature made her seem diminutive in comparison, he treated her as though she were a fragile china doll that might break during the gymnastics of love-making.

He was a passionate man and an accomplished lover. Eliza had no difficulty in responding to him, but she schooled herself to hold back, so as never to give him the feeling that he had made a complete conquest of her. She did not try to play the role of a virgin or even of a frigid woman, because she knew that this would be unbelievable to him.

Even in passion she felt somehow removed from him and looked at him critically, even though there was nothing for her to criticize. His strong body was lithe and beautiful, with little excess weight on it, and he had unusual control in postponing his climax until her own passion had peaked.

She was, as Pieter had called her, a "cock-chafer." But she did not tease without a purpose. She seized upon those expansive moments after love-making to mention casually some article of clothing or furniture that she wanted, and Stephen, like Sam Allen before him, always responded with a gift. Often, gifts would arrive unexpectedly without her even having asked for them.

But the matter of having her own coach and horses was something special. It was an event. Stephen himself took her to the carriage maker, Abraham Quick of Broad Street, and she chose a coach of shiny black enamel with a brilliant trim of gold plate. The team of horses were black Arabians, and the motif of gold was repeated on their harnesses. Her driver was, of course, Pieter, decked out in a new scarlet uniform with an elaborate tricornered hat to match.

One of her afternoon diversions, when the weather was fine, was to ride through the streets of the city, like a queen examining her domain. She made a point of driving past the houses that belonged to the city's richest and most outstanding citizens. It disturbed her that the ladies of these houses turned disdainfully away from their windows whenever she rode past. The men did not turn their eyes away. They smiled at her and doffed their hats, and that, to Eliza's way of thinking, was as it should be.

And yet, it upset her greatly that when Stephen gave their first dinner party, the men came but the women did not. There were excuses, of course: their wives were indisposed or ill, were out of town at the moment, or were staying with a sick relative.

It should have disturbed Stephen even more, because many of those he had numbered among his friends had summarily dropped him. Of those, not even the men accepted his invitation to dinner. The only ones he could count on were business associates, mostly Frenchmen, who came because they didn't dare not to.

He had foreseen that this would happen and had expected it from the moment Eliza became mistress of his household. He had moved in New York society long enough to know the rules that governed it. A woman of doubtful virtue was shunned as though she were a leper. Even in this sophisticated and unpuritanical society of New York, the old rules still obtained.

But after the guests of that first dinner party had left, Eliza was in tears—tears of disappointment and of rage.

"The bitches! The filthy bitches!" she stormed. "Who do they think they are? Too good for me, eh? Well, I'm not through!

170

Some day they will come begging to be invited to my house."

Stephen took her in his arms and tried to console her. He avoided mentioning the real reason why the ladies had not come. He said, "*Ma chère*, you must remember that you have been an actress, and members of the theatre are looked down upon as though they were all immoral gypsies."

She lifted her head and looked at him. "No, it is more than that, and you know it. I am your mistress, not your wife. Oh, Stephen, if you would only marry me."

Stephen's voice became suddenly cold. "No," he said with finality. "I do not wish to marry—not you, not any woman. I am a bachelor, and a bachelor I will be. You must accept that, because I will not change my mind."

"But if you loved me as much as you say you do—"

"I love you. You must know that. But marriage is out of the question."

On this subject Stephen was, she discovered, adamant. She could not understand why, but she did understand that it was useless to try to change his mind.

Just the same, that night Stephen slept alone, and Eliza cried herself to sleep in the privacy of her own small bedroom.

CHAPTER 16

As SUMMER APPROACHED, Stephen debated whether they should move northward to avoid the yearly plague of yellow fever. In the end, he decided to stay in the house on Whitehall Street. For some mysterious reason nobody in the houses on the fashionable southern tip of the island had ever contracted the disease. Stephen believed that the breeze that blew in from the harbor cooled the land so that whatever caused the illness was destroyed or blown away.

But Eliza was bored and restless. She had grown weary of her daily rides in her carriage, particularly since most of the people she wanted to impress had moved out of town for the summer. The theatre was closed, and there was little social activity. She still read books, but the heat of the summer was oppressive and she found it difficult to concentrate.

She often quarreled with Stephen, and the subject was always the same: she wanted marriage, and he did not.

"How will I ever be accepted by the people of this city?" she would ask. "Everyone knows I'm your mistress, and in their eyes I am still a disreputable woman!"

And Stephen would answer her only with another question. "What do you care?" he would ask. "You're *riche* and comfortable, and I have never denied you anything your heart desired. Why is it so important to you, as you say, to be accepted by society?"

"Because it is what I want more than anything in the world.

All my life I have been an outcast, even as a child. I want to be *accepted*! Do you understand what the word means?"

"I understand perfectly what it means, but it is a ridiculous idea. In any case, I like being a bachelor, and I have every intention of remaining one."

"I might as well have continued to be the mistress of Aaron Burr!"

Even now, Stephen was still jealous of Aaron. "I have asked you not to mention that name to me," he said coldly.

"And why not? I think he may well be our next President."

"Then God help us all!" said Stephen, who continued to have little empathy with the French since the Revolution and was therefore resentful of Burr's pro-French feelings.

"I would say God help us all if he does *not* become President. Aaron Burr is a great man!"

"I have already asked you not to mention his name in my presence!" said Stephen angrily.

"And I refuse!"

"Well, at least, will you promise me never to see him again?"

"Never is a long time." Eliza had grown weary of the argument. "Very well, I will give you my promise."

Stephen was pleased. He thought he had won the argument. "Tell me, dear Eliza, why are you so irritable these days?"

"I am bored, bored, bored!" she screamed.

"Would it amuse you to go to France?"

She looked at him incredulously. "Me go to France? To Paris?"

"I see no reason why not. It is almost time for me to go to Bordeaux and see my agents there. You could come along, and from Bordeaux we could go to Paris."

She jumped from her chair in excitement. "Oh, Stephen!"

"Of course, there would be dangers. Ships of both England and France might stop us, or even privateers and pirates."

"But why would they stop us?"

"The British don't want us carrying supplies to France and Napoleon. And the French—well, we would not need to fear them so much, because the *Stephen* flies the American flag and is of American registry. As to pirates, it's a chance we would have to take."

"Oh, damn the pirates!" said Eliza.

"Do not damn them so lightly, my dear. They would take not only our cargo—they might take *you*, all of them, one after another!"

She wanted to say that while she had lived in Sally's brothel in Providence, she had taken on as many as a dozen men a night, sometimes more. The thought of a mass rape did not disturb her at all.

"Well," she said, "it's a chance that I will have to take."

Immediately, Eliza began to make plans for the voyage. Stephen had provided a small cabin for her and told her that she could decorate it and furnish it in any way she pleased. But he cautioned her that all furniture would have to be capable of being bolted to the floor, and he advised that she bring only the simplest of clothing. The deck of a ship was no place to wear a hoopskirt. He assured her that when they arrived in Paris she could order a whole new wardrobe, and in the latest fashions.

Eliza went into a frenzy of shopping. She bought light, gaily colored material to make curtains for the porthole and ordered two comfortable chairs upholstered in green and yellow velvet. The bed was a simple affair without a canopy, and it had sturdy wooden legs that could be bolted to the floor. She bought all kinds of cosmetic supplies and could not resist the purchase of two new silk gowns without hoopskirts.

When Eliza broached the subject of bringing Pieter along on the voyage, Stephen was surprised.

"But we do not need him. I could understand if you wanted to bring Marie along as your maid—"

"I don't need a maid. I dislike having a woman fussing over me. Pieter would be useful. He could even serve with your crew. And during our journey from Bordeaux to Paris, an extra coachman might come in handy."

Stephen was puzzled by her insistence, but offered no further protest.

"Besides, dear Stephen, you know that I have been teaching him to read and write, and his lessons should continue."

174

"He would be better served, I think, if you taught him to speak French, so that he could understand my orders to the crew."

"A splendid idea!" said Eliza. "I'll begin French lessons for him as soon as we sail."

Stephen shrugged his shoulders noncommittally. But there was nothing noncommittal about Pieter's response to the news that he would accompany them on the voyage to France. He almost danced with excitement, not only at the prospect of visiting France, but because of the chance it gave him to be near Eliza. It was not often that he was able to go to bed with her now. On only two occasions had he visited her bedroom at midnight, while Stephen was out of town on business. But he did not care. It was enough for him merely to be near her, and he had no desire to bed one of the young girls in town. Alongside his beloved "madame" they all seemed plain and unattractive.

And so, on June 14, 1800, the *Stephen* sailed out of New York harbor bound for France. A stiff breeze set it quickly on its northeast course, and the square-rigged brig, laden with tobacco and cotton, moved steadily and smoothly.

Stephen had feared that Eliza might become seasick, but to his delight she enjoyed the motion of the ship. She learned to move with its rhythm as easily as any sailor, and she spent most of her time on deck, accompanied by Stephen or Pieter.

She liked to watch the crew as they went about their duties, and she remembered those days as a child in Providence when Sam Allen had taken her to the port and she had watched the loading and unloading of cargoes, while the sea gulls cried overhead.

She was never bored now. The sight of a group of dolphins leaping rhythmically in the sun fascinated her, and she wondered how they managed to time their curving gambols in unison without the use of speech or command. Whale sightings were an event to be marveled at, and one day, as their course moved farther northward, Stephen pointed to an iceberg glittering on the horizon.

175

"Oh!" she cried. "I hope that we can see it up close."

"We had better not," said Stephen with a smile. "We'll give it a wide berth, you may be sure."

"But why? It's only a little thing, after all."

When Stephen explained that only one-ninth of an iceberg appeared above water and that a collision would destroy their ship completely, Eliza became frightened.

"Oh, there is no danger, Stephen, is there?"

"There would be if we didn't have this fine wind to keep us on course."

She looked at him in admiration. "Oh, Stephen, you know so much, and I am so stupid. Why, I don't even know how you steer the ship in the right direction."

"Come with me, then, and I shall show you."

He took her to the bridge and explained to her how the sextant worked, and the declinations of the ship to the horizon in ascertaining longitude and latitude. She understood none of it and said so.

As Stephen began his explanation again, she said, "It is no use, Stephen. I have not a mind for such things. It's enough that I understand the difference between latitude and longitude. I'll leave the steering to you."

Stephen laughed, feeling rather pleased by his show of superiority. "There's no reason why you should bother your pretty head with it, *ma chère*. But it amazes me that you find it difficult to understand, when you are so good at common arithmetic."

"But that's different," she said. "Arithmetic is about buying and selling things, especially clothes."

He was going to say that it seemed to make little difference in the amount of money she spent, but he said nothing. He would never deny her anything that she wanted, and she knew it.

At the end of five weeks, land was sighted, and the *Stephen* steered toward the mouth of the Gironde River, and thence to the Garonne River, which ran southward to the city of Bordeaux.

The sight of land excited Eliza after the many days of an

empty horizon. But more than that, she was ecstatic to know that at last she was in France and that much nearer to Paris. She looked with curiosity at the vineyards that were planted almost to the edge of the river, and the land that was abloom with wild flowers.

Stephen planned to stay with his brother and two sisters in Bordeaux while he transacted his business. His younger brother, Victor, was married, and so were his younger sisters, Thérèse and Yvonne. They welcomed Stephen's arrival, and for propriety's sake, he introduced Eliza as his wife. She played the role successfully, hoping that he would realize what an excellent wife she would make. All of the Jumels were charmed by her beauty, and the fact that she could speak some French delighted them even more.

By the end of a week Eliza had become restless and urged Stephen to conclude his business quickly so that they could be on their way to Paris.

Stephen had decided to hire a coach and driver for the journey, because the stagecoaches were uncomfortable and lacked privacy. He outlined the itinerary to Eliza. From Bordeaux they would go to Périgueux and Limoges, thence to Châteauroux and Orléans. Then before going to Paris, he suggested that they make a short side trip to the cathedral at Chartres.

Eliza objected. "But that will delay us."

"Only by one day, and the cathedral is very beautiful. People come from all parts of Europe to see the famous Rose Window."

"Oh, to hell with the Rose Window! I want to see Paris, and the sooner the better."

"Well," said Stephen with a smile, "at least we will have to pass through Fontainebleau. It is where Queen Marie Antoinette gave her famous balls before the Revolution."

"It will be lots more interesting than a musty church," said Eliza.

So they traveled in leisurely fashion to the north, stopping in the best *tavernes* and *auberges*.

But it was a long and tiring journey, and to pass the time, Eliza, as she had done all her life, made up dreams of what would happen to her in Paris. At Bordeaux, the Jumel family had been wildly excited by Napoleon's latest conquest; he had defeated the Austrians at Marengo on June 14. And so, Eliza dreamed of meeting the great Napoleon himself. He was, by this time, the idol of the whole European continent.

Eliza had followed his meteoric career from the time of his early victories in Italy: Lodi, Milan, Mantua, Naples, Arcole and Rivoli. When he set out to destroy the British Empire itself, she admired his audacity and courage. He had invaded Egypt and won the Battle of the Pyramids in July 1798, although his whole fleet was destroyed by Admiral Nelson in Aboukir Bay. But when Turkey declared war on him, he had defeated their forces decisively in 1799.

Stephen joined Eliza in her enthusiasm for Napoleon, but not for romantic reasons. It was more important to him that when Napoleon became First Consul of France, he had brought an end to the bloody Revolution and a stability to the government.

Eliza not only imagined a meeting with him but also envisioned making a conquest of him. She saw no reason why she should not become his mistress, displacing Josephine. She had no qualms about deserting Stephen.

It took well over a week to travel the more than six hundred *kilomètres* to Paris. When they reached Fontainebleau, they stopped, and Eliza looked at the gardens and the splendid edifice that Marie Antoinette had built for her pleasure when, in the years before the Revolution, she and the nobility had dressed in peasant costume for balls.

For Eliza, it was not a deserted place; the gardens, still maintained in all their glory, were populated in her imagination by magnificently gowned beautiful women and elegantly costumed and handsome men of the court. It did not enter her head that all those imagined people were now dead, their heads lopped off by the guillotine.

As they got nearer and nearer to Paris, a fever invaded her. Her eyes were bright, and her nerves were taut with excitement. They entered Paris through the Porte d'Orléans, one of the historic old entrances to the ancient city.

She was strangely disappointed. Here, in the harsh August sunlight, the buildings seemed oddly small and dusty. She could not understand her reaction until she remembered that always, when she had dreamed of Paris, it had been a city of twilight, bathed in a mysterious blue light, so that its lines were softened and romantic.

Her disappointment did not last for long. When she saw the cathedral of Notre Dame, rising majestically from the Seine, she became aware that this was truly Paris, not exactly as it had been in her dreams, but still very beautiful.

As they passed the Tuileries, with its bright-flowered formal gardens, Stephen said, "It was from here that King Louis and Marie Antoinette were driven by a mob of revolutionaries. The palace is now the residence of Napoleon."

Eliza had Stephen stop the carriage so that she could get out. She ambled through the gardens, her eyes fastened on the windows of the building. She hoped to catch a glimpse of Napoleon, or, even better, to see him leave the building with his equipage. If he did, she resolved to throw herself before his carriage and force a meeting with him.

But the occasion did not present itself.

Reluctantly, she returned to the carriage, and they continued on their way until they reached the Place de la Concorde. Eliza had half expected to see the guillotine still erected in the center, but the large square was deserted except for pedestrians. They continued up the Avenue des Champs Elysées, and Eliza marveled at the width of the great thoroughfare, lined with its many cafés, expensive shops and huge chestnut trees.

Stephen explained that the avenue had been built at the order of King Louis XV. Now, Napoleon planned to erect a magnificent arch at the end of it, to be called the Arc de Triomphe, in commemoration of his many victories.

They then crossed the Seine to the Left Bank. Here, in the fashionable Faubourg St. Germain, Stephen had rented a whole floor in the house of a former marquis on the Rue de Grenelle, and they drove into its large courtyard.

Eliza was impressed by the opulence of the building that would be her home during their stay in Paris. Never had she seen such spacious and exquisitely furnished rooms. There was not an article of furniture that in the United States would not be looked upon as an antique.

By late afternoon Eliza was worn out by the excitement of their arrival in Paris. Stephen suggested that she lie down for a nap before they went out to dine, and Eliza reluctantly agreed. She fell asleep on the large and comfortable feather bed and did not awaken for several hours. When she found out that it was eight o'clock, she expressed her wonderment that it was still bright daylight outside.

"You must remember," said Stephen, "that Paris is much closer to the North Pole than New York is." He then embarked on a lesson in geography and the role of the Gulf Stream and the North Atlantic Drift in keeping these northern countries temperate in climate.

Eliza was ravenously hungry and did not even attempt to understand Stephen's geographical explanations. And so they went out to dine in an expensive café near the Palais Royale, and Eliza gorged herself on dishes that were, to her, new and even exotic. She was especially fond of lobster in a sauce that Stephen told her took two days to prepare. The desserts were incredibly luscious and rich, often made with thick whipped cream. She took care to memorize the name of everything she ate: *gigot* was lamb, *jambon* was ham, *champignons* were mushrooms. But she was disappointed in *truffes*, or truffles, which seemed so tasteless that she could not imagine why they were considered a delicacy, and when Stephen explained that they were rooted up by pigs, she took an active dislike to them.

The next day Stephen took her on a lengthy shopping tour. The gowns in the new neoclassic mode delighted Eliza, and she bought a dozen of them in as many shades, while Stephen looked on smilingly. He seemed not in the slightest concerned by what Eliza thought were the exorbitant prices.

The following day, while Stephen met with his agents, Eliza launched into the second day of extravagant shopping. It was the

180

shops in the narrow streets that she liked most, and she bought all kinds of trinkets and accessories. She even climbed the twisting alleys that led up the hill to Montmartre, until she could look back and see the city spread out below her.

When she returned to the quarters in the Faubourg St. Germain, she was exhausted. Stephen was waiting for her with good news. He had looked up Charles Talleyrand, whom he had befriended when both men had come to New York as refugees. In November 1795, after the Directoire had been established, Talleyrand had left the United States, had eventually made his way to Paris, and had found himself a place in the Napoleonic régime. He had been very friendly toward Stephen, and Stephen had taken advantage of the man's prominence to introduce Eliza to Parisian society.

"I hope, dear Eliza, that you can spare one day of shopping to be free next Thursday morning. You have been invited to attend a *levée* of the celebrated Madame Récamier."

"A *levée*? What's that?"

"In Paris it is one of the most popular social functions. *Levée* in French means a rising, or getting up in the morning. Instead of an afternoon tea, the guests gather to have a late breakfast with a socially prominent lady."

"But how am I to dress?" asked Eliza.

"In one of your loveliest gowns."

"And this Madame Récamier—who is she?"

"She is a beautiful and accomplished young woman of about your age. She was married at the age of fifteen to Jacques Récamier, a wealthy middle-aged banker, but it was an arranged marriage, not a marriage of love. Her *salon* is the most important in Paris, especially now that Madame de Staël has lost popularity because she lacks sympathy with Napoleon."

"I suppose that this woman has many lovers," said Eliza.

"It is strange, but though she has many suitors, she is not known to have a lover."

"She's strange, all right," commented Eliza. "But I am terrified of meeting her, if she is such a great lady."

Stephen patted her reassuringly. "You need not be. I have met

181

her. As beautiful and influential as she is, she is most gracious and gentle in manner. I think you will like her."

Nevertheless, Eliza was apprehensive as Thursday approached, and when, dressed in one of her new gowns, she alighted from her coach to attend the *levée*, she was trembling.

She was ushered into the grand drawing room and was dumbfounded at the scene before her. Here, at this hour of the morning, was congregated a collection of ladies and gentlemen attired as though for a royal event. At the center of the room Mme. Juliette Récamier lay on a large chaise lounge. Propped up on pillows, she received her visitors, who stood in line waiting to greet her.

Eliza looked curiously at the woman who was the center of all this attention. Her face was strikingly beautiful, framed with curls of shining chestnut hair that gleamed in the sunlight streaming through the spacious open windows. Her body, clad only in an elaborate nightdress of light-blue silk, was clearly outlined, and it was obvious that it was well shaped, her firm young breasts generously filling the low bodice that she wore.

As the liveried footman announced, "*Monsieur et Madame Jumel de New York aux États-Unis*," Eliza approached the chaise, kissed Mme. Récamier's outstretched hand and performed a low curtsy.

"I very much love the Americans," said Mme. Récamier in halting English, "and I welcome you to my *salon*."

Eliza replied in French, saying that she hoped Madame would some day visit the United States and be her guest.

"Ah, you speak French, and with such a delightful American accent. Thank you for your kind invitation, Madame Jumel. One day *peut-être* I shall make a *visite* to your country so wild and *farouche*."

Stephen spied Talleyrand in the gathering and took Eliza to meet him. He surveyed Eliza with voluptuous, heavy-lidded eyes.

"Stephen," he said, "you did not tell me that you had found for yourself a wife so *ravissante*. Leave her with me, and I will see to it that she meets all the young men who would make the most suitable lovers." He winked good-naturedly at Stephen, who gave him a formally stiff smile.

Talleyrand took Eliza by the arm, and leaving Stephen behind, he went the rounds and introduced her to the other guests.

Eliza noticed that he limped and said, "Monsieur Talleyrand, have you had an accident to your foot?"

"Oh, that was many years ago, when I was just a child. Because of it, I studied for the priesthood and became a bishop."

"Oh, I did not know that you were a *religieux*."

Talleyand laughed so that the rolls of fat on his belly jiggled in sympathetic merriment. "Oh, I am not a bishop anymore, madame. My scandalous behavior with the ladies soon put an end to that. Finally, I was excommunicated from the Church by the Pope himself, and so then I became a diplomat. But here are some assorted *ducs* and *marquis* that you must meet. *Vous voyez*, France once again has a nobility."

And so Eliza, thoroughly dazzled by the array of titles, met most of the guests. For the first time in her life, she felt thoroughly accepted by society. Here in Paris, no one knew her Providence background and her unsavory reputation, and she gloried in the feeling of freedom it gave her. She was the equal of anyone in the room, even if she did not have a title.

That afternoon, back in the apartment on the Rue de Grenelle, she questioned Stephen about the matter of getting a title for himself.

"A title?" he said. "Whatever for? A title is something you are born with, unless Napoleon decides to give you one. That reminds me of a story that I heard at the *levée* this morning. One of Napoleon's followers made a nuisance of himself asking Napoleon to give him a title, and finally Napoleon decreed that he would become the Duc de Mer."

"There," said Eliza, "you see? All you would have to do is ask, Stephen."

"But, my dear, you are missing the point of the story. If you reverse the words '*de mer*,' you have '*merde*.' "

Eliza gasped. "But that means shit."

"Exactly. Perhaps he might give me an even worse title. Anyway, although I am still a citizen of France, I have become an American, and a title would be meaningless."

"It would not be meaningless in New York," said Eliza.

"No matter. I have no plans to become one of the new nobility under Napoleon, and that's an end on it."

But it was not the end of the matter for Eliza. Someday and somehow, she would get a title for Stephen. She desperately wanted a *de* before his name. It would help her, she thought, in her battle for acceptance by the first families of New York.

As a result of Eliza's introduction to society at Mme. Récamier's *levée*, invitations began pouring into the house on the Rue de Grenelle. The Jumels were invited to balls, to *soirées* and to more *levées*.

Eliza lived in a state of frenzied activity that bordered on mania. She arose early every morning to prepare for the social functions of the day and evening. She fussed over herself, arranging her hair first one way and then another. She would try on as many as three different gowns, not being able to make up her mind as to which was most becoming or more suitable for the occasion.

Stephen watched all this with a bemused smile, patiently waiting for her to complete her *toilette*. He had never seen her so happy and vivacious, and that pleased him. It also pleased him that she was more responsive to him in bed than she had been in a long while.

Eliza had become the moment's latest darling in French society. Her beauty, her sprightliness and her spontaneous coquetry all endeared her to men and women alike, and they found her quaint and imaginative use of the French language deliciously amusing. The very fact that she was an American gave her distinction, and people were full of questions about the *peaux rouges*, or redskins, and about the vast wilderness of unexplored country that extended beyond the eastern coast to the western lands near the Mississippi and beyond.

A young man named François René Chateaubriand was utterly fascinated by the western part of the continent. He was a writer, only recently returned from exile in England. A great favorite of Mme. Récamier's, there was much speculation as to whether or not he might be her lover, but to the best of anyone's knowledge the relationship was purely platonic and based mostly on his talent as a writer. He had already published in England an essay on "the historic, political and moral aspects of revolutions," and it was widely read in Paris.

But it was America that interested him the most, and he plied Eliza with questions, many of which she could not answer.

He was a man in his early thirties, not quite handsome, but with an arresting face dominated by the intense expression in his eyes, which burned with an inner fire.

He told Eliza that he planned to visit America in search of material for a novel that he was writing, and Eliza extended an invitation for him to stay with her and her husband. He thanked her and said that he would be happy to stay with them in New York before he set out on his travels. It was not the cities that interested him but the wilderness beyond, and as he talked about Indians and explorers, his eyes became feverishly bright. Eliza was rather disappointed that he seemed so little taken with her and her charms.

But if Chateaubriand was not interested in her, most of the other men were. She politely refused their repeated suggestions for a rendezvous. Talleyrand himself suggested that she come to his house for refreshments after a ball—without Stephen, of course. The lustful look about his large mouth faded when Eliza told him that she never accepted engagements unless her husband accompanied her.

The Comtesse Henri Tascher de la Pagerie took a special interest in Eliza. She was a woman in her forties with a face that bore evidence of having once been very beautiful. But in her middle years she had put on weight and the muscles of her face had fallen so that her cheeks sagged and there was the beginning of a double chin. But her blue eyes were still young and glittered brightly, particularly if she had a choice bit of gossip to pass on to Eliza.

Through her, Eliza learned which *marquise* was having an

185

affair with which *duc*, which *marquis* was sleeping with which *duchesse*. There was nothing really malicious in the Comtesse's scandalmongering. She took a gleeful delight in it, as though it were a game, and the delight was contagious. Eliza enjoyed the knowledge that a virginal-looking woman she had met was actually an insatiable wanton between the silk sheets of her lover's bed.

As the time drew near for the Jumels to leave Paris and start on the journey home, Eliza begged Stephen to prolong their visit for another two weeks. He had concluded his business and had no need to stay, but the sight of Eliza enjoying herself more than she had ever done since he met her made him assent. He knew that once back in New York, she would become bored and irritable.

So, they stayed on in Paris, and on the night before they were finally to depart, Stephen gave a large dinner at the apartment on the Rue de Grenelle. Although it was difficult because he had no kitchen staff or serving help, he felt it was the least he could do in return for the generous hospitality that Parisian society had shown them. He had employed the necessary help for the evening, and the invitations had gone out.

It was a splendid dinner with many courses—fish, game and small roasted piglets. The wines, of course, were the very choicest from his own supply. All the people they had met, from Mme. Récamier and Talleyrand to Eliza's special friend, the Comtesse de la Pagerie, were there.

Eliza proved herself to be a superb hostess. For the first time in her life she was giving a dinner party which nobody made excuses not to attend. Her gaiety and exuberance were boundless, and she knew, without asking, that the affair had been a great success.

After the last guest had gone, Eliza went to her bedroom. Exhausted and in low spirits, she sat on the edge of her bed and made no move to undress until Stephen came into the room.

"What is the matter, *ma chère?* The party was enjoyed by everyone, you know."

"Yes," said Eliza. "But tomorrow now comes, and we shall leave Paris."

"But don't you want to go home? We have been away for a long while."

"No!" she said with anger. "I don't want to go home! It would suit me splendidly if I never had to see New York again. I hate New York and all the people in it!"

Stephen sat down on the bed with her and took her hand in his. "Maybe things will be better now," he lied. "And just think, the summer is almost over and soon the theatre will begin a new season."

"I would rather stay here and go to the Odéon, even if I can hardly understand a word of those plays by Racine and Corneille. It is more exciting than going to the Park Theatre and having people look the other way when they see me."

"But when they learn that you have been to Paris, when they see you in gowns that are in advance of the fashion there—"

"It will make no difference. Yes, the women will look at the gowns, so that they can get their dressmakers to imitate them. But I shall be the same—the mistress of the rich Stephen Jumel, a woman of tarnished virtue, not a wife as I have been here."

Stephen was silent, and so she pursued her point. "Why in God's name will you not marry me and make what they call an honest woman of me?"

"Because I do not wish to marry," said Stephen. "Not you or anyone else."

He got up and left the room.

Eliza's prediction about her life back in New York proved to be accurate. Her new wardrobe attracted the attention that she had foreseen, since the new neoclassic mode of women's dress had not yet arrived from France, and hoopskirts, though modified in size, were still being worn. She was correct, too, in how little this would affect her social standing.

When the theatre season opened, the Jumels attended the first performance. And as usual, Eliza was a target for the admiring glances of the men, while the women openly turned their eyes away from her.

Stephen's suggestion that they give a dinner party for their

187

French friends in the city stirred no enthusiasm in her. Indeed, it was not until the balloting for president in November that she took any interest in anything.

The astonishing news was that the Federalist Party lay in ruins, and the two Republicans who vied for the presidency were Thomas Jefferson and Aaron Burr. President Adams and Hamilton had continued their bitter feud, and whole segments of former Federalists had crossed over to the Republican Party.

And then came word that Burr and Jefferson had the same number of electoral votes for president and that the contest would be decided by the House of Representatives in Washington. Voting began on February 11, 1801, and by noon of the following day, after twenty-eight ballots, the tie was still unbroken.

Eliza could not understand why Aaron had not gone to Washington in an attempt to win delegates to his side. Instead, he had remained in Albany, tending to his duties as a member of the New York State Legislature.

When she read in the newspaper that Theodosia had married Joseph Alston on February 2, she realized that Aaron had set Theodosia's happiness above his career.

On February 16 the deadlock in Washington was finally broken by James A. Bayard of Delaware, and after thirty-six ballots, Jefferson was elected president with Burr as his Vice-President.

Eliza was sure that if Aaron had gone to Washington, he could have broken the deadlock by obtaining additional votes. Just the same, that night when Stephen made love to her, her thoughts were only of Aaron. Indeed, it was not Stephen who was sleeping with her. It was the new Vice-President of the United States.

CHAPTER 17

O<small>N AN AFTERNOON</small> in March 1804 Eliza alighted from her coach at her dressmaker's shop on Pearl Street. Two boys stopped in the street to watch her.

One of them turned to the other and said, "Who's that pretty woman?"

"Oh, that's the wine merchant's whore. Everybody knows that."

Pieter jumped from his seat on the box and went after them, with Eliza not far behind, horsewhip in her hand. Pieter caught the boys and held them by their collars while Eliza lashed them with the whip.

"So I'm a whore, am I?" she screamed. "Well, take that and that, and blast your loose goddamn tongues!"

Her fury had become a madness as she struck the boys again and again. They fell crying to the ground.

Pieter, seeing that a small crowd was gathering, grabbed Eliza by the elbow, took the whip away from her and ushered her back to the carriage. She got in and they drove quickly back to Whitehall Street before the incident could attract the constabulary.

When Eliza entered the house, she was shaken and still trembling with rage. Pieter attempted to console her and poured her a glass of brandy, which she gulped in one swallow.

At last she said, "Thank you, Pieter. I'll be all right now. Go tend to the horses and the coach."

He left reluctantly, and Eliza sat very still, trying to compose her thoughts. She knew that telling Stephen about the incident would in no way change his mind about marrying her. She had used all her weapons: temper tantrums, arguments, threats of leaving him. Nothing had worked. The time had come to force the issue, and she saw no way to do it except by trickery.

Her plan became clear when she learned that Stephen would be going to Philadelphia on business, a twenty-nine-hour trip by stagecoach. Two days before he was to leave, she took to her bed, complaining of a severe headache and nausea.

When Stephen brought supper up to her on a tray, she said that she had no appetite and could not eat. And the next morning she seemed no better. She drank some tea but refused food.

Stephen was concerned and insisted on calling Dr. Romayne to come see her. The doctor could find nothing seriously wrong beyond a slight digestive upset, for which he prescribed small doses of laudanum.

On the day that Stephen was to set out for Philadelphia he delayed his departure. "I don't want to go, dear Eliza, while you are feeling so poorly."

"Oh, it's nothing, Stephen. It will pass. This time of the month I never feel well, you know."

When he still insisted on staying, Eliza became angry. "I command you to go, Stephen! I am tired of your fussing over me like a mother hen. By the time you get back, I'll be fit as a fiddle."

Stephen knew better than to contradict her when she was in a mood like this. He shrugged his shoulders and bent over to kiss her goodbye.

"If you insist, Eliza, I will go. But my thoughts will be always with you, and I'll hurry back, you may be sure."

He had no sooner left the house than Eliza called Pieter to her bedside.

"I am sorry you don't feel good, madame."

"There is nothing at all wrong with me, Pieter."

"You mean you're not sick?"

"Not in the slightest. Since Monsieur Jumel will not willingly marry me, I will make him do so unwillingly. And you will be able to help me."

"But how, madame?"

190

"This afternoon you will bring me a flat cordial bottle filled with very hot water, and I'll put it under my pillow. Then, you will go get Dr. Romayne and tell him I've taken a turn for the worse. Next, you will get on your horse and ride to Philadelphia to overtake Monsieur Jumel and bring him back. You will tell him that I am dying and that the priest has been called for the last rites."

"But, madame, I don't understand."

"You will, dear boy. When Stephen finds that his mistress is dying and that her only wish is to be made an honorable woman before she leaves this earth, I believe that he will make me Madame Stephen Jumel, and I'll no longer be the wine merchant's whore!"

"But what is the wine bottle full of hot water for?"

"When I put the doctor's thermometer on it, it will show a high fever. It must be very hot water, Pieter, almost boiling."

As Pieter finally understood, he doubled up with laughter. "Madame, you are the goddamnedest humbugger I ever saw!" He had another spasm of laughter, and now Eliza could not help joining him.

She reached out her hand to grasp his and then said, "But not a word of this to anyone, Pieter. We are conspirators."

Pieter was not sure what a conspirator was, but whatever it was he liked being one. Then his face became serious as he said, "But, madame, when he finds out the truth—"

"Maybe he will not. I'll just make a miraculous recovery as soon as I have a wedding ring on my finger."

The plan went off on schedule. When Dr. Romayne arrived, Eliza turned away from him onto her side and slipped the thermometer for a moment against the wine bottle under her pillow and then placed it quickly back in her mouth.

Dr. Romayne's eyebrows raised in alarm when he took a reading. "Madame," he said, "you are a seriously ill woman. I would advise you to bring your husband back as quickly as possible. Shall I send for a priest?"

In a faint, barely articulate voice, Eliza said, "Yes, please do."

As soon as the doctor had left, Pieter was dispatched on horse-

191

back to overtake Stephen on the road to Philadelphia. Then Eliza got out of bed and removed all her make-up. She covered her face with a thin layer of white powder and mussed her hair to a wild tangle. As she surveyed herself in the mirror of her dressing table, she smiled. "Damned if you don't look like a corpse," she said.

When Stephen returned late that evening, the sight that met his eyes filled him with terror. Eliza lay flat on her back on the bed, her eyes closed, her breath coming in rapid gasps. Father O'Malley sat by her bedside mumbling prayers in Latin. He had already administered extreme unction. Dr. Romayne was pacing up and down anxiously. As for Eliza, all she knew was that she was voraciously hungry, and her feeling of weakness was real enough.

Stephen tiptoed to her side. "Eliza, *chère* Eliza. It is Stephen. I came back from my journey as soon as Pieter gave me the news."

Eliza opened her eyes, fluttering her eyelids, as though she did not recognize him. At last she said, "Stephen, thank God you are here. I fear that I am dying." Her eyes closed again.

Dr. Romayne stepped forward. "I am sorry, sir. I have done everything possible. I have bled her and cupped her, but her fever remains dangerously high. There is no explanation for it, but a person cannot live long with such a temperature, that is certain."

"Is it—is it yellow fever?" asked Stephen.

"No, not at this time of year. She has none of the symptoms of yellow fever. It is perhaps a toxic condition brought on by spoiled food. I do not know."

Stephen knelt by the bed and prayed in a low voice. Then he looked again at the face he loved so much.

"Eliza, for the sake of *le bon Dieu*, speak to me!"

Her eyes opened, the soft violet eyes that he had adored from the moment he met her. They stared at him now with a fixity that made him wonder if she saw him.

"Eliza, *ma chère* Eliza, before you leave me, is there anything that I can do for you?"

Her head moved slowly back and forth on the pillow. "Dear Stephen," she said in such a low voice that he could barely hear her, "before I die, I would like to go to God as an honest woman —a married woman—not a whore."

The barely audible words from her pale lips brought Stephen quickly to his feet, and he turned to Father O'Malley.

"Father, could you marry me to this dear woman whom I should have married years ago? I do not wish her to go to Heaven with this grievous sin upon her head."

"Certainly, Monsieur Jumel. Do you have a ring?"

"Darling Eliza, do you have a ring? We are to be married."

She raised her head. "There are rings in my jewelry box."

Stephen dumped the contents of the jewelry box onto the dressing table and returned with a simple gold ring set with a ruby. And so, with Stephen kneeling at the side of the bed, Father O'Malley intoned the marriage ceremony. Eliza's responses were weak but surprisingly clear.

When they were at last declared man and wife, Eliza turned to Stephen and gave him a wan smile. "Thank you, my dear husband. Now I shall be at peace."

Tears were running down Stephen's face as he kissed her tenderly on the mouth. Father O'Malley and Dr. Romayne stood nearby, watching the sad scene. Both of them offered to spend the night.

Eliza roused herself and lifted her head from the pillow. "Please go. You have both been very kind. But during these last moments I wish to be alone with my dear husband."

Stephen nodded his assent and ushered both men from the room. He returned to the bedside and sat in a chair, holding fast to Eliza's hand.

A few hours later, Stephen asked her whether she could take any nourishment. He had noticed that her hand did not seem hot.

Eliza opened her eyes and looked at him. "Maybe I could, Stephen. Send Pieter up to me, and you—you must be very tired. Go to your room and nap for a while."

"But I don't want to leave you alone, my dear wife."

"Pieter will stay with me and call you if I should take a turn for the worse."

Stephen left the room, and soon Pieter appeared at the door.

Eliza sat up in bed quickly. "Pieter," she whispered, "I am now Madame Jumel."

His face broke into a joyous smile. "Oh, that is good news, madame. So the plan worked!"

"And now, dear Pieter, Madame Jumel is as hungry as a lion. Bring me some tea, three sweet buns, and a glass of Madeira!"

When Pieter returned with a tray, Eliza grabbed at the buns and washed them down with the tea so fast that she scarcely chewed them. Then she tossed off the Madeira and asked for more.

Pieter returned with the wine and another sweet bun. He sat down in a chair and watched her with a broad grin on his amiable face.

At last, she settled back in the bed. "You'd better take this stuff away now, Pieter. Then come back and sleep in that chair over there. It was the only way I could persuade Stephen—my husband, that is—to take a nap."

Pieter picked up the tray, but before he left, he said, "Madame Jumel, you are *still* the goddamnedest humbugger I ever saw!"

She smiled at him. "But I am no longer the wine merchant's whore! I am his wife!"

Pieter nodded, laughed softly to himself and left.

When Dr. Romayne came the next morning and took Eliza's temperature, he was astonished to find that it was normal. Stephen, who stood anxiously at the side of the bed, asked, "Is she any better, doctor?"

Dr. Romayne looked at him in bewilderment. "Her temperature has dropped to normal, Monsieur Jumel. It is nothing less than a miracle of God."

"Then she will live?"

"I am sure of it, monsieur. But we must remember that she has been very ill and without food for more than two days, so her diet must be a light one. Do you have any appetite, Madame Jumel?"

"Yes, a little," said Eliza. It was one of the few times in her life that she had made an understatement. She could have eaten a huge beefsteak with relish.

"A cup of tea, then," said the doctor, "and a slice of bread and butter, perhaps, if she can hold it down. I shall come back this evening to see how she is."

Dr. Romayne left then, still muttering to himself, "It is a miracle, a miracle!"

Stephen stayed at her bedside, waiting for Pieter to bring a tray with tea and a slice of bread and butter. She ate slowly, remembering that she must still play the role of invalid. It was, she decided, the finest dramatic performance she had ever given.

Stephen was delighted to see that she was eating and murmured encouraging endearments in her ear.

"I am very weary, my dear husband. I would like to nap now. Please leave me. I am feeling much better. You may send Pieter up again to watch over me, if you wish."

Stephen left, and when Pieter appeared a few moments later, he found Eliza at her dressing table. She was powdering her face with the white powder.

"Madame," said Pieter, "you are supposed to be getting well now. Why do you powder your face so that you look like a dead woman?"

"I must not recover too quickly or Monsieur Jumel might became suspicious."

She got back into bed and drew the sheet up to her chin. Then she suddenly reached under her pillow and brought out the cordial bottle.

"Here, Pieter. For God's sake, get rid of my fever bottle, and don't let anybody see you with it."

Pieter grabbed the bottle and left quickly. When he returned, he brought another sweet bun and a glass of Madeira. As soon as Eliza had devoured the food, he left with the tray.

A little later Stephen came in to see her. She was propped up against the pillows and smiled wanly at him.

He went over to her and kissed her joyfully. "Oh, my darling, you seem so much better. But you are still so pale."

"Maybe it is the white powder I put on my face when the fever was so high. It made me feel more comfortable."

Stephen looked at her acutely. "But you never use white powder, Eliza. It certainly made you look very sick."

"I suppose it did. I never thought of that. But it was soothing to my hot skin."

He patted her hand. "Of course." Had her illness been a trick to get him to marry her? But he dismissed the thought as being too outlandish. The fever had been real enough, and Dr. Romayne was no fool. The important thing was that she was recovering.

He took her hand and held it in his. "My dear, dear wife—and I was the man who would remain forever a bachelor! But now, would you believe that I am *vraiment* proud to be your husband?"

Eliza forced tears to come to her eyes. "Oh, Stephen, those are the kindest words you have ever said to me."

Stephen felt guilty as he watched her crying. He got up and moved toward the window. When he turned and came back to the bed, he said, "When you are well recovered from this horrible illness, *ma chère*, I think our marriage should be a proper one in a church."

Eliza had difficulty controlling the excitement in her voice. "Oh, Stephen, a church wedding! Whatever for?"

"Because I wish to announce our marriage to all of New York, and I want to walk down the aisle with my beautiful bride on my arm!"

For a moment Eliza felt guilty. But not guilty enough to refuse a church wedding. She was already choosing the color of her wedding gown.

And so, on April 9, 1804, the wedding took place in the original St. Patrick's Cathedral at Prince and Mott Streets. Eliza, dressed in a gorgeous wedding gown of peach-colored silk and with a pure white lace cap, made what one witness called "a stunning bride—a beautiful blonde, with a superb figure and a graceful carriage."

196

Only a few of the people who had been invited to the wedding reception on Whitehall Street had accepted the invitation. But Eliza, for once in her life, did not care. She had the marriage certificate framed, with its announcement in Latin of the union of "Stephanus Jumel and Elizabethum de la Croix," and she hung it in a conspicuous place in the drawing room.

She glowed at the thought that now, after so many years, she was a respectably married woman and could begin again her never-ending fight to be accepted by the best families of New York.

But before the summer was over, scandal had once again touched her name.

CHAPTER 18

ON THE EVENING OF JUNE 27, 1804, Aaron Burr sat in his study and wrote a letter to Theodosia in South Carolina. He told her that he was to fight a duel with Alexander Hamilton on July 11 and he gave her instructions, in the event of his death, to burn all his correspondence, especially the letters from women. Then he bade a fond farewell to her and to his beloved Gampy.

It was odd, he reflected, how an apparently trivial event last April had been blown up until now it was a matter of life and death.

On April 4, Dr. Charles Cooper had written a letter to his friend Philip Schuyler. He mentioned having attended a meeting of Federalists at the Tontine Coffee House in the course of which General Hamilton had attacked Burr with his usual vitriolic scorn. At the conclusion of the letter, Dr. Cooper had written, "I could detail to you a still more despicable opinion which General Hamilton has expressed of Mr. Burr."

The matter would have rested there, if the Albany *Register* had not printed the letter, which was then copied by other newspapers, including those in New York.

Gossip flared as to what the "more despicable opinion" consisted of. It was evidently not of a political nature, but of a highly personal one concerning the Vice-President's morals. Some people said that the remark referred to Eliza's affair with Burr, that he had thrown her out because as his mistress she stood in the way of his presidential ambitions. Still other opinions hinted at incest between Burr and his daughter, Theodosia.

198

And so Aaron had sent his friend William Van Ness with a letter to General Hamilton at his home. In it, Burr requested "a prompt and unqualified . . . denial of the use of any expression which would warrant the assertions of Dr. Cooper."

On June 20, Hamilton replied with a vague and confusing letter about definitions of the terms "despicable" and "derogatory," but refused to comply with Burr's request.

Burr's answer was prompt. He wrote, "The common sense of mankind affixes to the epithet adopted by Dr. Cooper the idea of dishonor. The question is . . . whether you have [uttered] expressions or opinions derogatory to my honor. . . . Your letter has furnished me with new reasons for requiring a definite reply."

At this point Hamilton could easily have avoided a duel by a prompt disavowal of having used any language of a despicable nature against Burr. But he made no answer to Burr's letter, possibly because too many Federalists at the meeting remembered the remark, and such a denial could cause him to lose face in the ranks of his own party.

But no answer had come from Hamilton, and so Aaron had drafted a formal challenge that morning. He had no wish to fight a duel with Hamilton, but there seemed no other honorable way out.

There was a knock at the front door, and he went to answer it. Eliza stood there, with a black cape thrown over her shoulders and wearing a veil so heavy that at first he did not recognize her.

"Eliza!" he exclaimed. "What are you doing here?"

"I know it is late, Aaron. I had to wait until Stephen was asleep."

"Come in." He closed the door and bolted it.

She lifted the veil, and he said, "Black is very becoming to you, my dear."

She disregarded the compliment and said earnestly, "Aaron, I had to see you. It is rumored that you are to duel with Alexander Hamilton."

"It is not a rumor, Eliza. My letter of challenge has gone to him."

She had sat down in the chair he offered her, and now she leaned forward tensely. "It must not happen, Aaron. They say that it is because of me."

"I know that is what they say. In fact, it is true. I have learned that Hamilton, undoubtedly carried away by too much wine, called me a whoremonger and said that I picked you up from the streets and then, when I tired of you, threw you out."

"But that isn't true, Aaron!" she said with indignation.

"And since *when* has the truth mattered to General Hamilton, especially where I am concerned?"

"But you mustn't do this, Aaron—endangering your life in defense of my name!"

"In April you married Monsieur Jumel. You are now what this town would call a respectable woman."

"Respectable woman, indeed! In their eyes I'll always be little better than a whore, and well you know it."

"Perhaps. But that is not the important thing. It is my *own* honor that is at stake! For years now I have endured this man's lies, suffered in silence whatever injuries to my character he chose to invent. And the hypocrisy of the man, when only a few short years ago he found himself involved in a scandal with the Reynolds woman and her husband, and there was even a question whether he may not have used government money to answer their blackmailing demands."

"But he did finally make a public admission of his guilt, you must admit."

"Yes, when he was forced to. I will not defend Alexander Hamilton. Why do you?"

Her eyes blazed. "I hate the man! Do you know that when he sees me, he averts his eyes?"

Aaron suddenly laughed. "Why shouldn't he? You must remember that you got rid of him, and not long after that you became my mistress. He has always been jealous of me, you may be sure. His excessive vanity was cut to the quick."

Eliza was silent a moment. "He is more than vain. He is evil!"

"All the more reason why I should take a pot shot at him."

Eliza's voice took on a pleading tone. "But, Aaron, he could

200

just as easily kill *you*! And I will not have you risking your life for my name. It's hardly worth it."

Aaron's voice took on a serious tone. "Until now, he has called me every kind of name from Catiline to unprincipled rake, and I did not even honor him with a denial. But never, until now, has he mentioned a woman's name in his calumnies."

"But why is that so bad, Aaron?"

He drew himself up proudly. "I shall never permit any woman's reputation to be injured in any way because of me. I have taken maidenheads, but never intentionally; I have slept with other men's wives and am therefore an adulterer. But no woman's *name* has ever been blemished by me!" He paused. "I am writing a letter of farewell to Theodosia and have requested that as my executrix she destroy all my personal correspondence, especially letters from women."

"That is all very well, Aaron," said Eliza, "but you are being far too gallant."

He raised his eyebrows. "Gallant? Yes, I suppose I am gallant, if you want to use that word. But you must remember what I told you when I first met you. Women have rights. They have intelligence and should have education and respect. Do you think I am likely to change my opinion because of a blabbermouthed busybody like Hamilton? It is not just *your* name, Eliza. It would be the same if he had slurred any woman's name."

Eliza could not repress a twinge of disappointment, but she said, "You are carrying your idealism too far."

"Idealism and high principles can never be carried too far. Do you know that in all my life if a woman came to me and told me she had become pregnant by me, I never questioned it? I provided for her and the child, even if there was no certainty that the child was indeed mine."

Eliza smiled. "No wonder you have always been so poor."

"It was jokingly said at the time of the election, you know, that if all my bastard children had been old enough to vote, I would have been elected by an overwhelming majority." He laughed and added, "It could almost be true, I suppose."

"But this duel, Aaron—is there no way that you can avoid it?"

"Yes, if Hamilton were to make a public retraction of what he said. But a week has gone by, and he has not done so, nor is it likely that he will. And so, tomorrow morning Mr. Van Ness will deliver my formal challenge, and that is that."

Eliza saw that she could not turn him from his decision and got up from her chair. "I have come on a fool's errand, Aaron. But at least I'll be able to say goodbye."

She went over to him and threw her arms around him. She kissed him lovingly and tenderly. He responded with passion, and she looked at him in surprise.

He said, "And does not a doomed man have some privileges?"

"You mean you want to—"

"Yes. Eliza, I want to make love to you. After all, it may be the last time," he whispered.

"But with so many things on your mind—"

"All the more reason why I should have a bit of love, especially when you look so fetching in that black gown."

She could think of no reason to deny him. Anyway, she did not really want to. In spite of everything, she still loved him, would always love him. She could not bear the thought that he might soon be dead.

It gave her a perverse kind of pleasure to think that she might be the last woman to receive the love of the Vice-President of the United States.

The ecstasy he gave her was sweet and prolonged, but as she kissed him goodbye, she began crying. And she cried even after she had reached the street and rounded the corner, where Pieter waited for her with the coach.

She was still upset when she reached home, and Pieter wisely said nothing. He knew that there was nothing he could do to comfort her.

But as she alighted from the coach, he came down from the box and pressed her hand. Softly, he said, "I know now that you really love him, madame. And I know, too, that he is worthy of it, risking his life to defend your name."

Her "Thank you" was barely audible, and she fled up the steps and opened the door to her house, which was still and quiet, as quiet as the tomb it seemed to be.

The dawn on July 11 was misty and red, presaging another hot summer day. The rowboat that moved across the Hudson River to Weehawken held two passengers: Aaron Burr and his second, William Van Ness. Burr's eyes were fastened on the Jersey shore. He was thinking of Theodosia and his grandson, whom he called Gampy, and wondering what would become of them in the event of his death. He had no money to leave them.

General Hamilton, accompanied by his second, Nathaniel Pendleton, did not arrive for another twenty minutes.

Hamilton and Burr saluted each other and exchanged formal greetings. The seconds inspected and loaded the pistols. Then the antagonists turned and faced each other.

There was a silence, and then Pendleton shouted, "Fire!" Both men raised their pistols, and two shots rang out.

Burr still stood erect, but Hamilton had fallen to the ground. Burr moved slowly toward the prostrate body, and momentarily a look of regret, even pity, was on his face.

Dr. David Hosack, the attending physician, had rushed to Hamilton's side. He found that the ball had entered on the right and fractured a rib, but it was clear that much greater damage had been done.

Hamilton raised his head and said in a weak voice, "This is a mortal wound, doctor." Then he lapsed into unconsciousness.

Burr still stood looking down at the wounded man, until Van Ness grabbed him by the shoulder. "Aaron, we must get out of here with all possible speed."

As they left for their rowboat, Dr. Hosack and Pendleton picked up the unconscious form of Hamilton and carried it to their boat.

Halfway across the river, Hamilton revived momentarily and said, "My vision is indistinct." He paused and then added, "Pendleton here knows . . . that I did not intend to fire at him."

Hamilton had written this in his diary before the duel, and Pendleton did know it. But nobody had told Burr.

Hamilton was taken to the house of his friend William Bayard, and a message was sent to Hamilton's wife at The Grange. Elizabeth, who had not suspected a thing, was frantic with grief.

Hamilton was dying. The bullet had passed through his liver and diaphragm and lodged in a lumbar vertebra.

The news spread through the city, and friends came to see their dying leader. Dr. Hosack administered sedatives to ease the pain. A Dr. Post was called in, as well as surgeons from a French frigate then in the harbor. The ball could not be removed, and Hamilton's suffering was intense, in spite of the sedatives. He clung to life for thirty-one hours of agonizing pain. At two o'clock the next afternoon he died.

The city went into mourning, and the newspapers outdid one another in expressions of grief. Church bells tolled, and the clergy used the duel as the subject for sermons. Mass meetings were held not only in New York but in Trenton, Philadelphia, Boston and Albany. Angry crowds filled the streets and in a frenzy called Burr a murderer. They threatened to burn down his house. They chanted vicious doggerel:

> *"Oh Burr, oh Burr, what hast thou done?*
> *Thou hast shooted dead great Hamilton!*
> *You hid behind a bunch of thistle,*
> *And shooted him dead with a great hoss pistol!"*

Hamilton's death in the duel had awakened in the people a devotion that had never been shown during his lifetime. It was an irony that those very Federalists who had been covertly working against Hamilton's domination of the party were now the most demonstrative in their sorrow. Politically, Hamilton's martyrdom could serve to unite them.

While the people were calling for an indictment of murder against the Vice-President, there were a few voices raised in his defense. Judge Peters, a staunch friend of Hamilton's, said, "As an old military man, Colonel Burr could not have acted otherwise than he did. I never knew Colonel Burr to speak ill of any man, and he has a right to expect a different treatment from what he is getting."

But the voices of sanity were drowned out by the enraged people, and on July 14, the day of the funeral, the public outcry for revenge reached new heights. All stores and businesses had been closed, and the city was draped in mourning. The ships in the harbor lowered their flags to half-mast. The procession moved slowly through the streets to the muffled beat of drums.

Gouverneur Morris, in his funeral oration, tried to calm the passions of the mob, but failed. The services were read by Bishop Moore at Trinity Church, and it was there that Hamilton was buried, while the ships in the harbor gave a farewell salute with their guns.

Burr had not dared to leave his house since the day of the duel. There was little doubt that an indictment for murder would be brought against him. He stayed in his house for eleven days, seen only by his good friends Van Ness and the Swartwout brothers. They advised him to leave the city before the indictment could be drawn up. And so, on July 21 he left New York with John Swartwout for Perth Amboy.

On the day before Burr left, Pieter arrived with a note for him from Eliza. She expressed anger at the unjustified reaction of the people and wished him well. She told him that if he wished to write her, he could write Pieter Van Zandt at Box 92 in the New York Post Office. She signed the note "With all my love, Eliza."

On August 2, New York State indicted Burr for the murder of Hamilton, and New Jersey followed a few days later. Burr, then in Philadelphia, decided to go south, where the people looked upon him as a hero who had downed his man in a fair duel.

And so, sometime in the middle of August he adopted the pseudonym of R. King and, in the company of Samuel Swartwout and a slave named Peter, secretly embarked on a ship bound for Georgia, where he could stay with his friend Senator Pierce Butler, who lived on an island near Darien.

Eliza received a brief note to this effect, signed R. King, and she cried with joy at the knowledge that Aaron was safe.

She did not know anything further until she read in the newspaper that he had arrived in Washington on November 5 and as Vice-President had quietly taken his seat as presiding officer in the Senate.

He was surprised to receive a warm welcome from the President and the other Republicans, who seemed actually to be courting his favor. He soon found out why.

In March of that year Samuel Chase, a justice of the Supreme Court, had been impeached by the House, mostly because he was out of sympathy with the Republicans and they wanted to be rid of him. President Jefferson himself felt that the Supreme Court was "undemocratic" and wanted to break its spirit.

The trial opened on January 2, 1805, with Burr as the presiding officer. Burr refused to be dominated by the politics of the situation and conducted a fair and impartial trial. One of his colleagues said, "He conducted with the dignity and impartiality of an angel but with the rigor of a devil."

The trial ended on March 1, 1805. To Jefferson's consternation, Justice Chase was acquitted. The next day Burr gave a speech of farewell to the Senate, since his term of office would expire on March 4. He rose quietly from the chair that he had occupied for four years.

It was the greatest speech of his career. The *Washington Federalist* reported: "It is said to be the most dignified, sublime and impressive speech that ever was uttered. The whole Senate were in tears and so unmanned that it was half an hour before they could recover themselves sufficiently to come to order and choose a Vice-President *pro tem*."

The Annals of Congress reported: "He challenged their attention to considerations more momentous than any which regarded merely their personal honor and character—to the preservation of law, liberty and the Constitution. . . . 'This House . . . . is a sanctuary; a citadel of law, of order and of liberty; and it is here . . . in this exalted refuge; here, if anywhere, will resistance be made to the storms of political frenzy and the silent arts of corruption; and if the Constitution be destined ever to perish by the sacrilegious hands of the demagogue or the usurper, which God avert, its expiring agonies will be witnessed on this floor.' "

Then, in touching accents, he took leave of his colleagues, "perhaps forever," with personal respect and prayers, consoling himself and them with the thought that, though separated, "they would still be engaged in the common cause of disseminating principles of freedom and social order."

Then Burr rose quietly from his chair and, his figure trim and erect, left the room. He did not hear the resolution of thanks to him "for the impartiality, integrity and ability with which he had presided in the Senate, and their unqualified approbation of his conduct in that capacity. It passed unanimously."

Burr's swan song had been brilliant, even glorious. But he knew that his career was over. Senator William Plumer of New Hampshire, a devoted follower of Hamilton, wrote at the time: "I saw him after he was no longer in office. And my pity involuntarily was excited . . . he appeared dejected, gloomy, forsaken by all parties. Mr. Jefferson owes the presidency to the conduct of Mr. Burr. Mr. Jefferson is in power, but he will not give Mr. Burr any office. Governor of the Territory of New Orleans, or Attorney General of the United States, either of them would have been acceptable. But these are given to men of far less talents than Burr. Mr. Jefferson appears to afford no countenance to the man who served him so effectually. The reasons for this, 1st, it would be unpopular; 2nd, jealousy of his talents; and 3rd, fear that if Burr had the means he would injure him."

But Aaron Burr had never bowed to defeat, and he did not now. There were still frontiers in his nation, and fame and power beckoned to him from the western boundaries of the continent.

Aaron Burr, age forty-nine, was ready to build all over again from the rubble of his smashed career.

PART IV

Return to Providence

CHAPTER 19

O𝑵 ᴀ ᴅᴀʏ ɪɴ Mᴀʏ three years later, in 1808, Eliza Jumel received a letter from Freelove Ballou, the midwife who had delivered her illegitimate son some thirteen years ago in Providence and who had undertaken the child's care when Eliza left for New York.

Freelove was concerned about the fact that she was receiving no money for the support of the boy from the Wyatt family, and she was also troubled by the illness of Eliza's oldest and dearest friend, Polly Clarke.

Eliza decided to leave immediately for Providence in her coach, newly painted gold and drawn by four black horses. She told Stephen that Captain Carpenter, an old friend of her family, had died and that she wished to attend his funeral. The lie was necessary because Stephen knew nothing about her early life in Providence and certainly not that she had a bastard child there.

The journey was long and tiring, and Eliza was glad when her coach finally drew up before the finest hostelry in Providence, the Golden Ball. She asked that a messenger be sent in search of Polly Clarke.

Two hours later, she descended the grand staircase and passed the liveried footman standing in attendance at the newel post. As he bowed, she inclined her head graciously.

"I beg pardon," said the footman, "but I am not sure you will wish to see the woman who is waiting in the sitting room. She is poorly dressed and—"

"It is the woman I sent for, and I would like the curtain drawn so that we may converse in private."

The footman ushered her into the small sitting room and announced, "Madame Stephen Jumel will see you now, miss."

Polly Clarke stared in disbelief at the resplendently gowned and beautiful woman who stood before her. She opened her mouth to speak but could not.

Eliza laughed gaily. "Polly, whatever be the matter with you? You're still my dearest friend, though my name is no longer Betsy Bowen."

Eliza threw her elegant manners to the winds, pulled Polly to her, and encircled her in a hug that expressed more than just recognition of an old friend.

When Polly drew herself away, her face was wet with tears. "Madame—I—I—"

"Enough of the madame nonsense. To you I shall always be Betsy Bowen, whose bastard child you helped birth."

"But you've become such a lady—and even more beautiful now than you were at nineteen. How did you ever get to be so—so— But it's none of my business."

Eliza laughed. "Why not? It's very simple. Eight years ago I met a Frenchman named Stephen Jumel, a rich wine merchant, and the most eligible bachelor in New York."

"And you got him!"

"Truth to tell, Polly, it wasn't that easy. I was his mistress for four years and then—well, I persuaded him to marry me."

"And now you are happy and rich!"

"Rich," said Eliza pensively, "and almost happy."

Eliza turned toward the little girl who was standing at Polly's side. The child was pretty and about seven years old. She stared at Eliza in wonderment.

Polly said, "That's me daughter, Mary Bownes."

"So you are married then?"

"Men don't marry me, Betsy. David Bownes left me a month after Mary was born."

Polly choked back a sob of shame, and this sent her into a coughing fit that lasted several moments. When she spat into her handkerchief, Eliza noticed that the sputum was bloody.

"Polly! You are sick! Have you seen Dr. Bentham?"

"No, I ain't got the money. Anyway, 'tis nothing. When the warm weather comes—"

"Come, lie down on the sofa for a while, and we can talk." Eliza turned to the child. "And you, Mary Bownes, would you like to sit on my lap?"

Mary nodded and eagerly climbed onto Eliza's lap. Eliza hugged the child to her affectionately and then turned once more to Polly.

"You've lost a lot of weight," she said.

Polly smiled. "My customers find me more attractive now that I'm thin. But let's talk about you. Why would you ever want to come back to Providence?"

"Freelove wrote me that you were sick and in need. The other reason—" She paused and clasped Mary more tightly to her bosom. "The other reason has to do with my son, George Washington Bowen. Freelove wrote that since her husband died six years ago, the boy has had to give up school and go to work."

"Yes," said Polly. "He went to Deacon John Dexter's school until he was eight, and then, after the money stopped coming from the Wyatts for his support, he tried working for two or three farmers. But the boy never did take to farm work, and so he got Danny Woodhull's old job, peddling water crackers for Mr. Weeden, the baker. He's still living with Freelove."

"I would like to take him home with me," said Eliza, cradling little Mary still more closely in her arms.

Eliza's words had a strange effect on Polly. She got up from the couch abruptly and said, "Well, Betsy love, I'd best be goin' now." She reached out to take Mary from Eliza's lap, but Mary was reluctant to leave.

"Mama, I like this pretty lady," she said.

"But you like your own mama better, don't you?" asked Eliza. As the child nodded her head vigorously, Eliza's eyes filled with tears.

When Eliza went over to say goodbye to Polly, she pressed several gold coins into her hand.

"Betsy! I did not come to see you for money!" Polly's voice rose in anger as she said, "Take it back!"

213

"I am not a fool!" said Eliza. "I well know that you didn't come here for money. But you are going to take it because you need it, and I can well afford it."

"But I am your friend, and I cannot—"

Eliza's voice became imperious. "You will take it, and that's an end on it!" It was a voice that Polly scarcely recognized, the voice of a woman who was used to giving commands and having them obeyed. "And furthermore, dear Polly, you will give me your promise that you will go see Dr. Bentham this very afternoon. You must become well again!"

Polly was silent.

"Long ago," Eliza continued, "I told you that I would repay you for your kindness to me, for the loving friendship you gave me when I was sorely in need of it. And the debt is not yet fully paid."

Polly, so overcome by emotion that she could say nothing, fled from the room in tears. Eliza, lost in her memories, stood looking after her. She was suddenly aware that Mary was still there, tugging at her skirt.

"Why did you make my mama cry?" she asked.

Eliza knelt down and placed her hand on the child's cheek. "Because—because she is my oldest friend I gave her some money. Can you understand that?"

Mary pondered this. "I don't know why she should cry about that. We are very poor, and we need money."

"You're a bright little girl, Mary Bownes." On impulse she hugged the child to her and kissed her.

Mary moved toward the door. "Well, goodbye. I must go to Mama now." She paused. "You are a very nice lady, especially because you smell so good."

Eliza smiled, but as soon as the child had left, her eyes again filled with tears.

Later that afternoon, Eliza walked along Benefit Street on her way to see Freelove Ballou. The street had changed very little over the years. As she passed the house that had once belonged to Sam Allen, a wave of nostalgia swept over her. It seemed only yesterday that she had lived in that house where she had passed much of her childhood. The memory of Sam, her foster father, and his tortured passion for her still had the power to move her. But she had learned not to dwell on past unhappiness and to turn her mind to the day before her. And today, she told herself, a girlhood dream was becoming a reality. She was walking down Benefit Street as a rich and renowned woman.

The townspeople who passed looked at her in astonishment. Some of them recognized her. If they smiled at her in a friendly way, she smiled back. If they averted their eyes, she raised her head and walked on proudly.

The Ballou house on Charles Street seemed even more dilapidated than Eliza remembered it. As she walked up the path to the door, she found herself hoping that Freelove would not be drunk in her bedroom the way she had once found her. She knocked loudly on the door, and there was a sound of footsteps inside. The door opened, and Freelove stood before her. She stared at Eliza for a moment, and then her mouth dropped open in a toothless grin, and she stepped forward to embrace her.

"My God, it's Betsy! Damned if you *don't* look like George Washington's daughter!"

Freelove appeared older, but her figure was still enormous, like that of an overstuffed goose, and her movements were even slower than before.

"Well," said Eliza, "aren't you even going to give me a kiss?"

"No. My face is all dirty."

Eliza seized Freelove by the arms and planted a firm kiss on the dust-begrimed face. They hugged each other and then went into the big cluttered downstairs room to the hearth. Freelove set about brewing some tea and stirred up the fire to toast some johnnycake. Meanwhile, she chattered away, enumerating the deaths of people whom Eliza had known.

Bobby Brown, the town sergeant who had been Eliza's ancient enemy, had died of the pox in 1796. A year later, Eliza's sister, Polly, had gotten pregnant by Richard Wyatt and had died of an abortion. Not long after that, news came to Providence that

Eliza's mother and her beloved stepfather, Jonathan Clarke, who had first taught her to love Shakespeare, had died of yellow fever in Williamston, North Carolina.

"North Carolina?" asked Eliza. "But how did they get there?"

"Walked, I suppose. They was always wanderers, you know, always figgerin' their luck would change if they moved someplace else. And then my dear husband, Reuben—the Lord took him to his bosom on April 3, 1802. He died easy and no pain. He was drunk, of course, God bless him."

Eliza's eyes were full of tears, and she blew her nose gently on her perfumed silk handkerchief. At last she said, "I hope they all died easy and no pain—even my bitch of a sister."

After Freelove had served the tea and johnnycake, she sat down wearily in a chair opposite Eliza. "Well, anyway, I still keep a-goin', God knows why. Dr. Bentham told me that if I kept at the rum like I was doin', I'd join Reuben in the graveyard in less than a year. He said my liver was swoll up like a millstone. So I gave it up."

"Entirely?" asked Eliza incredulously.

"Well, I take a little nip now and then when the rheumatism hurts bad."

There was a brief silence, and then Eliza moved forward anxiously in her chair. "I came because I got your letter about Polly and my son, George. I saw Polly Clarke this morning, and she told me that George had to leave school and go to work right after Reuben died. Didn't old man Wyatt hold to our agreement to support the boy?"

"Oh, he would have, if he'd lived, but he died right after my Reuben did."

"But surely Matt would have cared for his son, bastard though he was."

"Maybe. But Matt and the old man quarreled, and the old man cut him off without a cent. Matt's a lawyer in town now. He's had a hard time gettin' ahead, and he couldn't keep up the payments."

Eliza said nothing. She was remembering her love affair with Matt and how her pregnancy had broken it up when old man

Wyatt had threatened to disinherit Matt if they married. It was an irony that he had been disinherited, anyway, and she would have been glad except that it was George who had suffered as a result.

"And George, how is he?" she asked at last.

Freelove did not answer for a moment. "He lives here with me—but he hates you, Betsy. He has never forgiven you for deserting him when he was a baby. Maybe you better leave. Betsy."

"No," said Eliza, "I'll wait."

About half an hour later, George Washington Bowen stood before Eliza, staring at her fine clothes coldly and with an appraising air. A good-looking, stockily built boy of thirteen, he had scarcely acknowledged Freelove's introduction. He had Matt's thoughtful gray eyes and her own red-gold hair, which framed his freckled face.

Eliza was aware of the insolence with which he regarded her, and she was nervous. Her voice, when she spoke, quavered. "George, I would like to take you home with me to New York and right the wrong I have done you."

The boy still stared at her but said nothing.

"I know how you must feel," she said. "But I'd like to explain to you why I left you—"

The boy interrupted her. "There ain't nothin' to explain," he said tonelessly.

"But I'm your mother."

"Freelove is my mother."

She played what she hoped would be her trump card. "I am rich now, George. I can offer you advantages, education, a lovely home—" She paused, and then, drawing herself up, she added, "I am now Madame Stephen Jumel."

A corner of George's mouth turned up in Matt's one-sided smile. "You're nothin' but a stinkin' whore! And I don't want to see you again—ever!" He cleared his throat and spat at her feet. Then he turned and ran out of the house.

Eliza sat down quietly in her chair.

Freelove, her face streaming with tears, went over to her. "Oh, Betsy, my poor darlin', I knew this would happen." She put her arms around Eliza in an effort to console her, as she had done so many times before.

Eliza did not cry. At first she was too stunned even to speak, but when she did, her voice was steady and calm. "It is only what I deserve," she said. "The only mother's love he has known came from you, dear Freelove. The boy spoke truly. You are his mother. I'm leaving now." Eliza got up and moved toward the door.

Freelove followed her, a pleading look on her face. "But, Betsy, where are you going?"

"To see Matt. If he cannot afford to support our child, then I will. It's the least I can do. Where does Matt live?"

"It's a small house on Powder House Lane, just where it bends to go into Old Gaol Lane."

Eliza smiled at the mention of the old gaol. It was where Margaret Fairchild had kept a brothel, in which Eliza's mother was one of the girls. When it had been burned down by the angry populace, Eliza had been separated from her mother and adopted by Sam and Lydia Allen.

Eliza, turning again to Freelove, said, "It doesn't sound like a very fancy part of town."

"Well, it's not Benefit Street. But like I told you, Matt's been having a hard time. They say he's too fond of the bottle, but I could hardly blame him. That wife of his is a shrew. The house is painted white." Freelove grinned. "For purity, no doubt."

Eliza paused at the door. "I want you to listen to me carefully now, Freelove. There will be a monthly allowance for you and George. And Polly Clarke—she's not well. Make sure that she sees the doctor, and if she is ever in need, write to me. The address is on Whitehall Street in New York City."

Freelove threw her arms around Eliza. "God bless you, my girl. Even if you're not George Washington's bastard daughter—and maybe you are—you've got a noble and generous heart. And George—"

"You are not to scold him, Freelove. And I want you to promise me that you will not tell him that I am helping him and you."

"I promise," said Freelove tearfully. Eliza gently disentangled herself from Freelove's embrace. She said goodbye and then started up the path to the street.

As she turned her steps once again toward Benefit Street, she took a deep breath and walked quickly, in a determined fashion.

Eliza turned off Benefit Street and into Powder House Lane. When she knocked on the door of Matt Wyatt's house, a servant girl appeared. She looked at Eliza in awe. Then she curtsied and said, "Oh, yes, ma'am."

"Will you kindly tell Mr. Wyatt that Madame Stephen Jumel is here to see him on urgent business."

Eliza entered the small hall, while the girl disappeared upstairs. From somewhere in the rear of the house there came the sound of a baby's wailing.

Matt descended the stairs slowly, a puzzled frown on his face. As he reached the entrance hall, Eliza rose to greet him. He stared at her, and it was a few seconds before he recognized her.

"Betsy! What are you doing here? The girl said a fine lady—a Madame Somebody-or-other—"

"I am Madame Stephen Jumel now, Matt."

Matt was still recovering from the shock of seeing her after fourteen years, and nervously he said, "Won't you please come into the sitting room so that we can talk?"

Eliza sat down in the chair he offered her. She looked at him curiously. For a man of thirty-seven he was still very attractive and easily recognizable as the man she had once loved, although he had put on some weight, his hair was thinning, and his boyish look had all but disappeared except when he smiled. His face was tired and careworn, but at the moment it wore an expression of animation.

Eliza found herself strangely moved by the sight of the first man she had ever loved—and loved deeply. She remembered the ecstasy of their love-making, and then the tragic outcome of their

219

affair, when she had become pregnant and he had abandoned her because of his father's threat to disinherit him. But most vividly, she remembered her anger and her hatred of him. Rather than accepting his offered charity, she had taken to the streets as a prostitute. There was a bitterness there that would never leave her.

Now, Matt was saying, "You were always beautiful, Betsy. But now, you are—you are more beautiful than ever."

"Thank you, Matt," she said. She looked about the room, which was comfortably but not expensively furnished. "I was sorry to learn that things hadn't been going well for you."

"Not as well as I had hoped. I quarreled with my father two years before he died. I was a fool. It began with an argument about nothing, really. But I was hotheaded the way I always have been, and said some daft and thoughtless things. And then I was too proud to apologize."

"And so," said Eliza, "you ended up by being disinherited." She paused for emphasis and added, "*Anyway*."

"Yes." He was silent. There was a thoughtful look on his face. "As things turned out, I could have married you as I wanted to—"

"But you didn't want to *enough*," said Eliza. The tone of her voice was not critical, merely factual.

"I suppose so. But I wish—well, I wish I had."

"Your marriage is not a happy one?"

"I am married to a woman who thinks of nothing but her house, her clothes, and her children. She is a nagger and a shrew."

Eliza smiled faintly. "Well, at least she is a good mother."

Matt shrugged his shoulders. "Yes. But to me—well, she is not a loving, affectionate woman, as you once were." He leaned forward in his chair, and his gray eyes looked straight into hers. "I am still a passionate man, Betsy."

There was no mistaking the look in his eyes. It stirred unexpected and unwanted memories of his once beautiful young body and his gentleness as a lover.

She looked away quickly. "I came here, Matt, to talk about our son, George."

The words had their intended dampening effect on him. He sat back in his chair and said, "Yes, I expected that you had. My father left no provision for the boy in his will, and my brothers flatly refused to continue payments for his support."

"And you?" asked Eliza.

"I was finding it difficult to support myself and my family. I had only just begun to practice law. Times were hard, and my wife doesn't know about our child."

"And I suppose it is she," said Eliza with a touch of mockery in her voice, "who manages the finances."

"Well, as a matter of fact, she does. And if she doesn't get her way, she flies into a tantrum."

Eliza smiled. "Somehow, Matt, I'd never have thought of you as a henpecked husband." She paused, and her voice took on a businesslike tone. "But now I gather that your income is much better. Will you be able to take over the responsibility for the boy?"

Matt was silent. He stared at the floor in embarrassment. "It would be extremely difficult. I believe the boy is working now for Mr. Weeden, the baker. After all, he is thirteen."

"And his education?" asked Eliza.

"I am afraid I cannot help there, either. It's not just the money. It's the gossip—"

The years, Eliza thought to herself, had not changed him. He was still fearful of what the town might think of him, still conventional—still, in effect, a coward, as she had discovered when their affair broke up.

Eliza got up quickly and faced him. "Well, have no fear, Matt. I am very well-to-do now, and I will take over the whole responsibility." She moved toward the door, and Matt followed her.

"I am sorry, Betsy. I am truly sorry."

"Never mind," she said softly. "It is not the first time that you've disappointed me, Matt."

He reached out to her, almost in desperation. "Betsy, please don't go. Wait a moment. I still love you—I—"

He moved to her quickly, seized her in his arms and kissed her passionately. Eliza, against her will, found herself responding to

221

his kiss. The memory of him as a lover was not dead, and she knew that she wanted him. With an effort, she pulled herself abruptly away.

"Betsy," he said, "you cannot leave like this. Say that you will see me again."

"I'm leaving for New York tomorrow in my coach."

"We can at least have dinner together tonight." His voice was pleading.

As Eliza reached the door, she turned toward him. "Very well, Matt. I am stopping at the Golden Ball. Meet me there at nine."

As he opened the door for her to leave, he seized her hand and kissed it. "Oh, Betsy, thank God you've come back! This is a stroke of good fortune that I don't deserve!"

"No," said Eliza slowly, "you don't."

As she walked down the steps to the street, Matt stood in the doorway, his eyes watching every movement of her graceful body. When she reached the gate, she turned, waved, and gave him a dazzling smile.

That night, at ten minutes before nine, Matt went to the Golden Ball. He was dressed in his finest clothes—a plum-colored waistcoat and a shirt with ruffles down the front. His hair was neatly combed and shone with imported French pomade.

He approached the liveried head footman confidently, and there was a note of condescension in his voice. "I should like to see Madame Jumel," he said.

"Madame Jumel is not here," said the footman.

"But of course she is here. She is stopping here while in Providence."

"Yes, sir. But she left in her coach at six o'clock to return to New York."

Matt stared at the footman in disbelief. At last he stammered, "But she was going to have dinner with me. Perhaps she left a note?"

"No, sir. Nothing. She just went. She seemed to be in a great hurry."

Matt went through the doorway to the street. He suddenly

remembered her words of that afternoon, when he had said that this was a stroke of good fortune that he did not deserve. "No, you don't," she had said. And she had meant it.

He laughed ironically and said softly, "The bitch!" After all these years, she had had her revenge.

He wanted to get drunk, and quickly. He comforted himself with the thought that there would be women at the Bulldog Tavern, available women to ease the consuming disappointment that filled him.

Yes, there would always be available women. But none of them would be Betsy, the only woman he had ever loved.

CHAPTER 20

Two years later, in the spring of 1810, Eliza received a letter from Freelove Ballou. Eliza's friend Polly Clarke had died of consumption, and Polly's daughter, Mary Bownes, was being cared for by Freelove, who could not really afford to support the child. She wondered whether Eliza, who had been such a close friend of Polly's, might wish to adopt Mary, especially since she had no children except George, who did not want her.

Eliza was upset by the news. Of all the women she had known, it was Polly whom she had loved most, and the thought of little Mary without a mother upset her.

She went to Stephen and told him the news. She said she would like to adopt Mary but did not know how he would feel about it.

Stephen was surprised. "But I did not know you wanted a child, Eliza."

"As you know, I am barren," she said, "but I am not without maternal feelings. Having a child about the house would make me happy."

Stephen scratched his head. "You always have surprises for me, *ma chère*."

"There are many things that you don't know about me."

Supposing she were to tell him about her bastard child, or how she and Polly had worked as prostitutes in Sally Marshall's brothel? No, that was part of her past he must never know.

"It might be nice to have a child here. What's her name and how old is she?"

"Her name is Mary Bownes and she is eight or nine years old."

"Good. Not a *bébé*. Somehow, I could not imagine you changing diapers, Eliza."

Eliza smiled, remembering that she had changed George's diapers, much as she had hated it. "Very well, then, Stephen. I shall go to Providence and fetch her."

"In your coach?"

"No, by packet. The journey by coach is too long and tiring for a little girl."

And so, on the next sailing of Captain Curry's *Roger Williams*, Eliza was aboard. Captain Bill, who had put on weight and whose hair was completely white now, was, of course, delighted to see her.

That night he invited her to his cabin to have some rum, and she went.

"You are very rich now," Bill said. "Are you happy?"

"I guess so," said Eliza. "But I had only one real love, you know."

"Aaron Burr?"

She nodded. "I haven't heard from him in a long time now. I am told that after he was acquitted of the treason charges, he went to Europe, using an assumed name."

There was a silence, and then Bill said, "And why are you going to Providence?"

"Polly Clarke, my dearest friend, died a little while ago. I am going to adopt her daughter, Mary."

Bill was surprised. "But why?"

"Partly to pay off a debt that I feel I owe Polly, and partly because—well, because I am barren and can't have any children."

"But you already have your son."

"Yes. But he hates me. Two years ago, when I saw him, he called me a dirty whore and spit in my face. After all, I deserted him, and he has never forgotten it."

Bill got up and went over to Eliza. He put an arm around her. "My poor Eliza," he said affectionately. Then he turned up her head to his and kissed her.

"How old are you now, Eliza?"

"Thirty-four."

"That's hard to believe. You are still so very beautiful."

She looked at him and said bluntly, "Do you still want me, Bill?"

"Of course, I do. But I don't think I can perform any more."

She laughed. "That's what you said the first time you met me."

"Yes. But now I am sixty-eight—too old—"

"We'll see about that," said Eliza.

She opened her bodice so that her breasts were revealed. Then she reached over and unbuttoned his trousers.

Bill laughed. "This is the first time I was ever raped."

"You are so lacking in confidence, Bill, rape is necessary."

She was right. In spite of his sixty-eight years, his response was immediate. After they had made love, she lay back on his bunk completely naked and smiled at him.

"You see?" she said.

"Once again you have given me back my manhood, just like the first time."

"But then you proved your manhood three times, remember?"

"Yes, but I was sixteen years younger then!"

"You are still younger than you think," she said.

"Tell me, Eliza, why are you so good to me?"

"First, because I have always liked you. And second, I have not forgotten how you helped me when I first came to New York."

After they both had another swig of rum, she asked him whether he would like to make love again. "You had better, Bill, because on the return trip, the child will be with me."

With that as a challenge he did manage to make love a second time. He tried for a third time but failed. He had to admit that sixteen years had made a difference. But he was content. After all, he had proved his manhood twice and was very proud of it.

As soon as Eliza arrived in Providence, she took rooms at the Golden Ball and then went immediately to Freelove's house on Charles Street.

Mary was sitting in the dilapidated wing chair that Eliza herself had sat in when she was a little girl. As soon as Freelove's effusive greetings were over, Eliza went over to the child and knelt down.

"Do you remember me, Mary?"

Mary looked at her gravely. "Yes, you are the lady who smells so good. You were a good friend to my mama, who went to Heaven and left me alone."

Tears came to Eliza's eyes as she answered, "I know, dear Mary. Would you like a new mama?"

"Yes. But there is no one except maybe Freelove."

"Would you like me to be your new mama and to come back to New York with me?"

Mary looked at her in surprise. "You? But you don't know me, and I don't think I'd like to go to New York."

Mary surveyed Eliza studiously. Her eyes, warm and brown like her mother's, seemed large and lustrous in contrast to the fairness of her complexion. But there was a serious and thoughtful look in their depths, quite different from Polly's eyes, which had always seemed to be laughing.

A pleading note entered Eliza's voice as she said, "Will you think about it, Mary? I would love to have you as my daughter."

"Yes, I will think about it," said Mary quietly.

Eliza was delighted by the child and could not resist picking her up in her arms and kissing her.

Mary responded, but not enthusiastically. All she said was "You still smell good."

Eliza left her sitting there in the chair and joined Freelove, who could hardly wait to tell Eliza all the latest town gossip. But first, she said, "It is good of you to want to take the child, Betsy." Then she added in a whisper, "I think she will go. She likes you."

She then launched into a lengthy recital of the goings on about town, forgetting that Betsy had not even known some of the people she was talking about. But then she told Eliza the latest news about Matt Wyatt. His wife had kicked him out of the house because of his drinking and his many infidelities. The end had come when he infected her with the clap, which he had contracted from one of the loose women he associated with. He was now living in a room that Nate Mason had rented him in the

Bulldog Tavern, but he barely had enough money for that because his law practice had dwindled so seriously.

Eliza asked Freelove about George.

"Oh, he's doing right well, Betsy. He's not peddling water crackers anymore. Mr. Weeden has taken him into the bakery as a helper. I wouldn't be surprised if he became a baker himself. He loves the work."

"And his education?"

"He didn't want any more when I offered him the chance to go back to school. He said he hated books and studying."

Eliza sighed. "Well, at least he's happy."

In the afternoon, after a light lunch, she went over to the wing chair where Mary was sleeping. She woke her gently and kissed her. The child spontaneously put her arms around Eliza's neck.

"I think you would be a good mama to me," she said, "but not as nice as my real mama."

Eliza told her about New York and the lovely house she lived in, where Mary would have her very own room. She promised to buy her lots of pretty clothes to make her happy.

At last Mary said, "I thought it over, and I decided to go with you." Then she looked Eliza directly in the eyes and said, "Will you love me?"

Eliza's arms went around Mary and she hugged her. "But I already love you, dear Mary."

That night at the Golden Ball Eliza felt so elated that she ordered a bottle of champagne. She gave Mary a few sips of it after dinner, and within a few moments, the child had curled up on the bed and gone to sleep.

The news that Eliza was back in Providence had spread through the town, and around nine o'clock she was accorded a reception, but not of a pleasant kind. A group of boys in their early teens had gathered in the street below her balcony.

"Betsy Bowen, Betsy Bowen!" they chanted in unison. "Come out and give us some fun!"

Eliza tried to ignore them, but finally she could stand it no longer. She had almost finished the bottle of champagne and was by this time tipsy.

She went to the French doors that gave onto the balcony and thrust them open with a dramatic flourish. "Go away and stop your filthy language!" she screamed at them.

Her angry reaction was exactly what they wanted, and they cheered and booed her appearance. Then they began pelting her with rotten eggs and fruit.

Eliza went into a rage. "You rotten no-good bastids!" she shouted. "Go home before I call the constable!"

"Betsy Bowen, Betsy Bowen!" they continued to chant. "Got money from every man in Providence."

Eliza drew herself up a bit unsteadily because of the champagne and said, "I am not Betsy Bowen. I am Madame Stephen Jumel, a great and rich lady in New York!"

"And still a whore, I'll be bound!" one boy yelled.

"I have been presented at the French court. I have lived in Paris and been friends with the nobility!"

This statement was greeted by hisses and boos and a new barrage of stinking missiles.

A footman from the hotel had come out to quiet the disturbance, but the boys clouted him until he fell to the ground.

Eliza was desperate, and then, as though by magic, the figure of Matt Wyatt appeared on the scene. He carried a gun and pointed it threateningly at the young hoodlums.

"Get out of here and leave this lady alone, unless you want an arse full of buckshot!" he shouted.

The sight of the gun had its intended effect, and one by one the boys, still muttering to themselves, disbanded.

Matt stood there in the street looking up toward Eliza. She was shocked by his appearance. His face was unshaven and bloated, and he was so drunk that he swayed.

In a slurred voice, he said, "I was at the Bulldog Tavern, and somebody told me you were having trouble, so I came."

In a soft voice, Eliza said, "Oh, Matt, how can I ever thank you?"

"By inviting me up to your room," he said.

Eliza's voice was firm. "I can't do that. Polly Clarke's little girl is with me. I'm adopting her."

"I'll be quiet," he said.

Eliza's voice was imperious. "You will not come up at all, and that's final! You're drunk and dirty!"

He stared at her, as though he did not understand her words.

She leaned over the railing of the balcony, and in a soft and pleading voice, she said, "Matt, just look at yourself. You're turning into a drunkard and a good-for-nothing. Why can't you be the man you once were?"

He was silent, as the meaning of her words finally penetrated his befuddled mind. At last he looked up. "Because it's too late." Then he suddenly lurched on his way down the street. He turned once to look back at her.

"Goodbye, my beloved Betsy. I won't bother you again. I'm lost." Then he disappeared into the shadows.

Eliza returned to her room and closed the doors to the balcony. She was glad to see that Mary had slept through the commotion.

She had trouble calming herself and took a stiff swig from the bottle of brandy she had brought with her. Then she began to cry. The sight of Matt had upset her, and then she thought, "But he wouldn't have cared if he had given me the clap too." He was, as he had said, lost and past caring about anything except liquor.

But the group of boys and their jeers had been even more upsetting. In the eyes of Providence, she was still a whore, no matter how rich she might become or how famous. And she always would be. She resolved never to set foot in the town again, the town that she had always hated. There was no need to expose herself to further humiliation and shame.

She dried her tears and went over to the bed, where Mary still slept. As she got beneath the coverlet, she drew the child close to her. In spite of the unhappy ending of the evening, she still had Mary. And at the moment, that was the most important thing in the world.

CHAPTER 21

MARY'S REACTIONS to the new and beautiful world she had entered in New York were very like Eliza's own when, as a child, she had been adopted by Sam Allen and his wife. Regular meal hours were miracles that happened three times a day. The cleanliness of everything in the house, including herself, was something to be marveled at. And like Eliza, she loved taking a bath.

But she did not sing bawdy songs, because she knew none. Polly had been able to protect her from association with her sailor friends because she had worked out of Sally Marshall's brothel. Mary did not even know where babies came from, let alone the reasons for their coming. Also, unlike young Betsy, she did not use dirty words.

But she did not like having a room of her own. She insisted on sleeping with Eliza, whom she had begun to call "Mama." She felt alone and frightened in a room all by herself.

When she was introduced to Stephen, she was awed by his size and would not come to him at first.

"Are you a giant?" she asked.

Stephen smiled at her and got down on his knees. "Yes," he said, "but see how I can make myself small?"

Mary was still distrustful of him. "But you are a giant anyway."

"Maybe," said Stephen, "but I am a good giant, not a bad one. I love little girls."

Finally, Mary went over to him when he held out his hand

toward her. She touched his hand timidly and then ran back to Eliza.

Stephen got up and said to Eliza, "She is an enchanting child and very beautiful."

But it was still a while before Mary felt comfortable with him. With Pieter, it was a different story. She took to the young man at once and let him put his arms about her.

"What's your name?" she asked.

"Pieter."

"My name is Mary." She stroked his blond hair. "You have pretty hair." After a pause, she asked, "Will you play games with me, Pieter?"

When he nodded, she kissed him on the cheek before she went back to Eliza. "I like this man," she said seriously.

The feeling was plainly mutual. Pieter adored the child and spent time devising new games to play with her.

The sight of them playing together did not make Eliza jealous. It made her sad. Pieter was thirty-one years old now, old enough to be married and have children of his own. She knew that he would have married if it had not been for his unwavering love for her.

And so Mary became part of the Jumel household. She loved the pretty frocks that Eliza bought for her, and finally reached a point of assurance where she enjoyed sitting on Stephen's lap and calling him "Papa." The surprising thing was that she did not become spoiled. She never insisted on having her own way and never threw temper tantrums.

It was Eliza who was her goddess and the center of her life. Everything she did was in some way designed to hold Eliza's affection, and Eliza enjoyed being adored.

Selfishly, Eliza had other thoughts. It was possible that the acquisition of a child might improve her reputation and help her to be accepted by New York society.

But that didn't happen. The gossip was that the child was illegitimate, a product of one of her former love affairs. The fact that Eliza filed papers for legal adoption did not bring an end to the gossip.

Clearly, Eliza's battle was not won. She would have to do something more to establish herself as a reputable woman.

On a very hot day that summer Eliza persuaded Stephen to take the day off so that they could ride to the north, where the weather was cooler. They went out the Boston Post Road for several miles until they reached Washington Heights. As they rounded the corner at the Harlem River and the horses began to struggle on the uphill road, Eliza saw a majestic house that rose from the highest point on Manhattan Island.

"Stephen, look at that beautiful big house!" she said.

"It's the old Morris mansion," said Stephen. "Roger Morris built it just before the Revolution for his bride. It was taken over by the American troops, and Washington made it his head-quarters."

"George Washington? Stop the coach, Stephen. I want to look at it."

They got out of the coach and walked up the hill toward the house. The lawn was unweeded, and the shrubbery was over-grown and untended. When Eliza reached the verandah, she looked south to the city of New York, and in the summer haze she could even see Brooklyn and Staten Island. To the west were the Hudson River and the steep Palisades of New Jersey.

"The house looks deserted," said Eliza. "I want to go inside."

Stephen pounded on the front door, but it was several moments before a man of middle age came out of the basement.

"Are you the caretaker?" asked Eliza.

"I am the owner. Me name is Leonard Parkinson."

"I am Madame Jumel, and this is my husband, Monsieur Stephen Jumel. We would like to look at the house. We might like to buy it."

At the mention of the name and the possibility of a sale, Mr. Parkinson's ears pricked up. He had long ago given up the idea that anyone would take the house off his hands.

While Mr. Parkinson fumbled among his keys, Eliza looked in admiration at the entrance, with its portico supported by four columns, and under the portico a second-story railed balcony.

When Mr. Parkinson finally found the key that opened the large front door, they entered. In spite of the poor state or repair of the house, Eliza was impressed and drew in her breath sharply. The entrance hall was large and spacious and there was a beautiful staircase, which had been painted white. Eliza flaked off some of the paint with her fingernail. Underneath, it was solid mahogany.

To the right of the hall there was a large room, which Mr. Parkinson said was the dining room, with a pantry, closets and an alcove adjoining. The room on the left was the drawing room.

As they went through the fifteen rooms of the house, Mr. Parkinson prattled on about its history. When they went through a passage at the rear of the main hallway, they found themselves in a large octagonal room with six sash windows and a fireplace with a marble chimney piece.

In a reverential tone Mr. Parkinson announced, "This is the room where Washington had his headquarters until the British captured the city."

Eliza had already made up her mind that the house would be hers, but she continued on the tour of the house, looking at the seven bedrooms on the second floor and the three guest rooms on the third floor.

Last, they inspected the huge kitchen with its enormous hearth, and adjoining it, a serving pantry, a dairy room, a laundry room, and sleeping apartments for servants. All of these rooms were below the ground level.

Stephen wanted to know how many acres went with the house.

Mr. Parkinson said, "Thirty-six acres, mostly cleared, and there is a fine orchard of peach trees and quince. The price for the house and grounds is twelve thousand dollars."

"That's too much," said Eliza.

"But it is well known that Monsieur Jumel is a wealthy man."

"Perhaps so. But that doesn't mean that you can rob us. The house is in a very poor state of repair. If you don't come down on your price, there will be no purchase." Eliza's voice was firm.

Mr. Parkinson reflected a moment. "We'll make it ten thousand dollars then, madame."

The price was agreed upon. In fact, later on Stephen bought an additional thirty-nine acres for nine thousand dollars. As Stephen started moving back to their coach, Eliza stood for a moment on the verandah and looked down to the south at the city of New York. It was a great satisfaction to her that she would be above all the first families in town, geographically, if not socially. And furthermore, it seemed only right that she should own the house where George Washington had lived, even briefly. She still believed that she was his bastard daughter, and when he died in 1799, she had gone into deep mourning.

Eliza lost no time in starting the work of reconditioning. She had decided to do nothing to modernize the house. She loved its original lines and its woodwork. Workmen removed layers of paint so that the original woods were brought to life again. She even took samples of the original wallpaper in every room and sent these to Paris to be duplicated exactly—at a cost of fifteen dollars a roll.

Stephen was horrified at the expenses and protested feebly.

Eliza stood her ground. "This will be our mansion, Stephen, and I intend to make it the showplace of New York, no matter what the cost. It will be our permanent home."

The only change in construction that Eliza authorized was a beautiful large fanlight of amber and clear glass over the front door, and also two side lights, but these did not violate the Colonial charm that she sought to preserve.

In furnishing the interior she spent a great deal of money. There were Turkey carpets in most of the rooms. She moved some of the better Federalist furnishings from Whitehall Street and installed cut-glass chandeliers in both the drawing room and dining room.

She had the drawing room painted a pale green and installed draperies of a darker green. Over the marble mantelpiece she hung a painting of an American landscape done by Groombridge in 1793. There was also, in addition to a tea table and chairs, a piano made in America by Benjamin Crehore in 1789. The dining room was equally splendid, with brilliant gold draperies and an eighteenth-century mahogany table with eight chairs.

Eliza took special care in furnishing the octagonal room that she called the George Washington Room, where he had planned some of the early campaigns of the Revolution before the British captured New York. Over the fireplace were crossed swords and beneath them a bronze American eagle, wings outspread in anger. An eighteenth-century grandfather's clock stood at one side of the room and an eighteenth-century flat-topped desk at the other. There was also a table whose top became a drawing board when it was raised. It was on this board that Washington had planned the Battle of Harlem Heights.

In the autumn, the road leading down to the Boston Post Road was rolled, the lawns were reseeded, and the boxwood hedges were trimmed and new shrubbery was added.

By the spring of 1811, the restoration was complete, and Eliza surveyed her new home with pride. Even Stephen was impressed, and he marveled at Eliza's excellent taste in furnishings. But every time he thought of the cost, he heaved a sigh.

Eliza had outdone herself, and now the real test would come. She would give a gigantic reception and invite all the first families to come.

The date was set for an evening in early July, and more than a hundred embossed invitations in French were sent out three weeks in advance. The restoration of the house had excited a great deal of curiosity in the city, and often coaches would stop on the Boston Post Road and people would crane their necks to get a look at what was going on.

On the night of the reception, which began at dusk, there was an orchestra in the entrance hall, and the floor of the Washington Room had been polished with beeswax to a mirrorlike sheen.

Dinner was served continuously from long linen-covered tables that had been set up on the lawn. There were roasts of beef and a suckling pig with an apple in its mouth and cranberries for eyes. There were pheasants and partridges and even venison and a barrel of oysters. All varieties of Stephen's best wines were there, and apparently limitless bottles of champagne packed in ice. Imported French cheeses took up a whole table, and there were fruit-flavored ices for dessert.

236

Eliza wore an elaborate Paris gown of green silk, and her most valued jewels were on display: ruby earrings and a necklace of pearls and diamonds set in gold. She wore only two rings: her large, handsome gold wedding ring on her left hand and a small but very beautiful turquoise ring on her right hand.

She was in such a state of excitement that her face was flushed so becomingly that she needed no rouge. It was clear to her that the reception was a great success, and all of the city's first families were there. The last of the guests did not leave until it was almost dawn.

The next day there were glowing descriptions of the party in all the newspapers, and Eliza was in a state of great exhilaration. At last, she had been accepted.

But then, as the summer wore on and fall came, the only invitations to parties and balls came from some of the well-to-do French refugees in the city. There was not a single invitation from any of the first families. Mansion or no mansion, she was still an outcast.

She had been an outcast for as long as she could remember. Even as a child, she had been the little girl whom respectable children did not play with. The only children she had met were those of the Wyatt family, whom Sam took her to visit on special occasions like Thanksgiving. But even then, she had not felt like one of them. Their clothes were prettier than hers, even those of her sister, whom the Wyatts had adopted after the burning of the old gaol and the banishment of her mother from the town of Providence. Her only friend then had been Sam Allen, and even that friendship had been suspect because of his tortured passion for her while she was still a child.

Was it any wonder that she became the mistress of Sam after his wife's death, and then of Jacques de la Croix? Her affair with Matt Wyatt had been broken not by her pregnancy, but by his family's refusal to let Matt marry her, because she wasn't "the right kind." So she had turned to prostitution in order to support herself.

She had thought that when she came to New York, leaving her past behind her, she could marry and become rich and then she

237

would be "the right kind," accepted by society. But again, she had acquired a new reputation as a "tainted woman," because she had been the mistress of Jacques, then of Hamilton, Burr and finally of Stephen.

And so now she was rich, respectably married, and lived in a beautiful house on Washington Heights. Nothing had made any difference. She was still a veritable pariah, except in France, where at least her past had not followed her. But a bitter rage filled her that she could not be accepted in her own country, which she loved. But she would not, could not, admit failure.

And when war was declared with England on June 18, 1812, her angry feelings found an outlet. She wished that she were a man so that she could be a soldier and fight the detested British. Then she could distinguish herself in battle, and her morals would be of no account; in fact, they might even make her more acceptable than ever, as a devil with the ladies.

But while Eliza dreamed of becoming a soldier, a private battle was brewing close to home, not with the British, but with her husband.

CHAPTER 22

AFTER DINNER on a chilly October evening, Eliza asked Stephen
to get her a wool shawl from her bedroom. When he lighted a
candle in the room in search of the shawl, he noticed an opened
letter on Eliza's bedside table, a letter from Freelove Ballou that
she had forgotten to conceal. Stephen's curiosity was aroused,
and he read it. The letter mentioned how well Eliza's son, George,
was doing. He had begun to learn weaving.

Stephen forgot all about the shawl and stormed down the stairs
with the letter in his hand. He confronted Eliza and shouted,
"Who is Freelove Ballou?"

Eliza realized that she had forgotten to hide the letter. She
quickly decided that her only course of action was to make a
complete confession and ask Stephen for forgiveness.

"Freelove is an old friend of mine in Providence. She is a
midwife."

Stephen was surprised by the calmness of her voice. "The
midwife who no doubt delivered you of a son!"

"Yes. He was a bastard, the result of an unhappy love affair
with a rich man in Providence. He refused to marry me because
of my humble birth."

"But you told me that your family was prominent in Providence society!"

"It was a lie," she said, still calm and unflurried.

"And how many other lies have you told me, I wonder! And
you abandoned this child?"

"At the time he was born I hated his father for refusing to

239

marry me, and I—I hated the child too. I left for New York when he was less than two months old."

Stephen sat down in a chair. His face was red and sweat poured from his forehead. Then a great rage filled him.

"What kind of woman are you, Eliza—a woman who abandons her child at the age of two months. You must be a monster, a woman completely without love or feeling. I cannot continue to live with you as your husband. I despise you utterly!"

"Then you will have to despise me, and I'll have to leave." She rose from her chair. She herself was now becoming annoyed by what she considered an unchivalrous attitude on Stephen's part.

"I did not leave without making an arrangement with the father's family for George's care! And when I went back to Providence four years ago, I planned to bring him here and tell you about him."

"And why didn't you?"

"The boy hates me and looks upon Freelove as his mother." She decided that it was time for tears, and she began to cry. "He called me a stinking whore and spit in my face."

Stephen made no attempt to console her. "The boy showed excellent judgment!"

Eliza continued to sob. "When I found out that the boy's father was no longer contributing to his support, I arranged to take care of him by sending Freelove money every month. I made her promise not to tell him."

Stephen looked at her incredulously. "You mean you have been supporting your bastard son on my money?"

She stopped crying abruptly and said, "On *our* money!"

"What do you mean?"

"You may have forgotten, dear Stephen, that early this year you deeded half your holdings to me. The papers are perfectly legal."

Stephen felt defeated and sank back in his chair with a look of despair on his face. Then a glint of suspicion came into his eyes. "And I suppose you tricked me into marrying you eight years ago! I always thought that your recovery from that illness was a little too miraculous to be believed."

240

She was silent.

"Well, did you? Did you?" he continued.

She looked him directly in the eyes and said, "Certainly, I did. How else would I have been able to become your wife?"

"Oh, my God! How evil you are! Our marriage is finished! Take your holdings and leave this house!"

"And what will become of Mary?"

"I adopted her legally. She will stay here, away from you!"

"Very well, I'll leave you—once and for all!" She ran upstairs, but at the landing, she paused, "Say goodbye to Mary for me."

"And I suppose she is another one of your bastard children!"

"No, she is the daughter of my best friend in Providence, who is now dead. Since I wanted a child and my own would not have me, I adopted Mary. Farewell, my dear Stephen. I have always loved you. Remember that."

There was a note of finality in her voice that alarmed him.

"Eliza! What are you going to do?"

"I am going to kill myself—to pay for my sins."

She continued up the stairs. He did not believe that she would kill herself until he remembered that she kept a small pearl-handled pistol in her bedside table. Then he got up and hurried toward the stairs.

But he was too late. A shot rang out. He ran into her bedroom and found her lying on the bed in a pool of blood.

She was conscious and raised the pistol toward him. "Let me die in peace! If you come one step closer, I will kill you too!"

"Eliza, you have gone mad! Drop that pistol!"

Her hand dropped, as she lost consciousness and fell back onto the bed. Stephen called for Pieter and sent him to fetch the doctor. Meanwhile, he mopped up the blood with a towel and tried to find the location of the wound. It was not, he thanked God, anywhere near her head. He stripped off her skirt and bodice and finally located the wound on her upper left arm. It was only a flesh wound, but it was bleeding copiously. He used a towel to make a tourniquet at the shoulder.

When Dr. Romayne arrived, Eliza had regained consciousness and smiled weakly at Stephen. "Am I going to die?" she asked.

241

"No, *ma chère*. It is only a flesh wound."

Dr. Romayne confirmed Stephen's diagnosis and then washed the wound. After dousing it with gin, which made Eliza scream with pain, he instructed her to hold her arm above her head until the bleeding stopped. Then he dressed the wound and put the arm in a sling.

Dr. Romayne took Stephen aside. "How did this happen, Monsieur Jumel?"

Stephen blushed. "We—we had a quarrel and she threatened to kill herself. I didn't believe she would until I heard the shot."

"You may thank God that her aim is poor," said Dr. Romayne. Then, in a confidential whisper, he added, "Monsieur, we know that she is a woman with strong feelings. I would not leave any kind of firearms where she can get to them. She might try again —and succeed. If the bleeding hasn't stopped in an hour or so, you had better call me."

Stephen said, "I know how to make a tourniquet, Doctor."

"Good. But remember that a tourniquet must be loosened frequently. The circulation must not be cut off from the arm entirely. I will return tomorrow to see how she is. Give her only light foods and keep her in bed."

After the doctor had left, Stephen returned to Eliza's bedroom. She was lying back on the pillows and seemed to be sleeping. The arm, in its sling, was still bleeding, he judged, but not copiously.

Eliza opened her eyes, and, looking at Stephen, she began to cry softly. He went over to her and held her right hand between his own.

Sobbing, she said, "Oh, Stephen, will you ever forgive me?"

Tears came to his eyes. He bent his head and kissed her. "You are already forgiven, my dear Eliza. How could I live without you? Try to rest now. I will stay here in the room and watch over you."

As soon as she had gone to sleep, he picked up the pistol and put it in his pocket. He looked at her with a puzzled frown and came to the conclusion that he did not understand her and probably never would.

But of one thing he was sure: he would never again entirely believe anything she told him. She was a convincing liar.

By way of atonement for the quarrel, he gave Eliza a gift of two horses. He knew that this would please her, because her love of horses had increased over the years to the point where it was almost an obsession. He rationalized his indulgence of her by saying to himself that she had not, after all, abandoned her son entirely, having paid for his care. Furthermore, hadn't she gone to Providence in 1808 with the idea of returning with the boy and telling all? It was not her fault that her son had refused. Her adoption of Mary, her friend's orphan child, had certainly been a generous and compassionate act. And he himself had come to love the child as though she were his own.

But Stephen was taking no chances on being duped again. Pieter was relieved of his post as driver of Eliza's coach, and Nodine was given the job, with instructions to report the comings and goings of Madame. Eliza was furious. She stormed and raged, but Stephen stood his ground. Nodine would be his spy.

CHAPTER 23

ACTUALLY, ELIZA'S TRIPS in the coach were innocent enough until an afternoon in the early part of 1813. As her coach passed The Battery, she noticed a man in an overcoat with a spyglass held to his eye. Somehow, he resembled Aaron Burr, except for the fact that he did not have Aaron's erect posture. She stopped the coach, got out and walked through the slush over to the man. She tapped him on the shoulder, and he turned around.

It was indeed Aaron, but so changed that she could scarcely recognize him. He was unshaven, and his face was lined and haggard.

"Eliza!" he said. "What are you doing here?"

"Aaron, what has happened to you? You look sick—"

"I am sick," he said and added, "sick at heart!"

"What has happened?"

"My beloved grandson, Gampy, is dead, and Theodosia—" Tears rolled down his face. "I fear that Theodosia is dead too." He pointed to the spyglass. "I am still looking for the ship she sailed on at the end of December. It never arrived."

"But what happened to it?"

"Nobody knows. The *Patriot* left Charleston December thirtieth. It may have been shipwrecked in a storm off Cape Hatteras, or it may have been captured by pirates." He paused. "Theodosia was doomed to die, anyway. She had a canker in her womb, and it was spreading, as cankers do. But I had hoped that she could be with me during whatever time was left for her."

Eliza was moved, and there were tears in her eyes as she said,

244

"Oh, Aaron, how tragic! Come into the coach with me so that we can talk. It is cold out here."

He followed Eliza into the coach, and she ordered Nodine to drive out toward The Mansion on Washington Heights. As soon as they were under way, Eliza kissed Aaron and hugged him to her.

Finally, she said, "It has been so long since I have heard from you. When did you get back to New York, and where have you been all this time?"

Briefly, and in a voice that was toneless and lacking in all feeling, he told her what had happened to him. He had been tried for treason several times allegedly for trying to set up a new nation on the American continent. All the trials had resulted in acquittal for lack of evidence. The last one had ended in an acquittal by Chief Justice Marshall himself. President Jefferson had become his implacable enemy, hounding him from state to state in an effort to hang him, for reasons that he, Aaron, had never understood.

Finally, he had left for Europe in June 1808 under a pseudonym, since popular opinion still believed him to be guilty of treason because of his plan to conquer the land west of Louisiana with an army of his own. He had thought that he might find friends in Europe to support him in this plan, but all his efforts had come to nothing. He had not been well received in the courts of Europe, and he had been desperately poor and often ill.

Finally, he had returned home in 1812, staying with his old friends the Swartwouts. Almost immediately, he had received a letter from Theodosia telling him that Gampy had died that year at the age of ten. He had resumed his law practice at 9 Nassau Street, and nobody seemed to mind. The duel and the murder charge had evidently been forgotten.

Eliza ordered Nodine to turn the coach around and take Aaron to his law office. She held his hands tightly in her own and told him that she had never stopped loving him. But he said nothing.

When they reached the door of his law office, he got out, and then stood for a moment looking at Eliza with eyes that were lifeless.

245

"And so, you see, dearest Eliza, my life is over. All that I loved is gone, and I find it hard to go on living. Even you are happily married and rich and have no need for me. No one has."

"And where is that will power you used to tell me about, Aaron? You must recover your spirits and go on! Remember that there is one person who will always care what happens to you— me."

Tears came to his eyes again as he clasped her hand in farewell. She tried to give him all the money she had with her, but he refused to take it. "If you ever need money, get word to me, Aaron. I am rich now, you know."

He nodded, mumbled a thank you and then hurried off to the door of his office. As he disappeared inside, Eliza thought to herself, "Thank God, he still has his pride, and as long as he has that, there's a chance that he will recover." She consoled herself with this thought on the long ride back to The Mansion.

That night after dinner, while Stephen and Eliza sat in the drawing room sipping cordials, Stephen suddenly looked at her abruptly.

"Where did you go in your coach today, *ma chère?*" he asked casually.

"Oh, shopping as usual."

"And that is all you did?"

She realized that Nodine had given a full report on her meeting with Aaron, and so she said, "No, not quite all. I saw Aaron Burr and talked with him in the coach. He got back from Europe in May. I didn't know that he had returned until I saw him down at The Battery looking out to the harbor with a spyglass."

"And so you stopped and talked with him, *bien entendu*, although you knew this would displease me."

"Why should it?" she asked in annoyance. "You know that my relations with Aaron Burr were over even before I met you. He is still a friend, and his life is very sad now. He needed someone to talk to."

"And *naturellement*," said Stephen ironically, "it had to be you."

Eliza was becoming angry at Stephen's jealousy. "No, it didn't *have* to be me. I had Nodine stop the carriage. The man was thin and despondent, and he looked old." She then told Stephen what had happened to Aaron.

"That's very sad," said Stephen with a note of sympathy in his voice. "But tragic things happen to everyone, and they survive. How is he making his living?"

"He has a small office and is practicing law again. He is very poor."

"And I suppose that my generous Eliza gave him all her money?"

"Yes," she said. "I offered money to him, and he refused to take it. Aaron Burr is a very proud man."

"I'm sure of that—and a very foolish and untrustworthy one too."

Eliza said angrily, "He is neither foolish nor untrustworthy! He was acquitted of all treason charges many times, and President Jefferson—"

Stephen interrupted her. "I am not interested in your defense of Mr. Burr, and there is no reason for you to feel any responsibility for him or what happens to him! I forbid you *absolument* to see him again while I am alive!"

"You forbid me!" she screamed. "What right have you to forbid me—"

"The right of a husband who has given you everything you ever wished for, who has been true and faithful to you in every way!"

"I'll see him anyway, if I want to! I just won't tell you!"

Stephen's voice took on a harsh and dictatorial tone that he had never used with her before. "You will *not* see him under any circumstances! You will not leave this house in your coach without Nodine in attendance, even if I should be away in France!"

"That's contemptible! You are employing a spy to watch over me. You do not trust me!"

"Why should I? You have lied to me and tricked me in the past. I do not intend that it should happen again."

She rose to her feet now and shouted at him, "I hate you! I'll

take whatever holdings belong to me and leave this house!"
There were tears of fury in her eyes as she moved toward the
stairs.

Stephen's voice was cold and calculating. "Do as you please.
But if you leave, you will leave without Mary, who is my legally
adopted daughter." He had played his trump card, and Eliza
knew it.

She went to bed and cried herself to sleep. For once, Stephen
had won a battle.

PART V

The Mansion

CHAPTER 24

STEPHEN MAY HAVE WON a battle, but Eliza had no intention of being a humble loser. In her own way, she would avenge her defeat. During love-making she was so passive and unresponsive that Stephen made less frequent overtures to her. She feigned a poor appetite at meals and actually did lose some weight. She made few shopping trips and seemed not interested in going to the theatre. She was pale and depressed.

Meanwhile, she had started a new campaign. She did not feel that it was good for their social standing for Stephen to remain "in trade." His store could easily be managed by his assistants, and he could become what she called "a gentleman of leisure." After all, he was fifty-four years old now and could afford to retire.

Stephen became so weary of her constant nagging that he finally agreed. In fact, he sold his store at a very profitable figure. More than that, he began investing in real estate in northern sections of the city because he foresaw that as the city grew, these properties would become more valuable.

Although assenting to Eliza's wishes about his retirement, he changed his will without telling her. He left everything to her in trust for Mary so that she would actually own nothing.

Meanwhile, he was worried about Eliza's health, her paleness and her loss of weight. He called Dr. Romayne to the house to give her a thorough physical examination, which she endured impatiently.

Her spirits brightened noticeably when Dr. Romayne recommended that she spend a few weeks at Saratoga Springs, where

251

she could drink the health-giving waters and bathe in them as well. The prospect of getting away from New York pleased her.

She would go on the long journey in her coach, drawn by six horses, and the trip would be leisurely so that it would not tire her.

The only drawback was that she would be accompanied by Nodine and his wife, Marie. When she asked that Pieter be allowed to come, too, Stephen refused on the reasonable grounds that he would need Pieter in maintaining the house and grounds. She argued the point, but once again, she lost. When she asked that Mary come along with her for company, Stephen agreed. It did not even occur to Eliza that Stephen would be lonely in the big house all by himself. She doubted that he would be unfaithful to her, and in any case, she did not care.

She was possessive about Stephen's money, but not jealous about him amorously—providing he did not substitute another woman for her. She did not really care if he slept with a dozen women while she was gone, although she would like to know about it as possible ammunition in their increasing battles and arguments. And so she appointed Pieter as her own spy.

In 1814 Saratoga Springs was a small country village with a few stores, a small park, and one hostelry—the Union Hotel, where the wealthy summer residents and invalids stayed. The rates for food and lodging were high, because Gideon Putnam, who had built the hotel in 1803, could earn money only during the summer months.

Eliza was delighted by the charm and quiet of the village. There were some comfortable houses built by well-to-do families, and one of them was a beautiful Georgian structure of red brick that faced the park. It was for sale, and within a few days, Eliza had looked it over carefully and decided to buy it as a summer home. She sent Nodine and her coach back to New York to bring Stephen with the four thousand dollars that was the asking price. She had already christened the house The Tuileries.

Two weeks later, Stephen arrived—with money. He had obviously been anxious to join her. The Mansion was lonely and deserted, and he was in no mood to entertain when Eliza was gone. He agreed that the house would be a good investment and managed to get the price down to three thousand five hundred dollars.

Eliza was radiant with health and vitality. Whether it was the supposedly curative effect of the waters or the excitement of acquiring a new home, she had never been more alluring.

She was once again receptive to Stephen's love-making, and this made him happy and helped relieve the tension he had been under since their quarrel.

Mary, too, had thrived on the change of scene. She drank the waters at her mother's command, even though she found the taste of the minerals rather unpleasant. Mary, now thirteen years old, was a beautiful child with a quick intelligence. Under the instruction of a tutor whom Eliza had hired, she had learned not only to read and write but to speak French.

Eliza had continued to give lessons to Pieter, and Mary had been happy to be able to join them. Her adoration of Pieter had increased over the years. Pieter, now thirty-five years old, had become a kind of father to her. She loved Stephen, too, who was so patient in teaching her French. To Mary, he seemed to be a benevolent grandfather, because of his age, and she had even begun to call him Grandpapa. This pleased Stephen, even though he realized that he occupied third place in her affections, next to Eliza and Pieter. But Stephen was not possessive toward the child and was very proud that she had turned out to be both beautiful and intelligent.

It was still to Eliza that Mary looked for affection and warmth. Her early desire to please her mother in every way made discipline almost unnecessary, although the relationship was not altogether good in its effect on Mary. The little girl was too submissive and dependent; she always stood shyly in her mother's shadow, completely dominated by Eliza's overbearing personality.

Mary was happy at Saratoga Springs, but she missed the presence of her beloved Pieter. One night at bedtime she climbed onto Stephen's lap and asked him why Pieter could not join them. Stephen looked thoughtful. There was, after all, no need for both Nodine and Marie to stay in Saratoga, and Nodine might better be employed in readying The Mansion for the fall.

"Very well, my darling Mary," said Stephen, clasping the child close in his arms. "We'll send Nodine back home, and Pieter can drive the coach back here and stay until we return to the city."

Mary impulsively kissed Stephen on the cheek and then went to bed, singing herself to sleep. Eliza was pleased too. She missed Pieter as much as Mary did, though in a different way. He was, for her, not only an occasional lover, but a substitute for the son who had disowned her.

Eliza, at thirty-nine, did not have the sexual needs that she had had when she was young. Her real obsession was still to be accepted by society, and a year later, she almost succeeded, when fate offered her the most exciting adventure of her life.

CHAPTER 25

In the spring of 1815 Stephen decided on a trip to Paris to see whether he could collect indemnity from the French government for his burned plantation in Santo Domingo, and the loss of his ships, the *Prosper* and the *Purse*, which had been taken by the French during the Napoleonic Wars.

Eliza was anxious to go to France, too, not only to enjoy the social life in Paris but to place Mary in a French boarding school. And so, on June 1, the Jumels, along with Mary and Pieter, set sail on Stephen's new barque, the *Eliza*.

When they were seventeen days out of New York, on June 18, they had no way of knowing the momentous news that had burst upon all the nations of Europe.

The great Emperor Napoleon had been decisively defeated by Wellington and Blücher at Waterloo. He was declared an outlaw in France as a condition for any arrangements for peace in Europe, and his abdication had been demanded even by his marshals and almost all of his generals.

Napoleon went secretly to Malmaison, the palace he had built for the Empress Josephine, and the only real home he had ever known.

During the ten days he stayed at Malmaison, he came to a decision. He would flee to America. Secret arrangements were made for two French frigates, the *Saale* and the *Medusa*, to wait for him in the harbor at Rochefort.

On June 29 a closed *calèche* left Malmaison to travel the three hundred miles to the coast. Inside, there were three passengers besides Napoleon: Generals Becker, Bertrand and Savary. Shortly afterward, two other carriages set out from Malmaison to travel to Rochefort by a different route, and in them were Mme. Bertrand and her children, Count Montholon and his family, Las Cases and his son, and the loyal General Lallemand.

The trip was made quickly with only one stop, and all the carriages arrived at Rochefort on July 3. At four o'clock that afternoon, in spite of a brewing storm, Napoleon was rowed to the *Saale*. The violent storm finally broke, and for the next two days both frigates were marooned in Rochefort harbor.

Napoleon was cheered by the fact that at least he was aboard the *Saale* and could get the sleep and the regular nourishment he required for his ailing stomach. What he did not know was that he had been betrayed by his former Prefect of Police, Fouché, who had informed the British that Napoleon was at Rochefort, ready to escape.

The refugees aboard the *Saale* first knew that someone had betrayed their leader when a British cruiser, the *Bellerophon*, sailed into the harbor at Rochefort the next day, thus effectually blockading means of escape. The blockade lasted for ten days, during which Napoleon's brother Joseph Bonaparte joined those aboard the *Saale*.

Meanwhile, Stephen Jumel's barque, the *Eliza*, had taken refuge from the storm by sailing a short way up the Gironde River, some thirty-five miles south of Rochefort.

On the chance that there might be a ship for escape in the Gironde River, General Lallemand started a journey by horseback along the narrow, muddy roads on the shore. Arriving at Gironde Harbor, he used his spyglass to survey the lone ship anchored there. His heart leaped up as he could distinguish the name, the *Eliza*, New York, and saw the stars and stripes of her flag. From the shore he waved frantically and was finally seen by Stephen, who sent out a rowboat to fetch him.

Once aboard, General Lallemand introduced himself to the Jumels. He gave them the news of Waterloo and explained that Napoleon was waiting at Rochefort for transportation to the

United States. On an American ship he would be legally on American soil and could not be captured by the British. Would Monsieur Jumel consider taking Napoleon to New York as a passenger?

Both Eliza and Stephen were dumbfounded by the news, but before Stephen could reply, Eliza stepped forward.

"Of course, we can take him, General Lallemand!" she said in French.

Stephen hesitated. "But the indemnity for my plantation and on my ships from the French government—"

Eliza turned on him savagely. "You're thinking about money at a time like this!" she screamed. "What kind of man are you? The great Napoleon lies ill and defeated only thirty miles or so from here, and you are thinking of francs!"

"You are right, *ma chère*," said Stephen. "Yes, of course, we will take him, General. But you must hurry, because it is going to rain some more."

Eliza waited for Napoleon's arrival aboard the *Eliza* in a state of excitement. The thought of returning to New York with the Emperor as her guest started her on a spell of daydreaming that was wildly euphoric. Now, at last, not a door in New York would be closed to her. She saw it all as vividly as though it had already happened.

First, she would give a banquet such as the city had never seen, and the food would be served on solid-gold service and the most expensive china obtainable. The invitation would be engraved in French, and none of them would be sent to the high-ranking people of New York society. Now, instead of seeking out these people and courting them, she would let them come to her, begging for an invitation to The Mansion.

There would be an orchestra in the hallway between the drawing room and dining room, and only French music would be played. There would be dancing after dinner, and she would begin it with the great Napoleon as her chosen partner. It was not impossible that she would become his mistress.

Her most cherished dream would be fulfilled—acceptance at

257

last by the people of New York. She went to bed that night early so that she would be at her best the next day.

With the morning light, even the weather seemed to be favoring her. The storm had dissipated and the sky had cleared. Eliza, dressed in her loveliest gown, paced the deck in the sunshine. At about ten o'clock she saw that a man on horseback had arrived on the shore of the Gironde River. He was alone, and Eliza had misgivings. Where was the Emperor? She nervously waited until the man, General Lallemand, had arrived on the deck of the *Eliza*.

He stood at attention and saluted. "I could not bring the Emperor, as I had hoped," he said. "When I returned to the *Saale*, he had already surrendered to the British and is now aboard the *Bellerophon*."

Tears of disappointment came to Eliza's eyes. "But why? Why?"

"You must remember, Madame Jumel, that since Waterloo the Emperor has been a changed man. He is not only depressed and hopeless, but he has been seriously ill with stomach trouble which seems incurable. He just gave up."

Eliza now began to cry freely, and her make-up ran down her face in discolored streaks. The tears were not only of disappointment that her own plans had fallen through. The thought of Napoleon being carried into exile by the British, whom she hated, was unbearable.

"Please dry your eyes, Madame Jumel," said General Lallemand. "We are assured that the Emperor will be well treated, and there is a doctor aboard the ship. Napoleon may even recover from his present illness. He is, as you know, an unbelievably brave man."

"But at least," sobbed Eliza, "I wanted to see him and tell him how much we Americans loved him."

"It is better," said the General, "that you did not see him. He is so wasted and thin—a shriveled man who hardly resembles the Napoleon we knew. The skin of his face is pudgy and discolored. Only his eyes are still alive—those blazing eyes—" He broke off, so overcome by his own emotion that he could not speak.

Then his military figure became erect again, and he stood at attention. "We who are still loyal to our fallen leader wish that you and Monsieur Jumel should have some reward for your generous offer. We have no money—"

"Who would care about money at a time like this?" Eliza demanded.

"Perhaps you would like to have the Emperor's own private carriage and his trunk as mementos. We know without asking that he would want to give them to you, if he were here. But perhaps you would not want—"

Eliza looked at General Lallemand in astonishment. "Not want them? I would cherish them as long as I live!"

General Lallemand smiled at her sadly. From a pocket he drew forth a silver key and placed it in Eliza's hand. "Here is the key to the trunk, Madame Jumel."

She looked at the key that lay in the palm of her hand. Tears filled her eyes again as she said, "I will have a silver chain made for it, and I shall wear it around my neck for as long as I live! Napoleon touched it, and that will make it sacred to me."

General Lallemand looked at her curiously. "Indeed, Madame Jumel, you are more a Frenchwoman than an American. The Emperor will be happy to know that his *calèche* and his trunk are in the hands of someone who loved him."

Before leaving, General Lallemand saluted the Jumels again. Not knowing whether it was proper or not, Eliza saluted in return.

"I must go now," said General Lallemand, "since I intend to follow my emperor into exile, no matter where that may be."

Silently, Eliza watched the rowboat as it took the General back to shore. At last she turned to Stephen and said, "We shall ride to Paris in the Emperor's coach."

"But, Eliza—" Stephen said.

"We'll need a carriage for the trip, anyway, and the horses are there already. They will need feeding."

She still clenched the key to the Emperor's trunk in her hand, and the next day she found a chain for it among her jewelry. She suspended it around her neck. As she watched the *Bellerophon*

259

set sail from Rochefort harbor, followed by the French frigates, tears came to her eyes briefly, but then curiosity overcame her. She was wondering what might be in Napoleon's trunk.

Eliza said to Stephen, "We must sail to Rochefort as quickly as we can and take possession of Napoleon's great gifts to us."

When they disembarked at Rochefort, Eliza was so excited that she didn't wait for the rowboat to make a firm mooring. Lifting her skirt, she waded to shore in two feet of water.

With trembling hands she inserted the key into the lock of the trunk, which was large and handsome, five and a half feet long and of black cowhide with a rounded top on which a brass *N* was fastened.

Stephen helped her undo the strong leather straps and lift the heavy top. The trunk was empty except for a small silver traveling clock. She picked it up and looked at it in admiration. It was a beautiful clock with intricate scroll decoration, and it was still ticking.

She turned to Stephen, and there was awe in her voice as she said, "It is still ticking away the minutes, like the Emperor's great heart itself."

The interior of the carriage was more luxurious than any Eliza had ever seen. It was upholstered in soft scarlet velvet with black leather trim. All the ornaments on both the interior and exterior were of gold. Napoleon's eagle crest was missing from the door, but the holes where it had been mounted were visible. It had been removed to prevent easy identification. Eliza found it tucked under the driver's seat. It was carved of wood, the eagle's wings spread as though about to descend on its prey. Eliza vowed to herself that the eagle would soon be restored to the side of the carriage.

Grain to feed the horses was brought from the *Eliza*, and the six handsome black Arabian horses, still in harness, ate hungrily. When the horses had replenished themselves, the coach set off for Paris.

Eliza settled herself on the soft velvet cushions with Stephen next to her. Mary had insisted on riding in the driver's seat next to Pieter.

Stephen was tired, and as the afternoon wore on, he fell asleep. But Eliza could not sleep.

For her, an old dream was now a reality. She felt like a true queen. She was riding in the Emperor Napoleon's own *calèche* on her way to conquer Paris. Some peasants working in the fields at the side of the road recognized the carriage and cried out, "*Vive l'Empereur!*" They were disappointed that Napoleon himself was not the passenger. They still remembered his miraculous escape from Elba and the rule of the Hundred Days that followed. What could happen once could happen twice. But it had not happened. He had not escaped this time, and they knew that he would not return. They wept.

Eliza echoed their cries of "*Vive l'Empereur*" and waved graciously from the window. But it was not until they reached a *taverne* in the little village where they were to spend the night that she felt like a true celebrity. The townsfolk crowded around, anxious for news of the Emperor. When Eliza told them of Waterloo, many of them were moved to tears, and their hatred of the British was voiced in long and thundering curses.

It was the same in every village where they stopped. The news of Napoleon's capture by the British had already spread ahead of them and had reached even Paris. By the time they reached the city, the streets were lined with people waiting for their arrival. Their reception was tumultuous, in spite of the fact that the monarchy had been restored by the Congress of Vienna, and Louis XVIII, fat and foolish, had been crowned King in an elaborate ceremony at the Cathedral of Notre Dame.

The citizenry had divided itself sharply into Bonapartists and Royalists, and although Louis XVIII sat upon the throne, it was a shaky throne indeed, and his efforts to stifle the more vociferous of the Bonapartists met with little success. Of all things, he did not want a civil war.

Eliza was delighted to learn that all her closest French friends were Bonapartists and that to them she was a heroine. The key that she wore around her neck became a key to French society.

And so was Stephen's money. The impoverished nobility took the Jumels to their hearts. Stephen rented the whole second floor of the Hôtel Berteuil at 22 Rue de Rivoli, a relatively new street that ran from the Place de la Concorde past the Tuileries gardens to the Louvre.

Although the street was new, the building where the Jumels made their home was not. It had originally been the town house of Louis de Berteuil, one of Louis XVI's ministers, a man who had barely escaped the guillotine himself. An imposing edifice of brick and stone, it faced on the palace gardens, and the view enchanted Eliza.

Living in a house like this, it was hard for her to realize that she did not actually have blue blood. But in a way, she did, because she still believed that her father had been George Washington, and she no longer kept this belief to herself. She embarrassed Stephen on numerous occasions by casually letting it drop that she was Washington's bastard daughter. Parisians were hardly shocked at her illegitimacy. "Natural" children were well accepted, especially if they had money.

Once Stephen said, "Dear Eliza, why must you tell such outrageous lies?"

Her answer was merely an airy, "Because, my dear Stephen, it amuses me to tell lies."

Stephen, finally, was amused too. He had married an outrageous woman, knew it and enjoyed it. It added spice to what his life might otherwise have been, that of a respectable but bored wine merchant. And Stephen, at the age of fifty-five, reacted to the coming of middle age with a renewed zest for living.

And so the huge Jumel apartment on the Rue de Rivoli became a place where elaborate dinners and fancy balls were held at least twice a week. Eliza even began to have *levées* of her own. Although she herself was still an avid Bonapartist, she decided in true democratic fashion that the doors of her *salon* would be open to Royalists and Bonapartists alike. Anyway, she loved to hear all these well-bred aristocrats argue their heads off at one another. It gave added spice to her social functions.

Stephen spent money wildly, with little thought for the future. To see Eliza happy made him happy, and Eliza was happier than she had ever been in her life.

Happiness and power had made her arrogant. She felt herself at last to be in a position that was secure and unassailable, above the limitations that hemmed in other people's lives. It was a natural enough feeling, but it was to prove her undoing, and in a way that she least expected.

CHAPTER 26

ELIZA DID NOT WANT Mary to grow up without a formal education. Her own had been achieved only by the efforts of Sam Allen, Jonathan Clarke, and most of all, Aaron Burr. But it had been haphazard, and even now, her spelling was far from perfect.

So Mary was enrolled in an expensive private school in a suburb of Paris. Here, at the École de Jeunes Filles, Mary would receive the best education that France could provide and eventually be as much at ease speaking French as English.

Mary did not want to leave her mother, but after a storm of tears, she was left at the boarding school, and Eliza promised to visit at least once a month.

Meanwhile, the Jumels lived in high style on the Rue de Rivoli. Eliza renewed acquaintance with Estelle, the Comtesse Henri Tascher de la Pagerie, whose gossip about the boudoir behavior of the nobility still delighted her. And she made a close friend of the Duchesse de Berry, who had just married the second son of Charles X, thereby establishing herself as the most influential woman in France. In court circles her position was second to none because her children would continue the Bourbon royal line. Her middle-aged husband, the Duc de Berry, was a favorite of Louis XVIII's and commander of the royal troops.

When the Comtesse de la Pagerie's husband died, she became not only a grieving widow but an impoverished one. Eliza came to her rescue. She bought Estelle's magnificent collection of Napoleonic relics for the sum of twenty-five thousand dollars, and Estelle became part of the Jumel household.

264

In December of 1816, Eliza decided that it was time for Napoleon's crest to be replaced on his coach, but she wanted to make it even grander than it had been originally. She removed the head and body of the eagle, leaving only the wings. Then, in the center, she had a craftsman place a magnificent laurel wreath of victory, with a quiver of arrows, each of which represented a victorious battle.

Eliza's adoration of Napoleon had become an obsession. The thought of the Emperor living in exile on a rock island called St. Helena in the South Atlantic filled her with fury.

One crisp December morning she decided to give full vent to her feelings. She had the horses harnessed to Napoleon's carriage and asked Pieter to affix the crest to the carriage door.

"But where are you going?" asked Pieter.

"I am going to remind the people of Paris that they had a great leader who now spends a miserable life in exile!"

"Shall I come with you, madame?" asked Pieter.

"No. I shall drive the coach alone."

Dressed in one of her most expensive gowns, Eliza took the driver's seat, and with a snap of the whip, she was off.

It was nearly noon, and the streets were thronged with people as Eliza drove out of the Rue de Rivoli and headed toward the Place de la Concorde. She planned to drive up the Champs Élysées to the place where Napoleon's Arc de Triomphe was still under construction.

With her cries of *"Vive Napoléon!"* ringing in the air, she drove the coach like a madwoman. The people on the streets looked at this spectacle in astonishment. But when they saw the laurel wreath of victory on the side of the carriage, they reacted violently. Although there was some guarded applause by a few Bonapartists, most Parisians had bowed to the restoration of the Bourbon monarchy. Angrily, they shouted, *"A bas! A bas! Napoléon est fini!"*

Eliza spat in their faces and drove on toward the site of the Arc de Triomphe. Halfway there, she noticed that she was being followed by one of the King's guards on horseback. He quickly caught up with her, and coming alongside, he shouted, *"Arrêtez!*

265

Arrêtez!" He recognized her and added in broken English, "Madame, you are under arrest!"

She stopped the horses and from the driver's seat stared down defiantly at the guard. "Under arrest? Under arrest for what?"

The guard made it clear that in the eyes of the law she was a traitor to His Majesty, Louis XVIII.

Eliza laughed at him. "*Très bien. Je suis traître!* Arrest me! *J'irai en prison!*"

And to prison was exactly where she went. She was allowed to send word to Stephen, and that was all. Dazed and frightened, she found herself in the large cellblock where all female prisoners were kept. She was surrounded by filthy, foul-smelling women: prostitutes, thieves and ancient drunken females. She retreated to a corner, lifting her skirts in an effort to avoid contact with the piles of excrement and puddles of urine that covered the floor. But the women were curious and excited by the sudden appearance of a lady dressed in fine clothes. They clustered around her, pulling at her clothing and pinching her arms.

One of the prostitutes, her make-up smeared and running down her face, came over and pulled at Eliza's bodice so that her breasts were exposed.

"Look! She got teats just like the rest of us, no matter if she got fine clothes!" She pinched hard at one of Eliza's nipples, and Eliza screamed with pain. This seemed to delight all of them, and they pulled at her brocade skirt until they got it off.

"Let's look at her *con!*" One of them reached down and stuck her filthy fingers into Eliza. "I wager some pretty juicy big *bîtes* on dukes and barons have been in there, pushin' themselves in and out on a fancy bed with silk sheets!"

Eliza felt a blinding fury at these assaults. She began to fight all of the women, clawing and scratching and pounding her fists into their eyes.

The women began to scream and curse as the fight worsened, and soon a jailer appeared. He came into the cell with a bullwhip and thrashed all the women until they retreated and left Eliza alone and shivering in a corner of the cell.

With an effort she rose to her feet. She ran over to the jailer and seized him by the arm. In French, she told him who she was, that she was a friend of the Duchesse de Berry. She pleaded that he place her in a cell by herself.

The jailer laughed at her. "Why should you get *traitement spécial?*" He waved his arm at the other women. "Your crime is worse than theirs! You are a traitor to our king, Louis XVIII! These other women are only whores and pickpockets and drunks!" He turned his back on her and left.

For supper the prisoners received a potato stew heaped onto tin plates. They gobbled it voraciously and hurriedly, so that they might grab the food from the slower eaters. They quarreled like hogs in a pigpen, screaming and cursing at one another. Eliza could not eat, and her plate was swooped out of her hand and its contents were devoured.

At nightfall, there was a new horror. As though from nowhere a horde of huge rats came to scrape clean the tin plates. They scurried everywhere, and when one walked over Eliza's face and then bit her arm, she screamed. The other prisoners fought the rats with their plates and seemed to find this a diverting sport. Then they amused themselves by taking pieces of Eliza's torn gown and dressing themselves in outlandish fashion, with satirical courtly airs. Their comedy was lost on Eliza, who sat in a corner of the cell with her eyes shut, trying to sleep.

But her mind would not stop working. She might well have cursed herself as a fool to have indulged in what proved to be such a disastrous adventure. But she did not. She was proud of what she had done. Though it had been a futile gesture and only that, she saw it as a tribute to the memory of Napoleon. The horrors of being in this filthy jail became a kind of sacrifice in honor of her hero, who had endured worse indignities at the hands of his enemies.

Toward midnight, the large room quieted down, and most of the women slept. The only sound was their snores, and an occasional scream at a savage biting rat. Eliza fell into a light sleep, in which she dreamed that Stephen had arrived to rescue her.

She was cold, and when she felt a body moving close to her in a friendly way, she snuggled against it for warmth. Soon she was

267

aware that hands were exploring her and playing with her. She awoke with a start of fright. It was the woman who had assaulted her earlier in the day. She pushed the woman's hands away and turned over so that she lay on her belly. Finally, out of sheer exhaustion, she slept.

When morning came and daylight filtered into the cellblock, the mass of foul-smelling women was revealed in all its grotesqueness. But now, instead of nausea, Eliza felt only a profound pity for them all. They were the scum of the city, as she and her mother had once been in Providence. She thanked God, if there was a God, that she had been able to climb out of the gutter.

The jailer arrived, unannounced on his slippered feet.

"*Eh, bien*, you ladies of *merde*, get up and make yourselves ready for breakfast. Some of you will go before the judge. Which one of you is Madame Stephen Jumel?"

Eliza roused herself and said weakly, "I am."

"You will come with me." He opened the door with his key, and Eliza hurried out. She thought joyfully, "At last, I will be free! Stephen has come to save me."

She followed the jailer, but he stopped before a solitary cell. He seized her shoulder and sent her sprawling, and then locked the door behind him.

"You will stay here until your trial for treason. You are a prisoner of the King."

Eliza considered this special treatment as only due a woman of her position, but she did not understand why the charge against her was treason. Was it treason to drive a carriage decorated with Napoleon's crest down the Champs Élysées? Was it not a person's right to express a political preference in France, which was, after all, a democracy like the United States?

For the next two days, she waited. It was a relief at least to be alone, away from the riffraff of the cellblock. She could keep herself reasonably clean and regretted only that her gown was gone and that she had to wear the soiled chemise that was the only clothing left to her.

On the morning of the third day the jailer came for her, and she was led away to a courtroom. Stephen was there, and she threw herself into his arms, crying with joy at the thought that she would soon be free.

At last, she was taken before the Chief Prefect of Police. He spoke in a bored and toneless voice.

"You are Madame Stephen Jumel?"

As soon as she had murmured assent, the voice, stern and cold, said, "You are accused, Madame Jumel, of treason against our King, Louis XVIII. You drove down the Champs Élysées in a coach that once belonged to Napoleon. And on the carriage door of this coach was the Emperor's insignia with a laurel wreath of victory affixed to it. Are you part of a conspiracy to bring Napoleon back to France?"

"Oh, no, *Monsieur le Préfet!*" Eliza protested.

"Well, no matter. The King believes that you are. The monster Napoleon was once able to escape his exile from Elba, and the King is taking no chances on the possibility of an escape from St. Helena."

"But there is no conspiracy, I swear to you!"

"Yet you have many Bonapartist friends."

"Yes, but I also have many Royalist friends—the Duchesse de Berry—"

He interrupted her. "I know, and they have implored the King to show mercy on you. You will not be sentenced to jail."

Eliza sighed in relief. "*Oh, merci bien!*"

"Your sentence will be banishment from France. Never again will you be allowed to set foot on the soil of this country."

Eliza was stunned. "But I love France! I love this city of Paris as though it were my true home!"

"That is unfortunate, Madame Jumel. You will be taken to Bordeaux under armed guard and there you will board your husband's ship, the *Eliza*, and set sail for the United States as soon as possible."

Eliza was crying now, imploring the Prefect of Police for mercy, to allow her to stay in France on probation, until she could prove her allegiance to the king.

But all her tears availed her nothing. The brief trial was over, and Stephen led her from the courtroom. Napoleon's carriage had been confiscated and burned, but Stephen had salvaged the trunk.

When they reached home, Eliza bathed and put on fresh clothes. Stephen and Pieter helped her pack. Many of her things were stored in Napoleon's trunk, which was strapped to the back of the carriage.

The journey to Bordeaux under armed guard was a melancholy one. Eliza still could not believe that she would never see France again.

"But why have they done this to me, Stephen? Why?"

"Because the King still fears Napoleon. It is foolish, *bien entendu*, but Louis XVIII is a foolish man. He is not truly popular with the people, and he knows it. The restoration of the Bourbon monarchy has been accepted, but the King's crown sits uneasily on his head. That's why your stupid adventure seems to him a treasonable act."

"It was not a stupid adventure!" said Eliza angrily. "It was done because my Emperor is still the greatest man in the world, and somebody should keep his memory alive! It is the French people who are stupid!"

Stephen knew better than to contradict her, and it was certainly not a time when he wished to quarrel with her. He was fully aware of what the banishment meant to her.

Eliza looked from the carriage window as the fields and vineyards passed by. She was thoughtful. When she turned to Stephen, her eyes were once again full of tears.

"I'll be all alone at The Mansion. Even you are not coming with me."

Stephen patted her hand. "You know why I can't come, *ma chère*. I must wait to see what the French government will do about paying me for the loss of my ships and my plantation." He paused and then added, "We are not as rich as we once were, you know."

"I know," said Eliza. "You have explained it to me again and again. But the thought of being all alone—even having Pieter with me would be something."

Stephen pondered a moment. "You may take Pieter with you, dear Eliza. It's too bad that Mary cannot come."

"Mary's education must not be interrupted, no matter what!" said Eliza. "But thank you for letting Pieter come with me. He is like a son to me, you know."

"Speaking of Mary, I almost forgot. A letter came from her while you were in jail." He fumbled in his pockets and finally produced a rumpled letter.

It was dated December 8, and it read:

MY DEAR MAMA:
As the feast of Miss Laurau will take place on Thursday next, we will have a concert, and the mistress told me to ask you to come. . . . It would give me great pleasure if you would come and see me, and bring me my gauze frock with my shoes and gloves and lace vandyke. It is very cold upstairs, so please ask Miss Laurau to let us have a fire in our room. . . . My dear Mama, I embrace you with a thousand kisses. Believe me to be your fond and dutiful daughter,

MARY ELIZA JUMEL

Eliza's eyes were moist as she finished reading the letter. "Poor child," she said. "She must never know what happened. I will write her that I returned home because of ill health."

"Don't worry, my Eliza. I'll visit Mary as soon as I return to Paris, and I'll take her all the things she requested."

"And don't forget about the fire in her room," said Eliza, as she remembered how cold she had been in jail. "If it costs extra, pay it."

"Of course," said Stephen.

They reached Bordeaux and the end of their journey. It was a sad leave-taking, but Pieter was overjoyed that he would be alone with Eliza during the voyage.

Stephen tried to be cheerful as the *Eliza* made ready to set sail. "Do not despair, Eliza. A pardon for you is always possible. When the King is more assured of his throne, this will appear to him as too harsh a punishment for so minor a crime. Remember that you still have many powerful Royalist friends in France, thanks to your own belief in democracy, when you opened the doors of our home to everyone."

Eliza nodded, trying hard to believe him. But when the ship got under way, and the shores of France slowly receded in the distance, she began to cry again. It was only Pieter's hand in hers that gave her consolation.

Suddenly, she looked him full in the face. It had grown fuller with the years, but it was still handsome, and the eyes were still adoring.

She smiled at him. "It has been a long time since we have made love together, Pieter. Let's go to my cabin."

Pieter almost pranced with joy as he followed her along the deck until they reached her cabin. He was standing nude by the bed before she had even taken off her dress. As she stared at his erection, she said, "I have often wondered what you did when we could not be together." She looked at him archly. "A little lady's maid somewhere?"

"There has never been anyone but you, madame."

"But you must do something. You are a man in his prime—"

Pieter blushed and spoke with difficulty. "Sometimes, madame, to relieve my feelings, I—I—play with myself."

Eliza laughed and said, "Well, there's no need for that now. Come to bed."

But before Pieter got into bed with her, he said, "But when I play with myself, madame, I think only of you in my imagination."

As she felt him entering her, she kissed him tenderly on the ear. "You are very sweet, dear Pieter, and the one friend who has never failed me."

She gave herself to him with more than usual passion. They stayed together for the rest of the afternoon, until they were both exhausted and slept.

CHAPTER 27

THE THREE AND A HALF YEARS that followed Eliza's banishment from France were not as lonely as she had feared. There was Pieter, of course, for company, and in the spring of 1817 Mary finished her schooling in Paris and returned home to stay. Eliza was overjoyed to see her daughter again and did everything she could to make the homecoming a happy occasion. She bought Mary a whole new wardrobe in the latest fashions.

But she need not have bothered. For Mary, just being with her mother again was a source of deep happiness, and seeing Pieter again was a delight.

Mary was sixteen now, maturing physically as well as mentally. When she was alone with Pieter, Eliza became nervous. Pieter was thirty-eight and not quite as demanding sexually as when he had been young. But he was, after all, a man, and he could hardly be unaware of the fact that Mary was developing breasts. It was not impossible that Pieter's love might change to passion and that Mary, in all innocence, would respond to it. Just how innocent Mary was Eliza had no way of knowing, and she decided that the time had come for her, in her role of mother, to find out.

So one afternoon, as Eliza and Mary were having tea, Eliza began to question Mary in as casual a manner as she could.

"While you were at school, Mary, I suppose you had many beaux."

"Oh, no, Mama. They were very strict at the school. The only time I saw boys was once every two weeks when we had our dancing lessons. I did not like them very much."

"Why not?"

"I was a little afraid of them. They are quite different from girls, aren't they?"

Eliza laughed. "Quite different. They are different, too, in the way their bodies are made."

"Oh, I know about that. Miss Laurau explained to us about the monthly flux, and then she told us how babies were born, and what a husband and wife did with each other to make it happen. It seemed disgusting to me, Mama. Is it really disgusting?"

Mary's eyes looked into Eliza's with a directness that demanded an answer. Eliza, who had expected that it would be Mary who would be embarrassed by the discussion, found that it was she who began to stammer and blush.

"No, Mary, love is not disgusting. It is beautiful." Then, feeling like a complete hypocrite, she added, "But only when the man and woman are married and wish to have children."

Mary nodded her head. "If you say it, Mama, then it must be true. But I don't think I'll ever get married. I am happy just the way I am—with you and Papa."

Eliza waited a moment and then asked the question that was most on her mind. "But Pieter—how do you feel about him?"

"Oh, he is my very best friend, Mama, not like one of the boys at the dancing school. He is like a father to me. At least that's the way I think of him."

"Good," said Eliza. "I want you to promise me that if your feelings toward him should—should change, you will tell me."

"Oh, they will not change, Mama. How could they?"

Eliza was temporarily reassured. But only temporarily.

In the two years that followed, Mary continued to mature. Her face took on a quiet beauty, and her figure became more womanly. And the more womanly she became, the more Eliza worried.

During the summer, when they went to Saratoga Springs for their yearly holiday to avoid the heat and the plague, Eliza became especially concerned.

One day she discovered Mary and Pieter stretched out on the rocks near the springs. They had their arms around each other, and Pieter was kissing Mary on the mouth in a way that was hardly platonic.

That night Eliza called Pieter to come to her room. She felt that it was time she had a talk with him about Mary. She foresaw that it would be difficult, and it was.

"Pieter," Eliza began, "I must talk to you about Mary. It seems to me that you are becoming very familiar with each other."

Pieter looked away in embarrassment and said nothing.

Eliza went on. "Today I saw you kissing each other."

"We are good friends, madame," said Pieter.

"I know that. But you were kissing each other as though you were lovers."

"Well," said Pieter, "we are not. So set your mind to rest. I would never touch Mary in that way."

"But can you deny that you are beginning to think of her, as you say, in that way?"

Pieter said nothing for a moment. Then he raised his head and, blushing, he said, "I won't deny it, madame. It is true. She is very attractive to me now that she is becoming a woman."

"Thank you, Pieter, for being honest with me."

"But you don't understand, madame. I wish to—I wish to marry Mary." He blurted out the words quickly, and they took Eliza by surprise.

"Marry her?" she said.

"Yes."

"But, Pieter, you are forty years old. Mary is only eighteen. And how would you plan to support her and the children she may give you?"

He held out his two hands, and there was a note of pride in his voice as he said, "I will work."

Eliza fell silent. She knew that she would have to marshal all her arguments against the marriage. It was something that could not, must not, happen. She did not want to hurt Pieter, but it was unavoidable.

"Pieter, you must listen to me. Mary has been brought up with every luxury that Stephen and I could give her. She would not be happy as a carpenter's wife. But more than that," she paused, and

275

added gently, "Mary is now an educated woman. When she marries, she must have a husband who is her equal."

"And I'm not, is that it?" A note of anger had crept into his voice. "Be honest, madame. You are looking for a husband for Mary, a man who would raise your *own* social position in New York. Isn't that it? Isn't that it?" He spoke like a prosecuting attorney; he knew that he had hit upon the truth, and he was not going to let her escape. "All your life," he said, "that has been the one thing you wanted more than anything else in the world! And now you are willing to use Mary as a way of getting it!"

He was speaking the truth, and Eliza knew it. She did not answer him. Instead, she changed the subject. "You have told me how you feel about Mary, but how does Mary feel about you?"

"She loves me," he said simply.

"Enough to want to marry you?"

"I think so. I have not asked her."

Eliza stood up. "And you will not, Pieter! Tomorrow you will take the coach back to New York. This has already gone too far!"

"As you say, madame. After all, you are the boss. You have always been the boss. But when I go back to New York, I'll leave The Mansion and make my own way in the world!"

Tears came to Eliza's eyes. She did not want to lose Pieter. He had been her closest friend for so many years.

"Oh, Pieter, there is no need for you to leave. I would hate not having you near—"

"Why?" he asked. "Because you would lose a lover? Is that it? Well, madame, I have loved you all my life, but now I am in love with someone else, someone—"

She knew that he was going to say "someone younger," but he had not said it, and she was glad he hadn't.

She was forty-four and looked much younger, but she was aware that the years were beginning to show. There were some lines around her mouth, little wrinkles around her eyes, and she was no longer as beautiful as she had been as a young woman. But age was something that she tried to put out of her mind.

She made a last attempt to keep Pieter from leaving her.

"Pieter, dear, you have been my closest friend for more than twenty years. I wouldn't want to lose you. You could stay on at The Mansion—"

"No, madame, I couldn't. To be near Mary and know that I could never have her would be more than I could bear. It is best for me to leave, since you have forbidden the marriage. I know when I am beaten. I will leave tomorrow."

He turned to go, and Eliza went over to him, throwing her arms around him. "Pieter, I'm sorry this had to happen. Please— will you kiss me goodbye?"

"Yes." He did not take her in his arms as she had expected he would, but he kissed her on the lips. As she attempted to make the kiss a passionate one, he turned his head away.

"No, madame," he said softly. "That is over for us now."

After he had left, Eliza sat down in a chair. It had all happened so quickly that she felt dazed. She had not foreseen that Pieter would leave her, and she felt alone and saddened. Pieter, she knew, had been more than a lover to her. He had been a son, too, a replacement for her own abandoned son back in Providence. But a still greater problem faced her: how would she explain Pieter's sudden disappearance to Mary?

The next morning she found Mary alone in the drawing room. Her red eyes told Eliza that she had been crying. Evidently, Pieter had told her that he would not be returning to The Mansion.

Mary ran to Eliza's arms, and Eliza tried to comfort her. When the girl had quieted her sobs and dried her eyes, she looked at her mother with her direct, cool gaze.

"But I don't understand, Mama. Why did Pieter leave, and why isn't he coming back to The Mansion?"

Eliza decided to be honest. "Pieter has fallen in love with you, Mary."

"Is that bad? You told me that love was something beautiful."

"But he wants to marry you, dear Mary, and that is out of the question. Do you love him enough to marry him?"

277

Mary looked down at her trembling hands. "I—I don't know. He never asked me. But supposing he had. Why would that be wrong?"

"To my way of thinking, it would be most unwise. How would he support you and the children you might have?"

"Why couldn't he just stay on at The Mansion the way he always has?"

"You would expect me to support both of you?"

"You could afford it."

"Yes, but I plan to have you marry someone of your own station, a man with education and a career, not one of my servants. Think, Mary, of the differences between you, not just in age, but in education—"

"Pieter can read and write, Mama."

"Yes, but that is hardly the equal of the education that I have given you at Miss Laurau's school. You are used to a life of luxury. You have always had everything you wanted. If you were to marry Pieter, you would end by being very unhappy." Eliza paused. "Do you really love him so much that you would be willing to live the life of a carpenter's wife?"

Mary did not answer, and Eliza continued. "Tell me, how much do you really love Pieter?"

"He is the best friend I ever had," she said slowly.

"But love? Do you love him in the way he loves you?"

Mary reflected. "I—I don't really know, Mama. I think of him almost as a father."

"A father is not the same as a lover," said Eliza.

"But I like it when he kisses me. It makes me feel excited and—well, I don't know how to describe it."

Eliza put her arms around the girl. "Of course you don't, dear Mary. You are still too young."

"Oh, but, Mama, I shall miss him so!" Mary began to cry, and Eliza did her best to console her. She told her all the conventional things: that in time she would forget Pieter and become interested in other young men, that she was still young and attractive and would someday marry a man whom she would be proud to love. But all the while she was saying these things, she knew that Mary was hurt and miserable, and she could not change that.

In the days that followed, Mary was inconsolable. She moved listlessly about the house, refused to bathe in the spring waters and ate very little.

It was nearing the end of summer, and one day Eliza's coach reappeared. It was driven by Nodine. There seemed little point in staying at Saratoga Springs any longer. Nodine said that the days of the plague were over for the year and the crispness of autumn was already in the air in New York.

Eliza decided that it was time to return to The Mansion. The change might improve Mary's depressed spirits.

But Mary's spirits did not revive, and Eliza became worried about her health. On many days she would stay in bed, making no effort to get up. Eliza pampered her like a sick child, allowing her to do as she pleased and attempting, quite unsuccessfully, to cheer her up.

But Mary did not change. The depression that had settled over her did not lift.

Eliza felt guilty about what she had done. She well remembered how she had felt when her affair with Matt Wyatt had come to its abrupt end, the days of going through the motions of life without really living. But she had been able to recover, thanks to her anger and resentment. Mary had no anger toward anyone. In fact, she seemed to have no feelings at all.

Eliza was forced to realize that Mary was a very different sort of girl than she had been at eighteen. Mary had no fight in her; she had always accepted what life gave her with gratitude. Indeed, she had never had anything to fight against, whereas Eliza's whole life had been a struggle against the circumstances into which she had been born, and her life was still a struggle toward her goal to be accepted by the socially important people of New York.

"Perhaps," she thought, "I have spoiled her, giving her everything she wanted, not only love, but clothes and education. Even my own education was a struggle, something I fought to get."

But deep down, the thing that made her feel guilty was Pieter's own judgment of the situation, and his words still came back to torment her. "*You are looking for a husband for Mary, a man who would raise your* own *social position . . . All your life that has been the one thing you wanted more than anything . . . And now you are willing to use Mary as a way of getting it!*"

It was true, and Eliza knew it. She also knew that she could not have acted otherwise.

CHAPTER 28

MARY'S SPIRITS DID NOT IMPROVE until the following spring when the news came that Stephen had succeeded in getting a pardon from Louis XVIII. Eliza could now return to France.

Mary made a remarkable recovery from her depression at the prospect of going to Paris and seeing Stephen again. The voyage was uneventful and smooth, and when at last Eliza and Mary arrived at Bordeaux, Stephen was there waiting for them with a coach ready for the trip to Paris. He had aged since Eliza had last seen him. He was only sixty, but his hair, which had been gray, was now completely white, and his movements had become slow and deliberate.

He was amazed at the change in Mary, who was now nineteen years old, a lovely young woman, as beautiful in her quiet, demure way as Eliza had once been. But Eliza had had a charm that drew people to her immediately, and now, even at forty-four, she still had a sensual appeal and an unquenchable zest for life, qualities that Mary, with her reserve and air of innocence, had never had.

Stephen had moved from the house on the Rue de Rivoli to an even more splendid apartment at 16 Place Vendôme. Eliza was happy about the change. The Rue de Rivoli still held memories of her arrest, and she was especially pleased to find that the windows of the new apartment looked out on the statue of Napoleon that stood in the square.

The Jumels again plunged into a dizzying round of social activities. As before, Eliza held open house to Royalists as well as Bonapartists, though there was now only a handful of the nobility who held the memory of the Emperor in their hearts.

When the news finally reached Paris that Napoleon had died on May 5, 1821, Eliza went into a state of deep mourning. For two weeks she closed the house to all visitors and spent many hours sitting by the window and staring out at Napoleon's statue. She wanted to put a mourning wreath on the door, but Stephen advised against it. Her allegiance to the Emperor had already caused enough trouble, and Eliza had to agree with him. Her stay in jail was still vivid to her, and she had no wish to repeat it. In any case, the great man was now dead, and there was nothing further to be done for his cause. She thanked God that at least she had a priceless collection of mementos of him. The carriage was gone, but she still had the trunk, the silver traveling clock and all the relics that she had bought from the Comtesse de la Pagerie.

After the mourning was over, the house on the Place Vendôme was once again opened and social activities were resumed: balls, dinners and *levées*. Eliza made many new friends, but now she had new motives in selecting them: she wanted a title for Stephen and a husband for Mary.

But she soon abandoned her hopes of finding a nobleman for Mary. Mary attended all the social functions with her mother and father, but mostly as though she were a bystander. She enjoyed the show but clearly did not want to be part of it. With the eligible bachelors to whom her mother introduced her she was extremely shy. In fact, she looked upon all men with fear and nervousness, and in spite of her attractiveness, they soon lost interest in her.

Eliza tried to persuade Mary to be more responsive, but she realized from the beginning that this was a lost cause. It was hard for her to realize that Mary was the daughter of Polly Clarke, who had been anything but shy with men, especially during her time as a town prostitute in Providence. It was probable, too, that Mary still mourned the loss of Pieter, the only man with whom she had ever felt at ease.

So Eliza made up her mind that she would have to concentrate on somehow obtaining a title for Stephen. She would do what she had always done: use a man to obtain her ends. She would cultivate some nobleman close to King Louis XVIII; sleep with him, if necessary. She wanted a title for Stephen—and for herself.

She confided in her old friend the Comtesse de la Pagerie. Estelle thought it unlikely that a title could be procured for Stephen, no matter whom Eliza slept with. However, it was worth a try.

Two weeks later Estelle came to see Eliza in a state of excitement. On the following Tuesday the King was to go to the Grand Opéra on the Rue de Richelieu. He would not go to the royal box as he usually did but planned to hold a reception at the front of the auditorium. Here, all the princes and highest noblemen would gather to pay homage to their King.

Estelle obtained invitations for the occasion so that she and Eliza could attend, and on the evening when the reception was to be held, Eliza was gorgeously dressed in a gown of shining red satin.

There was a throng already gathered in anticipation of the King's arrival, and when he at last appeared with his noblemen in attendance, there was a great clapping of hands and cries of "*Vive le roi de la France.*"

Eliza had never seen the King before, and she found him as fat and foolish-looking as he had been described. The look in his eyes gave an impression of a slightly bewildered and even stupid astonishment that he should find himself to be King of France.

Estelle pushed herself through the crowd, with Eliza following. She then began pointing out the noblemen by name, giving Eliza a brief history of their affairs, and most particularly their *affaires de boudoir*.

Many of the men looked at Eliza admiringly, and one of them in particular aroused Eliza's interest. It was because of the way he looked at her. His eyes were dark, with a hypnotic intensity that reminded her of Aaron's eyes.

"Who is that man?" whispered Eliza to Estelle.

"Oh, that's the Baron d'Agrilly."

"Is he married?"

"Of course," said Estelle, "but that doesn't keep him from being a lion in all the bedrooms of Paris. It is said that he is a very rough lover."

"I have had rough lovers before," said Eliza. "Could you introduce us?"

But there was no need for an introduction. The Baron d'Agrilly had exchanged glances with Eliza and was now making his way toward her.

When he stood before them, Estelle hastily performed the introductions. "Baron," she said, "I would like to present my dear friend Madame Stephen Jumel, who is an American."

The Baron bowed low and kissed Eliza's extended hand, but before letting it go, he gave it a hard and painful squeeze. Eliza withdrew her hand quickly. She could understand now why Estelle had described him as being a rough lover.

The Baron looked at Eliza with hungry eyes. He reminded her of a wild animal that had seized its prey and was now surveying it with pleasurable anticipation.

"This affair is very boring, n'est-ce pas?" he said. "Would you ladies like to join me for dinner as soon as it is over?"

Eliza lowered her eyes modestly. "Whatever the Comtesse wishes," she said.

"But we shall be delighted to accompany you, Baron," said Estelle.

"Excellent!" said the Baron, and again he looked at Eliza with that strange fixity of gaze that made her uncomfortable.

After they had dined well at an expensive café, the Baron said to Eliza, "Would you like to accompany me to my apartment for an after-dinner liqueur?"

Eliza looked questioningly at Estelle, who said, "I am sure Madame Jumel would be delighted, but as for me, I must go home. I am very tired from the evening's festivities."

Half an hour later Eliza found herself in the Baron's apartment. She chattered aimlessly about the reception at the Opéra, while he listened attentively.

Then he got up and sat down close to her on the sofa. "I find you extremely attractive, Madame Jumel."

"I am not as attractive as I was twenty years ago," said Eliza.

"And who of us is?" said the Baron. "Actually, I am not fond of very young women. They are too flighty. A mature woman like you is, after all, more experienced in the art of love."

His arm went around her, and he drew her to him and kissed her passionately. Then he said, "Shall we go to bed, where we can be more comfortable?"

"But your wife, Baron—"

"My wife is not here. This is not my home, *ma chère*, it is an apartment I rent for my own diversions. I do not even keep a servant here. We are quite alone, so we need not fear any intrusion."

Instead of reassuring Eliza, this statement produced in her a vague sense of fear, but she brushed it aside. After all, she was here to obtain a title for Stephen and not for her own amusement.

When they reached the bedroom, the Baron lost no time in undressing, but when she began to take off her clothes, he stopped her.

"Please wait," he said. "It gives me great pleasure to take off a lady's clothing."

Nude now, he went over to the bed, where she lay waiting. He seized her bodice roughly and tore it from her. She protested, because he had made a rip in the cloth.

"What do I care for a rip in your bodice? I want to humiliate you and bend you to my will!" He seized the skirt of her satin gown and tore it open.

Again, she protested that he had torn her skirt. Estelle had told her that the Baron was reputed to be a rough lover, but this was more than she had bargained for. She was beginning to feel frightened.

Now that he had her naked on the bed before him, he thrust himself down on her. The attack was so sudden that she was not prepared for love-making, but this did not bother the Baron in the least. He attempted to penetrate her anyway, and his entrance

285

into her was painful. She cried out, "Wait, please wait until I am ready for you."

He laughed. "Why should I wait?" He continued his thrust, but she was so frightened now that she could not respond at all.

He got up suddenly and went over to the dresser near the bed. He returned carrying a small whip, which he waved at her threateningly.

"Perhaps this will persuade you to prepare yourself!" He snapped the whip in the air.

Eliza's terror turned into a cold anger, and she got up quickly from the bed to escape him. She had gotten as far as the door when she felt the whip lash across her shoulders. It stung, and she winced with pain.

"Please, Baron. I wish to go home."

His voice was contemptuous. "You will not leave until I have had my will of you! Come back to bed, and let there be no more nonsense."

As she moved back to the bed, the whip lashed through the air again and came down a second time on her back. She cried out in pain and then, at his command, stretched out on the bed. He was on top of her again, kissing her so roughly that her upper lip began to bleed. The taste of blood seemed to rouse him further, and he again made an attempt to penetrate her.

A fury was rising in Eliza at being subjected to this man's insane lust. She remembered the time that Sam Allen had tried to murder her, and that other time, when she was a prostitute in Sally Marshall's brothel and Bobby Brown had tried to force himself upon her. She did not have a blunderbuss under the bed now, but she looked about wildly for some kind of weapon. Her eye lighted on a heavy bronze vase on the bedside table.

The Baron was laughing. "Did you think I was through with you, madame? I have only just begun!"

While he continued to fumble about on top of her, she grabbed his testicles and squeezed them as hard as she could. As he doubled up with pain, she scrambled from the bed and seized the heavy vase. She smashed him over the head with it, and he fell back unconscious. Blood dripped from an ugly cut on his head, and she half hoped that she had killed him. Still nude, she grabbed her torn gown and ran to the drawing room. The door to the corridor was locked, but the key was still in place, and she turned it.

Meanwhile, the Baron had recovered sufficiently so that he was on his feet, lurching toward her, the whip again in his hand.

"You bitch!" he screamed. "You filthy American *con!*"

But Eliza was in the corridor now and running down the stairs. "*Aidez-moi, aidez-moi!*" she bellowed as loud as she could.

The Baron stood at the head of the stairs. Above all things, he did not wish a *scandale.* He had already appeared before a magistrate on a charge of assaultive behavior with a woman, and he had no wish to be charged with a second offense. He closed the door and returned to his bedroom. It amused him to think of the American hussy naked in the street.

But Eliza had quickly entered a doorway so that she could clothe herself in her torn gown. When she was sure that the Baron was not following her, she started walking along the street as fast as she could. She had not the faintest idea where she was and she would need a coach to take her home.

After walking almost a *kilomètre*, she found a *calèche* for hire. The driver stared at her with only slight surprise. He had learned to expect anything in the streets of Paris at night. Eliza got into the coach and gave the address on the Place Vendôme.

She heaved a sigh of relief, but then a frightening thought occurred to her. She was sure that the blows of the Baron's whip had left marks on her back, marks that she would have to explain to Stephen.

As soon as she reached home, she went to her bedroom and looked at her back in her long mirror. The deep red welts made by the Baron's whip were vivid and bleeding. She realized that she would have to tell Stephen the whole stupid story.

The next morning, when she did not come downstairs to breakfast, Stephen knocked on the door of her bedroom and entered.

"You do not feel well this morning, Eliza? Perhaps you drank too much last evening."

"No," said Eliza. She was lying on her back, painful though it was. Dramatically, she rolled over so that Stephen could see the welts.

He was shocked and went over to her. He sat on the edge of the bed and said, "How has this happened? Those scars look like the marks of a whip."

"That's exactly what they are, dear Stephen."

"But how—"

"After the royal reception at the Opéra, a gentleman invited Estelle and me to have refreshments with him. He was the Baron d'Agrilly, a man who is very close to the King. I thought it might be helpful to cultivate him so as to get you a title, and so we accepted. After dinner, Estelle was tired and left us. The Baron invited me to his home for a liqueur, and I saw no harm in going. He made advances to me, and when I fought him off, he tried to rape me."

"Rape you?" asked Stephen incredulously.

"He tore my clothes from me and began lashing me with a whip. He was a madman. Finally, I was able to escape him and come home."

"But, Eliza," said Stephen, "you should know better than to accept an invitation from a man whom you had only just met!"

"I know, but since he is a man close to the King, I thought he might be able—"

Stephen interrupted her. "Tell me the truth, Eliza! You must have been aware of the man's intentions when you went to his home. You were willing to sleep with him on the chance he might get me a title!"

"Yes, Stephen. I will not lie to you. I did it only for you."

"For *me*? But I don't *want* a title!" He was quiet, and when he spoke again, his voice was angry. "You didn't do it for me! You did it for yourself! *You* want a title!"

"But, Stephen, you deserve a title, and—"

He got up abruptly, and when he turned to look at her, his eyes were cold.

"You got only what you deserved—a good thrashing! Eliza, is there no end to your ambition for social position? It is *vraiment* an obsession, and I am too old and tired to cope with it. I will send for a doctor to tend to your wounds. Tell him that you were attacked by ruffians in the street. There will be no more social life in this house until your wounds are healed, and maybe not even then!"

He was more furious than she had ever seen him. She feared that he might send her back to the United States and sue for divorce. Then, she did not know what she would do. She was reconciled to the fact that she could not obtain a title for him. But she still told herself that she had been acting in Stephen's interests and that her frightening experience with the Baron was something she had endured for her husband's sake.

Stephen did not send Eliza back to America nor did he sue for divorce. Eventually, their home on the Place Vendôme was once again the scene of festivities, and life went on as before.

But after that night, Stephen had become curiously detached in his attitude toward her. She was able to rouse him to passion only now and then, and he apologized for his occasional impotence by saying that he was getting too old for love-making.

But Eliza knew that was not the real reason. She was aware that Stephen now felt little love for her and that her power over him was on the wane.

There were periods when they hardly spoke to each other, and during these times Eliza busied herself with correspondence. Some mail was forwarded from the United States, and one day she was astonished to find a letter with the return address of "George Washington Bowen, Providence, Rhode Island."

The first thought that occurred to her was that George had forgiven her, but this hope faded quickly as she read:

DEAR MADAME JUMEL:
This is to inform you that my mother, Freelove Ballou, died recently of a stroke, which she suffered while she slept. Before she died, she told me that you have been helping us with money. This was good of you, and I suppose I should be grateful for this consideration, which is the only one you ever

289

showed me. On her behalf and because she loved you I am sending this letter of thanks.

Sincerely yours,
GEORGE WASHINGTON BOWEN

The news of Freelove's death saddened Eliza, but the coldness and formality of George's letter saddened her even more. It was quite clear that he wanted no part of her, and yet, she answered his letter with warmth and affection. She offered to help him financially with his business and signed the letter, "Your loving mother, Eliza Jumel."

The letter was never answered.

CHAPTER 29

FOUR YEARS LATER, in 1824, Louis XVIII died, and Charles X, an ardent Royalist, became king. The Coronation Ball was held in 1825, and Eliza, in the company of her friend the Duchesse de Berry attended.

In all the years since her return to Paris, she had never been a guest at such an eminent court function, and she dressed for it accordingly. Her gown was of yellow silk, trimmed with silver tinsel and hand embroidery. She wore handsome and genuine emerald earrings, and around her neck a large square-cut emerald, along with the key to Napoleon's trunk, on a sterling silver chain. Although she was now forty-nine years old, there were only a few gray hairs in her still-radiant red-gold hair.

Stephen had not wanted to go to the ball, complaining that at the age of sixty-four, social occasions tired him. But Eliza and the Duchesse de Berry persuaded him that as a well-known figure in Paris society he had an obligation to pay his respects to the new King.

The Coronation Ball was by far the most exciting social event of Eliza's life, and she took full advantage of it. Her only moment of embarrassment came when she caught sight of the Baron d'Agrilly, who came over to her immediately and asked her to be his partner in the next quadrille.

Eliza looked at him haughtily. "I am sorry, monsieur, but I do not have the pleasure of your acquaintance. My partner will be my husband."

The Baron bowed from the waist. "*Mille pardons, madame,*" he said. "It is that I believed you were someone else." But before he left, he smiled ironically, and the corners of his sensual mouth turned upward in mockery.

She shivered as she remembered her encounter with him, but she quickly put it out of her mind, continuing her conversation with the Duchesse de Berry, who had been describing the writing talents of Chateaubriand.

When the ball was over, Eliza and Stephen returned to their apartment on the Place Vendôme. Stephen was tired, but more than that, he seemed deeply depressed.

"What is the matter, Stephen? Didn't you enjoy yourself?"

"Oh, well enough. But I have some serious matters to discuss with you."

"I am tired, Stephen. Can it not wait until tomorrow?"

"No," he said. "I have bad news, and I waited until after the ball to tell you. I wanted you to enjoy yourself."

The serious tone of his voice alarmed Eliza. "What is it, Stephen? Your health—"

"Not *my* health, *ma chère*, but the health of our finances. We have spent a great deal of money, and we are heavily in debt. Somehow we must cut our expenses to the bone."

Eliza found it hard to believe him. She had always believed that they were endlessly wealthy, especially since the French government had finally made financial restitution for the loss of the plantation in Santo Domingo and the two ships it had seized some twenty years ago.

"But surely, Stephen, things cannot be as bad as you say. The money the French government paid you—"

"That is gone, too. Our only resources are what we own in the United States. The first thing we shall have to do is to move from these expensive quarters and buy a small house to live in."

"But we'll still be able to entertain, won't we?"

"Yes, but on a very modest scale. I am sorry to give you such bad news, Eliza, but we cannot go further into debt. And now, if you will excuse me, I'll go to bed."

He left her sitting alone in the drawing room. She got up and poured herself some brandy. The news had been a shock, and she wanted to think things over and decide what she should do. Ever since her marriage to Stephen she had never given a thought to money. She had been extravagant, but she had seen no reason why she should not be. Stephen had assumed the care of their finances, and she had never worried about money.

Now, she would have to pay attention to their money, and more than that, she would have to take charge of it. She had complete confidence in herself as a businesswoman. She had long ago learned how to count pennies and budget herself. She agreed with Stephen that the first thing to be done was to move from their expensive establishment on the Place Vendôme.

They found a small house at Mount de Marsan and bought it. Within two weeks they had moved in, and Eliza busied herself arranging their furniture to her satisfaction. There was a fairly large drawing room downstairs, and on the floor above there were three bedrooms: one for Stephen, one for Mary and the third for herself.

They continued to entertain, but not on the lavish scale of the past. It was Stephen's plan to give up all his American real estate and to make this new house their permanent home.

In January 1826, Stephen decided to deed over The Mansion with its original thirty-six acres of land to Eliza, not so much because he felt kindly toward her, but because this would checkmate impending legal action by his creditors.

And so in April, Eliza and Mary sailed for New York with Stephen's instructions to sell all his holdings and then return to Paris. Along with her personal effects, Eliza took with her all the mementos of Napoleon and her collection of good paintings. She explained to Stephen that she might need to sell these things to raise cash.

When Eliza arrived in New York, she could hardly believe that it was the same city she had left six years ago. It had expanded northward to where Greenwich Village began, and to the east as well, to accommodate the mounting number of immigrants who had been arriving. The population of New York City was now 200,000.

The wharves and docks, which had once occupied only the

southern tip of the island, now extended far up the East River and up the Hudson River as well. Robert Fulton's steamboat, which had once been dismissed as impractical, had been perfected, and now new and much larger side-wheelers left New York to go up the Hudson as far as Albany. The Erie Canal had recently been completed, and its three hundred and fifty miles now connected the Great Lakes with the Atlantic Ocean.

As soon as Eliza landed in this burgeoning city, she conferred with Brunel, Desobrus and Bernard, the men who had been left in charge of Stephen's affairs. They had leased The Mansion to Moses Field and his family. She went over the books with them, and it was clear to her that they had been turning some of the revenues to their own interests. She fired them on the spot and wrote Stephen about it. She said that in order to straighten out the tangle of his financial affairs, she would need power of attorney.

Stephen agreed to this, and Eliza received the document, which authorized her to "transact . . . his affairs at New York [and] to sell . . . all or any part of the real estate . . . belonging to him."

Armed with this document, Eliza's plan of action became clear to her. To sell Stephen's New York holdings in this time of soaring real estate values would be ridiculous. She foresaw that a quick fortune could be made in real estate, and she intended to make it, with or without Stephen's permission. With the power of attorney, she could legally do whatever she pleased.

But she would need a lawyer to work with her. She thought of Aaron, but decided that she wanted a young lawyer, in tune with the changing times. The lawyer she found was Alexander Hamilton, Jr.

He resembled his father in looks, blond and handsome, but there the resemblance stopped. From his mother, Elizabeth Schuyler, he had inherited a character that was totally admirable. Unlike his father, he was scrupulously honest and straightforward.

He knew who Eliza was, of course, and guessed at her early relationship with Aaron Burr and probably with his father as well, but this did not bother him. He had loved his father and mourned his loss, but he felt that the subsequent treatment of Burr had been unjust and unfair.

Eliza and young Hamilton liked each other on sight, and she outlined her plans to him. The first thing she did, for her own protection, was to have all of Stephen's holdings deeded over to her daughter, Mary Eliza Jumel.

Her only income was the rent from Moses Field, who was still living in The Mansion. Meanwhile, for economy, Eliza and Mary went to live in the house of a Dutch farmer on Long Island, two and a half miles from Brooklyn. It was a long journey into New York City, but by arising at dawn, Eliza was able to get to town in time to carry out her real estate transactions.

Hamilton was in a good position to be an adviser. He had a close association with the members of Mayor Philip Hone's administration. When he told her that there were plans to build a new thoroughfare beyond Canal Street, Eliza bought a sizable piece of property there. Within a month she sold the land for double what she had paid for it. And so the transactions continued, and Eliza worked from dawn till dusk in her effort to recapture Stephen's lost fortune.

Meanwhile, in Paris, Stephen was having severe financial problems. To settle a debt of eight thousand francs, he had to sell all their sterling silverware.

He wrote Eliza a pathetic letter, which ended:

Be good enough, then, for the love of God, to send money to me for my living expenses. I am totally without resources.

Eliza had told Stephen nothing about her speculations in real estate, and she replied to his request by saying:

I have done everything in my power to procure money for you but it was impossible, money being so scarce, but since we have the house at Mount de Marsan, wouldn't it be better to sacrifice that, rather than what we have left here for old age?

Stephen sold the house, together with all its expensive furnishings, and when it became evident that Eliza was not going to send him any money and did not intend to return to Paris, he moved to Bordeaux to stay with his relatives.

Eliza had indeed made an effort to get some money for Stephen, but when she found that the interest rate would be 17½ per cent, instead of the usual 7 per cent, she put the idea out of her mind. In any case, she had better uses for any available cash and did not want to be held down by loans. She would have worried about the possibility of Stephen's relatives cajoling him into changing his will in their favor, but with all the New York properties in Mary's name, they would be powerless.

Eliza worked harder than she had in her whole life. If she were to become very rich, the people of New York would have to accept her. She had learned to be a hard and determined bargainer, and little by little she accumulated more and more properties. The procedure was always the same: to buy a lot and then sell it for almost double its original cost. Her acquisitions even included land in Washington Heights, which, along with the rest of the city, had grown. She now had three neighbors near The Mansion and finally decided to move back into the building herself and leave her temporary quarters with the Dutch farmer on Long Island. She took her collection of paintings and Napoleonic relics out of storage and set about making The Mansion a comfortable place in which to live again.

One day on the street she met Pieter Van Zandt. He was forty-seven years old now and looked it. He had put on considerable weight, and his boyish good looks had completely disappeared. He pretended that he did not see Eliza, but she stepped in his path.

"Pieter!" she said. "How are you? It has been so long—"

"Yes, madame. It has been a long time. Two years ago I got married, and I now have two sons."

"How splendid!" Eliza said with warmth. "And where do you live and what do you do?"

"I am still in grandfather's house on Moore Street," he said. He paused and then asked, "How is Mary?"

"Oh, Mary is here with me at The Mansion. Someday you and your wife must come and have tea with us."

"I don't believe we will, thank you," said Pieter. "I am only a carpenter, and I would not feel comfortable having tea at The Mansion. Is Mary married?"

"No. She is a very attractive young woman of twenty-five, but as you know, she has always been shy with men."

Pieter smiled ironically. "She was never shy with me, madame."

"I know. Sometimes, I am sorry—"

"That's all in the past and best forgotten. Well, it has been good to see you. I'll bid you good day."

As he turned to leave, Eliza on impulse said, "Your grandfather's house on Moore Street—would you be interested in selling it? That is a very valuable property now."

"I know. But it is my home, and it is not for sale."

He left abruptly. Eliza stood in the street, looking after him. Again she felt guilt for having broken up his attachment to Mary. That afternoon, in a gesture of atonement, she sent Pieter and his wife a silver-plated tea service as a belated wedding gift. But she never received so much as a note of thanks. She knew now that she had lost Pieter's friendship forever. It saddened her for a day or two, but then she threw herself into a frenzy of work.

Now she was beginning to acquire not only empty land but houses as well, houses that would bring income in rent. She bought a new coach and a pair of her favorite horses—black Arabians.

The coach was painted gold, of course.

CHAPTER 30

EARLY IN THE SUMMER of 1828 Eliza had titles to fourteen hundred properties in New York City. Two million dollars had been added to the original one million dollars of the Jumel fortune, including The Mansion. Eliza decided, like a cautious cardplayer, to quit while she was ahead.

She wrote Stephen telling him what she had done, and that they now had three times as much money as before. She wanted him to come home so that they could spend their old age comfortably together.

In early autumn, Stephen arrived in New York. He was delighted to see Eliza and Mary and pleased to know that they were once again rich. He had aged greatly in the two and a half years since Eliza had last seen him and looked older than sixty-eight. It saddened Eliza to realize that he was no longer the "laughing giant" that he had once been called. Now, he did little laughing. But he was content to know that all the money had been legally deeded over to Mary.

Mary, who had always loved Stephen, now became devoted to him and spent much of her time talking to him and caring for him. She no longer called him Grandfather, since she thought this might remind him of his advancing years. Now she called him Father, and this pleased the old man.

Meanwhile, Eliza had started an active social life. She decided to abandon further cultivation of the old New York families for the time being and to concentrate her attention on the many French political refugees who lived in New York. In spite of their exile, they were a convivial and entertaining group, even though most of them were not rich. She had arranged for her old friend Estelle, the Comtesse de la Pagerie, to come to New York and stay at The Mansion on an extended visit. With her interest in the arts, Eliza gathered around her the French-born painters, musicians and writers of the time.

When her new neighbor, Sheppard Knapp, made fun of her one day because her coach was drawn by only two horses, she went out and bought two more handsome black Arabian horses and then had a new coat of gold paint applied to her coach. She resumed her old habit of riding through town to show off in high style.

Whenever new friends made their first visit to The Mansion, Eliza would take them through the rooms of the house and show off her imposing collection of Napoleonic relics: the sofa and eight chairs that had belonged to the Emperor when he was First Consul; his trunk and ornamental traveling clock; and his chess set, each piece made of old ivory, bearing the initial *N* and with a carved head of Napoleon wearing his cocked hat. She had also bought the Gobelin tapestry rug on which his small feet had rested when he played chess with the Empress Josephine at Malmaison.

When the theatrical season began in the fall, Eliza once again was a regular patron of the Park Theatre. Now, there were not only productions of Shakespearean plays to delight her. There was Italian opera.

The Jumels left for Saratoga, as usual, as soon as the weather grew warm in June 1831. Mary, Nodine and Marie went along, and The Mansion was closed for the summer.

The town had grown over the years. A huge, wide thoroughfare called Broadway had been constructed, and there was another hotel, Congress Hall. The original spring near High Rock was protected by a wooden conical covering. The area had been dug out and the marshy land around it drained. New springs had been discovered, and now neat footpaths covered the area.

Along with this expansion of the original town, the number of summer visitors from everywhere in the United States had risen to six thousand, and the town was booming.

Eliza's house, The Tuileries, was no longer the most imposing house in town, but its interior could not be matched anywhere. Her collection of fine paintings and her Colonial furniture were showpieces for visitors from everywhere in the country, and she had brought along her collection of Napoleonic memorabilia.

At three o'clock every afternoon, there was a procession of carriages on Broadway. The women in the carriages were dressed in their finest gowns and some, in open carriages, carried parasols. Eliza saw to it that her own golden carriage, drawn by six horses with outriders and a coachman, always led the parade. Eliza was the acknowledged queen of Saratoga Springs.

The days of the summer passed slowly, and Eliza grew bored. One morning she decided that she and Mary would pay a visit to her old friend Judge Crippen, who lived in Worcester, in Otsego County. Stephen stayed behind to drink the spring waters, which seemed to help his rheumatism.

Judge Crippen had been a friend of Aaron Burr's, and now he lived in retirement in a large and comfortable house. He was delighted to see Eliza and Mary and offered them his hospitality for as long as they wished.

There was a law student staying in the house. His name was Nelson Chase, and within ten minutes of meeting him, Eliza had decided that he would make an ideal husband for Mary, who was now thirty years old. Nelson was perhaps a few years older than Mary, an intelligent and likable young man, though hardly handsome. More important was the fact that he was educated and well read and could talk to Eliza about the plays of Shakespeare. Like Mary, he was a little shy, very polite and not too forward. He treated Eliza with the respect she felt was due her.

After three days Eliza returned alone to Saratoga Springs. She left Mary behind in the hope that a courtship might follow. She had told Mary that Nelson Chase would, in her view, make an excellent husband. To Eliza's surprise, Mary had agreed, saying that Nelson was a very considerate and gentle young man, not unlike Pieter. With a final bit of advice not to let the relationship go "too far," Eliza had said goodbye, promising to come back in a month.

After Eliza's return to Saratoga Springs, she soon became bored again. Her carriage still led the daily parade at three o'clock, and for diversion she read some of the French books that the Comtesse had sent her. She particularly liked the romantic novels of Chateaubriand and a play called *Hernani* by a new writer named Victor Hugo.

Sometimes, she took a walk into town and shopped for trifles in the little stores that had sprung up everywhere as Saratoga Springs prospered. On one of these occasions she passed a distinguished-looking tall man in his mid-thirties. Something about his appearance caught her attention, and she realized with a shock that the man was her bastard son, George Washington Bowen.

She ran back and placed herself in his path.

"I beg your pardon," said the man.

"Forgive me, but aren't you George Washington Bowen?"

When he nodded, Eliza said, "I am Madame Jumel, Mr. Bowen."

George stood off and surveyed her coldly.

"Are you indeed?" he said, smiling Matt Wyatt's one-sided smile.

"I am your mother, George. It is so good—"

He interrupted her. "My mother was Freelove Ballou, whose death I informed you of when I wrote you to stop sending money."

"But I wanted to help. Perhaps I could still help—"

"Thank you, but I need no help, madame. I own a prosperous dry goods business in Providence. I am married and have two children."

"Oh, how splendid! Then I have grandchildren—"

Again, George interrupted. "Grandchildren whom you will never see. Good day to you, madame."

301

He turned his back on her and went quickly on his way.

Eliza stared after him sadly. As her eyes followed him, she noted the red-gold hair so like her own. But what had really surprised her was his face, long and thin, with a prominent jaw. It was the face of a young George Washington. This fact completely took away any sorrow she might have felt about his rejection of her. There was no longer any doubt in her mind that she was indeed George Washington's daughter. Her mother, Phebe, drunken harlot though she was, had told the truth, after all.

As Eliza walked back to The Tuileries, her step was brisk and cheerful, and she lifted up her face to the setting sun with a new pride.

When Eliza returned to Judge Crippen's house on her way back to New York, she was pleased to see that young Nelson Chase and Mary seemed to be in love and that a marriage was not far off.

With much stammering and many blushes, Nelson asked Eliza for Mary's hand.

Eliza beamed at him. "Why, certainly, dear Mr. Chase. I would like to have you as my son-in-law."

Nelson smiled in relief. "Thank you, thank you, madame. I shall do my best to make Mary a faithful and dutiful husband."

"I am sure you will," said Eliza. "To get you off to a good start, I'll give you an allowance of one thousand dollars a year, with the understanding that you both will live with me at The Mansion."

"That is very kind of you," said Nelson.

"The marriage will take place early next year. I would advise you to get to New York before snow falls, when travel becomes difficult."

"In November?" asked Nelson.

"That would be splendid."

On the day of departure for New York, Mary kissed Nelson goodbye with more feeling than Eliza would have believed possible. The courtship had clearly gone well.

In the carriage on the way back to New York, Eliza and Mary planned an elaborate trousseau. Mary had never seemed happier.

In November, Nelson Chase arrived on schedule at The Mansion, and the wedding was planned for early in January 1832. Eliza was in favor of an elaborate church wedding, but neither Mary nor Nelson liked the idea. Both of them, shy by nature, said they would prefer the wedding to take place at The Mansion. Eliza was disappointed, but finally gave in when they agreed to a large wedding reception.

The wedding and the reception that followed were elaborate. Eliza spared no expense, and engraved invitations were sent out to all of Eliza's French refugee friends, as well as the city's first families.

As usual, the guests were mostly French refugees, but there was a sprinkling of Livingstons and Clintons, whom Alexander Hamilton, Jr., and his mother had persuaded to attend. Eliza was well pleased, especially by the glowing reports of the occasion in the daily newspapers. She dared to hope that at last she had made a small inroad on the highway of New York society. She was happy that the young couple planned to make their home at The Mansion.

But that arrangement did not work out well. It lasted only two months. Eliza, in her zeal to do everything possible for the comfort of Mary and Nelson, treated them as though they were her children, incapable of doing anything for themselves. She was not only a solicitous mother, but, without realizing it, a demanding one. She ruled the household with an iron hand, even though it might be gloved in silk. Her fifty-six years had given her the airs of a *grande dame* who expected to be deferred to and obeyed.

Nelson reacted to this by becoming lazy and taciturn. He stopped reading his law books and spent much of his time reading novels or playing cards with Mary.

When Eliza took him to task for this, he lost his temper. "It is not good for me to live here, madame!"

"Why not?" asked Eliza. "All your needs are taken care of; you are given whatever you wish—"

"That's just it!" he replied. "A man likes to be his own master and run his own house!"

"You will not run *this* house, Nelson! This is *my* house, and my house it will remain!"

"Then I will move out of it and take Mary with me!" Nelson stomped out of the room.

The friction continued, and Mary was drawn into it. Unexpectedly, she stood with Nelson against her mother.

Eliza wept, saying, "Even my own daughter, my own child, is turning against me."

"But I am not a child, Mama. I am a married woman, and I must stand by my husband in this, as in all things."

Eliza was shocked by Mary's first declaration of independence, and she was angry too, because she felt that the young couple had betrayed her.

Finally, she said, "And how do you propose to live if you leave here?"

"I will get work in a law office," said Nelson.

"We will take rooms in town," said Mary.

"And what will you use for money?" asked Eliza coldly.

Mary had never defied her mother before now, but when she spoke, her voice was clear and definite. "You will lend us the money to get started, Mama."

Eliza was silent. She had been beaten, and she acknowledged defeat with the gracefulness and courage of Napoleon himself.

"Very well," she said curtly.

Within a week, Nelson had found rooms at 63 Chambers Street, and Eliza helped in furnishing them comfortably. She had accepted her Waterloo and gracefully mended the quarrel. But she had no intention of letting Mary and Nelson be free of her. She visited them almost every day, and she kept them where she wanted them—under her thumb. She presented them with gifts of furnishings for their apartment, new clothing for Mary and Nelson, and she took them to the theatre when the season opened. During the intermissions, she paraded them about proudly and never let them get very far out of sight. Although they no longer lived with her, they were still her children.

And the marriage was successful, not only for Mary and Nelson, but for Eliza herself. It had helped to establish her own respectability.

And that, after all, was the most important thing.

CHAPTER 31

In the spring of 1832, Stephen Jumel seemed to undergo an unexpected rejuvenation. He became spirited and cheerful, and one fine day in the middle of May he left the chair by the fireside and decided he would get out-of-doors and make some pretense of being the gentleman farmer that Eliza insisted on calling him. He decided to accompany his farmhands as they went about their work with a hay wagon. Riding atop a load of hay on the Old Kingsbridge Road, he dozed quietly in the sun.

Suddenly, he lost his balance, slipped and fell off the wagon. The farmhands stopped and picked him up. He was unconscious, and one of his arms had been broken. With Stephen back on the wagon with one of the workers to attend him, the men returned to The Mansion as quickly as they could.

Eliza was shocked by the accident but acted with her customary efficiency in times of crisis. The doctor was sent for, and Stephen was placed gently in his bed. Eliza tried to revive him with some cognac, but he refused to swallow.

Dr. Romayne, an old man now but still the family's doctor, examined Stephen and then bled him. He said that Stephen had evidently suffered a concussion and had a compound fracture of his left arm, with the bone jutting out through the skin. A splint was made, and the arm was set, bandaged and placed in a sling.

Dr. Romayne told Eliza that Stephen might soon regain consciousness and that when he did, light food should be given him. Meanwhile, it would be necessary for someone to watch over him.

For the rest of the day Eliza sat at the side of the bed, calling out his name again and again in an effort to revive him. But Stephen slept on.

When it was dinnertime, Eliza had Marie take her place at the bedside. After eating, she again watched over Stephen, until she grew sleepy and asked Marie to take over her post.

Dr. Romayne came the next morning and again bled Stephen, but he saw no signs of improvement; however, late that afternoon, Stephen seemed to be struggling to come back to consciousness. He opened his eyes and looked about him in bewilderment. Eliza went over to him, called his name and reached for his hand.

He recognized her. "Eliza, *ma chère* Eliza," he whispered.

Eliza wept tears of joy and sent a servant to prepare a light meal for him. She propped him up on pillows and fed him a spoonful or two of oatmeal and cream.

He did not want to eat more and murmured, "*Du cognac, s'il te plaît.*"

Eliza gave him some diluted brandy in a spoon, and this revived him somewhat. He wanted more, and she gave it to him.

He gradually became aware of the world around him and recognized that he was in his bedroom. "Eliza, what has happened? Why am I here? What is the matter with my arm?"

Eliza explained, and Stephen's only response was: "I am a fool. Why didn't you just let me die? I don't want to live anymore."

"Hush, *mon bien-aimé*. You must not say such things. Your broken arm will mend, and soon you will be as fit as a fiddle."

"I don't want to be." He smiled wanly. "Why is a fiddle supposed to be fit?" Then he closed his eyes and fell asleep again.

The next day, Dr. Romayne found Stephen much improved. He changed the bloodstained bandage on the arm and again bled him. He left a sedative medicine, which would keep Stephen quiet and help him to sleep.

Eliza sent a coach to bring Mary and Nelson to the house. She thought that a visit from them would improve Stephen's spirits. Mary was very much upset and cried.

At last, when Mary had composed herself, she and Nelson

entered Stephen's room. Eliza shook Stephen gently to wake him up. When his eyes opened and he saw Mary, he gave his first genuine smile and took her hand. But Mary could not hold back her tears and wiped her eyes with her handkerchief.

"Now, you see how stupid your father is, riding a hay wagon like a *brave garçon*, forgetting that he is an old man of seventy-two."

"You are not *stupide*, *mon cher papa*. And you are still *vraiment un brave garçon*." She smiled her slow, sweet smile and kissed him gently on the forehead. "You must get well, Papa—for me."

"Are you making a *bébé* for me, then?"

Mary smiled again. "No, not yet—but soon, maybe."

"You must hurry, *chère Mary*, because I will not be here very long." He closed his eyes then and drifted off into sleep.

Late that afternoon, Stephen became restless, and when he talked, his words did not make sense. In recurring hallucinations, he was reliving the past.

"Hurry, Eliza. We are already late for the ball at the Duchesse de Berry's. For the sake of *le bon Dieu*, stop that primping before the mirror! You already look more beautiful than any woman I have ever seen. *Dépêche-toi, dépêche-toi!*"

Eliza's efforts to bring him back to reality were futile. Though his eyes were open, they had a vacant look, as scenes from their life together flitted before him.

Once, when he re-enacted the scene of their first meeting at the horse race back in 1800, tears filled Eliza's eyes.

It was late, and she was very tired. She called Marie and gave instructions for her to watch over Stephen carefully during the night, since he was delirious.

In her bedroom, Eliza found it difficult to sleep. The memories evoked by Stephen's wandering mind, even the happy ones, made her cry. It took three cognacs to calm her sufficiently for sleep.

It was early morning when Marie hastened into Eliza's bedroom. "Get up, madame! For God's sake, madame, come quickly! Monsieur Jumel is bleeding to death!"

Eliza ran to Stephen's bedroom. The sight that met her eyes

sickened her. Stephen was unconscious, and his bed was drenched with blood. The bandage had been torn from his arm, and blood still spurted rhythmically from his wound, but very slowly. She tore a piece of sheet from the bed and applied a tourniquet above the wound, but she knew that it was too late. His face was drained of all color, and he breathed slowly in short, spasmodic gasps.

She sat down by his side on the bloodied bed and took his hand in hers. She called to him softly again and again, and finally he opened his eyes. He recognized her and whispered, "Ah, *ma chère, ma chère.* I am gone." Then he closed his eyes wearily and did not open them again.

"Marie! Get the doctor, quickly!"

Marie fled from the room and downstairs. Eliza did not leave the bedside. Stephen's hand was still in hers, and nervously she felt for his pulse. It was faint and increasingly irregular. Finally, it stopped altogether, and Stephen rose up in the bed as though fighting for his breath. Then he suddenly fell back, his mouth open, saliva drooling from his lips.

Eliza did not need a doctor to tell her that Stephen was dead. She got up and paced the floor, too stunned for thought. Marie entered the room. There was a look of fright and guilt on her face. Weeping, she went over to Eliza and put her arms about her.

"How is he, madame?"

"He is dead. It is all over. A doctor cannot help him now."

Marie moved away, continuing to weep. "Oh, madame, it is my fault. I was sleepy, and I dozed off. When I woke up, I saw that he had torn off the bandage and was bleeding. The bed was soaked in blood. Then I called you—"

Marie was standing a few feet from Eliza, her body bowed by grief and guilt. Eliza went over to her and roughly lifted her face. Then, with all her strength, she slapped Marie on the cheeks again and again.

"Stupid, lazy slut! Get out of my sight!"

Marie ran from the room, leaving Eliza alone. Eliza stared out the window, looking at the garden with its spring flowers lifting

309

themselves toward the morning sun. It struck her as absurd that life should be going on as usual, when Stephen lay there so quiet, so dead on that bloodstained bed.

She could not believe that it had happened. She was not crying now, but she felt faint and went over to a table where there was a brandy bottle. She gulped down two or three swigs of cognac. The burning in her throat made her aware that she was still alive, that she was not dreaming.

She sat down in a chair facing the window. Her head was down between her legs, and at last, she began to cry with great sobs.

"Oh, Stephen, Stephen, forgive me. I should have been at your bedside all night instead of letting that wretched Marie—"

But the same thing might have happened, anyway, she told herself. It was clear to her that Stephen, in his delirium, had torn loose the bandage. Or he might have done it deliberately. He had said that he did not want to live any longer. But this thought made her feel even more guilty. Why hadn't he wanted to live?

She had always been so busy seeking her own pleasures since he had returned from France that she had given him little of her time, and he had sat there by the fireplace, smoking his pipe and dozing. He scarcely seemed alive. How ironic it was that his attempt to get out of the house and to be active again should have been the reason for his death.

Eliza felt a great sense of loss. For thirty-two years he had always been at her side—generous, kind, loving. He had been utterly faithful and forgiving, even when she had been guilty of wrongdoing or headstrong foolishness. He had been not only her lover but a father as well, the only real father she had ever known. He had lavished money on her to the point of spoiling her, and when he was needed, he had always been there, steadfast and loyal.

And in return, what had she given him? Her body, her ability to amuse him, companionship? Yes, but love? As much as she was capable of, perhaps, in the early days of their marriage. But she had never really loved anyone except Aaron. Mostly, she told herself, she had used Stephen as a rung on the ladder of her ambition. And now, too late, she had a mounting sense of guilt.

To make amends somehow, she ordered the most expensive coffin to be found in New York, and a very imposing tombstone over which a handsome marble slab would rest on stone posts three feet high.

From the servants she learned that it was being whispered about town that she had murdered Stephen, had torn the bandage from his arm so that he would bleed to death. There was a brief inquest in which it was established that she was innocent of all wrongdoing, and the chief witness was Marie, who took the blame tearfully on herself.

But the gossip did not stop, and many people in the city believed that Eliza, in addition to being an immoral woman, was a murderess.

A high mass was said for Stephen at St. Patrick's Cathedral on the corner of Prince and Mott Streets. The church was crowded with Stephen's friends, and many of them shed tears of genuine sorrow at his passing.

In the churchyard, in front of the gate that opened on Mott Street, Stephen was laid to rest in consecrated ground. As the coffin was lowered, Eliza sobbed and was comforted by Mary, whose own eyes streamed tears.

Eliza was kneeling on the wet ground, not caring that her stunning mourning costume of black silk was being soiled. She rose unsteadily to her feet, and Nelson Chase rushed to her side to keep her from falling. But she brushed aside his arm and walked with lifted head toward her waiting coach.

The summer passed slowly at The Mansion. Eliza was lonely and depressed. After the visits of condolence had dwindled off, nobody came to see her except occasionally Mary and Nelson.

She had little appetite and spent most of her time thinking of the days that were gone, especially those wonderful days in Paris. To cheer herself, she drank too much cognac, and by day's end, she was often tipsy.

It was the nights that she dreaded most. Even the cognac could not help her to sleep peacefully, and soon she became a prey to terror. She had never believed in ghosts, but now she was certain that The Mansion was haunted. There were footsteps in the middle of the night on the staircase, and they were loud enough to awaken her from cognac-drugged sleep. It sounded like Stephen rushing up the stairs, two at a time, in the way he had done in his younger days.

The whole house groaned and creaked, even on those nights when there was no wind; and if there was an autumn storm, the house seemed to rock back and forth in the gale. In the morning she always told herself that these were daft fancies, and that Stephen's ghost would have no reason for haunting the house, unless the anger that he must have felt toward her and had seldom shown was now expressing itself.

If there was a ghost, and she increasingly became sure that there was, it could only be Stephen. When the noises continued, she took to prowling about the house with a candle in her hand, in the hope of catching a glimpse of him. She saw nothing. But one night she thought she heard his loud and boisterous giant's laugh. It echoed and re-echoed through her bedroom, and in it there was a jeering note of sarcasm that it had never held before.

Again, in the morning, with the reassuring October sunshine falling through the windows, she tried to tell herself that she was having hallucinations. But she did not convince herself.

Marie was aware that Eliza was troubled, and one morning said, "Beg pardon, mum, but are you sick?"

"Not sick, Marie, just frightened out of my wits."

"But what are you scared of, madame?"

"Of the ghost of Monsieur Jumel. It is in this house. Haven't you heard him? His footsteps, his laughing?"

"I ain't heard nothin', madame."

"You wouldn't—not down there below stairs. But he is here, I tell you!"

"Have you seen him?"

"No, and I don't want to." Eliza began crying, and Marie stroked the graying hair in an attempt to console her.

"Madame, you are very jumpy since the master died. I think you should talk to Miss Mary—that is, Mrs. Chase."

Eliza looked up. "Yes. That is what I'll do. Go to town in the coach and tell her that I must see her this afternoon."

When Mary and Nelson arrived, Eliza was sitting in the drawing room. She sipped nervously at a glass of cognac.

Eliza rose. "Mary, I cannot stand living here a moment longer."

Mary looked studiously at her mother, at the pale face without make-up, the dark rings under her eyes, the disheveled hair.

"Mother, what is the matter? You look ill."

"Oh, I am not ill—except perhaps in my head. The trouble is *him*!"

"Him? Who is 'him'?"

"Stephen, Stephen! Your father! He is here in this house!"

Mary was puzzled. "But Father died last May. He is in his grave. How could he be here?"

Eliza paused and then whispered, "It is his ghost. I hear him coming up the staircase to my bedroom. He laughs—oh, God, how he laughs! But it is not pleasant laughter; it is sarcastic, mean—"

Nelson went over to Eliza and patted her shoulder reassuringly. "Madame, you are overwrought. Ghosts do not exist."

Mary said, "It is only your imagination, Mama. I know how you must feel—"

"Know how I feel? I'll tell you how I feel, like Lady Macbeth in the sleepwalking scene." She began to wring her hands as she remembered the words. " *'Out, damned spot! out, I say! . . . Wash your hands; put on your nightgown; . . . I tell you yet again, Banquo's buried; he cannot come out on 's grave. . . . To bed, to bed; . . . what's done cannot be undone; to bed, to bed . . .'* " Eliza was silent. The only sound that came from her was of muffled sobs.

Mary looked at Nelson, who nodded his head. Then she went over to Eliza and put her arms around her. She was the mother now, treating Eliza like a frightened child.

"Mother, you cannot live here all by yourself. It is making you mad. You must come home with us."

Eliza lifted her tear-streaked face and shook her head dolefully. "There's no room in your little apartment."

313

"Then Nelson will find new quarters for the three of us. Meanwhile, I'll stay here with you. I'll sleep in the same bed with you so that you will be safe from the ghost."

Eliza's usual feeling of independence had utterly disappeared, and she seized Mary's hands in her own, kissing them gratefully.

"Oh, thank you, thank you, dear child. I have been so frightened."

As Nelson left the house to return to town, Mary led a weeping Eliza up the stairs to her bedroom.

"You will go to bed now, Mother dear, and get some rest," she said with quiet firmness. She seized the brandy bottle from the night table. "And you will have no more of this."

"But I need it. Please, Mary."

"You will have no more cognac," said Mary resolutely. "I will have Marie bring you a tray of food. You must eat, dear Mama."

Mary left with the bottle of brandy in her hand.

That night she slept with Eliza, who curled up against her like a child. Mary could hardly believe that this was her mother, the dominating, assured woman she had always known, bold, afraid of nothing in the world.

Mary lay awake long after Eliza had fallen into a sound sleep for the first time in weeks. She was listening for the sounds that Eliza had described. But there were no footsteps, no sounds of laughter. At last she fell asleep and did not awaken until the morning sun streamed through the window blinds.

Late that afternoon Nelson returned. He had found a large apartment on the corner of Grand and Elm Streets. Eliza and Mary had packed whatever clothing might be needed during the fall and winter.

When they were ready to leave, Eliza stood alone for a moment in the entrance hall, as though saying goodbye to the house.

Her eyes filled with tears as she murmured, "Goodbye, dear Stephen. Have mercy on me, because someday I shall come back —to stay."

She turned and walked quickly to the door, locking it behind her.

314

PART VI

Eliza
and
Aaron

CHAPTER 32

THE WINTER PASSED SLOWLY for Eliza, cheerless and bleak. But when spring came, she became her normal self and was homesick for The Mansion. She decided to go back there to live, and the servants were given orders to make the place ready for her return.

On a sunny day in April she drove up to Washington Heights with Mary. She was still fearful of the ghost and asked Mary to stay the night. But there were no footsteps on the stairs, no sounds of laughter, and Eliza slept soundly. And yet, after Mary had left the next morning, the house oppressed her. She wandered from room to room restlessly, and the complete quiet made her nervous.

She lay awake that night, feeling so alone that she almost wished the ghost would return. Quite unexpectedly, she thought of Aaron. Stephen was gone now, so there was no reason why Aaron should not come to visit her.

The next day, after she had had her noon meal, she dressed herself in a new gown from Paris and set out for Aaron's office on Nassau Street.

Molly answered her knock at the door. She recognized Eliza and admitted her.

"The master is in his office, Madame Jumel."

Aaron came out to greet her. He had aged since she last saw him, but he had quite recovered from his melancholia. His figure was trim and erect, and he could easily have passed for a man of sixty-five.

"Eliza, my love!" he said and took her in his arms. He started to kiss her, but she moved her head gently away.

317

"Ah, in mourning for your deceased husband, is that it? I was sorry to hear of his death, and I wanted to offer my condolences, but I was not sure they would be welcome. Sit down, my dear, and tell me how you are. You look as beautiful as ever."

She sat down in the office chair opposite him. "I see that you are as cheerful a liar as ever, Aaron. I have aged. No, don't say I haven't. After all, I have a mirror. I have put on enough weight so that my figure is matronly. My hair is all white now, and on my face there are many lines that cannot be covered by make-up. And here, at my throat, I now wear a velvet band to lift up the sagging skin. After all, I shall be fifty-eight in August."

"Birthdays should neither be counted nor celebrated after fifty. Perhaps I still see you as you were at twenty, and the memory is clearer than present reality. In any case, you are the most beautiful woman I have ever known." He paused and smiled before adding, "And, as you remember, I have known many."

"I know," she said.

Aaron stood up. "Let's have some tea, my dear. Would you like that?"

Eliza nodded, and as soon as Aaron had gone to the kitchen, she looked at his desk and was pleased to see that there was a large stack of briefs and other legal papers there. Evidently, he had no lack of business.

When she had settled herself on the sofa in the drawing room, Aaron returned. He did not take a chair but sat by her side. He sought her hand and clasped it tightly in his own. His head was close to hers, and she looked him in the eyes, which were still lustrous and black. The glint in them told her that he desired her, and she primly moved away from him.

He laughed. "Ho! So my Eliza has become the coquette, has she?"

It was true. It was coquetry that had prompted her to move, and as usual, he had read her mind.

When Molly brought in the tea, it was a welcome diversion. She had no intention of getting into bed with Aaron on the first day of their reunion.

"Shall I pour?" she asked.

"Please do," he said.

After they had had their tea, Aaron again attempted to make love to her. He kissed her with passion, but she resisted him forcefully and stood up.

"Whatever is the matter, Eliza? You don't find me attractive anymore?"

"You have lost too much of your hair," she said mockingly.

"So I have. At seventy-seven I have a right to lose my hair. But I have not lost my passion for you."

"I wonder," she said. She moved toward the door. "I must leave, Aaron. Would you like to come to The Mansion tomorrow night and have dinner with me?"

Aaron stood up and gave her a bow that was mockingly elaborate. "The bald-headed elderly gentleman would be delighted, but he would like to kiss you goodbye."

Again he seized her in his arms, and when he kissed her, his tongue moved between her teeth and into her mouth. She bit it gently.

"Enough of that, sir," she said, feigning indignation.

"*Au revoir*, my little virgin," he said.

She slammed the door in his face. Then, chuckling to herself, she got into her golden coach and rode back to Washington Heights.

Eliza had her chef prepare an elaborate dinner of seven courses. Two bottles of champagne were chilled as well as some Chablis for the fish course. She had spent the afternoon making herself as alluring as possible, and now, with all the candles lighted in the drawing room, she sat down to await Aaron's arrival.

It was seven o'clock. She had not told him exactly when dinner would be served, and as the minutes ticked by on the gold clock on the mantelpiece, she began to grow nervous. Perhaps he would not come. Perhaps he had taken her little game of coquetry seriously.

319

As the clock chimed eight, she felt sure that he was not coming. And then the sound of the door knocker thudded on the porch, and the liveried footman went to answer it.

As Aaron was ushered into the drawing room, she rose to greet him. "You are a little late, Aaron," she said.

"Late?" he said. "But surely ladies and gentlemen do not dine before eight?"

"Perhaps I am not a lady," she said.

"Oh, I had forgotten," he said with a smile. "And after all my instruction—"

"I am grateful for your instruction—in grammar, at least. Will you have some brandy?"

He nodded, and she poured him some in one of her Napoleon brandy glasses of sparkling crystal. When she handed it to him, she gave him a warm smile. "Shall we declare a truce?" she asked.

"I was not aware that there was a war. I would never do battle with you, dear Eliza."

"I'm not so sure of that," she said.

After dinner they returned to the drawing room to have cordials and coffee.

Aaron stretched out full length on Napoleon's sofa.

"Your chef, Eliza, is a wizard. It has been a long time since I had such a delicious dinner."

"I'm sure that if you ate as much every night, you would soon lose your trim figure."

"Yes, my body is still lean and fit. I should thank the Lord for it. He took most of my hair, but he left a few other things: my hearing, my sight and the ability to make love."

"At seventy-seven?"

He nodded. "I may not be as insatiable as I once was, but I still perform very well. In fact, I intend to prove it to you. Come over here and sit by my side."

She wanted to say no, but she couldn't. The old magic was at work in her, and she went to his side as though drawn by a magnet. He drew her face down to his and kissed her full on the lips. She was lost then, and knew it. And did not care. He moved

320

her hand to his crotch, where he was beginning to have an erection.

"Aaron, you are really shameful," she said breathlessly.

"Shameful or not, I wish to take you to bed."

He led her by the hand to the staircase, and she followed dutifully.

Aaron had not been boasting. He was as lusty as a man half his age, and Eliza responded with an abandon that she had not felt in years. She caressed him tenderly, and he, naked above her now, buried his face in her breasts, kissing her nipples savagely.

Before he entered her, he murmured, "It has been a long time, dear Eliza—too long." Then, with long strokes, he moved slowly up and down on her pliant body. The pleasure was so intense for her that she began to moan softly.

"Oh, give it to me!" she cried.

"I'll give it to you, bitch—every last inch of it!"

His movements began to accelerate as he plunged back and forth in her. She locked her legs across his hard buttocks and gave herself to him utterly. She would not have believed it possible, but her feelings were the same as the first night she had gone to bed with him. No man had ever been able to make her reach the delirious ecstasy that he gave her, that she now felt again, as though she were young and experiencing sexual pleasure for the first time.

As before, he was able to hold his erection for a long time, so that she had already had two climaxes before he eventually had his own. When he did, he seized her by the shoulders roughly, holding her so close that she could not breathe.

"Take it! Take all of it, right into you, you goddamned whore!" he bellowed.

Finally, he lay quietly on top of her, unwilling to withdraw himself. Eliza, sweating and shuddering with the last pulsations of her climax, was motionless beneath him.

When she could talk, she said, "Oh, that was glorious, Aaron. I have never had a lover like you. I've been to bed with many men, but none of them could make me feel the way you do."

She did not see the smile of satisfaction that turned up the

321

corners of his still-voluptuous mouth. At last, she squirmed out from under him.

"Why did you do that, love?" he said drowsily.

"Because my legs were getting numb," she said. With a smile, she added, "Though you may be still slim, you are also heavy."

He moved toward her on the bed and took her in his arms again. "It's strange, but I have the feeling that you don't really like the position of being under me."

"Oh, but I do," said Eliza. "Except that—well, when you come, you are so violent that I feel possessed, as though I were your slave."

He laughed softly. "And you don't like that?"

"Well, I do and I don't. I don't understand it. And when you curse at me and call me names—"

He shrugged. "I cannot help it, my dear." He paused and reflected. "Perhaps that is part of every man's feelings. He hates at the same time that he loves. He even despises the woman, with a momentary contempt for the enemy that he has conquered."

"Enemy? I don't understand."

He kissed her with tenderness. "And neither, my love, do I."

As spring turned into summer, Aaron continued to be a weekly visitor at The Mansion. Promptly at seven every Wednesday evening he came to dinner at Eliza's invitation and invariably stayed until morning.

One night in early July, after they had made love, he looked at her thoughtfully and said, "I think we should get married, my dear. I offer you my hand, Eliza—my heart has long been yours."

She was taken by surprise. "Marry?" she repeated. "But why should we marry?"

"Why should we not?" he asked.

"It would never work, Aaron. We are too much alike."

"And so we would always understand each other."

"I'm not so sure of that," she said.

"But your answer is yes?"

"I must think about it."

"But it is not no?"

322

She was silent, trying to gather her thoughts together. Why, she asked herself, was he proposing marriage at this late date? The thing that troubled her was the feeling that he wanted to marry her because she was rich and he was still poor, mostly because of his extravagant and spendthrift ways. But there were advantages on her side too. Aaron would give her his name. She would become Mrs. Aaron Burr, wife of an ex-Vice-President of the United States. She would like that. But she still had reservations.

The reservations were dissipated the following evening when Aaron arrived uninvited with the Reverend Bogart in tow. "Are you ready, my adorable wife-to-be? I am ready, and the Reverend Bogart is ready."

"But, Aaron—" she protested feebly.

The Reverend Bogart acted with dispatch. "Now, if the two of you will just come before me, hand in hand."

Eliza found herself being led by Aaron's outstretched hand. She took it in her own, and its warmth was somehow reassuring.

She sighed. "Very well." She looked deeply into Aaron's eyes, which danced in boyish excitement. She bowed her head.

When the ceremony was concluded, Aaron left to take the Reverend Bogart to his gig. Eliza, alone in the drawing room, stood looking after them in a daze.

"Well," she said to herself, "I am Mrs. Aaron Burr." She drew herself up proudly and then, suddenly wilting, she added, "God help me."

Two evenings later, the ceremony was repeated, with Mary and Nelson Chase as witnesses. The drawing room was filled with wedding guests who repeatedly toasted the bride and groom with champagne.

Eliza was wearing a wedding gown of pearl satin and gold-threaded slippers trimmed with kid. Her jewelry consisted of brilliant rubies: in her earrings, in the comb that held up her white hair, and in the golden pendant she wore about her neck.

Aaron, smiling and courtly, was in full evening dress: bottle-green broadcloth coat and trousers, buff waistcoat, white ruffled shirt and a starched collar so high that it hid half his cheeks.

The wedding feast was spread out on tables before The Mansion and continued until dark. Nelson Chase grew rather tipsy, and the prospect of having Aaron Burr as a father-in-law led him into extravagant statements that Eliza found obnoxious. Her eyes flashed indignation at him, but she could not dampen his drunken enthusiasm.

Eliza had hoped that the newspapers would carry feature stories on the event, but there was only brief mention of it in the *Evening Post* and the *Commercial Advertiser*:

> On Monday evening last, at Haarlem Heights, by the Rev. Dr. Bogart, Col. Aaron Burr to Mrs. Eliza Jumel.

Eliza was furious at this mere notation in the marriage column, as though she and Aaron were only ordinary people. She would have been even more furious if she had known what Philip Hone, an ex-mayor of New York, wrote in his diary:

> The celebrated Col. Burr was married on Monday evening last to the equally celebrated Mrs. Jumel. It is benevolent of her to keep the old man in his latter days. *One good turn deserves another.*

Hartford, Connecticut, was to be the scene of the honeymoon. Eliza had decided on this because there was business that she wished to settle there. For some time she had owned a block of shares in a toll bridge that spanned a Connecticut river, and she wanted to know the financial condition of the bridge company.

Aaron offered no objection, since Hartford was the home of John Trumbull, the celebrated artist, a friend whom he had not seen in a long time.

So early the next morning, the wedding trip began, with Eliza wearing an enormous Leghorn hat, its broad brim turned up behind, and decorated with fluttering ribbons and gaudily colored artificial flowers. And Aaron was equally dashing in a new single-breasted bright-blue coat with shiny gilt buttons. The golden coach was Eliza's finest, drawn by six jet-black Arabian horses with shining brass-studded harnesses.

They were royally received by John Trumbull in his large country house, and Eliza immediately bought one of his most expensive paintings. This pleased the old man immensely.

That afternoon she made arrangements to meet with the officers of the bridge company. She told Aaron about her holdings and insisted that he come along.

She had originally planned to buy more shares in the company, but at the meeting she changed her mind and told the directors that she wished to sell all her holdings. They were surprised, because the company was doing well. But she insisted, and so a check was made out for six thousand dollars.

"Please to give it," she said grandly, "to Mr. Aaron Burr, my husband."

Aaron did not say thank you. He merely smiled and took the check. He already knew how he was going to spend it. There was a projected plan to populate Texas with German immigrants. "Texas" was still a magic word to Aaron, and investment in a venture to promote its growth and development was irresistible. He took the money as though it were his own and told Eliza nothing of how he planned to spend it.

After the return from Hartford, things went happily at The Mansion. Aaron needed more money to pay off his debts and for personal reasons. He continued to support his many illegitimate children, some of whom were probably not even his.

Eliza was indulgent whenever he requested money. As with Mary and Nelson, she seemed to enjoy the role of benefactress. But Aaron did not enjoy the role of suppliant. One day he sold a new carriage and a pair of horses that Eliza had recently bought for a thousand dollars. The fact that he received only five hundred dollars in the transaction only increased Eliza's anger when she discovered what had happened.

At tea that afternoon, she upbraided him. "You have as good as stolen a thousand dollars from me!" she said furiously.

"Stolen? How, stolen? I am your husband, am I not?" he replied coolly.

"Being my husband hardly gives you the right to sell my

horses and a carriage whenever it pleases you!"

"As your husband, I am in charge of your affairs, monetary and otherwise," said Aaron, as though stating an established fact.

"You are *not* in charge of my affairs, and you never will be!" she said. "And by the way, whatever happened to the six thousand dollars I gave you from the sale of my bridge stock in Connecticut?"

"I invested it," he said.

"You invested it in what?"

"In a plan to colonize Texas with German immigrants."

"Oh, my God!" she moaned. "Why must you be a gull for every wildcat scheme that comes your way?"

"It was a good investment," he said hesitantly.

"And how much is it paying you?"

He was silent. At last he said, "Nothing. The whole thing fell through, and I lost every penny."

She got up triumphantly. "And this is the man who wants to handle all my affairs!" she sneered. "Why, with you at the helm, my three million dollars would be gone in no time!"

Aaron was beginning to get annoyed. He rose and drew himself up with dignity. "Madame, I would have you know that I am master in this house and intend to remain so!"

Eliza's rage now burst forth in physical action. She stormed at him, seizing him by his coat. "Master are you? I'll show you who is master! You do not love me! You married me for my money! How could I have been so blind?"

"Perhaps because you are a vain and pompous old woman!"

She struck him then, a smart blow across the mouth. "Get out of here, you swollen-headed jackass! I never want to see you again!"

He moved quickly to the door. "I shall borrow one of your ridiculous golden coaches to get downtown, and it will be returned. Later, I shall send for my things."

His voice was cold, its tone utterly serious. He turned on his heel and slammed the door behind him as he left.

Eliza, still trembling with rage, called the servants. "Nodine," she said, "Mr. Burr has left the house. He will not be returning. See that all his belongings are placed on the front verandah."

Nodine could not believe his ears. "But, madame, you have been married only four months—"

"Four months too long!" she snarled. "Do as I say!"

She ran upstairs and flung herself on her bed. She began to cry, not softly and sadly, but in fury. She pounded her pillow as she mentally calculated how much her marriage had cost, and the total was something like thirteen thousand dollars.

But the loss of money was not the cause of her tears. It was the knowledge that marriage to Aaron was utterly impossible. Being Aaron, he would have to be master—of her and of everything she owned. And that she could not and would not endure.

It was curious that a man who had always believed in the rights of women and their liberation through education should insist on operating as a superior being in his household—as well as in bed.

His words had hurt her. Was it true that she was "a vain and pompous old woman"? She was no longer young, she knew, nor as beautiful as she had been. She could no longer rely on her physical charms to get what she wanted. She had reconciled herself to this; her mirror told her that it was true.

But the thought that Aaron had married her for her money, and not, as he had said, because he loved her, was hard to face. But now that she had lost her beauty, perhaps money was the only thing that could attract a man.

In youth, men had loved her for her beauty, and now they loved her for her money. But who had ever loved her for herself? Only Stephen, whom she had so lightly valued while he was alive; Stephen, whom she had betrayed not once but many times. She mentally listed the lovers with whom she had committed adultery during her marriage. If there was a God in Heaven and if adultery was indeed a sin, she was condemned to Hell three times over.

But what concerned her now was not the sinfulness of her behavior but guilt for her many betrayals of Stephen. He had given her everything, not only his heart but his money, and in return she had given him nothing. Yes, she had always amused him, had rarely turned him away from her bed, but she had never loved him really, certainly not in the way he loved her.

A November storm had been brewing all afternoon, and now

327

suddenly it struck. Rain pelted at the windows, and the wind made low, moaning noises as it blew around the house.

Eliza grew frightened. Perhaps Stephen's ghost would reappear. She dried her tears and hunted for the brandy bottle.

When Marie appeared with a tray of food, Eliza refused it and asked only for more brandy. Marie brought a fresh bottle, and Eliza looked at her pleadingly.

"Could you sleep in my room tonight, Marie? I am very much upset."

Marie looked at her sympathetically. "Of course, madame." She sat down on the side of the bed and took Eliza's hand in her own. "Is it true, madame, that Mr. Burr has left us, never to return?"

"Yes, Marie." She took several swallows of the brandy and sank back on the pillows.

"But, madame, it's maybe only a lovers' quarrel, which will be mended before the week is out."

Eliza shook her head. "It is more than that. Mr. Burr does not love me. He married me for my money."

"But how can you be sure of that, madame?"

Eliza sat up in bed, and her face showed her indignation. "He spent thirteen thousand dollars of my money without even asking. I wouldn't mind that so much, but he insists that he is the master in this house and that in future he will manage me and all my affairs, especially my finances! When I told him that that would never happen, he just got up and left—without even saying goodbye."

Marie bowed her head. "Oh, that is terrible" was all that she could say.

"But it is not Mr. Burr that I am worrying about now." Eliza looked fearfully at the windowpanes, where the rain still drummed loudly. "I am afraid of—of the ghost, Marie. I am sure it will come again tonight."

"Oh, I don't think so, madame. Surely, Monsieur Jumel has gone to his rest by this time." She crossed herself and murmured a prayer as she clutched tightly to her rosary.

Eliza drank more of the brandy, and the alcohol began gradually to calm her. She relaxed at last and sank back upon the silk-covered pillows.

"Thank God you are here, Marie. You are a good and faithful servant."

She closed her eyes, but it was not until after two in the morning, when the storm abated, that she fell into a drunken, disturbed sleep.

During the next three days Eliza wandered disconsolately about the house, lonely and deserted now without Aaron's cheerful presence. She had no appetite for food and continued to drink brandy.

On the third night, under the cheering influence of the alcohol, she decided that she must make a move to get Aaron back, in spite of everything. She wrote him a conciliatory note, saying that she was willing to accept whatever accounting he might wish to give her for his use of her money.

An answer came late the next day, delivered to her by Nodine. Aaron's note was politely formal:

My dear Madame Burr:

I am in receipt of your letter, in which you suggest that you would accept whatever accounting I wish to give for my expenditures.

But there is no need for an accounting. What I did with these monies is no business of yours.

You have a husband to manage your affairs—and indeed, a husband who *will* manage them.

Until you accept this simple fact, there can be no reason for further communication between us.

Sincerely yours,
A. Burr

Eliza stared at the letter in anger. She hated herself now for having been so weak as to offer conciliation. Crumpling his note savagely in her hand, she got up and tossed it into the hearth fire.

329

Her face was set and determined, and the lines about her mouth were hard and fixed. She knew that there was no kind of relationship open to them now, not even friendship. She would have to kill whatever love was left in her. But she did not know how to do it nor even how to begin.

As the days moved into winter, she contemplated leaving The Mansion. But she did not. As lonely as she was, The Mansion was still her home, and she knew that she would be just as unhappy in town.

She passed the time by reading French novels, and even some English ones. Twice a week she went to the new Park Theatre, which had been built over the fire-charred ruins of the old one. And there were two new theatres now to choose from, and a small playhouse devoted to light opera.

Her life was hardly a full one, and her only visitors were, every now and then, Mary and Nelson. She received occasional news of Aaron from Nelson, who was now working in the Burr law office. The news was uneventful—until one wintry day in January.

CHAPTER 33

UNANNOUNCED, Nelson arrived in the early afternoon. He was in a state of agitation and did not even remove his overcoat.

When Eliza appeared to greet him, he rushed over to her and seized both her hands in his.

"Oh, madame, a terrible thing has happened. Colonel Burr has suffered a stroke!"

Eliza's head raised in alarm. "How bad is it?"

"Bad enough, I would say. His right side is partially paralyzed, and his speech is slurred."

"Has a doctor seen him?"

"Yes. The verdict was rather cheerful than not. There is a chance that he may regain some use of his right side, and the slurring of his speech will probably disappear."

"Thank God for that! I could not imagine Aaron struck dumb."

"But he will make no progress at all, madame, without proper care and encouragement. He is alone, except for Molly."

Eliza did not hesitate. "He will be brought here, whether or not he wants to come!"

"But who will nurse him, madame?"

Eliza drew herself up. "I will!"

Aaron was brought to The Mansion that evening, borne on a stretcher. His eyes were closed, and he seemed to be asleep.

"Put him there on Napoleon's sofa," ordered Eliza.

331

As the men carried the limp body to the sofa, Aaron opened his eyes and looked about him in bewilderment. "Oh," he said at last, "I am home."

Tears came to Eliza's eyes as she realized that Aaron still thought of The Mansion as home. "As long as you men are here, perhaps it would be better if you carried him to his bedroom."

With an effort, Aaron raised himself. "No!" In spite of his impaired speech, there could be no doubt about what he had said.

Brokenly and speaking like a man who has had too much to drink, he said, "I would *die* in a bedroom! I will stay here or nowhere!"

Eliza went over to him and took his hand in hers. His face was pale and haggard.

"Now, Aaron, you have had a slight stroke, but you will not die. It will be better if you are in bed."

"No!" he screamed, with such an effort that he fell back exhausted.

"Leave him here, then," said Eliza. "I'll get a blanket to cover him."

Aaron smiled his gratitude and tried to blow her a kiss with his left hand. She was grateful for even this show of affection.

Aaron's recovery was slow, and there were great fluctuations in his condition. He would sometimes seem to improve in the morning, only to relapse in the afternoon. As his speech gradually improved, he began to curse and swear at the useless, offending limbs as though they did not belong to him.

Sweating and straining, he tried in vain to move them. "Move, you sons of bitches! *Move*, you bastards!"

The doctor had instructed Eliza on how to massage his leg and arm, and she became adept at it. Aaron loved it.

"I cannot feel your beautiful fingers, Eliza, but I can see them, and that is almost as good." One day he guided her hand to his crotch. She was reluctant to touch him there but gave in to his insistence.

Then, suddenly, he threw back the blanket. "There! Look at

that!" He pointed to a partial erection. "At least *that's* not entirely dead!" he said triumphantly.

Eliza smiled in spite of herself. "No, it is certainly not. I don't think that thing will ever die."

"On the day it does, I shall be happy to leave this earth. It has served me well over the years, and I would wager that it will continue to do so. Play with it, please, dear Eliza."

Eliza clamped her lips together firmly. "No, I will not. You know that it's beginning to work, and that's enough." She threw back the blanket so that it covered him once again.

She got up. "It is time for your dinner," she said.

The day came when he was able to move his right leg, but only slightly, and a short time after that he insisted on trying to walk. Sometimes he fell down, but Eliza helped him to his feet again, and he continued to move about slowly. He tired easily and still worried because his right arm continued to be useless.

Eventually, he was able to walk alone with a cane, although he still limped, and his right arm flopped about uselessly at his side. His spirits improved with his health, and he became restless. His mind was as alert as ever, and he asked Eliza for books to read. She gave him some of her novels.

"Do you have nothing but novels in your house? You have become as illiterate as a scullery maid, my dear."

"Perhaps. But as you know, Aaron, philosophy and things like that bore me. But I like poetry, especially this new poetry by Hugo and Lamartine."

"And De Vigny. Have you read the *Poèmes Antiques et Modernes?*"

"No."

"You should do so at once. He is not as popular as the other romantic poets, but he has greater depth and will last longer. I suppose you have read some Jean Jacques Rousseau?"

"I tried, but it was too dull."

Aaron exploded like the stern schoolmaster that he would always be. "Dull? Do you realize that if Rousseau had not lived, none of your romantic movement would have happened? It was he who influenced not only French literature but French politics, and even American politics as well! His love of nature, his belief in the essential goodness of man and the corruption of society— these ideas gave birth not only to the French Revolution but to our own!" He was standing now, waving his left arm at her excitedly. "*Le Contrat Social* was written in 1762, and you have never read it! For shame!"

Eliza, once more in the role of the penitent pupil, bowed her head. "I will do so at once. I am older now, and perhaps I will not find it so boring."

"Good! Of course the man's personal life was shameful, and he was probably mad, as we know from his *Confessions*, in which he even admits to constant masturbation." He paused and looked at her with sudden lust. "Which reminds me, my dear, since I am not yet able to make love, perhaps you would play with my jolly roger."

She got up. "Do it yourself, if you need to. I wish no part of such childish goings on."

He harangued her, calling her a puritanical bitch.

She said, "I will not, Aaron, and that's an end on it!"

A month later Aaron was much recovered and had even regained some use of his right arm. One night after dinner, he sat next to Eliza and began to kiss her and fondle her. Against her will, she found herself responding.

But she knew that if she gave in to him now, the whole love affair would begin all over again and with the same inevitable ending. If Aaron were to master her physically, he would begin trying to take over her affairs and her money. And that was something she would never permit.

She stood up suddenly, averting her gaze from the piercing glow of his black eyes. Then, with firmness, she said, "It is over between us, Aaron. I will not go to bed with you again, and that's final."

"Never?" he said incredulously.

"No, never." But as she said the words, she thought how easy it would be to give in to him, to go to the bedroom and make love. It was what she wanted to do. But she repeated, "No, never."

He sat back on the sofa and sighed. "Well, you have beaten me at last, haven't you?" He paused, frowning. Then he continued softly, "I am deeply grateful for your care of me in my hour of need. I shall not forget it, dear Eliza. But I thought—" He stopped again. "Well, never mind what I thought. If I cannot make love with you, then it will have to be with some other woman. I shall leave in the morning, Eliza."

"You are free to go. I still love you, but—"

He laughed. "But you will not bed with me. That's a strange kind of love."

Her curiosity made her say, "But where will you go?"

He smiled. "To Jersey City, I expect—to Jane McManus. She has been good to me since our separation and will no doubt be grateful to have me back as her lover."

"So you love her then?"

He laughed. "Certainly not! But what has that got to do with it?"

She could not help smiling. "Of course. You may not be too old to *make* love, but I think you are too old to *love*."

He could not meet her eyes and looked down at his feet in embarrassment. He said nothing.

After Aaron's departure The Mansion again seemed deserted and lonely, and Eliza almost regretted having refused to make love with him. By March she decided that she could not stand the isolation of her life any longer, even if spring was only a couple of months away.

She moved back into the city and took rooms at the Tontine City Hotel, since the Chases had made it clear that there was no room for her in their apartment at 16 Chambers Street. This was not quite true, but both Nelson and Mary had found the presence of Eliza an irritation. Her domineering ways were a constant source of friction, and they saw no reason to put up with her,

335

since she could well afford to live apart from them.

As for Eliza, she found life at the hotel at least stimulating, and although the meals were not as good as her own chef could prepare, they were well cooked and satisfying. She was most gregarious and made friends with many of the visitors who stopped at the hotel, regaling them with long and rambling stories of her life in the French court.

She saw to it that these stories were a bit more dramatic and exciting than they actually had been. Her arrest for treason and her banishment from France became incidents that had had a shattering impact on all French social life under Louis XVIII. Her eventual return was nothing less than triumphal, since her absence had been deplored by the entire French nobility, who had virtually gone into mourning for her.

She did not realize that her stories often bored her listeners, and that some guests actually avoided her because they did not wish to hear the same stories over again.

Eliza's sexual encounters were few. She was not interested in the middle-aged travelers whom she might have had, and the younger men, whom she found increasingly attractive, were not attracted to her.

But every now and then, there would be a young man poor enough so that he could not afford to dine at the hotel, and he would be Eliza's guest at dinner, and later, in return for her generosity, he would be her guest in bed. But she was well aware of the basically monetary nature of such liaisons and took them for what they were—an evening's diversion. She longed for the days when a mere nod of her lovely head would have had these young fellows running to her side. But she was beginning to accept her age philosophically. After all, there was little that could be done about it, and she would live through these years as gracefully as possible.

On July 12, 1834, Eliza instituted a suit in chancery for absolute divorce from Aaron Burr. She engaged Alexander Hamilton, Jr., as her lawyer.

The divorce was not an act of revenge on Eliza's part. It was purely financial. She did not want there to be any chance that Aaron could ever again touch her money. To this end, Hamilton obtained an immediate injunction to prevent Aaron from any control of her property, and this was quickly granted. The divorce action then went on to mention statutory grounds, charging various matrimonial offenses "at divers times with divers females," and specifically, "at Jersey City with one Jane Mc-Manus."

When the papers were served on Aaron, he reacted with fury —which did not keep him from commenting humorously, "Methinks the lady pays me a great compliment." He not only denied the charge of adultery but countered with charges of his own. He threatened to prove that Eliza had "misconducted herself with one or more persons," and proceeded to mention four correspondents to Eliza's one.

But when his temper had cooled, he withdrew all his charges and refused to contest the suit, possibly because of the chance that Eliza might well be able to prove his adultery with Jane McManus.

He was quite correct, because Alexander Hamilton, Jr., had already made contact with Maria Johnson, one of Burr's servants who had accompanied him to Jersey City. She had been an eyewitness to his love-making with Jane McManus.

As she later testified in court: "He was sitting there and had his trousers all down. I got up on the shed and turned the window blind and looked through it. I sat down on my hunkies and looked in."

When the court asked how close together Mr. Burr and Miss McManus were, she replied, "About as close as they could get together. I looked at them till they got through with their mean act."

She said that on another occasion, on a Sunday, she had watched again, but this time Burr had caught her in the act. She said that Colonel Burr had given her a new pair of shoes in return for her silence. But Maria Johnson was righteously angry, because it had happened on a Sunday.

"I did tell and will tell and always meant to tell, because I was

337

ready to go to church, and he had given me orders to go to the Bear Market and get oysters for their dinner."

Obviously, in Maria Johnson's eyes, eating oysters, especially on Sunday, was proof positive of the licentiousness of her aging master, Colonel Aaron Burr.

CHAPTER 34

Late in 1834, Aaron's amorous life came to an abrupt end. He suffered a second and completely disabling stroke. Jane McManus was unable to give him the care he needed, and so his friends arranged to have him brought from Jersey City back to New York, where he was placed in a room in the old Jay Mansion, which had now become a boardinghouse.

Here, he was nursed tenderly by Mrs. Newton, the housekeeper. Although all movement now was impossible for him, his mind remained alert as ever. He insisted on receiving clients while propped up in bed and applied his still agile talents to the solution of their difficulties.

Meanwhile, Eliza had leased The Mansion and did not know when she would return. Her winters were spent in town at the Tontine City Hotel, her summers in Saratoga Springs. Her life was placid and uneventful until an evening in December 1835.

Not long after dinner, gusts of smoke began to blow in through the window of her hotel bedroom. Then she heard a fire alarm ring, the signals locating the fire somewhere in the business section of the city. She went downstairs and asked the manager where the fire was. He said it was nothing, merely a small fire in one of the warehouse lofts near the southern tip of the island.

But then there was a second alarm, and a third, and when the fourth alarm rang, Eliza went downstairs again.

"Four alarms!" she said to the manager. "Where is this *small* fire? My room is full of smoke."

She did not wait for him to open the front door of the hotel but opened it herself. To the south she saw that the whole business district was on fire and that the Merchants' Exchange Building was a flaming cauldron. She was frightened, particularly because a gale was blowing from the west, and the temperature was below freezing.

She rushed back to the manager and took him to the door. He looked at the fire in astonishment. "My God," he said, "the fire is not far from us!"

In an imperious tone, Eliza said, "Evacuate the hotel, you jackass!"

Eliza and all the members of the hotel staff went from room to room alerting the guests, some of whom were already sleeping. They were told to dress warmly.

The streets were full of people now, and they milled about in a stunned and helpless way. It was unthinkable to them that their city was on fire. Fire engines from the upper part of New York were joining those from downtown, and soon the ferries from Brooklyn and Jersey City were bringing in additional fire-fighting equipment.

The flames had spread to the warehouses on Broad Street, and tons of valuable merchandise went up in smoke. Burning embers caught up by the wind carried the fire across the narrow streets to other buildings, until the city was now burning in a dozen places at once.

Eliza saw men in silk hats and evening dress working alongside rough men in corduroy and overalls as they manned the pumps or passed buckets of water along. She joined them in the bucket line, and a man looked at her in astonishment.

"But this is no job for a woman of your age," he said.

"Never mind my age!" shouted Eliza, as she passed him a bucket of freezing water. "New York is my goddamned city as well as yours!"

It became apparent very soon that water was useless in fighting the fire because it froze almost as soon as it fell, and soon the ice-covered pumps were paralyzed.

Eliza heard the chief constable say that there was only one way that the remainder of the city could be saved: the buildings in the path of the fire would have to be blown up. But the only explosives were in the Navy Yard in Brooklyn, and the trip across the East River would be a perilous one in the turbulent waters churned up by the wind.

When a boat was finally launched, Eliza ran to it and begged to be allowed to go. The men roared with laughter and would not let her climb aboard. She waited all night at the shore, but the boat did not return.

When dawn came, the lower part of the city was hidden by a pall of black smoke, and Wall Street, from William Street to the East River, was completely destroyed. According to an extra issued by *The Courier* at nine o'clock, almost a thousand buildings had burned to the ground.

The gale still blew from the northwest, and the fire continued to move eastward. Finally, the newspaper office itself lay in the path of the blaze, and there was only one more extra from *The Courier*. It said that the boat with the gunpowder from the Navy Yard had arrived.

There were no more newspapers published that day. But as the news reached other cities in the country, the response was immediate. Philadelphia and Baltimore sent all the fire-fighting equipment they had and almost a thousand firemen as well, but both men and fire engines were stranded at Perth Amboy in an inextricable congestion.

Meanwhile, the blowing up of buildings had begun, and finally on the third day, the fire was stopped. But the old part of the city, including all of the original Dutch houses, was a mammoth wasteland of blackened ruins. Looting began and had to be checked by the constables, who were given orders to shoot to kill.

Eliza wandered through the streets, her face begrimed and her clothes tattered and scorched. She thanked God that The Mansion had been nowhere near the conflagration. At least she had a house to live in. She paid a boy to go to The Mansion with orders to have her coach and a pair of horses sent to her. She waited at the entrance of the Jay Mansion, which had been left untouched, like most of the buildings to the west: Trinity Church, St. Paul's and City Hall.

She did not know that inside the Jay Mansion, Aaron Burr lay helpless on his bed. But he had insisted on watching the fire, and Mrs. Newton had gotten him to a chair by the window.

He had watched, and tears had streamed down his face. He loved New York above all the cities he had ever lived in, and the sight of the destruction had filled him with despair. Although his stroke had paralyzed his limbs, he was still able to talk.

He had turned to Mrs. Newton and said, "Put me back to bed, if you please. I cannot watch it any longer. My heart is burning along with the city. It is time for me to die, too."

For Aaron, the city would be forever gone, and when the Jay Mansion was slated to be torn down, he scarcely cared what would happen to him. But his friends and relatives cared, and Judge Ogden Edwards, who lived on Staten Island, thought that the island's clear air and ocean breezes would have a beneficial effect on Aaron's depressed frame of mind.

And so, on a warm, sunny day in the summer of 1836, he was carried to a boat in the bay and was moved to the Continental Hotel at Port Richmond. His room was large and comfortable, and the windows overlooked the harbor and Newark Bay.

The change did improve Aaron's spirits greatly, and although still confined to bed, he cheerfully joked with visitors and made improper advances to the chambermaids, all of whom adored him.

And yet, in spite of his clowning, Aaron knew that his days were numbered. That did not truly worry him. He had said that when he could no longer make love, he would be happy to leave this earth. And that time had come.

To some of Aaron's friends it seemed only proper that he should have the counsel of a man of religion as the end approached, and one day a Catholic priest arrived and tried to convert Aaron to his faith.

Aaron looked at the priest with a tolerant smile. "But, Father," he said, "I am not a Roman Catholic and have no wish to be one."

"You must repent, my son," said the priest.

"Why?" asked Aaron innocently.

"So that you can be saved from the hellfire that awaits you for your sins. The Almighty has already visited you with this illness as a punishment, and there is more to come!"

For an instant Aaron's eyes lighted with their old fire at the prospect of an argument. Then, quite abruptly, the fire in his eyes died, to be replaced by a mischievous twinkle.

"My good man," he said, "I think that God is a great deal better than some people suppose. Good day to you, sir."

Reluctantly, the priest rose and departed. Clearly, he told himself, this man had no fear of death and was a most unlikely candidate for conversion.

The next afternoon the Reverend William Hague, a newly ordained Episcopal minister, came to visit. While he was a schoolboy, he had known and worshipped Aaron, who remembered him and was pleased to see him.

"I hope," said Aaron warily, "that you have not come to see me in your capacity as a clergyman."

"I have come to see you as a friend, Colonel Burr. I have always admired you greatly, as you know. I have always thought of you as a stoic, and I see that even now you are imperturbable and calm."

"Should the proximity of death make me hysterical, then?"

"No, thank heaven." He pointed to the book on Aaron's bedside table. "I see you are still an avid reader."

"Yes, it is Laurence Sterne's *Tristram Shandy*. Have you read it?"

"No."

"You should. Like you, Sterne began life as a man of the cloth, but he was a great sinner, I suppose. He adored women and was highly promiscuous. But his books are charming and delightful." He paused. "Had I read Voltaire less, and Sterne more, I might have thought the world wide enough for Hamilton and me." It was the only time Aaron had ever been known to express the slightest regret for the duel.

They continued to talk about books until Aaron's head began

to nod, and he fell asleep. The Reverend Hague stooped and kissed Aaron's limp hand. Then he tiptoed from the room.

On September 14, 1836, the final divorce papers were delivered to Aaron in Staten Island. He was in a weakened state, but not so weak that he could look at the papers without comment.

"Well, my love," he murmured, "you have had your way. You are free of me now, and I trust you will be happy."

Aaron was now fading so fast that the Reverend Hague was called for. He arrived late in the day and was quickly ushered into Aaron's room.

Aaron was sleeping, but as though sensing his young friend's presence, he opened one eye. It twinkled. "William, it is good of you to come. I shall not last the day."

Hague sat down and took Aaron's hand in his. His eyes were full of tears.

"Sir, I have not talked of religion to you, because I thought it would displease you. But the hour grows late. I must ask you one question."

Aaron nodded, and the Reverend Hague said. "Sir—tell me, are you sure of salvation?"

Aaron opened both eyes and looked at him with a wry smile. "On that point—I am coy," he said. He closed his eyes again and began to struggle for breath.

He was fast losing consciousness, but with a last desperate effort he roused himself to a sitting position. "Tell Madame—tell Eliza—"

But he never finished the sentence. He fell back on the bed, utterly exhausted, and soon his breathing had ceased. The Reverend Hague closed the ancient eyes, and then, kneeling by the bedside, he prayed long and earnestly that God would look in mercy on this man who had sinned so much with his body, but whose mind had been honest and true, and whose heart had been unfailingly generous.

CHAPTER 35

ELIZA STARED AT THE NEWSPAPER and then let it fall to the floor. It could not be true. COL. AARON BURR IS DEAD the headline said, but her mind could not grasp the words. Aaron dead! Aaron Burr dead, but it could not be!

She poured herself a stiff drink from the cognac bottle at her side and swallowed it in one gulp. She picked up the newspaper again and forced herself to read the whole article.

It had happened in Staten Island. He had been alone with some minister whom she had never heard of. He was to be buried in Princeton, New Jersey, on September 16. The funeral was to be held in the chapel of the College of New Jersey, from which he had been graduated and of which his father had been the second president.

She read the rest of the newspaper article with mounting fury. In death, as in life, he was maligned—as the murderer of Alexander Hamilton, as a traitor to his country. Not a word was said about his many accomplishments, his complete integrity as a politician and statesman. The fact that he had been a notable Vice-President under Jefferson was briefly mentioned. His outstanding military career as one of George Washington's bravest aides during the American Revolution was dismissed with a grudging line.

She called for her coach and went to the office of Alexander Hamilton, Jr. She asked him whether he would accompany her to Princeton for the funeral. He declined on the grounds that his appearance would only serve to open old wounds that were better left alone.

"Very well, Alex. I'll go alone, then."

But she was angry at him. At the door, she said, "He did not murder your father, you know. He killed him in a fair duel, which was fought to protect my name."

Alexander hung his head. "I am sorry, Eliza. I know that Colonel Burr was a wronged man and will continue to be a villain in the eyes of history. But my presence at his funeral would not change that and would, I think, be in poor taste."

"Death is in poor taste too!" she flung at him and slammed the door.

On the afternoon of September 16, Eliza arrived at Princeton in her coach, which had been draped in black. She herself was dressed in deep mourning and wore a dark veil over her face.

The service in the chapel of the college had already begun. For once in her life she did not make a spectacular and dramatic entrance. All by herself, she took a seat in the last row of pews.

The chapel was almost full. All of Aaron's relatives and his many friends were there, and so were the entire student body of the college and many citizens of the town.

The Reverend Carnahan preached a moving sermon that befitted the man who lay in the coffin before the altar. Then the mourners started filing by for a last look at the body. Eliza did not know whether she could stand to see Aaron in death, but she decided that she must. It was the last and perhaps only honor that she could pay him.

When she reached the coffin, she lifted her veil, and there was a gasp as some of the mourners recognized her. She looked down at the waxlike face in the casket. She had expected to be shocked by the sight, but she was not. Strangely, the lines of Aaron's face had composed themselves into a peaceful look that his face had never worn in life. And there was just the suggestion of a mischievous and mocking smile around his mouth.

It was then that Eliza found tears for the first time since the news had reached her. She began to sob and fell to her knees. The chapel was utterly quiet. She looked up as a hand was placed on her arm. It was General Robert Swartwout, and he looked at her in a comforting way.

"Come now, Mrs. Burr. He is gone, God rest his soul, and we must let him go to a peace that he never knew in life."

Tenderly, he lifted Eliza to her feet, urging her to follow the moving procession.

"One moment, General." She plucked a solitary blood-red rose from the side of her gown and placed it gently on Aaron's breast.

"Goodbye, my only love," she whispered, and then she added, "My sweet bastard."

After the last of the mourners had returned to the pews, the coffin was closed, and the funeral procession began to form. The pallbearers were mostly old and faithful friends, men who had witnessed the swift and dazzling flight of Aaron's career and the equally abrupt descent into oblivion.

The military led the procession, followed by the hearse and pallbearers, and then the clergy, and all the professors and students of the college. Aaron was buried in the college cemetery, next to his father, and as the coffin descended into the freshly dug grave, the Mercer Guards fired a volley of shots.

At last, the restless spirit of Aaron Burr was at rest, oblivious of honors and vilification alike.

Eliza was no longer weeping. Her grief was replaced by a fiery pride for the man whom Aaron had been. She walked staunchly and unassisted to her coach and ordered her driver to return to The Mansion.

The next day Mary and Nelson Chase came to visit. They wanted to offer their condolences and their apologies for not attending the funeral. Mary was big with her first child, and Nelson had decided that the journey might be perilous during this late stage of her pregnancy.

Eliza sat in Napoleon's chair in the drawing room. Her face was pale and drawn, and her eyes were ringed with shadows from a sleepless night. She wore no make-up. In a wavering voice she thanked them for their sympathy.

"Mother," said Mary, "you must not stay here alone. There is room for you with us, and I shall be needing your advice during my pregnancy."

347

Eliza lied, "But I know nothing about pregnancy and child-birth, since I have never been pregnant."

Mary continued, "Perhaps not, Mother, but it would be a great comfort to have you near."

"I would be no comfort, my dear. The whole idea of child-birth frightens me half to death." This was no lie. The memory of George's painful birth was still vivid to her. "I would be worse than useless to you, dear Mary." She smiled wanly. "I would be hysterical. All you will really need is a good midwife."

"But what are you going to do here, so alone?"

"But I am not really alone, Mary. There are Marie and Nodine, and all the rest of my devoted servants. It's just that for the time being, anyway, I want no social life. If people should come to call, I will receive them. Otherwise, the house will be closed in mourning for my husband."

The Chases were unable to change her mind and finally left. Eliza made an attempt at cheerfulness as she waved goodbye to them.

"Let me know as soon as my first grandchild is born. Perhaps I may make myself useful then." She closed the door and leaned against it for a moment.

Suddenly, she laughed. "My grandchild! But in truth I have no grandchild. Not even dear Mary is my child. My only child, my only living blood relation in this whole world, is George, and he will not even let me see my true grandchildren."

Eliza's only solace was the brandy bottle, and she kept it somewhere near at all times. She did not allow herself to become intoxicated, taking only enough alcohol to soften the harsh edges of reality. As hard as she tried to escape memories of Aaron, she could not. He was always with her, and she even began to believe that his spirit, if there was such a thing, had not left the earth and still hovered somewhere near.

One afternoon as she sat in the drawing room, there was a gentle knocking at the door, and Nodine went to open it. William Hague, the Episcopal minister, stood there.

"I am William Hague. I was with Mr. Burr when he died, and I would like to talk with Mrs. Burr for a few moments."

"Tell him to come in," Eliza called from the drawing room, and William Hague came into the hallway. After giving his coat to Nodine, he was ushered into the drawing room.

Eliza looked thoughtfully at the good-looking blond man who stood before her. For some strange reason he reminded her of Pieter.

"I am sorry to intrude on you, Mrs. Burr. I wanted to speak to you at Colonel Burr's funeral, but I didn't think it was the proper time."

"Please sit down, sir. What is it that you have come to tell me?"

He sat down and spoke softly. "I have known Colonel Burr since I was a boy, and he once tutored me in Latin. I don't know quite why, but he became to me—a kind of hero. I worshipped him. When I heard that he was very ill on Staten Island, I went to visit him." He paused. "I was with him at the moment he died."

Eliza smiled. "I trust you did not convert him to your religion?"

William laughed. "No, Mrs. Burr, that would have taken a much more zealous man than I. I went to see him because I admired him so much—yes, even loved him. But what I wanted you to know, Mrs. Burr, was that you were on his mind at the moment of death. The last words he said were 'Madame—Eliza—' He did not finish the sentence. He was gone, and I closed his eyes."

Eliza sat very still, staring straight ahead of her. Then tears came, and she buried her face in her lap and sobbed. The Reverend Hague went over to her and patted her gently on the shoulder.

Eliza sat up and dried her eyes. "It was kind of you to visit me, Reverend Hague. You see, I was never sure of Aaron's love. Now, I know that, in spite of everything, he did love me. It gives me courage to go on with my life. How can I thank you, sir?"

"There is no need to thank me, Mrs. Burr." He rose, preparing to leave. As he moved toward the door, Eliza followed him, and then closed the door softly after him.

349

She walked slowly back into the drawing room. A great joy filled her. She knew now that although Aaron had loved her first for her beauty and then for her money, he had never stopped loving her for herself—because she was his Eliza.

She sat down in Napoleon's chair and stopped her hand as it reached for the brandy bottle. There was no need for brandy now. All her life she had been searching for acceptance—through money and power and position—and she had never found it.

Suddenly, those things no longer mattered, because she had had something that few women, no matter what their position, ever knew. Not even Napoleon, in whose chair she was sitting, had found it: an enduring love that had survived infidelity and years of separation, and even more, her own fear of Aaron's dominance and power over her.

Some twenty-five years later she described Aaron to a reporter from *The Times*, saying, "He was short, five feet six inches in height, but he had a martial appearance . . . He was a combined model of Mars and Apollo. He conquered all feminine hearts, and no woman could resist falling in love with him, but he never took any unfair advantage of this fact."

But now, it was as though he stood before her, bowing as he kissed her hand. He had loved her, had always loved her. She knew that and knew it deeply.

And perhaps that was enough.

Author's Note

Except for the years 1794 through 1800, the facts of Eliza Jumel's life are well established in William Cary Duncan's *The Amazing Madame Jumel*, the excellent and only definitive biography that exists, and to which I am once again greatly indebted.

During the first six years of Eliza's life in New York, it is known only that she was Aaron Burr's mistress (from Philip Hone's *Diary*) and that she had a brief career on the stage (from William Dunlap's *Diary*). It was, therefore, necessary for me to fictionalize during this period (1794–1800).

I am grateful to Tressie Horton and her associates at the Lakeside Library in Lakeside, California, for their great assistance in helping me to research the historical background of the novel.

Last of all, I wish to thank Nora DeWitt, who was extremely helpful in preparing and typing the manuscript.